Praise for the novels of Anne Bishop

The Invisible Ring

"Entertaining otherworlds fantasy adventure. Fresh and interesting."　　　　　—*Science Fiction*

"A weird, but highly diverting and oddly heartwarming mix."　　　　　—*Locus*

"A formidable talent, Ms. Bishop weaves another intense, emotional tale that sparkles with powerful and imaginative magic."　　　—*Romantic Times*

"Plenty of adventure, romance, dazzling wizardly pyrotechnics and [a] unique and fascinating hierarchical magic system. The author's overall sublime skill [blends] the darkly macabre with spine-tingling emotional intensity, mesmerizing magic, lush sensuality, and exciting action, all set in a thoroughl detailed, invented world of cultures in conflict. . . . It and its predecessors are genuine gems of fantasy much to be prized."　—The SF Site

continued . . .

Daughter of the Blood

"Anne Bishop has scored a hit with *Daughter of the Blood*. Her poignant storytelling skills are surpassed only by her . . . deft characterization. A talented author."
—*Affaire de Coeur*

"Vividly painted . . . dramatic, erotic, hope-filled. A promising debut."
—Lynn Flewelling, author of *Stalking Darkness*

"A fabulous new talent . . . a uniquely realized fantasy filled with vibrant colors and rich textures. A wonderful new voice, Ms. Bishop holds us spellbound from the very first page."
—*Romantic Times* (4½ stars)

"Lavishly sensual . . . a richly detailed world based on a reversal of standard genre clichés."
—*Library Journal*

"Mystical, sensual, glittering with dark magic, Anne Bishop's debut novel brings a strong new voice to the fantasy field."
—Terri Windling, coeditor of *The Year's Best Fantasy and Horror*

Heir to the Shadows

"A wonderful story . . . amply peopled with interesting and nearly always dangerous characters."
—*Romance Reader*

"Bishop seems to delight in turning fantasy conventions on their heads . . . still darkly opulent, often exotic."
—*Locus*

Queen of the Darkness

"As engaging, as strongly characterized, and as fully conceived as its predecessors . . . a perfect—and very moving—conclusion."
—*The SF Site*

"A storyteller of stunning intensity, Ms. Bishop has a knack for appealing but complex characterization realized in a richly drawn, imaginative ambiance."
—*Romantic Times*

"A powerful finale for this fascinating, uniquely dark trilogy."
—*Locus*

QUEEN OF THE DARKNESS

The Black Jewels Trilogy
Book III

ANNE BISHOP

A ROC BOOK

ROC
Published by New American Library, a division of
Penguin Group (USA) Inc., 375 Hudson Street,
New York, New York 10014, USA
Penguin Group (Canada), 90 Eglinton Avenue East, Suite 700, Toronto,
Ontario M4P 2Y3, Canada (a division of Pearson Penguin Canada Inc.)
Penguin Books Ltd., 80 Strand, London WC2R 0RL, England
Penguin Ireland, 25 St. Stephen's Green, Dublin 2,
Ireland (a division of Penguin Books Ltd.)
Penguin Group (Australia), 250 Camberwell Road, Camberwell, Victoria 3124,
Australia (a division of Pearson Australia Group Pty. Ltd.)
Penguin Books India Pvt. Ltd., 11 Community Centre, Panchsheel Park,
New Delhi - 110 017, India
Penguin Group (NZ), 67 Apollo Drive, Mairangi Bay,
Auckland 1311, New Zealand (a division of Pearson New Zealand Ltd.)
Penguin Books (South Africa) (Pty.) Ltd., 24 Sturdee Avenue,
Rosebank, Johannesburg 2196, South Africa

Penguin Books Ltd., Registered Offices:
80 Strand, London WC2R 0RL, England

First published by Roc, an imprint of New American Library,
a division of Penguin Group (USA) Inc.

First Roc Printing, January 2000
20 19 18

Copyright © Anne Bishop, 2000
All rights reserved

Cover art by Matthew Innis

ROC REGISTERED TRADEMARK—MARCA REGISTRADA

Printed in the United States of America

for
Pat and Bill Feidner
and
Grace Tongue

ACKNOWLEDGMENTS

Thanks to Lorna Czarnota and Tom Heim for the archery lesson; to Pat Feidner for always knowing a funny story when I needed to hear one; to the Circle for their celebration and support of creative endeavors; to Kandra and Tatianna for all their help with the webpage; and to all the readers who have shared in the wonder of Story.

Jewels

White
Yellow
Tiger Eye
Rose
Summer-sky
Purple Dusk
Opal*
Green
Sapphire
Red
Gray
Ebon-gray
Black

*Opal is the dividing line between lighter and darker Jewels because it can be either.

When making the Offering to the Darkness, a person can descend a maximum of three ranks from his/her Birthright Jewel.

Example: Birthright White could descend to Rose.

Author's Note

The "Sc" in the names Scelt, Sceval, and Sceron is pronounced "Sh."

Blood Hierarchy/Castes

Males:

landen—non-Blood of any race

Blood male—a general term for all males of the Blood; also refers to any Blood male who doesn't wear Jewels

Warlord—a Jeweled male equal in status to a witch

Prince—a Jeweled male equal in status to a Priestess or a Healer

Warlord Prince—a dangerous, extremely aggressive Jeweled male; in status, slightly lower than a Queen

Females:

landen—non-Blood of any race

Blood female—a general term for all females of the Blood; mostly refers to any Blood female who doesn't wear Jewels

witch—a Blood female who wears Jewels but isn't one of the other hierarchical levels; also refers to any Jeweled female

Healer—a witch who heals physical wounds and illnesses; equal in status to a Priestess and a Prince

Priestess—a witch who cares for altars, Sanctuaries, and Dark Altars; witnesses handfasts and marriages; performs offerings; equal in status to a Healer and a Prince

Black Widow—a witch who heals the mind; weaves the tangled webs of dreams and visions; is trained in illusions and poisons

Queen—a witch who rules the Blood; is considered to be the land's heart and the Blood's moral center; as such, she is the focal point of their society

PART 1

CHAPTER ONE

1 / Terreille

Dorothea SaDiablo, the High Priestess of the Territory called Hayll, slowly climbed the stairs to the large wooden platform. It was a bright morning in early autumn, and Draega, Hayll's capital, was far enough south that the days were still warm. The heavy black cloak that shrouded Dorothea's body made her sweat. Under the deep hood, her hair was damp and her neck itched. No matter. In a few minutes, she could shed the cloak.

When she reached the platform, she saw the lumpy canvas that stretched across the front, closest to the waiting crowd, and automatically began taking shallow breaths through her mouth. Foolish. She'd used every spell she knew to keep what was beneath that canvas a secret until the proper time. Forcing herself to breathe naturally, she walked across the platform, stopping a few feet behind the canvas.

Watching her, with wariness and resentment, were the Queens of all the Territories in the Realm of Terreille. She had demanded that each Territory Queen bring her two strongest Province Queens and any Warlord Princes who served her. She knew that many of the Queens, especially those from the far-western Territories, had come expecting a trap of some kind.

Well, the bitches were right. But if she presented the bait in the right way, they would throw themselves into the trap without a second thought.

Dorothea raised her arms. The crowd's rippling murmurs

faded to silence. Using Craft to enhance her voice so that everyone would hear her, she began the next move in a deadly game of power.

"My Sisters and Brothers, I called you here to warn you about a terrible discovery I made recently, something that threatens every one of the Blood in the entire Realm of Terreille.

"In the past, I've done some unspeakably cruel things. I have been responsible for the destruction of Queens and some of the best males in the Realm. I have bred fear into the Blood in order to be the controlling power in Terreille. Me. A High Priestess who knows better than anyone that a Priestess can't be a substitute for a Queen, no matter how skilled or how strong she is in her Craft.

"I will shoulder the sorrow and burden of those acts for the rest of my life. But I tell you this now: I HAVE BEEN USED! A few weeks ago, while using my skills as a Black Widow to spin a tangled web of dreams and visions, I inadvertently ripped through a mental shroud that had surrounded me for all the centuries I've been the High Priestess of Hayll. I fought my way through that mental fogging and finally saw what my tangled webs had been trying to tell me for so very long.

"There *is* someone who wants to dominate Terreille. There *is* someone who wants to subjugate all the Blood in this Realm. But it isn't me. I've been the instrument of a monstrous, malevolent being who wants to crush us and consume us, who plays with us the same way a cat plays with a mouse before it strikes the killing blow. That monster has a name—a name that has been feared for thousands upon thousands of years, and with good reason. Our destroyer is the Prince of the Darkness, the High Lord of Hell."

Uneasy murmurs rose from the crowd.

"You doubt me?" Dorothea shouted. She tore off the cloak and tossed it aside. Her wispy, white hair, which had been thick and black a few weeks ago, fell around her shoulders. Her sagging, deeply lined face twisted, and tears filled her gold eyes as the murmurs changed to shocked exclamations. "Look what happened to me when I fought to free myself from his insidious spells. *Look at me.* This is the price I paid, so that you would be aware of the danger."

Dorothea pressed a hand against her chest, gasping for breath.

Her Steward stepped forward and gently grasped her arm to support her. "You must stop, Priestess. This is too much for you to endure."

"No," Dorothea gasped, still using Craft to enhance her voice. "I must tell them everything while I can. I may not have another chance. Once he realizes I know about him . . ."

The crowd grew silent.

Lowering her hand, Dorothea stood as straight as she could, ignoring the ache in her spine. "I was not the High Lord's only instrument. There are those among you who have had the misfortune to have had Daemon Sadi or Lucivar Yaslana serving in your courts. May the Darkness forgive me, I sent those monsters into fragile Territories, and because of them, Queens have died. Sometimes whole courts were torn apart. I, like Prythian, Askavi's High Priestess, thought we were sending them into service in other courts by our own choice, in the hope that they could be controlled. But we were manipulated into sending them to those Territories *because they are the High Lord's sons*! They are that bestial creature's seeds, and they have grown up to be his tools of destruction. The control Prythian and I thought we had over them was nothing but an illusion, a blind to conceal their true purpose.

"Both of them disappeared several years ago. Most of us hoped they had died. Not so. I've learned from some brave Brothers and Sisters who are now living in the Kaeleer Territory called Little Terreille that both Yaslana and Sadi are in the Shadow Realm, where the High Lord has been living under the guise of being the Warlord Prince of Dhemlan. The viper's children have returned to the nest.

"There's more. The High Lord has an unhealthy influence over most of the Territory Queens in Kaeleer, as well as absolute control over a young woman who is the strongest witch in all the Realms. With her strength behind him, he will overwhelm us—unless we strike first. We have no choice, my Brothers and Sisters. If we don't crush the High Lord and everyone in his service, the cruelty I have done as his instrument will seem like a child's game in comparison."

Dorothea paused for a moment. "Many of you have

friends or loved ones who have fled to Kaeleer in order to escape the violence that has been strangling Terreille. Look at what has happened to many of those who have run straight into the High Lord's seductive embrace."

Using Craft, she whipped away the canvas covering the front of the platform. Then she clamped her hand over her mouth to keep from gagging as the flies rose from the mutilated corpses.

Screams filled the air. A piercing shriek of grief and rage rose above the other voices. Then another, and another, as the people nearest the platform recognized what was left of a face or recognized a distinctive piece of jewelry.

Using Craft again, Dorothea gently drew the canvas over the bodies. She waited several minutes for the screams to fade to muffled sobs.

"Know this," she said. "I will use every bit of Craft I have learned, every drop of strength that I have in me to defeat this monster. But if I stand alone, I will surely be defeated. If we stand and fight together, we have a chance to rid ourselves of the High Lord and those who serve him. Many of us won't survive this fight, but our children—" Her voice broke. It took her a moment to continue. "But our children will know the freedom we paid so dearly to give them."

Turning around, she stumbled. Her Steward and Master of the Guard supported her across the platform and down the steps. Tears and a fierce pride filled their eyes as they gently settled her into her open carriage for the short ride back to her mansion. When they tried to go with her, she shook her head.

"Your duties are here," she said weakly.

"But, Priestess—" the Master of the Guard started to protest.

"Please," Dorothea said. "Your strength will serve me better if you remain here." Calling in a folded piece of paper, she handed it to her Steward. "If these Queens ask to see me, arrange for an audience this afternoon." She saw the protest in his eyes, but he said nothing.

Her coachman clucked softly to his horses.

Dorothea leaned back against the seat and closed her eyes to hide her glee. *Well, you son of a whoring bitch, I've made the first move. And now there's nothing you can do that can't be used against you.*

2 / Terreille

Alexandra Angelline shivered despite the morning sun's warmth as she waited for Philip Alexander to return from his examination of the torn bodies lying on the wooden platform. She put a warming spell on the heavy wool shawl, knowing it was useless. No outer source of heat was going to thaw the cold inside her.

It's too soon, she thought desperately. *Wilhelmina had gone through the Gate yesterday morning. She can't be among . . .*

Vania and Nyselle, the two Province Queens she'd brought with her, had already returned to the inn, along with their escorts. They hadn't offered to wait with her. A few years ago—a few *weeks* ago—they would have. They had still believed in her then, despite the problems in her family.

But a few weeks ago, someone had sent cryptic messages to the thirty strongest witches in Chaillot—excluding herself and her daughter, Leland—inviting them to take a tour of Briarwood and promising to solve the riddle of what had happened to the young girls in their families who had been admitted to the hospital and then disappeared without a trace. Briarwood, which had been built to heal emotionally disturbed children, had been closed for several years now, ever since that mysterious illness started consuming dozens of men from the aristo families in Beldon Mor, Chaillot's capital—an illness that had seemed linked to that place.

The witches had arrived on the specified night, and they had learned the secrets and the horrors of Briarwood. Their guide, a demon-dead girl named Rose, showed no mercy as she introduced them to the ghosts. One Priestess found her cousin, who had disappeared when they were children, bricked up inside a wall. A Province Queen recognized what was left of a friend's daughter.

They saw the gaming rooms. They saw the cubicles that contained the narrow beds. They saw the vegetable garden and the girl with one leg.

Numbed by what they saw, they followed Rose, who smiled at them and told them in precise detail how and why each child had died. She told them about the other demon-dead children who had gone to the Dark Realm to live with the rest of the *cildru dyathe*. She recited the list of Briarwood's "uncles," the men who had supported and used that twisted carnal playground. And she recited a list of broken witches from aristo families who had been "cured" of their emotional instability—and stripped of their inner power—and then returned home.

One of the men Rose had named was Robert Benedict, Leland's former husband and an important member of the male council—a council already decimated by that mysterious illness.

When a Healer in the group had asked about the illness, Rose had smiled again, and said, "Briarwood is the pretty poison. There is no cure for Briarwood."

Alexandra clutched her shawl and kept shivering.

The rage that had swept through Chaillot had torn it apart. Beldon Mor became a battleground. The members of the male council who had not yet died from the illness were viciously executed. After several men from aristo families died of poison, many others fled to inns or one of their clubs because they were terrified to eat or drink anything that might have passed through the hands of the women in their families.

And after the first wave of rage had passed, the witches had turned their fury on her. They didn't blame her for Briarwood, since it had been built before she had become Queen of Chaillot, but they *did* blame her, bitterly, for her blindness. She had been so intent on keeping Hayll's influence out of Chaillot and trying to retain some power in the face of the male council that she hadn't seen the danger that already existed. They said it was like arguing with a man about groping your breast when he already had his cock sheathed between your legs.

They blamed her because Robert Benedict had lived in her house for all those years and had bedded her daughter. If she couldn't recognize the danger when it sat across from her day after day, how could she protect her people against any other kind of threat?

They blamed her for Robert Benedict and for all the young witches who had died or were broken in Briarwood.

She blamed herself for what happened to Jaenelle, her younger granddaughter. She had allowed that strange, difficult child to be locked away in that place. She hadn't known Briarwood's secrets, but if she hadn't dismissed Jaenelle's fanciful stories, if she had accepted them as a child's plea for attention instead of an annoying social problem, Jaenelle never would have been sent to Briarwood. And if she hadn't dismissed the girl's hatred for Dr. Carvay, would she have learned the truth sooner?

She didn't know. And it was too late to find the answers.

Now she had another family problem. Eleven years ago, Wilhelmina Benedict, Robert's daughter by his first marriage, had run away after claiming that Robert had made a sexual advance. Philip Alexander, Robert's bastard half brother, had found his niece, but he had refused to say where she was. At the time, Alexandra had been furious with him for keeping Wilhelmina's location a secret from her. Lately, she had wondered if Philip had had some inkling about what lay beneath Briarwood's solicitous veneer, especially when it had been his vehemence that had been the final push to close the place.

A couple of days ago, she had received a letter from Wilhelmina, informing her that the girl was going to Kaeleer, the Shadow Realm. No—Wilhelmina was twenty-seven now, no longer a girl. That didn't matter. She was still family. Still her granddaughter.

Alexandra shook her head to break the pattern of her thoughts and noticed Philip walking toward her. Holding her breath, she searched his gray eyes.

"She's not among them," Philip said quietly.

Alexandra released her breath in a sigh. "Thank the Darkness." But she understood what hadn't been said: *not yet.*

Philip offered his arm. She accepted, grateful for the support. He was a good man, the opposite of his half brother. She had been pleased when he and Leland had decided to handfast, and had been even more pleased when they chose to marry after the handfast year was done.

Alexandra looked back at the platform where Dorothea SaDiablo had made her horrifying speech. "Do you believe her?" she asked softly.

Philip guided her through clusters of people who were still too shocked to do more than huddle together while they gathered the courage to look at the mutilated bodies. "I don't know. If even half of what she said is true . . . if Sadi . . ." He choked.

She still had nightmares about Daemon Sadi. So did Philip, for different reasons. Sadi had threatened her when Jaenelle had been put in Briarwood for the last time, had given her a taste of the grave. When he unleashed his dark power in order to break the Ring of Obedience, he had destroyed half the Jeweled Blood in Beldon Mor. Caught in that explosive unleashing, Philip's strength had been broken back to the Green Jewel that was his birthright.

"We can get a Coach this evening," Philip said. "If we buy passage on one that rides the darker Winds, we'll be home by tomorrow."

"Not yet. I'd like you to talk to Dorothea's Steward. See if you can set up an audience for me."

"You're a Queen," Philip snapped. "You shouldn't have to beg an audience from a Priestess, no matter who—"

"Philip." She squeezed his arm. "I'm thankful for your loyalty, but right now we *are* beggars. I can't afford any more assumptions. I'm not convinced that Dorothea isn't the monster she's always appeared to be, but I *am* convinced that the High Lord *is* a greater threat." She shuddered. "We have to go to Kaeleer to find Wilhelmina. We can't afford to go there without having as much knowledge of the enemy as we can gain, no matter what the source."

"All right," Philip said. "What about Vania and Nyselle? Will they go with us?"

"They'll stay or go as they choose. They certainly won't care what I do." She sighed. "Who would have thought, even a month ago, that I would have to entertain the idea of Dorothea being an ally?"

3 / Terreille

Kartane SaDiablo wandered through the formal gardens, trying hard to ignore the speculative or pitying glances of the few people who hadn't retreated indoors.

He had waited until Dorothea's carriage was out of sight

before walking away from the platform. The mutilated bodies that had been left for grisly inspection didn't bother him. Hell's fire, Dorothea had done that much—or worse—to people when she was feeling playful. But no one seemed to remember that. Or, perhaps, most of the fools here had never witnessed one of the High Priestess's moods.

But the Steward and the Master of the Guard . . . Ball-withered idiots. They had actually had *tears* in their eyes when they helped her into the carriage. How could they believe she'd been under a spell for all these centuries, that she hadn't reveled in her victims' pain?

Oh, she had certainly sounded sincere and remorseful. He didn't believe it for a moment. Any man who had ever had to pleasure Dorothea in a bed wouldn't have believed it. Daemon wouldn't have, that's for sure.

Daemon. The High Lord's son. That explained a great deal about his "cousin." All those years, when Daemon had been raised as a bastard in Dorothea's court, had she known? She must have. Which meant that the High Lord of Hell would have no love for the High Priestess of Hayll.

Which circled back to his own concerns.

The mysterious illness that had started almost thirteen years ago was consuming him. All the other men who had enjoyed Briarwood's secret little playground were already in the grave. Because he was Hayllian, one of the long-lived races, and because he had never gone back to Chaillot, he was the only one left. And he could feel that he was running out of time.

After the connection between the illness and Briarwood had been revealed a few weeks ago, he had started thinking—when his mind wasn't so consumed in nightmares that he *could* think—and he always came to the same conclusion: the only Healers who might be powerful enough to cure this illness before it destroyed him, and the only ones who would be ignorant of the cause, were in Kaeleer. They would probably be serving in the courts of the Territory Queens, who, if Dorothea hadn't been lying about *that,* were under the High Lord's control. Which meant he had to find something that would buy the High Lord's assistance. Thanks to Dorothea's little speech, he now had information he thought the Prince of the Darkness would find very interesting.

Pleased with his decision, Kartane smiled. He would spend a few more days sniffing out information and then pay a little visit to the Shadow Realm.

4 / Terreille

Alexandra Angelline gingerly settled into a chair, relieved that Dorothea had chosen a private receiving room instead of a formal audience room. This meeting was going to be difficult enough without enduring a court full of sneering Hayllians.

But being alone with Dorothea also had disadvantages. She'd heard that Hayll's High Priestess had been a handsome woman. Oh, the ghost of that loveliness was still there, but there was a definite stoop to Dorothea's shoulders, a twistiness to her spine. Age spots dotted the backs of her brown hands, and the face and hair . . .

It happens to all of us, eventually, Alexandra thought as she watched Dorothea pour tea into delicate cups. But what would it feel like to go to bed one night a woman in her prime and wake the next morning as a crone?

"I'm . . . grateful . . . you granted me an audience," Alexandra said, trying not to choke on the words.

Dorothea's lips curled in a slight smile as she handed Alexandra a cup of tea. "I'm surprised you asked for one." The smile faded. "We haven't seen eye to eye in the past. And considering what happened to your family, you have good reason to hate me." She hesitated, took a sip of tea, and continued softly, "It wasn't my idea to send Sadi to Chaillot, but I can't remember who suggested it or why I agreed. There's a veil over those memories that I still can't pierce."

Alexandra lifted her cup toward her lips, but put it down again without drinking. "You think the High Lord arranged it?"

"Yes, I do. Sadi is a beautiful, vicious weapon, and his father knows how to use him well. And they did achieve their goal."

"What goal?" Alexandra said angrily. "Sadi tore my family apart and killed my younger granddaughter. What was achieved by *that*?"

Dorothea sat back, took a sip of tea, and said quietly, "You forget, Sister. The girl's body was never found."

Something about the expectant way Dorothea was looking at her made Alexandra shiver. "That doesn't mean anything. He's a very discreet gravedigger." She put the cup and saucer on the table, the tea untouched. "I didn't come here to talk about the past. Just how dangerous is the High Lord?"

"Daemon Sadi is his father's son. Does that answer your question?"

Alexandra tried but couldn't suppress a shudder. "And you really think he wants to destroy the Blood in Terreille?"

"I'm sure of it." Dorothea touched her white hair. "I paid a heavy price to be sure of it."

"My other granddaughter, Wilhelmina Benedict, recently went to Kaeleer," Alexandra said softly.

Dorothea stiffened. "How recently?"

"She went through the Gate yesterday."

"Mother Night," Dorothea said, collapsing in her chair. "I'm so sorry, Alexandra. So very, very sorry."

"Prince Philip Alexander and I intend to go to Kaeleer as soon as that 'service fair' is over and visitors are permitted again. Hopefully, we'll be able to find her and convince whatever Queen she's signed a contract with to release her."

"She's in far more danger than that," Dorothea said worriedly.

"There's no reason for her to draw anyone's attention," Alexandra said, fear making her voice sharp. "There's no reason for her to accept a contract outside of Little Terreille."

"There are two reasons: the High Lord and the witch he controls. If you don't find her quickly, Wilhelmina will end up in his dark embrace, and there will be no hope for her then."

Despite the warm room, a chill ran down Alexandra's spine.

Dorothea just looked at her for a long moment. "I told you—Sadi and the High Lord achieved their goal. No one hunts very long for a corpse when the living need care. And your granddaughter's body was never found."

Alexandra stared at Dorothea. "You think *Jaenelle* is this powerful witch under the High Lord's control? *Jaenelle?*" She laughed bitterly. "Hell's fire, Dorothea, Jaenelle couldn't even do *basic* Craft."

"If you know how to read between the lines of some of the . . . less available . . . records of the Blood's history, you'll find that there have been a few women—very few, thank the Darkness—who had enormous reservoirs of power that they were unable to tap by themselves. They required an . . . emotional . . . bond with someone who had the skill to channel the power in order to use it. But they didn't always have the choice about *how* it was used." Dorothea paused. "The gossip that has recently filtered in from Little Terreille about the High Lord's pet describes her as 'eccentric,' 'somewhat emotionally disturbed.' Does that sound familiar?"

Alexandra couldn't catch her breath. There wasn't enough air in the room. Why wasn't there enough air?

"If you'll take it, I'll give you whatever help I can." Dorothea looked at her sadly. "You can't ignore this, Alexandra. No matter what you want to think or what you want to believe, you can't ignore the fact that the High Lord's pet witch, the witch Daemon Sadi helped him acquire, goes by the name Jaenelle Angelline."

5 / Terreille

Dorothea pulled aside the dark, heavy curtains and stared out at the night-shrouded garden. She felt drained, physically and emotionally. Oh, how she had wanted to dig her nails in and scratch out the pathetically hopeful look in the eyes of the males in her First Circle. They wanted to grasp at any excuse for her behavior over the past centuries. They wanted to believe that a *male* had made her cruel, a *male* had manipulated her and controlled her thoughts, a *male* had been behind her rise to power and the viciousness afterward that had made it possible to soften and harvest most of the other Territories in Terreille.

They didn't want to give her any credit at all. They wanted her to be a victim so that they wouldn't feel ashamed of serving her, so that they could pretend they served out of a sense of honor instead of avarice and fear.

Well, once Kaeleer fell, she would make a few changes in her court. Maybe she would even arrange for the fools to die in battle, choking on their bloody honor.

"You did well today, Sister," said a harsh but still girlish voice. "I couldn't have done better myself."

Dorothea didn't turn around. Looking at Hekatah, the demon-dead Dark Priestess and self-proclaimed High Priestess of Hell, always turned her stomach. "They were your words, not mine, so it's not surprising that you're pleased."

"You still need me," Hekatah snarled as she shuffled to a chair near the fire. "Don't forget that."

"I never forget that," Dorothea replied softly, keeping her eyes focused on the garden.

It had been Hekatah who had seen her potential when she was a young witch still learning a Priestess's duties as well as the Black Widows' Craft. It had been Hekatah who had nurtured her ambitions and dreams of power, who had pointed out the possible rivals who could interfere with those dreams. And it had been Hekatah who had helped eliminate those rivals. The Dark Priestess had been there, every step of the way, guiding, advising.

She couldn't remember just when she realized that Hekatah needed her just as much as she needed Hekatah. That need made them despise each other, but they were bound together by the common dream of ruling an entire Realm.

"Do you really think, after all we've done to gain control of Terreille, those Queens will believe it was all the High Lord's fault?"

"If you cast the persuasion spells correctly, there's no reason they won't believe it," Hekatah said with sweet venom.

"There's nothing wrong with my Craft skills, Priestess," Dorothea replied with equal venom, turning to face the other woman.

"Your skills didn't help you elude the spell Sadi wrapped around you, did they?"

"No more than your skills protected you or have helped you reverse the damage."

Hekatah hissed angrily, and Dorothea turned back to the window, feeling a brief satisfaction at the well-aimed barb.

Seven years ago, Hekatah had tried to gain control of Jaenelle Angelline and eliminate Lucivar Yaslana. Something had gone wrong with her scheme, and the backlash of that confrontation had stripped away her ability to pass as one of the living, had made her look like a decaying, desiccated corpse. For the first couple of years, she had insisted that all she needed was to consume large quantities of fresh blood in order to restore her body. But the demon-dead were, in a sense, spirits that still had too much psychic power to return to the Darkness and were now housed in dead flesh. While the power lasted and could be renewed, the body could be maintained by consuming blood. But nothing was going to restore Hekatah's looks. The juice had been wrung out of her dead flesh, and the past seven years had been a slow decay of a body that had died 50,000 years ago.

"They'll believe the High Lord has been responsible for all the perversion in Terreille," Hekatah said, coming up behind Dorothea close enough for her reflection to be visible in the window's night-darkened glass. "They *want* to believe it. He's a myth, a terrifying story that has been whispered for thousands of years. And anyone who has doubts about *him* will have no doubts at all about Yaslana and Sadi. The thought of the three of them coming together and having the use of a strong witch as their tool will be enough to unite Terreille against Kaeleer. In the end, it doesn't matter *why* they join the fight, only that they fight."

"We've gained one reluctant ally this afternoon—Alexandra Angelline, the Queen of Chaillot." Dorothea's lips curled in a vicious smile. "She was shocked to discover that her younger granddaughter has been under the High Lord's thumb for all these years, thanks to Daemon Sadi."

Hekatah frowned. "She's a fool, but she isn't stupid. If she convinces Jaenelle to help her maintain control of Chaillot . . ."

Dorothea shook her head. "She doesn't believe Jaenelle has any power. I could see it in her eyes. I spun her a little story about women who are reservoirs of raw power—she didn't believe that either. She can accept that Sadi and the High Lord might have wanted Jaenelle for their own twisted reasons, but she'll continue to believe what she *wants* to believe about Jaenelle Angelline. Once she gets to Little Terreille, Lord Jorval will be waiting to offer his assistance. *He'll* never mention that Jaenelle is the Queen of Ebon Askavi. And I doubt Alexandra will believe anything *anyone* at the Hall tells her."

Hekatah laughed gleefully.

"And I imagine that once she actually meets Prince Saetan Daemon SaDiablo, the High Lord of Hell, she'll be more than happy to send along any information she thinks will be useful to us."

"And if he discovers her deceit . . . ." Hekatah shrugged. "Well, we would have had to get rid of her after the war anyway."

Dorothea stared at their reflections in the glass. They had been lovely women once. Now Hekatah looked like a corpse that the worms had been feasting on, and she . . .

Sadi had created some kind of spell to age and twist her body, but he hadn't done anything to diminish her sexual appetite. The Blood called him the Sadist, but she hadn't really appreciated the depths of his cruelty. He had known her appetites—how could he not since he'd had to satisfy them when he was young? He had also known the humiliation she would feel when she saw revulsion in the eyes of the males she rode instead of that exciting combination of lust and fear. Now, after her tearful confession, she wouldn't even be able to indulge in that much.

"You've informed your pet Queens that they'll have to abstain from their more—imaginative—pleasures for the time being?" Hekatah asked.

"I've told them," Dorothea replied irritably. "Whether they *will* restrain themselves is difficult to say."

"Any who indulge will have to be eliminated."

"And how do we explain *that*?"

Hekatah made an impatient sound. "Obviously they, too, have been under the High Lord's spell. Your gallant struggle to free yourself from his power also freed a number of your Sisters, but, unfortunately, not all of them. All it will take is one or two of them being killed for the others to understand the message and behave properly."

"And after we've won?"

"After we've won, we can do whatever we damn well

please. We'll rule the Realms, Dorothea. Not just Terreille, but *all* of them—Terreille, Kaeleer, and Hell."

Wanting to savor that possibility, Dorothea didn't say anything for several minutes. Then finally, reluctantly, she asked, "Do you really think that fear of the High Lord will be enough to start a war? Do you really think this will work?"

What was left of Hekatah's lips pulled back in a terrible smile. "It worked the last time."

6 / Kaeleer

The Queen of Arachna settled next to the shoulder of the weary, golden-haired woman who leaned against a flat-sided boulder.

Is bad? the large golden spider asked in her soft voice.

Jaenelle Angelline brushed her hair away from her face and sighed. Her haunted sapphire eyes narrowed a little against the early-morning sunlight as she once again studied the delicate strands of the tangled web that she'd woven during the night. "Yes, it's bad. A war is coming. A war between the Realms."

Can stop?

Jaenelle shook her head slowly. "No. No one can stop it."

The spider shifted uneasily. The air around the woman tasted of sadness—and a growing, cold rage. *The two-legs have fought before. Is more bad this time?*

"You may look."

Accepting the formal invitation, the Arachnian Queen opened her mind to the dreams and visions in the large tangled web Jaenelle had spun between a boulder and a nearby tree.

So much death. So much pain and sorrow. And a creeping taint that soiled the ones remaining.

Pulling back from the dreams and visions, she studied the web itself and noticed two odd things. One was the delicate silver ring set with an Ebony Jewel that had been placed in the center of the web. A Jewel chip was rarely woven into a tangled web because the magic that shaped those webs was powerful—and dangerous—enough, and this particular Jewel belonged to Jaenelle, who was Witch, the living myth, dreams made flesh. The other odd thing was the triangle. Many threads were connected to that ring, but overlying them were three threads that formed a triangle around it.

Intrigued, the spider continued to study the web. She had seen that triangle before. Strength, passion, courage. Loyalty, honor, love. She could almost taste the male tang in those threads.

"If Kaeleer accepts Terreille's challenge and goes to war," Jaenelle said softly, "it will destroy the Blood in both Realms. All the Blood. Even the kindred."

Some will live. It is always so.

"Not this time. Oh, there will be some who will physically survive the war, but . . ." Jaenelle's voice broke. She took a deep breath. "All of my Sisters, all of my friends will be gone. All of the Queens will be gone. All of the Warlord Princes."

All?

"There will be no Queens left to heal the land, no Queens left to hold the Blood together. The slaughter will continue until there's no one left to slaughter. The witches will be as barren as the land. The gift of power that had been given to us so long ago will be the final weapon that destroys us. If Kaeleer goes to war with Terreille."

Must fight. the spider said. *Must stop creeping taint.*

Jaenelle smiled bitterly. "War won't stop it. I know who nurtured the seeds, and if eliminating Dorothea and Hekatah would stop this from coming, I'd destroy them right now. But it wouldn't stop anything, not anymore. It would only delay it, and that would be worse. This is the right place and the right time to cleanse that taint out of the Blood."

You speak paths that go no place, the spider scolded. *You say can't fight but must fight. You confused? Maybe you read web wrong.*

Jaenelle turned her head toward the spider, a dryly amused look on her face. "And where did I learn to weave a tangled web? If I'm not reading it right, maybe I wasn't taught correctly."

The spider used Craft to make a harsh, buzzing sound that indicated severe disapproval. *Not fault of teaching spider if little spider pay more attention to catching fly than doing lesson.*

Jaenelle's silvery, velvet-coated laugh filled the air. "I never once tried to catch a fly. And I *did* pay attention to the teaching spider. After all, she *was* the Dream Weavers' Queen at the time."

The Arachnian Queen resettled herself, somewhat mollified.

Jaenelle's humor faded as she turned her sapphire eyes back to the web. "Terreille will go to war."

Then Kaeleer will war.

"This web shows two paths," Jaenelle said very quietly.

No, the spider replied firmly. *One web, one vision. That is the way.*

"Two paths," Jaenelle insisted. "Following the second path, Kaeleer doesn't go to war with Terreille, and the Queens and Warlord Princes survive to heal and protect the Shadow Realm."

Then who war with Terreille?

Jaenelle hesitated. "The Queen of the Darkness."

But you are Queen!

Jaenelle exhaled sharply. "A war that cleanses the Realms, calls in the debts, takes back the gift of power that was given. There's a way. There *must* be a way, but the web can't show me yet because of that." Her finger pointed to the triangle. "That's not the Queen's triangle." Her finger traced the left side of the triangle. "That thread is the High Lord." She traced the bottom thread. "And that thread is Lucivar." Her finger hesitated at the triangle's right side. "But that thread isn't Andulvar. It should be, since he's the Master of the Guard, but it's someone else. Someone who isn't here yet, someone who can guide me to the answers I need to walk that other path."

The thread not tell you its name?

"It says the mirror is coming. What kind of answer is—" Tensing, Jaenelle scrambled to her knees. "Daemon," she whispered. "*Daemon.*"

The spider shifted uneasily. Witch had flavored the air with intense pleasure when she had whispered that name—but underneath the pleasure there was a little taste of fear.

"I have to go," Jaenelle said hurriedly as she leaped to her feet. "I still need to stop at a couple of kindred Territo-

ries before I return to the Hall." She hesitated, glanced at
the spider. "With your permission, I'd like to keep this one
for a while."

Your webs be welcome among the Weavers of Dreams.

Raising her hand, Jaenelle used Craft to put a protective
shield on the tangled web's threads. She looked back at the
spider. "May the Darkness embrace you, Sister."

And you, Sister Queen, the spider replied formally.

The Arachnian Queen waited until Jaenelle caught one
of the Winds, those psychic pathways through the Darkness, before she used Craft to float gently toward the tangled web.

One web, one vision. That was the way. But when Witch
spun a web . . .

Using instinct and all of her training, the spider cautiously brushed a leg against a small thread that floated
loose from the Ebony ring. The tangled web showed her
the second path.

The spider quickly backed away. *No!* she called, sending out her psychic communication thread as far as it would
reach. *No! Not a second path. Not an answer! You not
walk this path!*

No answer. Not even a flicker from Witch's powerful
mind to indicate that she had heard.

You not walk this path, the spider said again sadly,
seeing clearly where that path would end.

Perhaps not. Witch could weave a tangled web better
than any other Black Widow, but even Witch couldn't always sense all the flavors in the threads.

The Arachnian Queen turned back to the web and felt
a mild tug. Walking on air, she followed the tug to a thread
near the tree-anchored side of the web. Cautiously, she
brushed a leg against the thread.

Dog. The brown-and-white dog she had seen in the first
web she had spun after the cold season had passed. She
had asked Witch to bring the dog, Ladvarian, to the Weavers' island. She had wanted to see this Warlord—and she
had wanted him to see her.

She plucked the Ladvarian thread and felt its vibration
run through the web. Many of the threads connected to the
Ebony ring—the kindred threads—began to shine brightly.

The human threads shone, too, but not so bright, not so sure. She must remember that. And that triangle . . .

With her leg still resting on the Ladvarian thread, the spider let her mind sail to the secret cave, the sacred cave in the center of the island. There the Arachnian Queens had gone time after time to listen to dreams—and to weave, thread by thread, the very special webs that bound dreams to flesh, that were the first tangible step in creating Witch.

Small webs. Larger webs. Sometimes only one race, only one kind of dreamer, had dreamed Witch into being. Other times the dreamers had come from different places with different needs that somehow had fit together to become one dream.

When that dream's time in the flesh was done and it no longer walked the Realms, the Arachnian Queen would respectfully cut the anchor threads that held the web to the cave walls, roll the spidersilk into a ball, deposit it in a niche, and then use Craft to coax crystals to grow over the opening. There were many closed niches, more than the human Blood realized. But then, the kindred had always been far more faithful dreamers.

There was one web in the cave that had been started long, long ago. Generation after generation after generation, the Arachnian Queens had brushed one of the anchor threads of that web, had listened to the dreams, and then had added more strands. So many dreamers in this web, so many dreams that had fit together to become one. Twenty-five years ago, by human reckoning, that dream had finally become flesh.

In the center of that special web was a triangle. Three strong dreamers. Three threads that had been reinforced so many times they were now thick and very powerful.

And each Queen, as she consumed the freely offered flesh of the one who had come before her, had been told the same thing: Remember this web. Know this web. Know every thread.

The spider pulled her mind back to the new web.

Dreams made flesh. A spirit nurtured in the Darkness, shaped by dreams. And a tangled web, equally nurtured and hidden in a cave full of ancient power, that guided that spirit to the right kind of flesh.

There had been times, when the spider had seen terrible things in her webs of dreams and visions, when she had wondered if that particular spirit had, in fact, found the right flesh; had wondered if, perhaps, some of the threads had been too old. No, there had been a reason why this one had been shaped into this flesh. The pain and the wounds had not been the fault of the dreaming—or the dreamers.

The spider drew silk out of her body and carefully attached it to the Ladvarian thread.

So. Witch would choose the second path, blind to the fact that, while she would save Kaeleer and those she loved, she would also destroy Kaeleer's Heart.

There *had* to be a way to save Kaeleer's Heart.

Spinning out an anchor thread between the tree trunk and a sturdy branch, the Arachnian Queen began to weave her own tangled web.

CHAPTER
TWO

1 / Kaeleer

Lucivar Yaslana flipped the list back to the first page of neatly written names and stepped away from the table, faintly amused by the men who were caught between wanting to review the lists at that table and *not* wanting to get too close to *him*.

That was one advantage he had over the other males who were drifting from table to table to check the service fair lists. No one jostled him or complained about how long it took him to scan the names, because no one wanted to tangle with a Warlord Prince who wore Ebon-gray Jewels, was an Eyrien warrior bred and trained, and had a vicious temper and a reputation for unleashing that temper—and his fists—without a second thought. When added to his belonging to one of the strongest families in the Realm and also serving in the Dark Court at Ebon Askavi, it was little wonder that other men quickly yielded.

But even all of that didn't help him feel comfortable while he was at the service fair in Goth, Little Terreille's capital. No matter what they called it, this fair had too much of the flavor of the slave auctions still held in the Realm of Terreille.

Slowly making his way to the door, Lucivar took a deep breath and then wished he hadn't. The large room was overcrowded, and even with the windows open, the air stank of sweat and fatigue—and the fear and desperation that seemed to rise up from the hundreds of names on those lists.

As soon as he was outside the building, Lucivar spread his dark, membranous wings to their full span. He wasn't sure if it was out of defiance for all the times that natural movement had earned him the cut of a lash or just that he wanted to feel the sun and wind on them for a moment after being inside for several hours—or if it was simply a way to remind himself that he was now the buyer, not the merchandise.

Folding his wings, he set off for the far corner of the fairground that was reserved for the Eyrien "camp."

He'd noted several Eyrien names that were of interest to him, but not the one name—the Hayllian name—that was the main reason he'd spent the past several hours searching through those damn lists. But he'd been searching the lists for Daemon's name for the past five years, ever since the idiots in the Dark Council had decided this twice-yearly "service fair" was the way to funnel the hundreds of people who were fleeing from Terreille and trying to find a fingerhold in Kaeleer. And he thought, as he did every time, about why Daemon's name wasn't there. And he rejected, as he did every time, all the reasons except one: he wasn't looking for the right name.

But that wasn't likely. No matter what name Daemon Sadi used to get to Kaeleer, once at the fair he would use his own name. There were too many people here who would recognize him, and since the penalty for lying about the Jewels one wore was immediate expulsion from the Realm—either back to Terreille or to the final death—changing his name while admitting that he wore the Black Jewels would only make him look like a fool because he was the *only* male besides the High Lord who had worn the Black in the entire history of the Blood. The Darkness knew Daemon was many things, but he wasn't a fool.

Pushing aside his own stab of disappointment, Lucivar wondered how he was going to explain this to Ladvarian. The Sceltie Warlord had been so insistent about Lucivar checking the lists carefully this time, had seemed so certain. Most people would think it odd to feel apprehensive about disappointing a dog that just reached his knees, but when that dog's best friend was eight hundred pounds of feline temper, a smart man didn't dismiss canine feelings.

Lucivar put those thoughts aside as he reached the Eyrien "camp": a large corral of barren, beaten earth, a poorly made wooden barracks, a water pump, and a large trough. Not so different from the slave pens in Terreille. Oh, there were better accommodations on the fairground for those who still had the gold or silver marks to pay for them, with hot water and beds that were more than a sleeping bag on the ground. But for most, it was like this: a struggle to look presentable after days spent waiting, wondering, hoping. Even here, among a race where arrogance was as natural as breathing, he could pick up the scents of exhaustion brought on by too little food, too little sleep, and nerves frayed to the breaking point. He could almost taste the desperation.

Opening the gate, Lucivar stepped inside. Most of the women were near the barracks. Most of the men were in small groups, nearer the gate. Some glanced at him and ignored him. A few stiffened in recognition and looked away, dismissing him in the same way they had dismissed the bastard boy he'd believed himself to be.

But a few of the males moved toward him, every line of their bodies issuing a challenge.

Lucivar gave them a slow, arrogant smile that blatantly accepted the challenge, then turned his back on them and headed for the Warlord whose concentration was focused on the two boys moving through a sparring exercise with the sticks.

One of the boys noticed him and forgot about his sparring partner. The other boy pounced on the advantage and gave the first one a hard poke in the belly.

"Hell's fire, boy," the Warlord said with so much irritation it made Lucivar grin. "You're lucky all you've got is a sore belly and not a dent in that thick head of yours. You dropped your guard."

"But—" the boy said as he started to raise his hand and point.

The Warlord tensed but didn't turn. "If you start worrying about the man who hasn't reached you yet, the one you're already fighting is going to kill you." Then he turned slowly and his eyes widened.

Lucivar's grin sharpened. "You're getting soft, Hallevar. You used to give me the bruised belly and then a smack for getting it."

"Do you drop your guard in a fight?" Hallevar growled. Lucivar just laughed.

"Then what are you bitching for? Stand still, boy, and let's take a look at you."

The youngsters' mouths were hanging open at Hallevar's disrespect for a Warlord Prince. The males who had noticed him and had decided to talk—or fight—had formed a semicircle on his right. But he stood still while Hallevar's eyes traveled over his body; he said nothing in response to the older man's small grunts of approval, and he bit back a laugh at Hallevar's glaring disapproval of the thick, black, shoulder-length hair.

His hair was a break from tradition, since Eyrien warriors wore their hair short to deprive an enemy of a handhold. But after escaping from the salt mines of Pruul eight years ago and ending up in Kaeleer instead of dead, he had shrugged off quite a few traditions—and by doing so, had found others that were even older.

"Well," Hallevar finally growled, "you filled out well enough, and while your face is nowhere near as pretty as that sadistic bastard you call a brother, it'll fool the Ladies long enough if you can keep that temper of yours on a tight leash." He rubbed the back of his neck. "But this is the last day of the fair. You haven't left yourself much time to draw anyone's attention."

"Neither have you," Lucivar replied, "and putting those pups through their paces isn't going to show anyone what you can do."

"Who wants gristle when they can have fresh meat?" Hallevar muttered, looking away.

"Don't start digging your grave," Lucivar snapped, not pleased with how relieved he felt when anger fired Hallevar's eyes. "You're a seasoned warrior and an experienced arms master with enough years left in you to train another generation or two. This is just another kind of battlefield, so pick up your weapon and show some balls."

Hallevar smiled reluctantly.

Needing some balance, Lucivar turned toward the other men. Out of the corner of his eye, he noticed some of the women coming over. And he noticed that some were bringing young children with them.

He clamped down on the emotions that started churning

too close to the surface. He had to choose carefully. There were those who could adjust to the way the Blood lived in Kaeleer and would make a good life for themselves here. And there were those who would die swiftly and violently because they couldn't, or wouldn't, adjust. He had made a few bad choices during the first couple of fairs, had offered a trust that he shouldn't have offered. Because of it, he carried the guilt for the shattered lives of two witches who had been raped and brutally beaten—and he carried the memory of the sick rage he'd felt when he'd executed the Eyrien males who had been responsible. After that, he'd found a way to confirm his choices. He hadn't always trusted his own judgment, but he never doubted Jaenelle's.

"Lucivar."

Lucivar honed his attention to the Sapphire-Jeweled Warlord Prince who had moved to the front of the group. "Falonar."

"It's *Prince* Falonar," Falonar snarled.

Lucivar bared his teeth in a feral smile. "I thought we were being informal, since I'm sure an aristo male like you wouldn't forget something like basic courtesy."

"Why should I offer you basic courtesy?"

"Because I'm the one wearing the Ebon-gray," Lucivar replied too softly as he shifted his weight just enough to let the other man see the challenge and make the choice.

"Stop it, both of you," Hallevar snarled. "We're all on shaky ground in this place. We don't need it yanked out from under us because you two keep wanting to prove whose cock is bigger. I thumped both of you when you were snot-nosed brats, and I can still do it."

Lucivar felt the tension slide away and took a step back. Hallevar knew as well as he did that he could snap the older man in half with his hands or his mind, but Hallevar had been one of the few who had seen the potential warrior and hadn't cared about his bloodlines—or the lack of them.

"That's better," Hallevar said to Lucivar with an approving nod. "And you, Falonar. You've had a couple of offers, which is more than most of us can say. Maybe you'd better consider them."

Falonar's face tightened. He took a deep breath and let it out. "I guess I should. It doesn't look like the bastard's going to show."

"What bastard is that?" Lucivar asked mildly. More of the women and some of the men who had refused to acknowledge him had wandered over.

It was a young Warlord who answered. "The Warlord Prince of Ebon Rih. We'd heard . . ."

"You heard . . . ?" Lucivar prodded when the Warlord didn't finish, noticing the way the man shifted a bit closer to the witch who was holding an adorable little girl in her arms. Lucivar's gold eyes narrowed as he opened his psychic senses a little more. A little Queen. His gaze shifted to the boy who had a two-fisted grip on the woman's skirt. There was strength there, potential there. He felt something inside him shift, sharpen. "What did you hear?"

The Warlord swallowed hard. "We heard he's a hard bastard, but he's fair if you serve him well. And he doesn't . . ."

It was the fear in the woman's eyes and the way her brown skin paled that honed Lucivar's temper. "And he doesn't plow a woman unless she invites him?" he said too softly.

He felt a flash of female anger nearby. Before he could locate the source, he remembered the children who probably already carried too many scars. "You heard right. He doesn't."

Falonar shifted, bringing Lucivar's attention—and his temper—back to someone who could handle it. Then he gave Hallevar a sharp look, and a couple of other men that he'd known before centuries of slavery had taken him away from the Eyrien courts and hunting camps.

"Is that what you've been waiting for?" It took effort, but he kept his voice neutral.

"Wouldn't you?" Hallevar replied. "It may not be the Territory that we knew in Terreille, but they call it Askavi here, too, and maybe it won't feel so . . . strange."

Lucivar clenched his teeth. The afternoon was fleeing. He had to make some choices, and he had to make them *now.* He turned back to Falonar. "Are you going to choke every time you have to take an order from me?"

Falonar stiffened. "Why should I take any orders from *you*?"

"Because I *am* the Warlord Prince of Ebon Rih."

Shock. Tense stillness. Some of the men—a good number

of the men who had wandered over—looked at him in disgust and walked away.

Falonar narrowed his eyes. "You already have a contract?"

"A longstanding one. Think carefully, Prince Falonar. If serving under me is going to be a bone in your throat, you'd better take one of those other offers, because if you break the rules that I set, I'll tear you apart. And you—and everyone else who was waiting—had better think about what Ebon Rih is."

"It's the Keep's Territory," Hallevar said. "Same as the Black Valley in Terreille. We know that."

Lucivar nodded, his eyes never leaving Falonar's. "There's one big difference." He paused and then added, "I serve in the Dark Court at Ebon Askavi."

Several people gasped. Falonar's eyes widened. Then he looked at the Ebon-gray Jewel that hung from the gold chain around Lucivar's neck, but it was a considering look, not an insulting one. "There's really a Queen there?" he asked slowly.

"Oh, yes," Lucivar replied softly. "There's a Queen there. You should also know this: I present her with my choices about who serves me in Ebon Rih, but the final decision is hers. If she says 'no,' you're gone." He looked at the tense, silent people watching him. "There's not much time left to make a decision. I'll wait by the gate. Anyone who's interested can talk to me there."

He walked to the gate, aware of the eyes that watched him. He kept his back to them and looked at the corrals set up as waiting areas for other races. He observed everything and saw nothing.

It shouldn't matter anymore. He had a place here, a family here, a Queen he loved and felt honored to serve. He was respected for his intelligence, his skill as a warrior, and the Jewels he wore. And he was liked and loved for himself.

But he had spent 1,700 years believing he was a half-breed bastard, and the insults and the blows he'd received as a boy in the hunting camps had helped shape the formidable temper he'd inherited from his father. The courts he'd served in as a slave after that had put the final vicious edge on it.

It shouldn't matter anymore. It *didn't* matter anymore. He wouldn't allow it to hurt him. But he also knew that if Hallevar decided to go back to Terreille or accept whatever crumbs were offered in another court instead of signing a contract with him, it would be a long time before the Warlord Prince of Ebon Rih returned to the service fair.

"Prince Yaslana."

Lucivar almost smiled at the reluctance in Falonar's voice, but he kept his face carefully neutral as he turned to face the other man. "The bone's choking you already?" The careful wariness he saw in Falonar's eyes surprised him.

"We never liked each other, for a lot of reasons. We don't have to like each other now in order to work together. We've fought together against the Jhinka. You know what I can do."

"We were green fighters then, both taking orders from someone else," Lucivar said carefully. "This is different."

Falonar nodded solemnly. "This is different. But for the chance to serve in Ebon Rih, I'm willing to set aside the past. Are you?"

They had been rivals, competitors, two young Warlord Princes struggling to prove their dominance. Falonar had gone on to serve in the High Priestess of Askavi's First Circle. He had gone to slavery.

"Can you follow orders?" Lucivar asked. It wasn't an unreasonable question. Warlord Princes were a law unto themselves. Unless they gave their hearts as well as their bodies, following orders wasn't easy for any of them. Even then, it wasn't easy.

"I can follow orders," Falonar said, and then added under his breath, "When I can stomach them."

"And you're willing to follow the rules I've set, even if it means losing some of the privileges you may have come to expect?"

Falonar narrowed his gold eyes. "I suppose you don't break any rules anymore?"

The question surprised a laugh out of Lucivar. "Oh, I still break some. And I get my ass kicked for it."

Falonar opened his mouth, then closed it again.

"The Steward and the Master of the Guard," Lucivar said dryly, answering the unspoken question.

"Those Jewels would give you some leverage," Falonar said, tipping his head to indicate Lucivar's Ebon-gray Jewel.

"Not with those two."

Falonar looked startled, then thoughtful. "How long have you been here?"

"Eight years."

"Then you've already served out your contract."

Lucivar gave Falonar a sharp-edged smile. "Plant your ambitions somewhere else, Prince. Mine's a lifetime contract."

Falonar tensed. "I thought Warlord Princes were required to serve five years in a court."

Lucivar nodded and clamped down on the pleasure that jumped through him when he saw Hallevar coming toward him. "That's what's required." He smiled wickedly. "It only took the Lady three years to realize that wasn't what I agreed to."

Falonar hesitated. "What's she like?"

"Wonderful. Beautiful. Terrifying." Lucivar gave Falonar an assessing look. "Are you coming to Ebon Rih?"

"I'm coming to Ebon Rih." Falonar nodded to Hallevar and stepped aside for the older man.

"I'd like to come with you," Hallevar said abruptly.

"But?" Lucivar said.

Hallevar looked over his shoulder at the two boys who were hovering out of earshot. He turned back to Lucivar. "I said they were mine."

"Are they?"

Hallevar's eyes filled with heat. "If they'd been mine, I would have acknowledged them, whether or not the mothers denied paternity. A child isn't considered a bastard if a sire is listed, even if the man doesn't get a chance to be a father."

The words stung. Prythian, the High Priestess of Askavi in Terreille, and Dorothea SaDiablo had spun their lies in order to separate him from Luthvian, his mother, and they had altered his birth documents because they hadn't wanted anyone to know who his father really was. It had stunned him to learn that the hard feelings he carried inside him because of that deceit were nothing compared to Saetan's rage.

"One has a mother who's a whore in a Red Moon

house," Hallevar said. "Stands to reason she wouldn't know whose seed she carried. The other woman was the known lover of an aristo Warlord. The witch he'd married was barren, and everyone knew he made sure his mistress didn't invite another man to her bed. He wanted the child, would have acknowledged the child. But when it was born, she named a dozen men in the court that she claimed might have been the sire. She did it on purpose, and because she wanted revenge on the father, she condemned the child."

Lucivar just nodded, fighting the anger that burned in him.

"This is a new place, Lucivar," Hallevar pleaded. "A new chance. You know what it's like. You should understand better than anyone. They're not strong like you. Neither of them will wear dark Jewels. But they're good boys, and they'll carry their weight. And they are full-blooded Eyriens," he added.

"So they don't carry the stigma of being half-breeds?" Lucivar asked with deadly control.

"I never used that word with you," Hallevar said quietly.

"No, you didn't. But it's an easy enough word to say without thinking. So I'll give you fair warning, Lord Hallevar. It's a word you would do well to forget, because there's nothing I could do to save you if you said it within my father's hearing."

Hallevar stared at him. "Your father is here? You know him?"

"I know him. And believe me, you haven't seen temper until you've been on the receiving end of my father's rage."

"I'll remember. What about the boys?"

"No lies, Hallevar. I'll take them for themselves, subject to the Queen's approval just like any other male."

Hallevar smiled, obviously relieved. "I'll tell them to fetch our things." A curt wave of his hand had the two boys racing toward the barracks. Without looking at Lucivar, he asked, "Is he proud of you?"

"When he doesn't want to throttle me or kick my ass."

Hallevar tried to swallow a laugh and ended up wheezing. "I'd like to meet him."

"You will," Lucivar promised dryly.

Whether it was seeing the first ones being accepted or

needing a little time to gather their courage, others approached him.

There was the young Warlord, Endar, and his wife, Dorian, their son, Alanar, and their little Queen daughter, Orian.

The woman was frightened, the man tense. But the little girl gave him a sweet smile and leaned away from her mother, her arms reaching for him.

Lucivar took her, settled her on his hip, and grinned. "Don't get any ideas, bright-eyes. I'm taken," he told her as he tickled gently and made her giggle. When he gave the girl back to her mother, Dorian stared at him as if he'd grown another head.

Next came Nurian, a Healer who hadn't completed her training yet, and her younger sister, Jillian, who was on the cusp of changing from girl to woman.

There was Kohlvar, a weapons maker. And there were Rothvar and Zaranar, two warriors Lucivar remembered from the hunting camps.

One thought nagged at him as he talked with them. Why were they here? Kohlvar had been a young man, by the standard of the long-lived races, when Lucivar was first sent away from Askavi. Even then, when Kohlvar was just past his journeymanship, he'd been known for the strength and the balance of the weapons he made. He should have made a good living in Terreille, and he could have stayed away from court intrigue if he'd chosen to. Rothvar and Zaranar were seasoned warriors, the kind who could have found a position in most of the courts in Askavi or accepted any independent work they chose.

And why would an aristo Warlord Prince like Falonar leave Terreille?

The wariness inside him grew. Were things far worse in Terreille than anyone here suspected, or were these men here for another reason?

Lucivar pushed those thoughts aside. He hadn't sensed anything in the people who had approached him that would make him decide against them, so he would let the questions rest for now. And he would let Jaenelle pass judgment.

By the time the last man left to fetch his things from the

barracks, Lucivar had agreed to take twenty males and a dozen females.

How many of these people would survive the full term of their contracts? he wondered as they hurried toward him with the meager belongings they had been allowed to bring with them. There were other dangers in Kaeleer beyond the ones they expected. And there were the demon-dead. Considering where he was taking them, they would quickly have to come to terms with having the demon-dead walk among them.

He took a deep breath and let it out slowly. "Ready?"

It amused him, but didn't surprise him, when Falonar looked over the group and answered him as if he'd already accepted the man as his second-in-command.

"We're ready."

2 / Kaeleer

Daemon Sadi crossed his legs at the knee, steepled his fingers, and rested his long, black-tinted nails against his chin. "What about the Queens in the other Territories?" he asked in his deep, cultured voice.

Lord Jorval smiled wearily. "As I've explained before, Prince Sadi, the Queens outside of Little Terreille are not eager to accept their Terreillean Brothers and Sisters into their courts, and even the immigrants who do get contracts are made to feel less than welcome."

"Did you inquire?" Daemon's gold eyes glazed slightly. A stranger or slight acquaintance might have thought he looked tired or bored, but that sleepy look would have terrified anyone who really knew him.

"I inquired," Jorval said a bit sharply. "The Queens didn't reply."

Daemon glanced at the four sheets of paper spread out on the desk in front of him. In the past two days, he and Jorval had sat in this room six times. Those sheets of paper, listing the four Queens who were interested in obtaining his services, had been offered to him at the first meeting. They had been the only ones offered.

Jorval folded his hands and sighed. "You must understand. A Warlord Prince is considered a dangerous asset, even when he wears a lighter Jewel and is serving among his own people. A man with your strength and reputation . . ." He shrugged. "I realize your expectations might be different. The Darkness knows, there are so many who have an unrealistic idea of life in Kaeleer. But I can assure you, Prince, that having four Queens who are willing to accept the challenge of having you serve in their courts for the next five years is unusual—and not an opportunity that should be brushed aside."

Daemon didn't give any indication that the warning had been felt as much as a physical jab would have been. No, he couldn't brush aside the narrow choices if he wanted to stay in Kaeleer. But he wasn't sure he could stomach any of those women long enough to do what he had originally come here to do. And he couldn't help wondering how large a gift Jorval would receive from whichever Queen he chose.

Suddenly it was too much: the lack of sleep, the pressure to make an unpalatable choice, the nerves that were strained because of what he had planned to do—and the questions that had arisen from the gossip he had sifted through as he walked around the service fair.

"I'll consider them and let you know," Daemon said, moving toward the door with the graceful speed that tended to make people think of a feline predator.

"Prince Sadi," Jorval called sharply.

Daemon stopped at the door and turned.

"The last bell will ring in less than an hour. If you haven't made a choice by then, you will no longer have a choice. You will have to accept whatever offer is made or leave Kaeleer."

"I'm aware of that, Lord Jorval," Daemon said too softly.

He left the building, slipped his hands into his trouser pockets, and began walking aimlessly.

He despised Lord Jorval. There was something about the man's psychic scent, something tainted. And there were too many things hidden behind the dark, flat eyes. From the moment he'd met Jorval, he'd had to fight against the instinctive desire to rise to the killing edge and tuck the thin Warlord into a deep, secret grave.

Why had Lord Magstrom handed him over to Jorval?

He had talked to the elderly man briefly when he arrived
in Goth late on the third day of the fair and had been
cautiously willing to trust the man's judgment. When he
had expressed his desire to serve in a court outside of Little
Terreille, Magstrom's blue eyes had twinkled with
amusement.

*The Queens outside of Little Terreille are very selective in
their choices,* Magstrom had said. *But they do have an advantage for a man like you—they know how to handle dark-
Jeweled males.*

Magstrom had promised to make some inquiries, and
they had arranged to meet early the following morning. But
when Daemon arrived for the meeting, it was Lord Jorval
who was waiting for him with the names of four Queens
who wanted to control his life for the next five years.

Questionable food smells that he caught in passing sharpened an already keen temper by reminding him that he'd
eaten almost nothing in the past two days. The clash of
strong perfumes mingled with equally strong body odors
helped him remember why he hadn't eaten.

More than that, the inability to sleep and the lack of
appetite were due to the questions that had no answers. At
least, not here.

It had taken him five years after walking out of the
Twisted Kingdom to come to Kaeleer. There had been no
hurry. Jaenelle had not been waiting for him as she had
promised when she had marked the trail to lead him out
of madness. He *still* didn't know what had really happened
when he had tried to bring Jaenelle out of the abyss in
order to save her body. His memories of that night, thirteen
years ago, were still jumbled, still had pieces missing. He
had a vague memory of someone telling him that Jaenelle
had died—that the High Lord had tricked another male
into being the instrument that had destroyed an extraordinary child.

So when Jaenelle *hadn't* been on the island where Surreal and Manny had kept him safe and hidden, and when
Surreal had told him about the shadow Jaenelle had created
in order to bring him out of the Twisted Kingdom . . .

He had spent the past five years believing that he had
killed the child who was his Queen; had spent the past five
years believing that she had used the last of her strength

to bring him out of madness so that he would call in the
debt owed to her; had spent the past five years honing his
Craft skills and allowing his mind to heal as much as it
could for only one reason: to come to Kaeleer and destroy
the man who had used him as the instrument—his father,
the High Lord of Hell.

But now that he was here . . .

Gossip and speculation about the witches in the Shadow
Realm flowed through this place, currents of thoughts easily
plucked from the air. The currents that had unnerved him
as he'd walked around the fair yesterday were the specula-
tions about a strange, terrifying witch that could see a
man's soul in a glance. According to the gossip, anyone
who signed a contract outside of Little Terreille was
brought before this witch, and anyone found wanting didn't
live to see another sunrise.

He might have dismissed that gossip except that it finally
occurred to him that, perhaps, Jaenelle *had* been waiting
for him, but not in Terreille. He'd let grief cloud his thinking, locking away all but the best memories of the few
months he had known her. So he'd forgotten about the ties
she already had to Kaeleer.

If she really *was* in the Shadow Realm, he'd already lost
five years he could have spent with her. He wasn't going
to spend the next five in some other court, yearning from
a distance.

If, that is, she really *was* alive.

A change in the psychic scents around him pulled him
from his thoughts. He looked around and swore under his
breath.

He was at the far end of the fairgrounds. Judging by the
sky, he'd have to run in order to get back to the administra-
tors' building and make a choice before the bell ending the
last day of the fair rang. Even then, he might not have a
choice if Jorval wasn't waiting for him.

As he turned to go back, he noticed one of the red ban-
ners that indicated a station where court contracts were
filled out. There were a few Eyriens standing to one side,
and a line of them waiting their turn. But it was the Eyrien
warrior watching the proceedings that froze Daemon where
he stood.

The man wore a leather vest and the black, skintight

trousers favored by Eyrien warriors. His black hair fell to his shoulders, which was unusual for an Eyrien male. But it was the way he stood, the way he moved that felt so painfully familiar.

A wild joy filled Daemon, even as his heart clogged his throat and tears stung his gold eyes. *Lucivar.*

Of course, it couldn't be. Lucivar had died eight years ago, escaping from the salt mines of Pruul.

Then the man turned. For a moment, Daemon thought he saw the same fierce joy in Lucivar's eyes before it was lost in blazing fury.

Seeing the fury and remembering that the unfinished business between them could only end in blood being spilled, Daemon retreated behind the cold mask he'd lived behind for most of his life and started to walk away.

He'd only gone a few steps before a hand clamped on his right arm and spun him around.

"How long have you been here?" Lucivar demanded.

Daemon tried to shake off the hand, but Lucivar's fingers dug in hard enough to leave bruises. "Two days," Daemon replied with chilly courtesy. He felt the mask slip and knew he needed to get away from here before his emotions spilled over. Right now, he wasn't sure if he would meet Lucivar's anger with tears or rage.

"Have you signed a contract?" Lucivar shook him. "Have you?"

"No, and there's little time left to do it. If you'll excuse me."

Lucivar snarled, tightened his grip, and almost yanked Daemon off his feet. "You weren't on the lists," he muttered as he pulled Daemon toward the table under the red banner. "I checked. You weren't on any of the damn lists."

"I apologize for the incon—"

"Shut up, Daemon."

Daemon clenched his teeth and lengthened his stride to match his brother's. He didn't know what kind of game Lucivar was playing, but he'd be damned if he'd go into it being dragged like a reluctant puppy.

"Look, Prick," Daemon said, trying to balance Lucivar's volatile temper with reason, "I have to—"

"You're signing a contract with the Warlord Prince of Ebon Rih."

Daemon let out an exasperated huff. "Don't you think you should discuss it with him beforehand?"

Lucivar gave him a knife-edged look. "I don't usually discuss things with myself, Bastard. Plant your feet."

Daemon felt the ground roll unexpectedly and decided it was good advice. "Have long have you been in Kaeleer?" he asked, feeling weak.

"Eight years." Lucivar hissed as an older Eyrien Warlord signed the contract and stepped away from the table. "Hell's fire. Why is that little maggot taking so long to write a line of information?" He took a step toward the table. Then he turned back, and said too softly, "Don't try to walk away. If you do, I'll break your legs in so many places you won't even be able to crawl."

Daemon didn't bother to respond. Lucivar didn't make idle threats, and in a physical fight, Daemon knew he couldn't beat his Eyrien half brother. Besides, the ground under his feet kept shifting in unexpected ways that threatened his balance.

The Warlord Prince of Ebon Rih. Lucivar was the Warlord Prince of the territory that belonged to Ebon Askavi, the Black Mountain that was also called the Keep—that was also the Sanctuary of Witch.

That didn't necessarily mean anything. The land existed whether a Warlord Prince watched over it or not—or a Queen ruled there or not.

But Lucivar being alive here nourished the hope in Daemon that he had been wrong about Jaenelle's death as well. Had she sent Lucivar to the service fair to look for him? Had one of Lord Magstrom's inquiries reached her after all? Was she . . .

Daemon shook his head. Too many questions—and this wasn't the time or place to get answers. But, oh, how he began to hope.

As Lucivar approached the table, someone called, "Prince Yaslana. Here are two more for the contract."

Turning toward the voice, Daemon felt the ground shift a little more. Two men, a Sapphire-Jeweled Warlord and a Red-Jeweled Warlord Prince, were pulling two women toward the table. A brown-haired man with a black eye patch and a pronounced limp angrily followed them.

The frightened woman had dark hair, fair skin, and blue

eyes. It had been thirteen years since he'd seen Wilhelmina Benedict, Jaenelle's half sister. She had grown into a beautiful woman, but was still filled with the brittle fear she'd had as an adolescent. Her eyes widened when she saw him, but she said nothing.

The snarling woman with the long black hair, light golden-brown skin, delicately pointed ears, and blazing gold-green eyes was Surreal. She had left the island four months ago, giving no explanation except there was something she had to do.

At first, he didn't know the limping man. When he saw the flash of recognition in the man's blue eye, he felt a stab of pain under his heart. Andrew, the stable lad who had helped him escape the Hayllian guards after Jaenelle had been taken back to Briarwood.

"Lord Khardeen. Prince Aaron," Lucivar said, formally greeting the Sapphire-Jeweled Warlord and the Red-Jeweled Warlord Prince.

"Prince Yaslana, these Ladies should be part of the contract," Prince Aaron said respectfully.

Lucivar gave both women a look that could have flayed flesh from bone. Then he looked at Khardeen and Aaron. "Accepted."

Wilhelmina trembled visibly, but Surreal hooked her hair behind her pointed ears and narrowed her eyes at Lucivar. "Look, sugar—"

"Surreal," Daemon said quietly. He shook his head. The last thing any of them needed was Surreal and Lucivar tangling with each other.

Surreal hissed. When she tried to shake off Prince Aaron's hand, the man let her go, then shifted to block any attempt she might make to leave. Eyeing Lucivar with intense dislike, she moved until she stood beside Daemon. "Is that your brother?" she asked in a low voice. "The one who's supposed to be dead?"

Daemon nodded.

She watched Lucivar for a minute. "*Is* he dead?"

For the first time since he'd arrived in Kaeleer, Daemon smiled. "The demon-dead can't tolerate daylight—at least according to the stories—so I would say Lucivar is very much alive."

"Well, can't you reason with him? I have a mark of safe

passage and a three-month visitor's pass. I didn't come here to sign a contract for court service, and the day I jump when that son of a bitch snaps his fingers is the day the sun is going to shine in Hell."

"Don't make any bets on it," Daemon muttered, watching Lucivar study the member of the Dark Council who was filling out the contract.

Before Surreal could reply, Wilhelmina sidled over to them. "Prince Sadi," she said in a voice that trembled on the edge of panic. "Lady."

"Lady Benedict," Daemon replied formally while Surreal nodded in acknowledgment.

Wilhelmina glanced fearfully at Lucivar, who was now talking to the older Eyrien Warlord. "He's scary," she whispered.

Surreal smiled maliciously and raised her voice. "When a man wears his pants that tight, they tend to pinch his balls, and that tends to pinch his temper."

Aaron, who was standing near them, coughed violently, trying to muffle his laughter.

Seeing Lucivar break off his conversation and head toward them, Daemon sighed and wished he knew a spell that would make Surreal lose her voice for the next few hours.

Lucivar stopped an arm's length away, ignoring the way Wilhelmina shrank away from him, focusing his attention on Surreal. He smiled the lazy, arrogant smile that was usually the only warning before a fight.

Surreal lowered her right hand so that her arm hung at her side.

Recognizing that as *her* warning signal, Daemon slipped his hands out of his trouser pockets and shifted slightly, prepared to stop her before she was foolish enough to pull a knife on Lucivar.

"You're Titian's daughter, aren't you?" Lucivar asked.

"What do you care?" Surreal snarled.

Lucivar studied her for a moment. Then he shook his head and muttered, "You're going to be a pain in the ass."

"Then maybe you should let me go," Surreal said with sweet venom.

Lucivar laughed, low and nasty. "If you think I'm going to explain to the Harpy Queen why her daughter's in another court when I was standing here, then you'd better think again, little witch."

Surreal bared her teeth. "My mother is *not* a Harpy. And I'm not a little witch. And I'm not signing any damn contract that gives you control over me."

"Think again," Lucivar said.

Daemon's hand clamped on Surreal's right forearm. Aaron clamped down on her left arm.

The bell indicating the end of the service fair rang three times.

Surreal swore furiously. Lucivar just smiled.

Then a man's voice, rising in protest, made them all turn their attention toward the table.

Daemon caught sight of the fussily dressed man who was busily straightening papers and ignoring the young Eyrien Warlord.

Snarling, Lucivar strode to the table, slipped through the line of confused, upset Eyriens, and stopped beside the man who was still pretending not to notice any of them.

"Is there a problem, Lord Friall?" Lucivar asked mildly.

Friall shook back the lace at his wrists and continued to gather up his papers. "The bell ending the fair has rung. If these people are still available when you arrive tomorrow for claiming day, you can sign them to a contract under the first-offer rule."

Daemon tensed. Lord Jorval had explained the first-offer rule of the service fair several times. During the fair, immigrants had the right to refuse an offer to serve in a court, or wait to see if another offer was made from a different court, or try to negotiate for a better position. But the day after the service fair was a claiming day. There was only one choice. Immigrants could accept whatever was offered by the first court to fill out a claim for them—and Jorval had implied that any position offered at a claiming was usually a demeaning one—or they could return to Terreille and attempt to come back for the next fair. He had spent two million gold marks in bribes in order to get on the immigration list for this service fair. He had the means to do it again if he dared risk going back to Terreille. But most had spent everything they had for this one chance at a hopefully better life. They would sign a contract for the privilege of crawling if that was the only way to stay in Kaeleer.

"Now, Lord Friall," Lucivar said, still sounding mild, "you know as well as I do that a person has to be accepted before the final bell, but there's an hour afterward for the contracts to be filled out and signed."

"If you want to sign the contract for the ones already listed, you can take them with you now. The others will have to wait until tomorrow," Friall insisted.

Lucivar raised his right hand and scratched his chin.

The rest happened so fast, Daemon didn't even see the move. One moment, Lucivar was scratching his chin. The next, his Eyrien war blade was delicately resting on Friall's left wrist.

"Now," Lucivar said pleasantly, "you can finish filling out that contract or I can cut off your left hand. Your choice."

"Shit," Surreal muttered as she moved closer to Daemon.

"You can't do this," Friall whimpered.

Lucivar's hand didn't seem to move, but a thin line of blood began to flow from Friall's wrist.

"I'll inform the Council," Friall wailed. "You'll be in trouble."

"Maybe," Lucivar replied. "But you'll still be without a left hand. If you're lucky, that's all you'll lose. If you're not . . ."

A hurried movement made Daemon glance to the left. Lord Magstrom, the Dark Council member he had first talked with, stopped at the other end of the table.

"May I be of some assistance, Prince Yaslana?" the elderly man asked breathlessly.

Lucivar looked up, and Magstrom froze. The color drained from his face.

"Mother Night," Aaron muttered. "He's risen to the killing edge."

Daemon didn't move. Neither did anyone else. A Warlord Prince who had risen to the killing edge was violent and uncontrollable. He wore the Black, the only Jewel darker than Lucivar's Ebon-gray, but any effort he made to try to contain his brother would only snap whatever self-control Lucivar still had. At the very least, Friall would die. At the worst, there would be a slaughter.

"Lord Friall says the contracts can't be filled out after the last bell," Lucivar said with deceptive mildness.

"I'm sure he misunderstood," Magstrom replied quickly. "There's an hour's leniency after the last bell in order to fill out the papers." When Lucivar said nothing, he took a careful breath. "Lord Friall seems to be indisposed. With your permission, I will finish filling out the contracts."

By this time, the white lace around Friall's left wrist was a wet, bright red. Snot ran from the man's nose as he wept silently.

At Lucivar's slight nod, Magstrom pulled the papers away from the small pool of blood on the table and picked up the pen lying next to them. Retreating to the other end of the table, Magstrom sat down.

Lucivar raised his left hand and pointed at Daemon. "He's first."

Magstrom filled out the top of the contract and then looked at Daemon expectantly. Beads of sweat dotted his forehead.

Move, damn you, move. For a tense moment, Daemon's body refused to obey. When his legs finally started working, he had the chilling sensation that he was walking on thin, cracked ice where one false step could lead to disaster.

"Daemon Sadi," Magstrom said quietly, writing the name in neat script. "From Hayll, isn't that right?"

"Yes," Daemon replied. To his own ears, his voice sounded hoarse, hollow. If Magstrom noticed, the man gave no indication.

"When we met, I recall that you said you wore a dark Jewel, but I don't remember which one."

When he'd met with Magstrom, he'd said the Red was his Birthright Jewel, but he had evaded mentioning his Jewel of rank. There could be no evading now. "The Black."

Magstrom looked up, his eyes wide with shock. Then he quickly filled in the space on the paper. "And you brought two servants?"

"Manny is a White-Jeweled witch. Jazen is a Purple Dusk Warlord."

Magstrom wrote down the information, then turned the contract around. "Just sign here and then put your initials in the spaces for the other two signatures to indicate that you accept responsibility for your servants." As Daemon bent down to sign the contract, he whispered, "This court would have been my choice for you. You belong here."

Saying nothing, Daemon stepped away from the table to make room for Surreal. He glanced once at Lucivar, whose glazed gold eyes just stared at him.

"Name?" Magstrom asked.

"Surreal."

When she didn't say anything else, Magstrom said gently, "While they are not often used in Kaeleer, it is customary to formally record a family name."

Surreal stared at him. Then she smiled maliciously. "SaDiablo."

Magstrom gasped. Khardeen and Aaron gaped at her for a moment before turning away from the table.

Daemon closed his eyes and didn't listen to the rest of her answers. Since she was Kartane SaDiablo's bastard daughter, she had probably intended it as a slap against his mother, Dorothea. There was no reason for her to know that the name had meaning in Kaeleer.

"Hell's fire, Mother Night, and may the Darkness be merciful," two voices said in unison.

Daemon opened his eyes. Aaron and Khardeen stood in front of him, watching Surreal move away from the table.

Aaron looked at him. "Is that really her family name?"

Daemon hesitated. He didn't know what kind of stigma being a bastard carried in Kaeleer, and he owed Surreal too much to reveal a potentially vulnerable spot. "The man who sired her goes by that name," he replied cautiously.

"What do you think we should do?" Aaron asked Khardeen.

"Sell tickets," Khardeen replied promptly. "And then find a safe place to watch the explosion."

Their amusement at Surreal's expense made Daemon's temper flash. "Is this going to be a problem?"

"You could say that," Khardeen said gleefully. Then he settled his face into a serious expression. "You see, what Lady Surreal hasn't realized yet is that by formally declaring herself as part of the SaDiablo family, she's just acquired Lucivar as a cousin."

"And if you think Lucivar has a dominating personality with other males, you should see him with the women in the family," Aaron added.

And with Jaenelle?

The question went unspoken because he didn't want to see a blank expression on their faces when they heard the name—and because he wasn't sure what he would do if he saw recognition. It would be better to ask Lucivar that question—in private. And the questions he now had about women and family . . . Those, too, would be asked later.

"And we're not even going to try to imagine what's going to happen when she tangles with the males on the Dea al Mon side of her family," Khardeen said.

"Why should they be involved at all?" Daemon asked.

"Because she's Titian's daughter, finally come home," Aaron said. Then he grinned. "Lady Surreal is about to find out that she now has male relatives from both her bloodlines who are going to make her life their business—and several of those males are Warlord Princes."

Mother Night! "She's never going to tolerate that," Daemon said.

"Well, she's not going to have a lot of choice," Khardeen replied.

"The Blood are matriarchal. Isn't that true in Kaeleer?"

"Of course," Aaron said cheerfully. "But males do have rights and privileges, and we take full advantage of them." He studied Daemon for a moment. "Why don't you try to keep her calm while we keep an eye on Lucivar. If nobody pushes him, he should be able to keep his temper leashed."

"Do you know him that well?" Daemon asked.

He saw the knowledge in their eyes that they had kept carefully masked until now. They knew he was Lucivar's brother. And they knew . . .

"We all serve in the same court, Prince Sadi," Aaron said quietly. "We all serve in the Lady's First Circle."

Then they walked away from him.

They might as well have shouted it from the rooftops. *She's alive!*

Joy and trepidation warred inside him, causing his heart to pound too hard, his blood to whip through his veins too fast. *She's alive!*

But what did she think of him? What did she *feel* for him?

No answers. Not here. Not yet.

With exaggerated care, Daemon walked over to Surreal. The moment he stopped moving, he swayed like a willow in a heavy wind.

Surreal wrapped her arms around his left arm and planted her feet.

"What's wrong?" she asked quietly, urgently. "Are you ill?"

She, better than anyone, would be able to guess exactly what was wrong, but he wasn't about to admit it. Not now. "I've had almost no sleep and very little food in the past few days," he said.

She narrowed her eyes but accepted the truth that was also a lie. "I can understand that. This place makes my skin crawl."

Daemon tapped into the reservoir of power stored in his Black Jewel. It rushed through his body, and for the first time since he'd seen Lucivar, he felt steady.

Surreal sensed the change in him. She loosened her grip, but still kept one arm companionably linked with his. "Why do you think the old Warlord doing the contracts looked so shocked when I said my family name was SaDiablo? Is that bitch Dorothea that well-known here?"

"I don't know," Daemon said carefully. "But I have heard that the name of the Warlord Prince of Dhemlan is S. D. SaDiablo." This wasn't the time to tell her that the Warlord Prince of Dhemlan was also the High Lord of Hell—and his and Lucivar's father.

"Shit," Surreal muttered. Then she shrugged. "Well, I'm not likely to meet him, and if someone asks, I can just say that we *might* be distantly related. Very distantly."

Remembering Khardeen's and Aaron's comments, Daemon made a sound that might have been a whimper.

"You sure you're all right?" Surreal asked, studying him.

"I'm fine." Just fine. More than fine. He would believe it, insist on it, until it was true. "Do me a favor. Ask Khardeen or Aaron if we're going to be traveling in the Web Coaches, and then contact Manny so that she and Jazen can meet us there."

She didn't ask why he didn't do it himself, and he was grateful.

Finally, the last Eyrien had signed the contract and moved away from the table. Lucivar, who hadn't moved or said anything since Lord Magstrom started filling out the contracts, called in a clean cloth, wiped the blood off his war blade, vanished both, and walked around the table to sign the contracts.

Holding his bleeding wrist against his chest, Friall wiped his nose on his clean sleeve and said in a sulky voice, "You have to make copies. He can't take the contracts until you make copies."

Lucivar slowly straightened up and turned toward Friall. A male voice swore softly.

Giving Friall a sharp glance, Magstrom said hurriedly, "I'll give Prince Yaslana blank contracts. The Steward of the Court can make the copies and return them to the Dark Council for the clerks to record." When Friall seemed about to protest, and surely get himself killed, Magstrom added, "I've seen Lord Jorval do this a number of times. He explained that the Stewards could be trusted to make an accurate copy, and it was the only way to expedite getting the immigrants settled in their new homes."

Calling in a thin leather case, Lucivar slipped the contracts inside and then vanished it. He nodded politely at Magstrom, turned to face the waiting immigrants, and snarled, "Let's go."

Daemon turned smoothly as Lucivar approached him and matched the Eyrien's stride.

They had walked like this before, side by side. Not often, because the Terreillean Blood, who were afraid of them individually, were terrified of them when they were together. Even the Ring of Obedience hadn't been enough to stop the destruction they had caused in Terreillean courts.

As they headed for the Coaches that were designed to ride the Winds, Daemon wondered how long they could put off the unfinished business between them.

It was almost full dark by the time they reached the two large, Ebon-gray shielded Coaches at the far end of the landing area.

Lucivar dropped the Ebon-gray shields, opened the door of the first Coach, looked at Daemon, and said, "Get in."

Daemon glanced around. "My servants aren't here yet."

"I'll look for them. Get in."

Looking at Lucivar's still-glazed eyes, and picking up a

strained urgency in his brother's psychic scent, Daemon obeyed.

Surreal, Wilhelmina, and Andrew quickly came in behind him, followed by several Eyriens. A minute later, Daemon breathed a sigh of relief as Jazen helped Manny up the steps into the Coach. A couple more Eyriens came in, and then an Ebon-gray shield snapped up around the Coach, effectively locking everyone but Daemon inside, since he was the only one who wore a Jewel darker than Lucivar's.

A Web Coach this size could usually accommodate thirty people, but Eyriens required more room because of their wings. Noticing the lack of seats, Daemon wondered if the Coach was usually used for conveying something other than humans, or if Lucivar, intending to bring Eyriens, had had the usual seats removed. The only thing that could be used for seats were a few sturdy wooden boxes pushed up against the walls, with cushions on top of them and an open front for storage.

After studying the people packed against the walls in order to leave a narrow aisle in the center, Daemon turned his attention to the Coach. At the front was a door that led to the driver's compartment. Maybe one other person could sit with the driver, giving the rest a little breathing room. Moving carefully, Daemon made his way to the short, narrow corridor at the back of the Coach. On the left was a small private room that held a narrow desk and a straight chair, an easy chair and hassock, and a single bed. The room on the right held a sink and toilet.

Daemon was about to step back into the main compartment when he heard Lucivar's voice just outside the Coach's open door.

"I don't give a damn what that sniveling little maggot says," Lucivar snarled.

"Lord Friall's conduct is not in question here," said a voice Daemon recognized as Lord Jorval's. "This will be brought before the Dark Council, and I can assure you we will not be intimidated into ignoring your vicious conduct."

"You have a problem with me, you can take it up with the Steward, the Master of the Guard, or my Queen."

"Your Queen fears you," Jorval sneered. "Everyone knows that. She can't control you properly, and the Steward and Master of the Guard certainly aren't going to demand any restraints on your temper since it suits their purpose so well."

Lucivar's voice lowered to a malevolent hiss. "Just remember, Lord Jorval, that while you and Friall are whining to the Council, I'm going to make the Territory Queens aware that there are some members of the Council who blatantly ignore their own rules about the service fair."

"That is an outright lie!"

"Then Friall is incompetent and shouldn't be given the task."

"Friall is one of the finest members of the Council!"

"In that case, was he just pissed because he'd expected to get his percentage of the bribes at the table and didn't realize you'd already pocketed them?"

"How dare you!" A long pause followed. "Perhaps Lord Friall was partly responsible for this unfortunate incident, but the Council will stand firm about this other matter."

"And what matter is that?" Lucivar crooned.

"We cannot allow you to have in your service a male who wears Jewels darker than yours."

"The Queens in Little Terreille do it all the time."

"They're Queens. They know how to control males."

"So do I."

"The Council forbids it."

"The Council can go to the bowels of Hell."

Lucivar suddenly filled the Coach's doorway.

"You can't do this!" Jorval yelled from behind him.

Lucivar turned and gave Jorval a lazy, arrogant smile. "I'm an Ebon-gray Warlord Prince. I can do anything I damn well want to." He shut the door in Jorval's face, then glanced at the driver's compartment at the front of the Coach, sending an order on a psychic thread. The Coach immediately lifted.

When Daemon took a step to reenter the main compartment, Lucivar shifted in front of him, effectively blocking the mouth of the corridor. Accepting the unspoken order, Daemon slipped his hands into his trouser pockets and leaned against the wall.

When he felt sure that Lucivar was through giving his silent instructions to whoever was driving the Coaches, he used an Ebon-gray spear thread to ask, *Will this get you into trouble?*

No, Lucivar replied. He looked over the immigrants. Every one of them quickly looked away in order to avoid meeting his eyes.

Won't this Council send a demand for some kind of discipline?

They'll send it. The Steward will read it, probably show it to the Master of the Guard, and then they'll ignore it.

Daemon realized his breathing was too quick, too shallow, but he couldn't change it as he forced himself to ask the next question. *Will they show it to your Queen?*

No, Lucivar said slowly. *They won't mention this to the Queen if they can avoid it. And if they can't, they'll try to minimize it without lying outright.*

Why?

Because the Dark Council has pushed her before, and the results scared the shit out of everyone. Lucivar shifted. "We're away from Goth," he said, raising his voice slightly. "Make yourselves as comfortable as you can. It'll be a couple of hours before we get to where we're going."

"Aren't we going to Ebon Rih?" someone asked.

"Not yet." Lucivar stepped into the small corridor, forcing Daemon to move back. He slid the door to the private compartment open, said, "Inside," and went through the doorway sideways to accommodate his wings.

Daemon followed reluctantly and slid the door closed.

Lucivar stood at one end of the room. Daemon remained at the door.

Lucivar took a deep breath, let it out slowly. "I'm sorry I lashed out at you. I wasn't angry with *you*. I—Damn it, Daemon, I checked every list I could think of, and I must have missed your name. If it wasn't for blind luck, you would've ended up in another court, and there might have been no way to get you out of that contract."

Daemon felt one layer of tension ease. He forced his lips to curve in a smile. "Well, luck favored us this time." Then he looked, really looked, at Lucivar, and the smile became genuine. "You're alive."

Lucivar returned the smile. "And you're sane."

Daemon felt a tremor run through his body and tightened his self-control. Tears stung his eyes. "Lucivar," he whispered.

He didn't know which of them moved first. One moment

they were standing as far away from each other as they could in the small room, the next they were in each other's arms, holding on as if their lives depended on it.

"Lucivar," Daemon whispered again, pressing his face against his brother's neck. "I thought you were dead."

"Hell's fire, Daemon," Lucivar said softly, hoarsely, "we couldn't find you. We didn't know what happened to you. We looked. I swear, we did look for you."

"It's all right," Daemon stroked Lucivar's head. "It's all right."

Lucivar's arms tightened around him so hard his ribs ached.

Daemon's hand fisted in Lucivar's hair. "Lucivar . . . I know there are things that need to be settled between us. But can we put them aside, just for a little while?"

"We can put them aside," Lucivar said quietly.

Daemon stepped back. Using his thumbs, he gently wiped the tears from Lucivar's face. "We'd better join the others." He turned and reached for the door.

Standing behind him, Lucivar's left hand gripped Daemon's left arm. Daemon placed his right hand over it for a moment. As his fingers slid away from Lucivar's, he looked down, and the significance of what he'd seen but hadn't really *seen* finally hit him.

"Daemon," Lucivar said urgently. "There's one thing I need to tell you. I think you may already know, but you need to hear it."

She's alive! Another tremor went through Daemon's body. "No," he said. "Not now." He slid the door open and stumbled into the corridor. Barely keeping his balance, he went into the bathroom and Black-locked the door. His body shook violently. His stomach twisted viciously. Leaning over the sink, he fought the need to be sick.

Too late.

If he had tried to find her five years ago, when he'd first returned from the Twisted Kingdom, maybe it would have been different. If he had searched for the High Lord and at least tried to find out what had really happened that night at Cassandra's Altar . . .

Too late.

He could hold on. He *would* hold on. His mind was far more fragile than he allowed anyone to realize. Oh, it was

intact. He had lost a few memories, a few small shards of
the crystal chalice, but he was whole, and he was sane. But
the healing would never be complete because he had lost
the one person he needed to complete it. It hadn't mattered
when he had only wanted to stay in one piece long enough
to destroy the High Lord. It didn't really matter now. He
could survive long enough to see her, just once.

There was nothing else he could do. If it had been any
other man, he would have used everything he was and everything he knew in order to be her lover. If it had been
any other man. But not Lucivar. He wouldn't become his
brother's rival.

So he couldn't let Lucivar tell him what he desperately
needed to hear. Not because he didn't want to know for
sure that Jaenelle was alive, but because he wasn't ready to
be told about the gold wedding ring on Lucivar's left hand.

3 / Kaeleer

Surreal pushed the last of the cushioned boxes together to
form a bench against one wall. "Sit down, Manny," she
said to the older woman.

"Wouldn't be right," Manny said. "A servant shouldn't
be sitting."

Surreal gave her a slashing look. "Don't be an ass.
You're a 'servant' because that's the only way Sadi could
bring you with him."

Manny tightened her lips in disapproval. "No need for
you to be using that kind of language, especially with children around. Besides, I was a servant for a good many
years. It was an honest living and nothing I'm ashamed of."

Unlike me? Surreal wondered. She had never denied that
she had been a very successful whore for centuries before
she quit thirteen years ago, no longer able to stomach the
bedroom games. That night at Cassandra's Altar had left
its mark on all of them.

Manny's feelings about women who worked in Red
Moon houses were ambivalent. What would she think if
she knew about Surreal's other profession? How comfortable would the older woman have been if she had known

that Surreal had been—and still was—a very successful assassin?

Didn't matter. They had become friends during the two years when Daemon had been rising out of the Twisted Kingdom, but after he regained his sanity. Manny had made a mental shift, treating both of them to the domestic affection that existed between a special servant and an aristo child. Daemon hadn't noticed anything odd about this behavior; maybe Manny had always treated him like that. But it had annoyed Surreal, who had grown up hard and fast on the streets. It had also given her a lot of practice in dealing with Manny's set opinions.

"Look," she said very softly. "Lady Benedict's servant doesn't look like he can stand up for two hours without being in pain. If you sit down, you can badger him into sitting."

A few minutes later, Manny, Andrew, Wilhelmina Benedict, and Surreal were sitting on the makeshift bench.

Surreal glanced at the remaining space on her right. Where in the name of Hell was Sadi? He wasn't as mentally stable as he pretended to be, and seeing Lucivar must have been a shock. But what had the *Eyrien* thought about seeing his half brother again? After Jaenelle disappeared thirteen years ago, Daemon had gone to Pruul, intending to get Lucivar out of the salt mines. For some reason, Lucivar had refused to go with him. She had always suspected, because of what Daemon wouldn't say, that there had been a vicious collision of tempers and that a rift had formed between them. And she had always suspected that the reason for that rift had begun, like so many other things, at Cassandra's Altar.

The driver's compartment door slid open. Lord Khardeen stepped out and glanced at the Eyriens, who tensed at his appearance. Saying nothing, he walked to the end of the makeshift bench and sat down beside Surreal.

Directly across from them was the woman with the two young children. They had the brown skin, gold eyes, and black hair that was typical of the three long-lived races, but the little girl's hair had a slight, natural curl. Surreal wondered if the girl's hair indicated that one of the parent's bloodlines wasn't pure Eyrien, if those curls had betrayed a secret, and if that was the reason these people had left their home Territory.

The older boy stayed close to his mother, but the little girl smiled at Khardeen and took a couple of steps toward him.

"Woofer," she said happily, holding out a worn stuffed animal.

Khardeen leaned forward and smiled. "That he is. What's his name?"

"Woofer." She gave the toy a squeezing hug. "Mine."

"Right you are."

Watching Khardeen apprehensively, the woman reached for the little girl. "Orian, don't bother the Warlord."

"She's no bother," Khardeen said pleasantly.

The woman pulled the girl close to her and tried to smile. "She likes animals. My husband's mother made her a girl doll before we left, but Orian wanted to bring this one."

And where was your own mother while that bitch was giving you a verbal knife? Surreal wondered as she watched shadows gather in the woman's eyes and picked up a flicker of shame in the psychic scent. Well, that answered which side of the girl's heritage was in question.

The Warlord who had protested when Friall refused to finish the contract turned away from his conversation with a couple of Eyrien males, glanced sharply at Khardeen, and then moved protectively closer to the woman and children.

Khardeen leaned back, returning that sharp glance with a mild look.

Sitting next to him, with his arm brushing hers, Surreal felt his tension—and anger?—but he gave no outward sign of it. When he looked at her, his expression was solemn, but his blue eyes held amusement.

"I wonder how the little Queen's mother will react when she sees the 'woofers' her daughter's going to be hugging," he said softly.

"Will they bite her?" Surreal asked.

"The girl? No. The mother?" Khardeen shrugged.

Hearing the warning underneath the amusement, Surreal shivered. Then Daemon approached them, and she took a sharp breath.

He moved carefully, like a man who had received a fatal wound and was quietly bleeding to death.

Khardeen stood up and gestured toward the vacated seat. "Why don't you sit down? I've got a couple of things to see to."

As soon as Daemon sat down, he wrapped his arms around himself.

She'd seen that protective gesture before, when he had been pushing too hard at his Craft studies, when dreams had haunted his sleep.

Khardeen gave her a questioning look. She shook her head. She appreciated his concern, but there was nothing anyone could do for Daemon just then except let him retreat until he felt strong enough to face the world again.

A minute later, Lucivar came out of the private room, his expression carefully blank.

For the rest of the journey, Daemon sat beside her with his eyes closed and Lucivar stood near the back of the Coach, talking quietly to the Eyrien males who cautiously approached him.

For the rest of the journey, she wondered what had happened in that private room. And she worried.

4 / Kaeleer

Lord Jorval cowered in the chair and watched the Dark Priestess storm around the outer room of the suite he'd rented for this meeting.

Red Moon houses hadn't existed in Kaeleer until four years ago—and *still* didn't exist anywhere outside of Little Terreille. But certain influential Council members, himself included, had argued that the stronger immigrating males, who had little chance of having a Kaeleer-born woman for a lover, needed some way to relieve their sexual tension. The Queens in Little Terreille had yielded to the argument with no more than a token protest since they quickly recognized the usefulness of such places. Now a visit to a Red Moon house became a way of rewarding males for good behavior in the Queens' courts. They could take their frustrations and aggressions out on women who couldn't refuse them, who couldn't demand courtesy and obedience. And no one noticed—or cared, if they did—that all the women in those houses were immigrants who had been claimed the day after a service fair.

And some Kaeleer males, himself included, had discovered the pleasure that could be had from a cringing woman's obedience.

He'd chosen this Red Moon house, on the edge of the slums that had sprung up near the fairground, because the proprietors wouldn't ask any questions. The two men who owned the place didn't care if a woman was damaged physically or mentally, as long as they were suitably compensated. And they wouldn't care about the youth who was now bound and gagged in the other room—the offering he had brought in the hopes it would lessen the Dark Priestess's rage.

Hekatah threw off the cloak that had shrouded her face and body.

Jorval swallowed hard. He had become violently ill once at the sight of her decaying, demon-dead body. Her punishment for his lack of control had given him nightmares for months.

There were times when he desperately wished he'd never met her or become entangled in her schemes. But she had been behind his rise to power in the Dark Council, and he had discovered that she owned him before he even realized he had agreed to serve her.

"There were four Queens suitable for our purpose," Hekatah snarled. "*Four.* And you still couldn't manage to get him tucked away until we found a way to use him."

"I tried, Priestess," Jorval said, his voice quivering. "I blocked the inquiries Sadi made about serving outside of Little Terreille. Those were the only names I offered him."

"Then why isn't he with one of them?"

"He walked out of the last meeting," Jorval cried. " I didn't know he had signed another contract until Friall told me."

"He signed another contract," Hekatah crooned. *"With his brother!"*

Jorval's chest jerked with the effort to breathe. "I tried to stop it! I tried . . ." His voice trailed off as Hekatah slowly approached him.

"You didn't handle him well," she said, her girlish voice

becoming dangerously gentle. "Because of that, he's now connected with the court we wanted unaware of his presence in Kaeleer, and we have no way of using that Black-Jeweled strength for our own purposes."

Jorval tried to get up. Fear clogged his throat when he realized she was using Craft to keep him pinned to the chair.

She settled gracefully in his lap and wrapped one arm around his neck. As her long nails brushed against his cheek, he wondered if he was going to lose an eye. Maybe that would be best. Blind, he wouldn't be able to see her. On second thought, no. She wore darker Jewels than he did. She could force his mind open and leave an image that was a hundred times worse than her actual appearance.

He whimpered as his stomach rolled ominously.

"Just as there are rewards for success, there are penalties for failure," Hekatah said as she stroked his face.

Knowing what was required, he whispered, "Yes, Priestess."

"And you did fail me, didn't you, darling?"

"Y-Yes, Priestess."

What was left of her lips curved in a smile. Using Craft, she called in a stoppered crystal bottle and a small silver cup. They floated in the air while she removed the stopper and poured the dark, thick liquid into the cup. She closed the bottle and vanished it, then held the cup up to Jorval's lips.

"I brought you a fresh offering," he said weakly.

"I saw him. Such a pretty boy, full of the hot sweet wine." She pressed the cup against his lower lip. "I'll get to him shortly."

Having no choice, Jorval opened his mouth. The liquid slid over his tongue like a long warm slug. He gagged on it, but managed to swallow.

"Is it poison?" he asked.

Hekatah vanished the cup and leaned back, her eyes widening in surprise. "Do you really think I would poison a man who's loyal to me? And you are loyal to me, aren't you, darling?" She shook her head sadly. "No, darling, this is just a little aphrodisiac brew."

"*S-Safframate?*" He would have preferred poison.

"Just enough to make the evening interesting," Hekatah replied.

He sat there, helpless, while she caressed skin that began to quiver at the slightest touch. Groaning, he wrapped his arms around her, no longer noticing the smell of decay, no longer caring about who or what she was, no longer caring about anything except using the female body that was sitting on his lap.

When he tried to thrust his tongue into her mouth, she pulled back with a satisfied laugh.

"Now, darling," she said while she caressed him, "you're going to bring one of those whores up here."

The lust-fog cleared a little. "Up here?"

"We still have to take care of your punishment," Hekatah said gently, viciously. "Get one that has golden hair and blue eyes."

The lust became fierce, almost painful. "Like Jaenelle Angelline."

"Exactly. Think of this as a little rehearsal for the day when that pale bitch has to submit to me." She kissed his temple, licked the throbbing pulse. "Will it excite you if I sip a little blood while you're locked inside her?"

Jorval stared at her, wildly aroused and terrified.

"I'll drink from her, too. By then you won't care if you're mounting a corpse, but I won't do that to you, darling. This is just a rehearsal, after all, for the night when you'll have Jaenelle under you."

"Yes," Jorval whispered. "Yes."

"Yes," Hekatah echoed, satisfied. She stood up and slowly walked to the bedroom door. "Don't worry about the whore telling anyone about our little game. I'll fog the bitch's mind so that she'll never be certain about anything except that she was well used."

Rising, Jorval moved unsteadily to the outer door, painfully aware that Hekatah watched him.

"The pretty boy will be the appetizer and the dessert," Hekatah said. "Fear gives blood such a delightfully piquant taste, and by the end of the evening, he'll be fully ripened. So don't spend too much time making your choice, darling. An appetizer doesn't take long to consume, and if I become impatient, we may have to adjust your punishment. And you wouldn't want that, would you?"

He waited until the bedroom door closed behind her before whispering, "No, I wouldn't want that."

5 / Kaeleer

A warm hand gently squeezed his shoulder.

"Daemon," Lucivar said quietly. "Come on, old son. We've arrived."

Daemon reluctantly opened his eyes. He wanted to withdraw from the world, wanted to sink into the abyss and just disappear. Soon, he promised himself. Soon. "I'm all right, Prick," he said wearily. It was a lie, and they both knew it.

Getting stiffly to his feet, Daemon rolled his shoulders. His muscles hummed with tension while a violent headache gathered behind his eyes. "Where are we?"

Saying nothing, Lucivar guided him out of the Coach.

Surreal stood just outside the Coach's door, staring up at the massive, gray stone building. "Hell's fire, Mother Night, and may the Darkness be merciful. What is this place?"

Prince Aaron grinned at her. "SaDiablo Hall."

"Oh, shit."

The ground spun under Daemon's feet. He flung out an arm. Lucivar grabbed him, steadied him. "I can't," he whispered. "Lucivar, I can't."

"Yes, you can." Holding his arm, Lucivar led him to the double front doors. "It'll be easier than you think. Besides, Ladvarian's been waiting to meet you."

Daemon didn't have the energy to wonder, much less care, why this Ladvarian wanted to meet him, not when the next step might bring him face to face with the High Lord again—or Jaenelle.

Lucivar pushed the doors open. Daemon followed him into the great hall, the rest of the immigrants crowding behind him. They'd only gone a few steps when Lucivar stopped suddenly and swore under his breath.

Daemon glanced around, trying to understand the flash of wariness he'd picked up from Lucivar. At the far end of the hall, a maid knelt under one of the crystal chandeliers, wiping the floor. A few feet away from them stood a large

Red-Jeweled Warlord dressed in a butler's uniform. His expression was more icy than stoic.

Eyeing the butler, Lucivar said cautiously, "Beale."

"Prince Yaslana," Beale replied with stiff formality.

Lucivar winced. "What—"

Someone giggled. They all looked up.

High overhead, a naked Eyrien boy, barely more than a toddler, balanced precariously on the nearest chandelier.

Lucivar glanced at Beale, sighed, and took a couple of steps forward. "What are you doing up there, boyo?"

"Flyin'," the toddler said.

"Take a guess," the maid growled as she dropped her cloth into a bucket and got to her feet.

"Slipped past your keepers, did you?" Lucivar muttered.

The toddler giggled again and then made a very rude noise.

"Come down, Daemonar," Lucivar said sternly.

"No!"

Tears stung Daemon's eyes as he stared at the boy. He swallowed hard to get his heart out of his throat.

Lucivar took another step forward and slowly spread his dark, membranous wings. "If you don't come down, I'll come up and get you."

Daemonar spread his little wings. "No!"

Lucivar shot into the air. As he passed the chandelier, he made a grab for Daemonar, who ducked and dove. The boy flew like a drunken bumblebee trying to elude a hawk, but he managed to stay out of reach.

"Boy's got some good moves," Hallevar said approvingly, moving to the front of the crowd.

Surreal glanced at the older Eyrien Warlord. "He seems to be getting the better of Yaslana."

Hallevar snorted as Lucivar swept past Daemonar and tickled his foot, making the boy squeal and dodge. "He could have caught him on the first pass. The young one will have to concede the battle, but it'll stay in his mind that he put up a good fight. No, Lucivar understands how to train an Eyrien warrior."

Daemon barely heard them. Hell's fire! Couldn't Lucivar see the boy was getting tired? Was he going to push until the baby fell to the floor?

As the toddler headed toward him, he stepped forward, reached up, and grabbed one chubby leg.

Daemonar shrieked and furiously flapped his little wings. Pulling down gently, Daemon wrapped his other arm around Daemonar, drawing the boy against his chest.

A small fist smacked his chin. The other small hand grabbed a handful of his hair and yanked, making his eyes water. An indignant shriek lanced his ear and made his head vibrate.

Lucivar landed and rubbed the back of his hand against his mouth. It didn't quite erase the smile. Hooking his left arm around the boy's middle, he carefully pried open the small hand. "Let go of your Uncle Daemon. We want him to like you." He stepped back quickly, then he tethered the boy's feet with one hand and growled, "That's not a good place to kick your father."

Daemonar made a rude noise and grinned.

Lucivar looked at the squirming boy and said ruefully, "At the time, you seemed like a good idea."

"Yeah!" Then Daemonar noticed the woman holding the little girl. "Baby!" he shouted, squirming to get loose. "Mine!"

"Mother Night," Lucivar muttered, turning to block Daemonar's view.

Two wet, disheveled women entered the hall. One of them held up a large towel. "We'll take him, Prince Yaslana."

"Thank the Darkness." With a little effort, Lucivar and the two women got Daemonar bundled up in the towel and out of the great hall.

Watching them, Daemon's heart ached. The boy looked like Lucivar. He wasn't sure if he felt regretful or relieved that there was no hint of sapphire in the child's gold eyes, no lightening of the black hair and brown skin, no trace of the mother's exotic beauty.

Lucivar returned quickly.

"Once the guests are settled in their rooms, dinner will be served in the formal dining room," Beale said.

"Thank you, Beale," Lucivar replied a bit meekly.

"Are there any arrangements the household should be aware of?"

Lucivar made a "come-here" gesture to the young Warlord who had remained protectively close to the woman with the two young children. "This is Lord Endar, Lady Dorian's husband."

Endar stiffened under Beale's scrutiny.

Prince Aaron wrapped a hand around Surreal's arm and pulled her forward. "I'll escort Lady SaDiablo and Lady Benedict to their rooms."

"Lady SaDiablo?" Beale said, startled.

Aaron grinned.

Surreal hissed.

"I'm sure the High Lord will be pleased to welcome the Lady," Beale said, a suspicious twinkle in his eyes.

Before Surreal could stop him, Aaron brushed her hair back, revealing a delicately pointed ear. "So will Prince Chaosti."

Beale's lips twitched. Then he resumed his stoic demeanor and turned to the immigrants. "Those of you who are here as servants will follow Holt," he said, indicating the waiting footman. "The rest of you will follow me."

As soon as all the Eyriens except Prince Falonar had left the great hall, along with Manny, Jazen, and Andrew, Surreal turned to Lucivar. "Shouldn't you have told him to let the children stay with their parents? I doubt they're going to feel easy, being in a strange place."

Prince Aaron vigorously cleared his throat.

Lord Khardeen tipped his head back and studied the ceiling.

Lucivar just stared at her for a moment before saying slowly, "If you want to tell Beale or Helene how to run this place, you go right ahead and try. Just let me get out of the line of fire before you do."

"Come on, Lady Surreal," Aaron said. "Let's get you settled in before you start bringing the place down around us."

Lucivar waited until Aaron and Khardeen had escorted Surreal and Wilhelmina out of the hall before turning to Falonar. "What?"

Falonar squared his shoulders. "Why did you single out Endar?"

"As long as the household knows that Endar is Dorian's husband, no one will challenge his being in her bed. And believe me, there are males here who won't hesitate to tear him apart if they aren't made aware that he's in her bed by her choice." He took a deep breath, let it out slowly. "I'll explain the rules tomorrow. For tonight, just tell the men to keep their distance from all the women." He paused, and then added, "You'd better get settled in. We'll be here for a few days."

After Falonar left, Lucivar turned to Daemon. "Come on. Let's finish this so we can both get some food and rest."

Daemon followed Lucivar up the staircase in the informal receiving room and through the labyrinth of corridors. After a couple of minutes of silence, he said, "You named him Daemonar."

"It was the closest I could come and still keep the name Eyrien," Lucivar said quietly, his voice a little thick.

"I'm flattered."

Lucivar snorted. "Well, you would have been when he was an infant. Once he got his feet under him, he turned into a little beast." He raked a hand through his shoulder-length hair. "And it is *not* all my fault. I didn't do this by myself. But nobody seems to remember that."

"I can't imagine why," Daemon said dryly, watching Lucivar swell with indignation.

"When he does something adorable, he's his mother's son. When he does something clever, he's the High Lord's grandson. But when he acts like a rotten little beast, he's *my* son." Lucivar rubbed his chest. "Sometimes I swear he does things just to see if my heart will stop."

"Like tonight?"

Lucivar waved his hand dismissively. "No, that was just . . . just . . . shit. What can I tell you? He's a little beast."

They turned a corner and almost ran into a lovely Eyrien woman. She wore a long, practical nightgown and clutched a thick book.

"Your son," she said, spacing out the words, "is not a beast."

"Never mind that," Lucivar said, narrowing his eyes. "Marian, why aren't you in bed? You should be resting today."

Marian let out her breath in an exasperated huff. "I dozed for most of the morning. I played with Daemonar for a little while this afternoon, and then we both took a nap. I just got up to borrow a book. I'm going to get tucked back in before Beale brings up a cup of hot chocolate and a plate of biscuits."

Lucivar's eyes narrowed a little more. "Didn't you eat today?"

Daemon stared at Lucivar in amazement. Even an idiot—or an Eyrien male—should be able to tell that this woman was silently sputtering.

"Uncle Andulvar checked on me to make sure I had eaten a good breakfast. Prothvar brought me a midmorning snack. I ate lunch with Daemonar. Sure that I must be starving, Mephis brought me a midafternoon snack. And your father already inquired about what I ate for dinner. I've been fussed over enough today."

"I'm not fussing." Lucivar growled—and then added under his breath, "I haven't had a chance to fuss."

Marian looked pointedly at Daemon. "Shouldn't you be looking after your guests?"

"He's not a guest. He's my brother."

Smiling warmly, Marian held out her hand. "You must be Daemon. Oh, I'm so glad you've finally come. Now I have another brother."

Brother? Taking her hand, Daemon gave Lucivar a quizzical look.

Running a possessive hand down Marian's waist-length hair, Lucivar said warmly, "Marian does me the honor of being my wife."

And Daemonar's mother. The floor dropped out from under Daemon and then came up again fast and hard.

Marian squeezed his hand, her eyes filled with concern. Lucivar's gaze was sharper.

Emotions collided in him, banging against his fragile sanity. Unable to offer them any reassurances, he took a step back and began, again, the exhausting effort of regaining control of his feelings.

Perhaps sensing that he needed time, Lucivar tugged at the book Marian held, trying to see the title.

She clutched it harder and stepped away from him.

"Is that a sniffle book?" Lucivar asked suspiciously.

Marian opened and closed her wings with a snap. "A what?"

"You know. One of those books that women like to read

and get all weepy over. The last time you read one of those, you got upset when I came in to find out what was wrong. You threw the book at me."

Marian's sputtering was no longer silent. "I didn't get upset because of the *book*. You came storming into the room with weapons drawn and you scared me."

"You were crying. I thought you were hurt. Look, I just want to know ahead of time if you're going to get weepy over it."

"When Jaenelle read it, I'll bet you didn't barge in on her when she got weepy."

Lucivar eyed the book as if it had just grown fangs. "Oh. *That* book." He curled an arm protectively over his belly. "Actually, I did barge in on her. Her aim was better than yours."

Marian's growl turned into a laugh. "Poor Lucivar. You try so hard to protect the women in the family, and we don't show our appreciation, do we?"

Lucivar grinned. "Well, if there are any interesting love scenes in that story, mark the pages and you can appreciate me in a few days."

Marian glanced at Daemon and blushed.

Lucivar gently kissed her, then stepped aside to let her pass. "Get into bed now."

"I'll see you tomorrow, Daemon," Marian said a little shyly.

"Good night, Lady Marian," Daemon said. It was all he could manage.

They watched her until she went into her and Lucivar's suite, then Lucivar reached out. Daemon stiffened, rejecting the touch.

Dropping his hand, Lucivar said, "The High Lord's suite is just down this corridor. He'll want to see you."

Daemon couldn't move. "I thought you married Jaenelle."

"Why would you think I married Jaenelle?"

The surprise in Lucivar's voice woke Daemon's temper. "You were here," he snarled. "Why wouldn't you want to marry her?"

Lucivar didn't say anything for a long minute. Then, quietly, "That was always your dream, Daemon. Not mine." Turning, he walked down the corridor. "Come on."

Daemon followed slowly. When Lucivar stopped and knocked on a door, he kept walking, drawn to the strong, dark, feminine psychic scent coming from a room on the opposite side of the corridor.

"Daemon?"

Lucivar's voice faded, muted by a powerful tide of emotions.

Daemon opened a door and walked into a sitting room. One wall had built-in bookshelves above a row of closed, waist-high wooden cabinets. A couch, two triangular side tables, and two chairs formed a bracket of furniture around a long, low table. A pair of sinuous, patinaed lamps sat on the side tables. Next to one chair was a large basket full of skeins of wool and silk and a partially completed piece of needlework. A desk sat in front of the glass doors that led out to the balcony. A tiered stand filled with plants occupied one corner.

The psychic scent washed over him, through him. Oh, he remembered that dark scent. But there was something different about it now, something delicately, deliciously musky.

His body tightened, then swelled with male interest before his mind understood the significance of that difference. Then he noticed the sapphire slippers near one chair. A woman's slippers.

Against all reason, despite all desire, even when he had thought that Lucivar had married her, he hadn't fully absorbed the fact that she was no longer the child he had known. She had grown up.

The walls of the room faded to gray, then darkened and began to close in, forming a tunnel around him.

"Daemon."

He remembered that deep voice, too. He had heard it amused. He had heard it full of rage and fierce power. He had heard it hoarse and exhausted. He had heard it plead with him to reach up, to accept the help and strength being offered.

Turning slowly, he stared at Saetan. The Prince of the Darkness. The High Lord of Hell. His father.

Saetan extended his hand, with its slender fingers and long, black-tinted nails. "Daemon . . . Jaenelle is alive," he said softly.

The room shrank. The tunnel kept closing. The hand waited for him, offering strength, safety, comfort—all the things he'd rejected when he'd been in the Twisted Kingdom.

"Daemon."

He took a step forward. He raised his hand, with its slender fingers and long, black-tinted nails. This time, he feared his own fragility. This time, he would accept the promises Saetan offered.

He took another step, reaching for the hand that mirrored his own.

Just before his fingers touched Saetan's, the room disappeared.

"Keep your head down, boyo. Breathe, slow and easy. That's right."

Calm strength and warmth flowed from the hand that stroked his head, his neck, his spine.

The effort made him queasy, but after a moment Daemon got his brain and body working together enough to open his eyes. He stared at the carpet between his feet—earth-brown, with swirls of young green and burnt red. Obviously the carpet couldn't decide if it was representing spring or autumn.

"Do you want some brandy or a basin?" Lucivar asked.

Why would he want a basin?

His stomach jumped. He swallowed carefully. "Brandy," he said, gritting his teeth and hoping it wasn't the wrong choice.

When Lucivar returned, Daemon got a generously filled snifter shoved into his hand and a basin shoved between his feet.

The hand rubbing Daemon's spine stopped moving. "Lucivar," Saetan said, his voice equally amused and annoyed.

"Helene won't be pleased with him if he pukes on the carpet."

Daemon didn't know the word Saetan used, but it sounded nasty. It was petty, but he felt childishly pleased that his father had taken his side.

"Go to Hell," he said, sitting up enough to take a sip of brandy.

"I'm not the one whose nose was heading for the floor a minute ago," Lucivar growled, rustling his wings.

"Children," Saetan warned.

Since his stomach didn't immediately reject the brandy, Dacmon took another sip—and finally edged around the questions that needed answers. "She's really alive?"

"She's really alive," Saetan replied gently.

"She's lived here since . . ." He couldn't bring himself to say it.

"Yes."

Daemon turned his head, needing to see the answer in Saetan's eyes as well as hear it. "And she healed?"

"Yes."

But he saw the flicker of hesitation in those gold eyes.

Taking another sip of brandy, he slowly realized that, while Jaenelle's dark psychic scent filled the room, it wasn't recent. "Where is she?"

"She's making her autumn tour of the kindred Territories," Saetan said. "We try not to interrupt her during that time, but I could—"

"No." Daemon closed his eyes. He needed some time to regain his balance before he met her again. "It can wait." It had already waited for thirteen years. A few more days wouldn't matter.

Saetan hesitated, then glanced at Lucivar, who nodded. "There is something you need to think about before she returns." He called in a small jeweler's box, then pushed the lid open with his thumb.

Daemon stared at the faceted ruby in the gold ring. A Consort's ring. He'd seen that ring in the Twisted Kingdom, circling the stem of a crystal chalice that had been shattered and carefully pieced together. Jaenelle's chalice. Jaenelle's promise.

"That's not for you to offer," Daemon said. He gripped the brandy snifter to keep from reaching for the ring.

"I'm not the one who's offering it, Prince. As the Steward of the Dark Court, it was given into my keeping."

Daemon carefully licked his lips. "Has it ever been worn?" Jaenelle was twenty-five now. There was no reason to think—to hope—it had never circled another man's finger.

Sactan's eyes held a mixture of relief and sadness. "No."
He shut the box and held it out.

Daemon's hand closed over it convulsively.

"Come on, boyo," Saetan said as he handed the brandy
snifter to Lucivar and helped Daemon stand up. "I'll show
you to your room. Beule will bring a tray up in a few
minutes. Try to eat and get some sleep. We'll talk again in
the morning."

Opening the glass door, Daemon stepped out onto the
balcony. The silk robe was too thin and couldn't stop the
night air from leaching the warmth he'd gained from a long
bath, but he needed to be outside for a moment, needed
to listen to the water singing over stone in the natural-
looking fountain at the center of the garden below. There
were only a couple of rooms surrounding the garden that
showed a soft glow of light. Guest rooms? Or did Aaron
and Khardeen occupy those rooms?

Saetan had said no man had worn the Consort's ring,
but . . .

Daemon took a deep breath, let it out slowly. She was a
Queen, and a Queen was entitled to any pleasure the males
in her court could provide.

And he was here now.

Shivering, he went into his room, secured the glass door,
and drew the curtains. He slipped out of the robe, got into
bed, then pulled the covers up over his naked body. Shifting to his side, he stared for several minutes at the jeweler's
box he'd set on the bedside table.

He was here now. The choice was his now.

He took the Consort's ring out of the box and slipped it
on the ring finger of his left hand.

6 / Kaeleer

As Surreal placed the last of her toiletries in the bathroom
cabinet, she paused, listening. Yes, someone had entered
her bedroom. Had the maid returned for another polite
verbal struggle? She'd *told* the woman she didn't need help
unpacking—and had wondered about the maid's muttered
comment. *No question about it, you're a SaDiablo.*

So maybe she'd been a little hasty. After all, she didn't want to have to launder her own clothes for however long she would be there.

Moving toward the bathroom door, Surreal sent a cautious psychic probe into the bedroom. Her lips curled into a snarl. Not the maid back for another round, but a *male* making himself comfortable in her room. Then she paused. The psychic scent was definitely male—but there was something about it that was just a little off.

Calling in her favorite stiletto, she used Craft to place a sight shield around it. With her arms down and her right hand curled loosely around the hilt, no one would suspect she had a weapon ready—unless they knew she was an assassin. More than likely, it was a male who had heard of her former profession and figured she'd be delighted to accommodate him—like those balless pricks at the service fair who kept pushing her to sign a contract to serve in an "aristo" Red Moon house.

Well, if this male was expecting a jolly, she would just inform him that she would have to talk to the Steward first about compensation. Unless it *was* the Steward. Did he really expect her to buy her way out of a contract she hadn't wanted to sign in the first place?

With her temper simmering, Surreal strode into the bedroom—and stopped short, not sure if she wanted to yell or laugh.

A large gray dog had his head buried in her open trunk. The tip of his tail wagged like a brisk metronome as he sniffed her clothes.

"Find anything interesting?" Surreal asked.

The dog leaped away from the trunk, heading for the door. Then he stopped, a nervous quiver running through his body as his brown eyes stared at her. His tail gave a couple of hopeful *tock-tocks* before it curled between his legs.

Surreal vanished the stiletto. Keeping one eye on the dog, she checked the trunk. If he'd done anything disgusting on her clothes . . . Seeing that he hadn't done more than sniff, she relaxed and turned to face him.

"You're big," she said pleasantly. "Are you allowed inside?"

"Rrrf."

"You're right. Considering the size of this place, that was a silly question." She held out her hand in a loose fist.

Accepting the invitation, he eagerly sniffed her hand, sniffed her feet, sniffed her knees, sniffed . . .

"Get your nose out of my crotch," Surreal growled.

He took two steps back and sneezed.

"Well, that's your opinion."

His mouth opened in a doggy grin. "Rrrf."

Laughing, Surreal put her clothes away in the tall wardrobe and mirrored dresser. After hanging the last piece, she closed the trunk.

Seeing that he had her attention again, the dog sat down and offered a paw.

Well, he seemed friendly.

After shaking his paw, she ran her hands through his fur, scratched behind his ears, and rubbed his head until his eyes started to blissfully close. "You're a pretty boy, aren't you? A big furry boy."

He gave her chin two enthusiastic, if sloppy, kisses.

Surreal straightened up and stretched. "I have to go now, boyo. Somewhere in this place is my dinner, and I intend to find it."

"Rrrf." The dog bounded to the door, his tail wagging.

She eyed him. "Well, I suppose you *would* know where to find the food. Just let me get ready, then we'll go hunting the elusive dinner."

"*Rrrf.*"

Hell's fire, Surreal thought as she washed her hands and brushed her hair. She must be more tired than she realized if she was imagining tonal qualities in the dog's sounds that made it seem like he was really answering her. And she would have sworn that last "Rrrf" was full of amusement. Just as she would have sworn that someone kept trying to reach her on a psychic communication thread and that *she* was the one who kept fumbling the link.

The dog's mood had changed by the time she came back. When she opened the bedroom door, he gave her a sad look, then slunk into the corridor.

Prince Aaron leaned against the opposite wall.

He was a handsome man with black hair, gray eyes, and a height and build women would find appealing. Standing next to Sadi he would come in a poor second—well, so would any other man—but she didn't think he'd ever lacked invitations to the bed.

Maybe that explained the wariness under the arrogant confidence.

"Since you don't know your way around yet, I stopped by to escort you and Lady Benedict to the dining room," Aaron said, looking like he was fighting hard not to smile. "But I see you already have an escort."

The dog's ears pricked up. The tail went *tock-tock*.

The corridor filled with annoying male undercurrents. Surreal briefly considered giving one of them a hard smack just to break up whatever was going on, but losing her escorts would mean trying to find the dining room on her own.

Fortunately, Wilhelmina Benedict chose that moment to leave her room, which was next to Surreal's. After Aaron explained about being their escort, he offered each woman an arm, and the three of them, with the dog trailing close behind, began the long walk through the Hall.

"The servants must be exhausted by the end of the day," Surreal said as they turned into another corridor.

"Not really," Aaron replied. "The staff works on a rotation and are assigned to a wing of the Hall. That way everyone gets to work in the family wing and the wings where the court resides when it's here."

"You mean I'm going to have the same argument with *another* maid?" Surreal almost wailed.

Aaron shot her an amused look. "You mean you drew your own bath?"

"I didn't bother to bathe," Surreal snapped. "Sit upwind."

Smart-ass.

He didn't have to say it out loud. His expression was sufficient.

Surreal glanced back at her furry escort. Well, animals should be a safe subject for small talk. "He is allowed inside, isn't he?"

"Oh, yes," Aaron said. "Although, I was surprised to see him. The pack tends to stay in the north woods when there are strangers here."

"The pack? What kind of dog is he?"

"He's not a dog. He's a wolf. And he's kindred."

Wilhelmina jumped and gave the wolf a frightened look. "But . . . aren't wolves wild animals?"

"He's also a Warlord," Aaron said, ignoring Wilhelmina's question.

Surreal felt a little queasy. She'd heard about the kindred, who supposedly had some kind of small animal magic. But calling him a Warlord . . . "You mean he's Blood?"

"Of course."

"Why is he in the Hall?"

"Well, offhand, I'd say he was looking for a friend."

Hell's fire, Mother Night, and may the Darkness be merciful, Surreal thought. What did *that* mean? "I guess he's not really wild then. If he's in the house, he must be tame."

Aaron gave her a feral smile. "If by 'tame' you mean he doesn't pee on the carpets, then he's tame. But then, by that standard, so am I."

Surreal clamped her teeth together. Screw small talk. In this place, it turned into verbal quicksand.

She echoed Wilhelmina's sigh of relief when they reached a stairway. Hopefully the dining room wasn't too far away and she could put some distance between herself and her escort. Escorts. Whatever.

Shit.

Maybe Khardeen would be in the dining room. He was a Warlord, which made him an equal caste, and her Gray Jewels outranked his Sapphire, which gave her an advantage. Right now, she wanted an advantage because she had the strong impression that, of her two escorts, the one with the more impressive set of teeth was really the less dangerous one.

Surreal stared at the closed wooden door and wished she'd done this before eating. The thick beef and vegetable stew had been delicious, as had been the bread, cheese, and slightly tart apples, and she'd consumed them with enthusiasm. Now, her tightened stomach was packing that food into a hard ball.

Snarling quietly, she raised her fist to knock on the door. Hell's fire, this was just a required meeting with the Steward of the court . . . who now had the authority to control her life . . . who was also the Warlord Prince of

Dhemlan . . . who was also the High Lord of Hell . . . whose name was Saetan Daemon SaDiablo.

"Rrrf?"

Surreal looked over her shoulder. The wolf cocked his head.

"I think you'd better stay out here," she said, giving the door one hard rap. When a deep voice said, "Come," she slipped inside the room, closing the door before the wolf could follow her.

The room was a reversed L. The long side contained a comfortable sitting area with tables, chairs, and a black leather couch. The walls held a variety of pictures, ranging from dramatic oil paintings to whimsical charcoal sketches. Intrigued by those choices, she turned toward the alcove.

Dark-red velvet covered the side walls. The back wall contained floor-to-ceiling bookshelves. A blackwood desk filled the center of the space. Two candle-lights lit its surface and the man sitting behind it.

At first glance, she thought Daemon was playing some kind of trick on her. Then she looked closer.

His face was similar to Daemon's, but handsome rather than beautiful. He was definitely older, and his thick black hair was heavily silvered at the temples. He wore half-moon glasses, which made him look like a benevolent clerk. But the elegant hands had long, black-tinted nails like Daemon's. On his left hand, he wore a Steward's ring. On his right, a Black-Jeweled ring.

"Why don't you sit down," he said as he continued making notes on the paper in front of him. "This will take a minute."

Surreal sidled over to the chair in front of the desk and gingerly sat down. His voice had the same deep timbre as Daemon's, had the same ability to reach a woman's bones and make her itchy. At least the sensual heat that poured out of Daemon even when he kept it tightly leashed was muted in the High Lord. Maybe that was just age.

Then he tucked the pen in its holder, laid the glasses on the desk, leaned back in his chair, and steepled his fingers, resting them against his chin.

Her breath clogged in her throat. She'd seen Daemon sit exactly that way whenever a conversation was "formal."

Hell's fire, what *was* the connection between Sadi and the High Lord?

"So," he said quietly. "You're Surreal. Titian's daughter."

A shiver went through her. "You knew my mother?"

He smiled dryly. "I still do. And since I am kin to her kin, she considers me a tolerable friend, despite my being male."

The words that had been rankling inside her all through the journey here burst out. "My mother is *not* a Harpy."

Saetan gave her a considering look. "A Harpy is a witch who died violently by a male's hand. I'd say that describes Titian, wouldn't you? Besides," he added, "being the Harpy Queen is hardly an insult."

"Oh." Surreal hooked her hair behind her ears. He made it sound so matter-of-fact, and there was no mistaking the respect in his voice.

"Would you like to see her?" Saetan asked.

"But . . . if she's demon-dead . . ."

"A meeting could be arranged here at the Hall. I could ask her if she would be willing."

"Since you're the High Lord, I'm surprised you wouldn't just order her to come," Surreal said a bit tartly.

Saetan chuckled. "Darling, I may be the High Lord, but I'm also male. I'm not about to give an order to a Black Widow Queen without a very good reason."

Surreal narrowed her eyes. "I can't picture you as submissive."

"I'm not submissive, but I do serve. You would be wise not to confuse those two things when dealing with the males in this court."

Oh, wonderful.

"Especially since you've formally declared yourself part of this family," Saetan added.

Mother Night. "Look," Surreal said, leaning forward. "I didn't know anyone was using that name here." *And I certainly didn't expect to meet them.*

"All things considered, you have as much right to that name as Kartane SaDiablo," he said cryptically. "And since you *did* list it, you're stuck with the results."

"Which are?" Surreal asked suspiciously.

Saetan smiled. "The short version is, as the patriarch

of this family, I am now responsible for you and you are answerable to me."

"When the sun shines in Hell," Surreal shot back.

"Be careful what conditions you set, little witch," he said softly. "Jaenelle has an uncanny—and sometimes disturbing—way of meeting someone's terms."

Surreal swallowed hard. "She really is in Kaeleer?"

Saetan held up the mark of safe passage that had been sitting on his desk. "Isn't that why you came?"

She nodded. "I wanted to find out what happened to her."

"Why don't you save those questions for Jaenelle. She'll be home in a few days."

"She lives *here*?"

"This isn't her only home, but, yes, she lives here."

"Does Daemon know?" she asked. "He wasn't at dinner."

"He knows," Saetan said gently. "He's feeling a bit unsettled."

"That's an understatement," she muttered. Then she thought of something else, something that had nagged at her curiosity for thirteen years. If there was anyone in the Realms who would know the answer, she figured it was the High Lord. "Have you ever heard of the High Priest of the Hourglass?"

His smile had a sharp edge. "I *am* the High Priest."

"Oh, shit."

His laughter was warm and full-bodied. "You're willing to snarl at me as the High Lord, the Steward, and the family patriarch, but knowing I'm the Priest knocks your feet out from under you?"

Surreal glared at him. Put that way, it *did* sound silly. But it was disconcerting to find out that the dangerous male she'd caught a whiff of that night at Cassandra's Altar was the same amused man sitting on the other side of the desk. "Then you can tell Daemon what happened that night. You can tell him what he doesn't remember."

Saetan shook his head. "No, I can't. I can confirm what happened while we were linked, and I can tell him what happened after. But there's only one person who can tell him what took place in the abyss."

Surreal sighed. "I'm almost afraid of what he'll find out."

"I wouldn't be too concerned. When Jaenelle formally set up her court, the Consort's ring was set aside for him, by her decree. So whatever happened between them couldn't have been that distressing. At least for her," he added solemnly. Rising, he came around the desk. "I still have to meet with several of the Eyriens tonight as well as get the reports from Aaron, Khardeen, and Lucivar. If you need any help understanding the Blood here, please come and talk to me."

Accepting dismissal, Surreal rose and glanced at the door. "There is one other thing."

Saetan studied the closed door. "I see you've met Lord Graysfang."

Surreal choked back a laugh.

"I know. Their names sound as strange to us as ours do to them. Although they may have more reason to think so. When kindred young are born, a Black Widow makes that mental sidestep into the dreams and visions. Sometimes she sees nothing. Sometimes she names one of the young according to the visions."

"Well," Surreal said, smiling, "he is gray, and he does have fangs. Aaron said he was in the Hall because he's looking for a friend."

Saetan gave her an odd look. "I'd say that's accurate. The kindred dogs and horses relate well to the human Blood since they've lived among them for so long, although, until eight years ago, in secret. The rest of the kindred tend to stay away from most humans. But whenever they come across a human who is compatible with them, they try to form a bond, to better understand us."

"Why me?" Surreal asked, intrigued.

"The Queens here have strong courts, and the males in the First Circle are entitled to the first share of their time and attention. A youngster like Graysfang has to wait for his turn and then has to share that time with other young males in the same position. But you're a Gray-Jeweled witch who does not, as yet, have any other male claims."

"Except the males in the family," Surreal said sourly.

"Except the males in the family," Saetan agreed. "On both sides."

She sputtered.

"But that claim isn't quite the same thing. You're not a

Queen, whose courts are set up by a different Protocol. So if you accept Graysfang before the other males realize you're here, he will hold the dominant position over any male except your mate, even if the other male wears darker Jewels. Since he's not old enough to make the Offering to the Darkness and still wears his Birthright Purple Dusk Jewel, the odds of a darker-Jeweled male becoming interested in you are rather high."

"Which still doesn't explain why he's interested in me in the first place."

Saetan reached out slowly. His left index finger hooked the gold chain around her neck and drew it out of her shirt until her Gray Jewel hung between them.

At first, she thought the caress accompanying that movement was a subtle kind of seduction. Then she realized that, for him, it wasn't meant to be seductive at all. It was simply a gesture that was as natural to him as breathing.

Which wasn't doing *her* breathing a whole lot of good.

"Consider this," he said. "He may not have been given that name because he's gray and has fangs but because he is Gray's fang."

"Mother Night," Surreal said, looking down at her Jewel.

He lowered her Jewel until it rested above her breasts. "The decision about him is yours, and I'll support any decision you make. But think carefully, Surreal. A Black Widow's visions should not be dismissed in haste."

Nodding, she savored the feel of his hand on her lower back as he guided her to the door. When he reached for the doorknob, she put her hand on the door to keep it shut. "What's your connection with Daemon?"

"He and Lucivar are my sons."

That figured.

"Daemon inherited your looks," she said.

"He also inherited my temper."

Hearing the warning in his voice, she noticed, at the back of his golden eyes, the same wariness she had seen in Aaron's. Hell's fire, she was going to have to find someone to talk to soon who could explain the male-female rules in Kaeleer. Being wary of her as an assassin was one thing. Being wary of her as a woman . . . She didn't like it. Not coming from him. She didn't like it at all.

"I'd like to meet my mother," she said abruptly.

Saetan nodded. "The court's coming in this evening, and I can't leave until the Queen approves the new arrivals, but I'll see that a message gets to Titian."

"Thank you." *Damn it, stop delaying. Get out of here.* She bolted from the room as soon as he opened the door.

As Graysfang anxiously trotted beside her, she kept feeling that odd psychic brush against her inner barriers.

She would have gotten lost twice without him, although she noticed there were footmen in all the major corridors. Each man rose from his chair, glanced at Graysfang, smiled at her, and said nothing. So she followed the wolf until, with a sigh, she was safely in her room.

When he left her a minute later to take care of his own nightly business, she quickly undressed and pulled on a pair of long-sleeved pajamas. She still preferred silky nightgowns most of the time, but there were times—like tonight—when she wanted to wear something that looked and felt asexual.

Dumping her soiled clothes into a basket in the bathroom, she hurried through her nighttime ritual, slipped into bed, and turned off the candle-light on the bedside table.

Someone had put a light warming spell on the sheets. Probably the maid. Silently thanking the woman, Surreal snuggled under the covers.

She was just starting to doze off when a shape passed through the glass door. She tensed, waiting, until a body landed lightly on the bed, circled three times, then settled next to her with a content sigh.

Twisting her upper body slightly, she looked at Graysfang. Feeling that odd psychic brush again, she followed it, too tired to think about what she was doing and more concerned with whether or not she was going to end up with fleas in the morning.

No fleas, said a sleepy male voice on a psychic thread. *Kindred know spells for fleas and other itchies.*

With a yelp, Surreal shot into a sitting position.

Graysfang leaped up, his teeth bared and hackles raised. *Where is the danger?* he demanded. *I smell no danger.*

"*You can talk!*"

Slowly, Graysfang's hackles smoothed. He covered his teeth. *I am kindred. We do not always* want *to talk to humans, but we can talk.*

Mother Night, Mother Night, Mother Night.

Wagging his tail, he leaned forward and licked her cheek. *You heard me!* he said happily. *You are not even trained yet and you can hear kindred!* He raised his head and howled.

Surreal grabbed his muzzle. "Hush. You'll wake everyone."

Ladvarian will be pleased.

"Great. I'm delighted." *Who in the name of Hell is Ladvarian?* "Let's just go to sleep now, all right?" And since she didn't know how she had made this link in the first place, how was she going to sever it so that her thoughts were private again?

She felt a gentle mental push, then that odd brush again. "Rrrf."

"Thank you," Surreal said weakly. In the morning, she thought as she snuggled back under the covers and felt Graysfang settle himself against her back. She'd think about this in the morn . . .

CHAPTER THREE

1 / Kaeleer

Daemon carefully adjusted the cuffs of his shirt and jacket. He felt steadier that morning, but not rested. His sleep had been broken by vague dreams and flashes of memory, by the knowledge that nothing but a door separated his bedroom from Jaenelle's, and by an aroused, restless body that knew quite fiercely what it wanted.

Slipping his hands into his trouser pockets made him aware of the Consort's ring on his left hand. As if he hadn't been aware of it from the moment he'd woken up. It wasn't just the unfamiliar feel of a ring on that hand; it was the duties and responsibilities that came with that ring that made him uneasy. Oh, his body would perform its duties eagerly enough. At least, he thought it would. And that was the point, wasn't it? He really didn't know how he would respond when he met Jaenelle again. And he didn't know how she would respond to him.

Finally aware that Jazen, his valet, was still dawdling through the morning tasks, Daemon studied the man.

"Did you get settled in all right last night?" Daemon asked.

Jazen made an effort to smile but didn't look at him. "The servants' quarters here are very generous."

"And the servants?"

"They're . . . polite."

Daemon felt the beginning chill of temper and reined it in, hard. Jazen had already endured enough. If he had to shake the Hall down to its foundation, he'd make sure the

man's life wasn't made more difficult by servants who had
no understanding of the brutality men faced in the Terreillean Territories under Dorothea's control.

"I'm not sure what's going to be required of me today."
Jazen nodded. "The other personal servants indicated
that dress would be relaxed today since the First Circle will
be assessing the new arrivals. Those who sit at the High
Lord's table do dress for dinner. Not formal dress," he
added when Daemon raised one eyebrow. "But I gathered
the Ladies are usually casual in their attire during the day."

Daemon turned that bit of information over and over as
he made his way through the corridors toward the dining
room. Based on his experience in Terreillean courts, casual
attire meant practical dresses made of fabrics only slightly
less sumptuous than those worn to dinner.

Then he turned a corner and noticed the fair-skinned,
red-haired witch coming toward him. She wore threadbare,
dark-brown trousers and a long, baggy, heather-green
sweater that was decoratively patched. There was approval
in the fast assessment her green eyes made over his body
but no active interest. "Prince," she said politely as she
passed him.

"Lady," he replied with equal politeness, wondering how
such a stickler as he suspected Beale to be would allow a
servant to dress like that. When he caught a whiff of her
psychic scent, he spun around and stared at her until she
turned the corner and disappeared.

A Queen. That woman was a *Queen*.

His stomach growled, which finally got him walking
again.

A Queen. Well, if *that* was the Ladies' idea of casual
attire, he wholeheartedly approved of the High Lord's insistence on dressing for dinner—a sentiment he strongly suspected he should keep to himself.

He had almost reached the dining room when he met up
with Saetan.

"Prince Sadi, there's something I need to discuss with
you," Saetan said quietly, but his expression was grim.

Saetan using the formal title caused a chill down Daemon's spine.

"Then shall we get it over with?" Daemon replied as he

followed Saetan to the High Lord's official study. He felt one layer of tension ease when Saetan leaned against the front of the blackwood desk instead of sitting behind it.

"Are you aware that your valet is fully shaved?" Saetan asked softly, ominously.

"I'm aware of it," Daemon replied with equal softness.

"There are very few of our laws that, when broken, justify that punishment. All of them are sexual."

"Jazen didn't do anything except be at the wrong place at the wrong time," Daemon snarled. "Dorothea did that to him to entertain her coven."

"Are you sure of that?"

"I was there, High Lord. There wasn't a damn thing I could do for him except slip past the drugs they'd given him to keep him aware and knock him out. His family took care of him for a while, but many of them are in personal service. Once the word got out—and Dorothea always made sure that it did—Jazen would have been considered tainted because, *of course*, it wouldn't have happened to him if he hadn't deserved it. If he had stayed with his family, they would have lost their positions as well. He's a good man, and a loyal one. He deserved far better than what happened to him."

"I see," Saetan said quietly. He straightened up. "I'll explain the situation to Beale. He'll take care of it."

"How much will you have to tell him?" Daemon asked warily.

"Nothing more than that the maiming was unjustified."

Daemon smiled bitterly. "Do you really think that will change the other servants' opinion of him? That they'll believe it?"

"No, all it will do is suspend judgment until the Lady returns." Saetan looked solemn. "But you have to understand, Prince. If Jaenelle turns against him, there's nothing you or I or anyone else can do or say that will make any difference. In Kaeleer, once you step outside of Little Terreille, Witch *is* the law. Her decisions are final."

Daemon considered this, then nodded. "I'll accept the Lady's judgment." As he followed Saetan to the dining room, he kept hoping that the woman Jaenelle had become wasn't too different from the child he remembered—and had loved.

2 / Kaeleer

Lord Jorval's heart pounded as he returned to the room where the sandy-haired man with worried gray eyes waited. He sat down behind the desk and clasped his hands together to hide the tremors of excitement.

"Have you already found out where my niece has gone?" Philip Alexander asked.

"I have," Jorval replied solemnly. "When you explained the family connections, I had a suspicion of where to look."

Philip gripped the arms of the chair hard enough to snap wood. "Did she sign a contract with a court in Little Terreille?"

"Unfortunately, no," Jorval said, struggling to put just the right amount of sympathy in his voice. "You must understand, Prince Alexander. We had no way of knowing who she was. A couple of Council members remembered her saying that she was trying to find her sister, but they had assumed the sister had immigrated earlier—and in a sense, that is true. But the Dark Council was never provided with a record of where Jaenelle Angelline came from before the High Lord acquired guardianship over her. There was no reason for them to link the two women, and by the time they began to wonder about the significance of her inquiries, it was too late."

"What do you mean, 'too late'?" Philip snapped.

"She was . . . persuaded . . . to sign a contract with the Warlord Prince of Ebon Rih—and *he* is Lucivar Yaslana."

Satisfaction warmed Jorval as he watched Philip's face pale. "I see you've heard of him. So you can appreciate the danger your niece is in. And it's not just Yaslana, although he's bad enough." He paused, giving Philip time to swallow the hook as well as the bait.

"She's trapped with all three of them, isn't she? She's trapped with Yaslana, Sadi, and the High Lord—just like Jaenelle."

"Yes." Jorval sighed. "To the best of our knowledge, Yaslana took her to SaDiablo Hall in Dhemlan. How long she'll remain there . . ." He spread his hands in a helpless gesture. "You may have some chance of slipping her away from the Hall, but once he takes her into the mountains that ring Ebon Rih, it's unlikely you'll ever get her back—at least while there's enough left of her to be worth the risk."

Philip sagged in the chair.

Jorval just waited. Finally, he said, "There is nothing the Dark Council can do officially to help you at this time. However, *unofficially*, we will do everything in our power to restore Jaenelle Angelline and Wilhelmina Benedict to their rightful family."

Philip got to his feet like a man who had taken a savage beating. "Thank you, Lord Jorval. I will convey this information to my Queen."

"May the Darkness guide and protect you, Prince Alexander."

Jorval waited a full minute after Philip left before he leaned back in his chair and sighed, well satisfied by their meeting. Thank the Darkness that Philip was a Prince. He would worry and brood, but, unlike a Warlord Prince, he *would* go back to Alexandra Angelline and abide by her decision. And how fortunate that Philip hadn't thought to ask if Yaslana served a Queen—or who she was. Of course, he would have lied if he'd been asked, but how interesting that Philip hadn't considered, even for a moment, that Jaenelle might be a Queen powerful enough to control the males in the SaDiablo family.

As for Alexandra Angelline . . . She would be useful in distracting the High Lord and dividing loyalties in the court at Ebon Askavi—as long as she didn't realize the *real* importance of getting Jaenelle away from the Dark Court.

3 / Kaeleer

Daemon wandered through the Hall's first floor rooms, distractedly noting each room's function, his mind too full of impressions he'd received during breakfast. When he came to a door that led to one of the open courtyards, he went outside and paced, hoping that the fresh air and greenery would help clear his head.

He'd expected to find the dining room full of people.

After all, the Eyriens would want to eat before going on
to whatever plans Lucivar had for them. And he'd expected
Khardeen and Aaron to be there and knew they would
notice, and understand the significance of, the Consort's
ring. He'd been prepared for that. But he *hadn't* been prepared for the *other* males who made up the First Circle.

There was Sceron, the Red-Jeweled Warlord Prince of
Centauran. The dark-haired centaur had stood near the
dining table, eating a vegetable omelet while talking with
Morton, a blond-haired, blue-eyed Warlord from Glacia.
Then there was the Green-Jeweled Warlord, Jonah, a satyr
whose dark pelt covered him from his waist to his cloven
hooves but didn't quite cover the parts of him that were
blatantly male. There was Elan, a Red-Jeweled Warlord
Prince from Tigrelan, who had tawny, dark-striped skin and
whose hands ended with sheathed claws. Watching Elan,
Daemon would have bet the man had more in common
with the dark-striped cat he'd glimpsed from a window than
just physical markings.

And then there was Chaosti, the Gray-Jeweled Warlord
Prince of the Dea al Mon, with his long silver-blond hair,
delicately pointed ears, and slightly too large forest-blue
eyes. Every territorial instinct in Daemon had come roaring
to the surface at the sight of Chaosti—perhaps because
Chaosti was the kind of man who could be a formidable rival
no matter what Jewels he wore or perhaps because Daemon
saw a little too much of himself in the other man. Only Saetan's presence had kept a sharp-edged greeting from turning
into an open confrontation. That meeting had left him edgy,
and far too aware of his own inner fragility.

Next came the older, Gray-Jeweled Warlord Prince who
had introduced himself as Mephis, his older brother. The
room had tilted a bit when Daemon realized that, as Saetan's eldest son, Mephis had been demon-dead for more
than 50,000 years. He might have recovered his balance if
Prince Andulvar Yaslana and Lord Prothvar Yaslana
hadn't walked in at that moment, and the collective shock
of the Eyrien males who realized who they must be—and
then realized *what* they must be—hadn't hit him like a run-
away wagon. After one raking look at the fearful Eyriens
and a murmured comment to the High Lord, the demon-
dead Warlord Prince and his grandson had left the room.

By that point, Daemon had sincerely wished for brandy instead of coffee—a wish that must have been apparent. The stuff Khardeen had poured into his coffee from a silver flask hadn't been brandy, but it had successfully furred his nerves enough for him to be able to eat.

Still too jangled to enjoy the meal, he'd just finished his modest breakfast when Surreal stormed in, muttering something about it taking more time than expected "to get us brushed." She had looked shocked when she saw Chaosti, who was the only person she had seen who came from the same race as her mother, but the moment he'd moved toward her, she had bared her teeth and announced that the next male who approached her before breakfast was going to get brushed with the edge of a knife.

She, at least, had enjoyed a quiet, and undisturbed, breakfast.

He was just about to leave the room when a tall, slender witch with spiky, white-blond hair walked in, took one look at him, and said loudly enough to be heard in every corner of the Hall, "Hell's fire, *he's a Black Widow!*"

That he was a natural Black Widow—and, besides Saetan, the *only* male Black Widow—was something he'd been able to successfully hide for all the centuries since his body had reached sexual maturity, just as he'd been able to hide the snake tooth and venom sack beneath the ring-finger nail of his right hand. Whatever he had done instinctively to suppress other Black Widows' ability to detect him had failed him now, when there was nothing he could do about such a public betrayal.

The tension in the room had faded when Saetan replied mildly, "Well, Karla, he *is* my son, and he *is* the Consort."

The witch's surprise had changed to sharp speculation. "Oh," she said. "In that case . . ." A slow, wicked smile bloomed. "Kiss kiss."

Brushing past Lucivar, he had escaped from the dining room and had spent the past hour wandering through the Hall, trying to get his churning thoughts and emotions under control.

"Are you lost?"

Daemon glanced over to where Lucivar leaned against a doorway. "I'm not lost," he snapped. Then he stopped pacing and sighed. "But I am very confused."

"Of course you are. You're male." Grinning at Daemon's snarl, Lucivar stepped into the courtyard. "So if one of the darlings in the coven offers to explain things to you, don't take her up on it. She'll sincerely be trying to help, but by the time she's done 'unconfusing' you, you'll be banging your head against a wall and whimpering."

"Why?"

"Because for every five rules you'd learned in Terreille about a male's proper behavior in a court, the Kaeleer Blood know only one of them—and they interpret it very differently."

Daemon shrugged "Obedience is obedience."

"No, it's not. For Blood males, the First Law is to honor, cherish, and protect. The second is to serve. The third is to obey."

"And if obedience interferes with the first two laws?"

"Toss it out the window."

Daemon blinked. "You actually get away with that?"

Lucivar scratched the back of his head and looked thoughtful. "It's not so much a question of getting away with it. For Warlord Princes, it's almost a requirement of court service. However, if you ignore an order from the Steward or the Master of the Guard, you'd better be sure you can justify your action and be willing to accept the consequences if they won't accept it, which is rare. I got into more trouble with the High Lord as my father than as the Steward."

Father. Steward. The ties of family and court.

"Why are you here, Prick?" Daemon asked warily. "Why aren't you at the practice field observing the warriors you selected?"

"I was looking for you because you *didn't* show up at the practice field." Lucivar shifted slightly, balancing his weight.

Not yet, Daemon thought. *Not now.* "And because we have unfinished business," he said slowly.

"And because we have unfinished business." Lucivar took a deep breath, let it out slowly. "I accused you of killing Jaenelle. I accused you of viler things than that. I was wrong, and it cost you your sanity and eight years of your life."

Daemon looked away from the regret and sadness in Lucivar's eyes. "It wasn't your fault," he said softly. "I was already fragile."

"I know. I sensed that—and I used it as a weapon."

Remembering the fight they'd had that night in Pruul, Daemon closed his eyes. Lucivar's fury hadn't hurt him as much as his own fear that the accusations might possibly be true. If he'd been sure of what had happened at Cassandra's Altar, the fight would have ended differently. Lucivar wouldn't have spent more years in the salt mines of Pruul, and he wouldn't have spent eight years in the Twisted Kingdom.

Daemon opened his eyes and looked at his brother, finally understanding that Lucivar wasn't offering to meet him on a killing field for something *he* had done, but as reparation for whatever pain he'd suffered in the Twisted Kingdom. Oh, Lucivar would fight, and fight hard because he had a wife and a young son to consider, but he wouldn't hesitate if Daemon demanded it, even knowing what the outcome would be when Ebon-gray faced Black.

He also knew why Lucivar was forcing the issue. His brother didn't want the wife and child weighed in the balance, didn't want Daemon to have enough time to develop feelings for them before making this decision. Following the old ways of the Blood, if he forgave this debt now, he couldn't demand reparation later. Otherwise, they would always be wary of each other, always feel the need to guard their backs while waiting for the unexpected strike.

And, in a way, hadn't the debt already been paid? His years in the Twisted Kingdom balanced against Lucivar's years in the salt mines of Pruul. His grief when he believed Lucivar was dead balanced against Lucivar's grief over Jaenelle's supposed death by Daemon's hand. And if their positions had been reversed, would he have believed any differently or acted any differently?

"Is that the only unfinished business between us?" Daemon asked.

Lucivar nodded cautiously.

"Then let it go, Prick. I've already grieved for the loss of my brother once. I don't want to do it again."

They studied each other for a minute, weighing the things that went beyond words. Finally, Lucivar relaxed. His smile was lazy, arrogant, and so irritatingly familiar that Daemon smiled in return.

"In that case, Bastard, you're late for practice," Lucivar said, gesturing Daemon toward a door.

"Kiss my ass," Daemon growled, falling into step.

"Not a good suggestion, old son. I have a tendency to bite, remember?" Smiling, Lucivar massaged his upper arm. "So does Marian. She tends to get feisty when she's riled."

Seeing the warmth and pleasure in Lucivar's eyes, Daemon ruthlessly suppressed a surge of envy.

Finally reaching an outside door, they headed for the Eyriens gathered at the far end of the expansive lawn.

"By the way," Lucivar said, "while you were brooding—"

"I wasn't brooding," Daemon snarled.

"—you missed the fun this morning."

Daemon clenched his teeth. He wouldn't ask. Wouldn't. "What fun?"

"See the embarrassed-looking wolf standing by himself?"

Daemon looked at the gray-furred animal watching a group of women going through some kind of exercise with Eyrien sticks. "Yes."

"Graysfang wants to be Surreal's friend. He's young and he doesn't have much experience with humans, especially the females. Apparently, in an effort to strengthen that friendship and improve his understanding of females, he joined Surreal while she was taking a shower. Since her head was under the water at the moment, she didn't realize he was there until he stuck his nose where he shouldn't have."

"That would have improved his understanding of females," Daemon said dryly.

"Exactly. Then, when he whined that he had soap in his fur, she dragged him all the way into the shower and washed him. So now he smells like flowers."

Daemon bit his lip. "There's an easy remedy for that."

Lucivar cleared his throat. "Well, there usually would be, but as soon as they got outside, she threatened to smack him if he got dirty."

"Everything has a price," Daemon said in a choked voice. Noticing the woman Surreal was talking to, he gave Lucivar a sharp nudge. "Should Marian be doing something that strenuous during her moon time?"

Lucivar hissed. "Don't you start." He stopped walking and studied the women through narrowed eyes. "I told her she could do one round of the warmup drill. She'll sneak a little more in under the guise of demonstrating the moves, but after that she'll be content to rest."

Daemon looked at the women and then at Lucivar. "You told your wife how much she could do?"

"Of course I didn't tell my wife," Lucivar said indignantly. "Do I look like a fool? The Warlord Prince of Ebon Rih told a witch who lives in his territory."

"Ah. That's different."

"Damn right it is. If I told my wife, she would have tried to dent my head with a stick."

Daemon laughed as they continued toward the Eyrien warriors. "Now I *am* sorry I missed it."

Lucivar focused his attention on Falonar and Rothvar, who had just stepped into the practice circle, while Daemon watched Surreal and Marian go through a couple of moves.

"Who is she?" Daemon asked when the spiky-haired witch joined the other women.

Lucivar glanced at the women, then turned his attention back to the Eyrien warriors. "That's Karla, the Queen of Glacia. She's a Black Widow Queen and a Healer. One of three who have a triple gift."

A triple gift and a big mouth, Daemon thought darkly.

"You're excused from the practice today, but I'll expect you to be on time tomorrow," Lucivar said.

Daemon sputtered. "I am *not* going to drill with sticks against Eyrien warriors."

Lucivar snorted and looked at Daemon's feet. "I've got some boots that will fit you until you can get your own made."

"I'm not doing this."

"Until the official transfer is made, I own the contract you signed, old son. You've got no choice."

Daemon swore quietly, viciously.

Lucivar started to step away from him to speak to Falonar.

"Give me one good reason why I should put myself through this." Daemon demanded through clenched teeth.

Lucivar turned back to him. "Do you understand how good I am with the Eyrien sticks?" he asked quietly.

"I've seen you."

"Jaenelle can put me in the dirt." Lucivar grinned when Daemon's jaw dropped. "Not often, I grant you, but she's done it."

Daemon thought about that little nugget of information while Lucivar talked with the Eyrien males. He thought hard. When Lucivar returned, giving him a questioning look, he stripped off his jacket, rolled up his shirtsleeves, and growled, "Where are the damn boots?"

4 / Kaeleer

Pulling her shawl more tightly around her, Alexandra Angelline wrapped her arms around her waist as she stared out the streaked inn window that overlooked the service fairgrounds. The rain that had started falling an hour earlier was more of a drizzle that only managed to smear the dirt that covered everything rather than a downpour that would wash it away.

This is Kaeleer? she thought bleakly. *This is the Shadow Realm that so many were so desperate to reach?* Oh, it was probably unfair to judge an entire Realm by ground that had been scraped bare by the hundreds of people who had waited there, hoping to be chosen for a service contract. But she knew that, no matter what else she saw, this is what she would always picture whenever someone mentioned Kaeleer.

She felt someone approach, but didn't turn when her daughter, Leland, joined her at the window.

"Why would Wilhelmina have wanted to come to this place?" Leland murmured. "I'll be glad when we can leave here."

"You don't have to stay, Leland. Especially now that Vania and Nyselle have so graciously insisted on accompanying me."

"They didn't come with us out of loyalty," Leland said quietly but bitterly. "They just wanted a chance to see the Shadow Realm and knew they might not get in any other way."

Alexandra clenched her teeth while the truth of Leland's remark gnawed at her. Vania and Nyselle, the two Province Queens who grudgingly had accompanied her to Hayll, had become sickening in their solicitousness as soon as she announced she was going to Kaeleer to look for Wilhelmina. So they and their Consorts had come with her, along with

Philip and Leland and a five-man escort. Four of the escorts had come with her from Chaillot. The other one, chosen by Dorothea SaDiablo, had been "borrowed" from one of Dorothea's pet Queens in another Territory. The man made her skin crawl, but Dorothea had assured her that he would be able to slip Wilhelmina away from her "captors" and deliver her to another loyal group of males already in position in Kaeleer.

It pains me to say it, Dorothea had said, *but if you can free only one of your granddaughters from the High Lord's control, it must be Jaenelle. She is the danger to Terreille.*

Alexandra didn't believe for a moment that Jaenelle was anything more than a stalking-horse being used to hide whoever—or whatever—was the *real* threat to Terreille. But, sweet Darkness, she hoped she wouldn't have to make a choice between Wilhelmina and Jaenelle—because she knew in her heart which child would be left behind.

"Besides," Leland added softly, "I need to stay. She was always such a strange child, but Jaenelle was . . . is . . . my daughter. To think she's been under that monster's control all this time . . ." Leland shuddered. "There's no telling what he's done to her."

And no way to tell what had been done to her in Briarwood. Had she really been mentally fragile or had that place made her so? No, she decided firmly. Jaenelle's stays at Briarwood might have weakened an already fragile stability, but the child's eccentricities had been the reason why she had decided to send the girl to Briarwood in the first place.

"What are we going to do?" Leland asked quietly.

Alexandra looked over her shoulder at the other people restlessly waiting for her decision. Philip, whose self-control had broken several times while he'd given her Lord Jorval's information, would go with her, not only because he had married Leland, but also because he genuinely cared for Wilhelmina and Jaenelle. Vania and Nyselle would go in order to see more of Kaeleer than this dirty piece of barren ground. The Consorts and escorts would follow the Queens out of duty. Would curiosity and duty be enough against something like the High Lord?

It didn't matter. She would take whatever help she could get.

As she turned back to the window, she said, "Prince Alexander, please arrange passage on a Coach as soon as possible. We're going to SaDiablo Hall."

5 / Kaeleer

Certain that he had more muscle aches than muscles, Daemon slowly made his way to the great hall where, Beale had informed him, the High Lord was waiting.

Never again. Never never never. He should have remembered what "I'll start you off easy" meant, should have remembered that other kinds of exercise didn't prepare the body for Eyrien weapons drills. Oh, if he wanted to be fair—and he had no intention of being fair in the foreseeable future—Lucivar *had* started him with the basic warmup drills. But even moving at the practice pace, when you had Lucivar as a working partner, you *worked*.

Then he opened a door at the far end of the great hall and forgot about his aching muscles when he saw Saetan brush the hair away from the face of an attractive Dhemlan witch. There was tenderness in that action, and affection as well. Wondering if he was reading things correctly, he moved forward as quietly as possible.

The witch noticed him first. Looking flustered, she took a long step back and watched him tensely. But it was the flash of anger he picked up from his father that made him wary.

Then Saetan turned, saw him, and relaxed for a moment before hurrying toward him.

"What happened to you?" Saetan demanded. "Are you hurt?"

"Lucivar happened to me," Daemon replied through gritted teeth.

"Why were you and Lucivar tangling?" Saetan asked in a deceptively neutral voice that had a strong undertone of parental disapproval.

"We weren't tangling, we were drilling. But I'm delighted that someone besides me has trouble understanding the distinction."

The witch turned away from them and started making funny noises. When she turned back, her gold eyes were bright with laughter. "I'm sorry," she said, not sounding the least bit sorry. "Having been on the receiving end of Lucivar's instruction, I understand how you feel."

"Why were you doing weapons drills with Lucivar?" Saetan asked.

"Because I'm an idiot." Daemon raised his hand to brush the hair off his forehead. His arm froze halfway through the motion, stuck. He slowly lowered his arm, grateful it would go back down. "I really want to be there the next time Jaenelle puts him in the dirt."

"Who doesn't?" the witch murmured.

Saetan let out an exasperated sigh. "Sylvia, this is Daemon Sadi. Daemon, this is Lady Sylvia, the Queen of Halaway."

Sylvia's eyes widened. "This is the *boy?*"

Daemon bristled until Saetan gave him a sharp mental jab.

" 'Boy' is a relative term," Saetan said.

"I'm sure it is," Sylvia replied, trying to school her face into an appropriate expression.

Saetan just looked at her.

"Well," Sylvia said too brightly, "I'll just go say hello to the coven and let the two of you sort this out."

"Are you going to lend me that book?" Saetan asked, his lips curving in a knowing, malicious smile.

"What book is that, High Lord?" Sylvia asked, attempting to look innocent while blushing furiously.

"The one you won't admit to reading."

"Oh, I don't think it would interest you," Sylvia mumbled.

"Considering your reaction every time I've mentioned it, I think I would find it very interesting reading."

"You could buy your own copy."

"I would prefer to borrow yours."

Sylvia glared at him. "I'll lend it to you on the condition that *you* admit to the *coven* that you're reading it."

Saetan said nothing. A faint blush colored his cheeks.

Satisfied, Sylvia smiled warmly at Daemon. "Welcome to Kaeleer, Prince Sadi."

"Thank you, Lady," Daemon replied courteously. "Meeting you has been highly instructive."

Saetan hissed. Sylvia didn't waste any time removing herself from their company.

As soon as she left, Saetan raked his fingers through his hair, then inspected the empty hand. "I understand perfectly why her father's hair fell out," he growled. "Mine just keeps getting grayer, for which, I suppose, I should be thankful."

"She's a friend?" Daemon asked blandly.

"Yes, she's a friend," Saetan snapped, putting too much emphasis on the last word. He gave Daemon a sour look. "Come on, puppy. You'd better sit down before you fall down."

Daemon obediently followed his father into the official study, amused by and intensely curious about the edgy, defensive tone in Saetan's voice.

By the time he'd gotten his rebelling muscles to yield enough to let him sit down, Andulvar Yaslana had joined him and Saetan.

"You didn't do too badly for a novice," Andulvar said.

"As soon as I can move again, I'm going to flatten his head," Daemon growled.

Saetan and Andulvar exchanged an amused look.

"Ah," Saetan said, "the centuries may pass, but the sentiment remains the same."

"You said much the same thing the first time you and Lucivar pounded on each other," Andulvar said.

Daemon studied the two men through narrowed eyes.

"The two of you were only a couple of years older than Daemonar," Saetan said. "You found a long pole that was the right diameter for a child's hand. cut it in half, and then Lucivar set out to show you the drills he'd been practicing."

"He's always had a natural talent for weapons," Andulvar said, "but at that age, he wasn't good at explaining the drills."

"So," Saetan said, "he got in a couple of good whacks, and you, by luck or temper, got in a couple of whacks yourself. At which point, the two of you tossed aside the sticks and started using your fists. Manny put an end to it by dumping a bucket of cold water over both of you."

Daemon had to make a conscious effort not to squirm. "Are you going to do this every time?" he growled at Saetan.

"Do what?" Saetan asked blandly.

"Trot out embarrassing stories from my childhood."

Saetan just smiled.

"Come on, puppy," Andulvar said. "You need a hot bath, a rubdown, and something to eat. The morning's still young, and you've got the rest of the day ahead of you."

Daemon's snarl turned into a yelp when Andulvar grabbed the back of his shirt and hauled him to his feet.

"One moment," Saetan said quietly.

Sensing the change in mood, Daemon turned to face Saetan squarely. "You sent for me."

Saetan studied Daemon for a minute. "I've received a request. Whether you want to honor it is totally your choice. If you decide you're not ready, or don't want to at all, I'll try to explain."

Daemon felt ice rush through his veins, but he resisted the urge to give in to the cold rage. He had a lot to learn about the give-and-take between males and females in Kaeleer. He shouldn't assume that a request made here meant the same thing as a request made in Terreille.

"What's the request?"

Saetan said gently, "Your mother would like to see you."

6 / Kaeleer

Sipping a cup of herbal tea, Karla wandered around the inner garden, hoping the sound of the fountain would soothe her. She looked up once, apprehensively, at the second floor windows on the south side of the courtyard. Was Sadi up there right now, watching her from behind the sheer curtains?

Hell's fire, I shouldn't have blurted out that he is a Black Widow. She'd realized that the moment she saw the cold fury in his eyes. But she'd been disturbed by the tangled web she'd woven a couple of days ago and so preoccupied with trying to understand the cryptic images she'd seen . . . Well, seeing Daemon Sadi certainly explained a lot of those images. She'd seen the High Lord looking into a mirror, but the reflection wasn't him. She'd seen truths protected by lies. She'd seen a Black-Jeweled Black Widow who became an enemy in order to remain a friend. And she'd seen death held back by a ring. Her death.

Troubled by her inability to interpret the vision of the

High Lord, she had begun to wonder if she'd misread the tangled web somehow. Now there were no more doubts.

She drained the cup and sighed. There was one more thing she'd better get straightened out before Jaenelle returned—for all their sakes.

Daemon reached for the black jacket he had laid on his bed, then paused when he heard the tapping again, a little louder this time. Someone was outside the glass balcony door of his sitting room.

Leaving the jacket, he went into the sitting room, pulled aside the curtain, and stared at the spiky-haired witch standing on the balcony. His first impulse was to release the curtain and ignore her. He didn't want her physical presence or her psychic scent in his rooms. He didn't want anyone wondering why he was entertaining another woman before he'd had a chance to be formally accepted by the Queen.

He didn't give a damn that she was a Territory Queen. But the fact that she was in the First Circle of Jaenelle's court *did* matter.

Reluctantly, he opened the door and stepped back to let her enter.

"I have an appointment in a few minutes," he said coldly.

"I came to apologize," Karla said. "It won't take long. I'm not very good at them, so I tend to keep them short."

Daemon slipped his hands into his trouser pockets and waited.

Karla took a deep breath. "I shouldn't have announced your belonging to the Hourglass so publicly. The First Circle would have been told in any case, but I shouldn't have blurted it out like that. I was thinking about something else that had been puzzling me, and when I saw you . . ." She shrugged.

"How did you know? No one in Terreille realized what I am."

Her lips curved. "Well, I doubt any of them has spent the past ten years annoying Uncle Saetan. Those of us who have would notice the similarities in your psychic scents and reach the correct conclusion."

Daemon blinked. "*Uncle* Saetan?"

Her lips finished curving into that wicked smile. "He adopted Jaenelle, and the rest of us adopted him. We came to stay for a summer and never quite went home again. You can imagine how thrilled he was to discover he'd acquired ten adolescent witches instead of just one—and the boyos, too, of course."

"Of course," Daemon said, fighting not to smile. "Some surprise."

"Mmm. That first summer, when we all piled in on him, the coven became very adept at brewing soothing tonics. It was so distressing to hear him whimper."

Daemon choked on a laugh. Then his amusement faded. She was clever, this Queen with the ice-blue eyes and spiky white-blond hair. She must realize how much he wanted to hear stories of Jaenelle's youth.

Karla studied him. "If it would make you feel better, you can threaten to throttle me."

He was speechless for a moment. "I beg your pardon?"

"In this court, it's the acceptable way for a male to express annoyance with a witch."

"Threatening to throttle a woman is considered acceptable?" Daemon asked, sure that he had misunderstood something.

"As long as he says it calmly so you know he doesn't mean it."

A male who could remain calm in this place must have an amazing amount of self-control, Daemon thought. He rubbed his forehead and began to understand Lucivar's warning about having one of the coven explain things to him.

"Having Lucivar threaten you doesn't bother you?" Daemon asked. Since Lucivar usually sounded calm when he threatened someone, only a fool wouldn't take him seriously.

Karla twitched her shoulders. "Oh. Well. *Lucivar*. He rarely says anything if he's annoyed with you. He just picks you up and tosses you into the nearest body of water." She paused. "Although to be fair—"

"Who wants to be fair?" Daemon growled.

"Spent the morning with him, didn't you?" Karla said knowingly. "If it's a watering trough or a fountain, he dunks you rather than tosses you so that you don't get hurt. However, that's Lucivar. We strongly discourage other males from acquiring that particular habit."

"If you didn't, you'd be wet most of the time," Daemon muttered.

Before Karla could respond to that comment, Morghann, the Queen of Scelt—the red-haired Queen he'd seen earlier that morning—and Gabrielle, the Queen of the Dea al Mon, gave the balcony door a token tap before walking in.

"The coven's rooms all face this inner garden, so it's quicker to use the balcony doors rather than walking all the way around inside," Morghann said at the same time Karla said, "Where's Surreal?"

Gabrielle hooked her silver-blond hair behind her pointed ears and grinned. "Chaosti claimed her on the pretense of giving her a tour of the Hall. She was still snarling about having to apologize to Graysfang for sounding like she meant it when she threatened to smack him."

"I was explaining some of the rules to Daemon," Karla said.

"I really do have an appointment," Daemon muttered, then said, "Come in,"—loudly—when someone knocked on the sitting room door.

Saetan walked in, took one look at the three women, and stopped.

"Kiss kiss," Karla said.

"We were going to explain the rules to Daemon," Morghann said.

"May the Darkness have mercy on Daemon," Saetan said dryly.

"I'll get my jacket," Daemon said, not about to ignore a chance to retreat. Pride kept him from bolting into his bedroom. Common sense made him linger far longer than necessary, so that when he finally walked back into his sitting room, Saetan was the only one waiting for him.

"Have they gone off to plague someone else?" Daemon asked sourly as they left his suite and started walking through the corridors.

Saetan chuckled. "For the moment."

Daemon hesitated. "Maybe you'd better explain those rules to me."

"I'll give you a book of court Protocol to review."

"No, I meant the rules that are peculiar to this court. Like—"

"I don't want to know," Saetan said quietly but firmly.

"You have to know. You're the Steward."

"Exactly. And if this court has some rules that I have been blissfully ignorant of for the five years that I've been the Steward, I do not want to know about them now."

"But—" Daemon said. The implacable look in Saetan's eyes stopped him. "That's a prissy attitude for you to take."

"From where you're standing, I suppose it is. From where I'm standing, it makes a world of sense. You're younger. Deal with it."

Before he could make a comment he might regret, a small brown-and-white dog raced up to them and stopped a few feet away, his tail wagging in effusive greeting.

He's here! Jaenelle's mate is finally here!

Daemon felt as if the wind had been knocked out of him, not only because he had heard the dog but because he'd seen the Red Jewel hidden in the white ruff.

"Daemon, this is Lord Ladvarian," Saetan said. "Ladvarian, this—"

A Black-Jeweled Warlord Prince, Ladvarian said as he danced around in front of them. *He's a Black-Jeweled Warlord Prince. I have to tell Kaelas.* The dog dashed down the corridor and disappeared.

"Mother Night," Saetan said under his breath. "Come on. Let's get out of here before you meet anyone else. You've already had a sufficient amount of education for your first day in the court."

"He's kindred," Daemon said weakly as he followed Saetan. "When Lucivar said someone named Ladvarian would be pleased to see me, I thought . . . Unless he meant someone else?"

"No, that's Ladvarian. He would have gone to the service fair to look for you himself, but kindred aren't well received in Little Terreille, and I wasn't willing to risk him. His ability to explain kindred behavior to humans and human behavior to the kindred makes him unique. And his influence on Prince Kaelas is not to be taken lightly."

"Who's Kaelas?"

Saetan gave him an odd look. "Let's save Kaelas for another day."

*   *   *

Daemon studied the well-kept cottage and neat yard. "I'd always wanted Tersa to live in a place like this."

"She's comfortable here," Saetan said, opening the front door. "A journeymaid Black Widow lives with her as a companion. And then there's Mikal," he added as they followed the sound of voices to the kitchen.

Daemon stepped into the kitchen, gave the boy sitting at the kitchen table a quick glance, and then focused on Tersa, who was muttering to herself as she busily arranged an assortment of food.

Her black hair was as tangled as he remembered it, but the dark-green dress was clean and looked warm.

The boy hastily swallowed a mouthful of nutcake before saying in a suspicious voice, "Who's he?"

Tersa looked up. Joy brightened her gold eyes and made her smile radiant. "It's the boy," she said as she rushed into Daemon's arms.

"Hello, sweetheart," Daemon said, feeling swamped by the pleasure of seeing her again.

"*He's* not a *boy*," the boy said.

"Mikal," Saetan said sternly.

Leaning away from Daemon, Tersa looked at Mikal, then back at Daemon. "He is a large boy," she said firmly. She pulled Daemon toward the table. "Sit down. Sit. There is food. You should eat."

Daemon sat across from the boy, who openly regarded him as an unwelcome rival. "Shouldn't you be in school?"

Mikal rolled his eyes. "It's not a school day."

"But you did finish the chores your mother assigned to you *before* you came here," Saetan said mildly, accepting the glass of red wine Tersa offered him while his eyes never left Mikal.

Mikal squirmed under that knowing stare, and finally muttered, "Most of them."

"In that case, after we've eaten, I'll escort you home and you can finish them," Saetan said.

"But I have to help Tersa weed the garden," Mikal protested.

"The weeds will still be there," Tersa said serenely. She looked at the two "boys," frowned at the glasses of milk she held, then put both of them in front of Mikal. She patted Daemon's shoulder. "He is old enough for wine."

"Thank the Darkness," Daemon said under his breath.

The meal was eaten with little conversation. Saetan inquired about Mikal's schoolwork and got the expected evasive answers. Tersa tried to make mundane comments about the cottage and garden, but each time the remarks became more disjointed.

Daemon clenched his teeth. He wanted to tell her to stop trying. It hurt to watch her struggling so hard to walk the borderland of sanity for his sake, and seeing the concern and resentment in Mikal's eyes as her control continued to crumble stabbed at him.

Saetan set his wineglass on the table and rose. "Come on, puppy," he said to Mikal. "I'll take you home now."

Mikal quickly grabbed a nutcake. "I haven't finished eating."

"Take it with you."

When they left, with Mikal still loudly protesting, Daemon looked at Tersa. "It's good to see you again," he said softly.

Sorrow filled her eyes. "I don't know how to be your mother."

He reached for her hand. "Then just be Tersa. That was always more than enough." He felt her absorb the acceptance, felt the tension drain from her body.

Finally, she smiled. "You are well?"

He returned the smile and lied. "Yes, I'm well."

Her hand tightened on his. Her eyes lost focus, became distant and farseeing. "No," she said quietly, "you're not. But you will be." Then she stood up. "Come. I'll show you my garden."

7 / Kaeleer

Saetan shifted to a sitting position on the couch in his study. He didn't need to use a psychic probe to know who was on the other side of the door. The scent of her fear was sufficient. "Come."

Wilhelmina Benedict entered the room, each step a hesitation.

Watching her, Saetan tightened the reins on his temper. It wasn't her fault. She had been barely more than a child herself thirteen years ago. There was nothing she could have done.

But if Jaenelle hadn't stayed in Chaillot in order to protect Wilhelmina, that last, terrible night at Briarwood wouldn't have happened. She would have left the family that hadn't understood or cherished what she was. She would have come to Kaeleer, would have come to *him*— and would have escaped the violent rape that had left her with so many deep emotional scars.

It wasn't fair to hold Wilhelmina in any way responsible for what had happened to Jaenelle, but he still resented her presence in his home and her reappearance in her sister's life.

"What can I do for you, Lady Benedict?" He tried, but he couldn't keep the edge out of his voice.

"I don't know what to do." Her voice was barely audible.

"About what?"

"All the other people who signed the contract have something to do, even if it's just making a list of their skills. But I—"

She wrung her hands so hard Saetan winced in sympathy for the delicate bones.

"He hates me," Wilhelmina said, her voice rising in desperation. "Everyone here hates me, and I don't know why."

Saetan pointed at the other end of the couch. "Sit down." As he waited for her to obey, he wondered how such a frightened, emotionally brittle woman had managed to make the journey through one of the Gates between the Realms and then tried to acquire a contract at the service fair. When she was seated, he said, "Hate is too strong a word. No one here hates you."

"Yaslana does." She pressed her fists into her lap. "So do you."

"I don't hate you, Wilhelmina," he said quietly. "But I do resent your presence."

"Why?"

Faced with her hurt and bewilderment, he was tempted to blunt the truth, but decided to give her the courtesy of honesty. "Because you're the reason Jaenelle didn't leave Chaillot soon enough."

Her swift change from frightened to fierce startled him,

and he realized it shouldn't have. He should have looked for the common ground between her and Jaenelle instead of letting the past cloud his judgment.

"You know where to find her, don't you? *Don't you?*"

She looked like she was about to shake the answer out of him. Intrigued by the change in her, he wondered if she would actually try.

"Not at the moment," he said mildly. "But she'll be home soon."

"Home?" Her fierceness changed back to bewilderment and then thoughtfulness as she looked around the study. "Home?"

"I'm her adopted father." When she didn't react to that, he added, "Lucivar is her brother."

She jumped as if he'd jabbed her with a pin. Her blue eyes were filled with something close to horror as she stared at him. "Brother?"

"Brother. If it's any comfort to you, while you're both related to the same woman, you're not related to each other."

Her relief was so blatant he almost laughed.

"Does she like him?" Wilhelmina asked in a small voice.

He couldn't help it. He did laugh. "Most of the time." Then he studied her. "Is that why you came to Kaeleer? To find Jaenelle?"

She nodded. "Everyone else said she had died, that Prince Sadi had killed her, but I knew it wasn't true. He never would have hurt Jaenelle. I thought she had gone to live with one of her secret friends or with her teacher." She looked at him as if she were trying to measure what she saw against something she knew. "It was you, wasn't it? She came to *you* for lessons."

"Yes." He waited. "What made you think of Kaeleer?"

"She told me. After." Wilhelmina brushed a finger against her Sapphire Jewel. "When Prince Sadi unleashed his Black Jewels to escape the Hayllians who had come for him, I heard Jaenelle yelling 'ride it, ride it.' So I did. When it was over, I was wearing a Sapphire Jewel. Everyone was upset about that because they thought I had somehow made the Offering to the Darkness. But it wasn't my Jewel. It was Jaenelle's. I couldn't actually use it, but it protected me. Sometimes, when I was scared or didn't know what to do, it always gave the same answer: Kaeleer. I left home because Bobby—" She pressed her lips together and took a couple of deep breaths. "I left home. As soon as I was twenty, I made the Offering. I got this Jewel. The other one disappeared."

"And you've spent these past years trying to find a way here?"

She hesitated. "I wasn't ready for a long time. Then, one day, I started wondering if I would *ever* be ready. So I came anyway."

Which meant this woman had more courage than was readily apparent.

"Tell me something, Wilhelmina," Saetan said gently. "If, thirteen years ago, Jaenelle had decided to leave Chaillot and had asked you to go with her, would you have?"

It took her a long time to answer. Finally, reluctantly, she said, "I don't know." She looked around the room, sadness in her eyes. "Jaenelle belongs here. I don't."

"You're Jaenelle's sister and a Sapphire-Jeweled witch. Don't judge too quickly." *And I, too, will try not to judge too quickly.* "Besides, you would have had a different opinion of this place if you'd been here while ten adolescent witches were in residence," he added in a deliberately mournful voice.

Her eyes widened. "You mean the Queens who are here?"

"Yes."

"Oh, dear."

"That's one way of putting it."

She ducked her head as she stifled a laugh. When she dared to look at him again, he could tell she was thinking hard, reassessing the Hall and the people who resided here.

"I still don't have anything to do," she said hesitantly.

The almost-hopeful expectation in her eyes made him realize she had taken a long step toward accepting him as the family patriarch—and expecting him to fulfill the duties of that position.

"Lucivar didn't say *anything*?" he asked, fully aware that the only reason Lucivar had brought her there was to keep her away from anyone who might try to use her relationship to Jaenelle.

For the first time, a bit of temper flashed in her eyes.

"He told me to try not to faint because it will upset the males if I do."

Saetan sighed. "Coming from Lucivar, that was almost tactful. He's right. Blunt, but right. Males react strongly to feminine distress."

Wilhelmina frowned. "Is that why that large striped cat keeps following me?"

Saetan looked at the study door. A quick question on a psychic spear thread gave him the answer. "His name is Dejaal. He's Prince Jaal's son. He's appointed himself your protector until you feel comfortable with the other males at the Hall."

"He's kindred? I had heard stories—"

"The Blood in Little Terreille don't have much use for the kindred, and the kindred have even less use for the Blood in Little Terreille," Saetan said, and then added silently, *Except when they're hungry.*

Rising, he offered a hand to Wilhelmina and led her to the door. He called in a grooming brush and gave it to her. "If you want to do something that will help all of us right now, take Dejaal out to one of the gardens and brush him. Once you get used to him, perhaps it will be easier for you to be around the rest of us."

"If it's supposed to make me feel easier, maybe I should brush Lucivar instead," she said with just a hint of tartness.

Saetan burst out laughing. "Darling, if you want to get along with Lucivar, just show him that bit of steel in your backbone. Since he's lived with Jaenelle for the past eight years, he'll recognize it for what it is."

8 / Kaeleer

"Are you sure this is the path back to the Hall?" Daemon asked as he ducked under a low-hanging branch.

We left the path. Ladvarian said. *We have to cross the creek, and the path has no bridge.*

"I don't need a bridge to cross the creek."

Ladvarian looked at Daemon's shoes. *You would get wet.*

"I'd survive." Daemon muttered.

When he left Tersa's cottage, he'd found Ladvarian wait-

ing to escort him back to the Hall. At first, he'd wondered
if this was a subtle kind of insult, implying that he couldn't
find his way back by himself. Then, when Ladvarian offered
to show him a footpath that ran between Halaway and the
Hall, he'd wondered if he was being set up for an ambush.
Finally he realized the dog just wanted to spend a little
time getting to know the male whose duties made him an
important part of the Queen's life.

What he didn't like was the growing impression that he
was being labeled as a human who needed to be coddled.

He stopped walking. "Look, this has got to stop. I may
not be an Eyrien warrior, but I'm perfectly capable of walking a couple of miles without collapsing, I can get across a
creek without getting wet if I choose to, and I don't need
a short furball treating me like I can't survive if I'm not
inside a house full of servants. Do you understand?"

Ladvarian wagged his tail. *Yes. You want to be treated
like a Kaeleer male.*

Daemon rocked back on his heels and studied the Sceltie. "Is that what I said?"

Yes. Ladvarian headed off at an abrupt angle. *This
way.*

A minute later, they arrived at the creek. Ladvarian trotted up to the bank and leaped. By rights, he should have
landed in the middle of the creek, but he kept sailing over
it, and when he landed, he was standing a foot above the
ground, a doggy grin on his face.

Daemon looked at the creek, looked at the Sceltie, and
then air walked over the creek to the other bank.

Did Jaenelle teach you that?

Remembering the afternoon when Jaenelle had shown
him how to walk on air, Daemon's chest tightened. "Yes,"
he said softly, "she did."

She taught me, too. Ladvarian sounded pleased.

As soon as they walked through another stand of trees,
Daemon saw the road. The drive, he amended. Once the
north road out of Halaway crossed the bridge, it became
the drive up to the Hall, and the land spread out before
him was the family estate.

He headed for the drive, then spun around when Ladvarian growled, half-expecting an attack despite the dog's
display of friendship.

But Ladvarian was facing the way they'd come. The bridge was out of sight because of the roll of the land, but the wind was coming from that direction.

"What is it?" Daemon asked, opening his first inner barrier enough to sense the area around them.

Humans are coming. Three carriages. I've warned the other males, but we have to get back now. Ladvarian started trotting in a direct line toward the Hall, forcing Daemon into a fast walk to keep up.

"What's wrong with humans coming to the Hall?"

Ladvarian's psychic scent became hostile. *They feel wrong.*

The sudden fierceness was a sharp reminder that the small male trotting beside him was also a Red-Jeweled Warlord, and if Lucivar had overseen some of Ladvarian's training, the Sceltie was a far more effective fighter than anyone might suspect.

Nighthawk will take you to the Hall. He runs faster.

Before Daemon could wonder about that cryptic remark, he heard the hoofbeats pounding toward him.

Under other circumstances, once he saw the black horse, he would have declined the offer—not only because riding a stallion bareback wasn't a healthy idea, but because, for just a moment, the wind and the horse's movement had lifted its forelock and he'd seen the Gray Jewel hidden underneath. Despite the difference in their species, he recognized the aggressive psychic scent of another Warlord Prince. But when he didn't move after the horse pulled up, Ladvarian nipped his calf.

Go, Daemon. Now.

He barely had time to mount and grab a fistful of the long mane before Nighthawk took off at a flat-out gallop cross-country. Wondering how Ladvarian was going to keep up with them at that pace, he glanced back and saw the dog balanced on the horse's rump.

When the horse angled toward the last, long, straight section of the drive, Daemon tugged on the mane, and shouted, "Ease up," worried that Nighthawk would slip on the gravel at that speed.

He felt a slight lift, and then heard . . . nothing. No pounding hooves, no scattering gravel. Looking over Nighthawk's left shoulder, he saw those driving legs racing on air straight for the front door.

They were close enough to see the details of the dragon's head doorknocker before Nighthawk sat back on his haunches and finally came to a stop a hand span away from the steps.

Daemon dismounted and walked up the steps, not sure if his legs were trembling from muscle tension or frayed nerves. When he reached the door and looked back, there was no sign of Nighthawk, but he could sense the stallion's presence nearby.

"Hell's fire," he muttered as a footman opened the door. Ladvarian rushed in ahead of him and disappeared.

Daemon entered more slowly, feeling the press of male hostility. Besides the footman, the only visible person in the great hall was Beale, the butler, but he doubted they were the only ones present.

"It seems we're about to have company," Daemon said as he smoothed back his hair and straightened his black jacket.

"So it would seem," Beale replied blandly. "If you would remain here, Prince Yaslana and the High Lord will be arriving shortly."

Daemon looked around, then stepped into the formal receiving room just far enough not to be seen by whoever walked through the door.

Observing the move, Beale shifted position, putting himself directly in Daemon's line of sight.

Lucivar, Daemon said, using an Ebon-gray spear thread.

I'm coming in through the servants' door at the back of the hall.

If any of them manage to slip past us, is there any way for them to reach the living quarters?

The only way to the upper floors from that part of the Hall is by using the staircase in the informal receiving room. Don't worry about it. Kaelas is there. Nothing's going to get up those stairs. And the High Lord is coming down from that direction.

Daemon heard the carriages pull up in front of the Hall, saw Beale nod to the footman when someone banged on the door.

Footsteps. Rustling clothes. Then a woman's voice.

"I demand to see Wilhelmina Benedict."

Cold rage slipped through him so fast he was riding the killing edge before he realized he'd taken the first step toward it. He hadn't heard her voice in thirteen years, but he recognized it.

"Lady Benedict is not available," Beale said in a bland voice.

"Don't tell me that. I'm the Queen of Chaillot and I—"

Daemon stepped out of the receiving room. "Good afternoon, Alexandra," he said too calmly. "Such a pleasure to see you again."

"You." Alexandra stared at him, her eyes wide and fearful. Then the anger came. "You arranged for that 'tour' of Briarwood, didn't you?"

"All things considered, it was the least I could do." He took a step toward her. "I told you I would wash the streets of Beldon Mor with blood if you betrayed me."

"You also said you would put me in my grave."

"I decided that letting you live was a more thorough punishment."

"You bastard! You—" Alexandra started shivering. All of her entourage started shivering.

The intense, burning cold hit him a moment later, stunning him enough that he slipped away from the killing edge.

A moment after that, Saetan stepped into the great hall.

Is that what I look like when I go cold? Daemon wondered, unable to look away from glazed, sleepy eyes and the malevolently gentle smile.

"Lady Angelline." Saetan's voice rolled through the Hall like soft thunder. "I always knew we would meet someday to settle the debt, but I never thought you would be foolish enough to come here."

Alexandra clenched her hands but couldn't stop shaking. "I came to take my granddaughters home. Let them go, and we'll leave."

"Lady Benedict will be informed that you're here. If she wants to see you, a meeting will be arranged—fully chaperoned, of course."

"You dare imply that *I* present some kind of danger?"

"I know you do. The only question is, how much of a danger."

Alexandra's voice rose. "You have no right—"

"I rule here," Saetan snarled. "You're the one who has no rights, Lady. None at all. Except those I grant you. And I grant you little."

"I want to see my granddaughters. *Both* of them."

Something savage flickered at the back of Saetan's eyes. He looked at Leland and Philip, then turned his attention back to Alexandra. His voice dropped into a singsong croon. "I had two long, terrible years in which to come up with the perfect execution for the three of you. It will take you two long, terrible years to die, and every minute of it will be filled with more pain than you can imagine. However, in this case, I must have my Queen's consent before I begin." He turned away from them. "Beale, prepare some rooms for our guests. They'll be staying with us for a while."

As he walked past Daemon toward his study, their eyes met.

Daemon looked at Leland, who was clinging to Philip and crying softly; at the other Queens and their males, who were cowering in a tight group; and, finally, at Alexandra, who stared at him with terrified eyes and whose skin was bleached of any color.

Turning on his heel, he headed for the study and noticed Lucivar standing quietly at the back of the hall.

If you go in there, be careful, Bastard, Lucivar said.

Nodding, Daemon walked into the study.

Saetan stood by the desk, carefully pouring a glass of brandy. He looked up, poured a second glass, and extended it toward Daemon.

Daemon accepted the glass and took a healthy swallow, hoping it would thaw him a little.

"Another male's rage shouldn't throw you so much it knocks you away from the killing edge," Saetan said quietly.

"I'd never felt anything quite like that before."

"And if you feel it again, will it throw you again?"

Daemon looked at the man standing an arm's length away from him and understood it was the Steward of the Dark Court and not his father who was asking the question. "No, it won't."

Moving carefully, as if he were too aware that any sudden movement might unleash the violence still raging inside him, Saetan leaned against his blackwood desk.

Keeping his own movements equally controlled, Daemon poured himself another brandy. "Do you think the Queen will give her consent?"

"No. Since her relatives inflicted harm on her and not someone else, she'll oppose the execution. But I'll still make the request."

Daemon gently swirled the brandy in his glass. "If, for some reason, she doesn't oppose it, may I watch?"

Saetan's smile was sweet and vicious. "My darling Prince, if Jaenelle actually gives her consent, you can do more than watch."

9 / Kaeleer

Lord Magstrom sighed as he laid his stack of files on the large table already filled with stacks of files. He sighed again when his elbow jostled a corner stack and the top bulging file spilled on the floor. Going down on one knee, he began collecting the papers.

Thank the Darkness claiming day had ended and the autumn service fair was officially over. Perhaps he should decline to work the service fair next spring. The grueling hours were taxing for a man his age, but it was the heartbreaking hope and desperation on the immigrants' faces that wrung him dry. How could he look at a woman no older than his youngest granddaughter and not want to help her find a place to live where the fear lurking at the back of her eyes would be replaced by happiness? How could he talk to a courteous, well-spoken man who had been horrifically scarred by repeated attempts to "teach him obedience" and not want to send him to some quiet village where he could regain his self-respect and not have to wonder what was going to happen to him every time the Lady who ruled there looked in his direction?

There weren't places like that in Little Terreille. Not anymore. But it was the Queens in this Territory that continued to offer contracts and stuff their courts with immigrants. The other Queens in Kaeleer, in the Territories that answered to the Queen of Ebon Askavi, were more

cautious and far more selective. So he did his best to find
the immigrants who had a skill or a dream or *something*
that might buy them a contract outside of Little Terreille,
and he brought those people to the attention of the males
in Jaenelle Angelline's First Circle when they came to the
service fair. As for the others, he filled out the contracts
and wished them luck and good life—and wondered if their
new life in Little Terreille would really be any different
than the life they had tried to escape.

And he tried not to think at all about the ones who
hadn't been fortunate enough to receive *some* kind of contract and were sent back to Terreille.

Magstrom shook his head as he shuffled the papers into
some kind of order. Such sloppy work, stuffing the immigration entry lists into the same file as the service lists and
the lists of those who were returning to Terreille. How
could the clerks be expected to—

His hand tightened on a sheet of paper. The Hayllian
entry list. But *he* had been in charge of the Hayllian list—
until the end of the third day, when Jorval had decided to
oversee that particular list. There had been twenty names
on the list he'd given Jorval. Now there were only twelve.
Had someone recopied the list and only put down the
names of the people who had been accepted into service?
No, because Daemon Sadi's name wasn't there.

Magstrom quickly shuffled through the papers for the
Hayllian list of people returning to Terreille which the
guards would use to make sure no one tried to slip away
and go into hiding. Four names listed. Since Sadi was now
in Dhemlan, that left three people unaccounted for who
had been on the entry list he had given to Jorval.

When he heard footsteps approaching, he stuffed the papers back into the file, grunted softly as he stood up, and
hurriedly placed the file on a stack where it wouldn't just
spill back onto the floor.

The footsteps stopped at the door, then continued on.

Magstrom listened for a moment, then used Craft to
probe the area. No one there. But a shiver of uneasiness
rippled down his back.

Pushed by that uneasiness, he left the building and hurried to the inn where he had been staying during the service
fair. As soon as he reached his room, he began to pack.

By rights, he should have sought out other Council members and mentioned the disparities in the Hayllian lists. Maybe it was a simple clerical error—too many names, too much work rushed through. But who would "forget" to put a Warlord Prince like Daemon Sadi on the list? Unless the omission had been deliberate. And if that were the case, who knew how many other lists had similar disparities, how many Terreilleans who had come to Kaeleer were now unaccounted for?

And who knew what might happen to the evidence of those disparities if he told the wrong Council members about it?

If he rode the White Wind, which would be the least demanding, he could still be at the Nharkhava border by dawn. Because one of his granddaughters lived there, Kalush, the Queen of Nharkhava, had granted him a special dispensation that allowed him to visit her Territory without having to go through the formalities every time. And if, once he reached the border landing web, he requested an escort to his granddaughter's house . . . The guards might think it an odd request, but they wouldn't refuse to assist an elderly man. After he had a little sleep, he would compose a letter to the High Lord, explaining about the disparities in the lists.

Maybe it *was* only a clerical error. But if it was, in fact, the first glimpse of trouble, at least Saetan would have some warning—and would also know where to look for the source.

Jorval looked at the sheet of paper lying under the table and the papers hastily stuffed back into the bulging file.

So. The old fool had gotten curious. How unfortunate.

Magstrom might have been a thorn in the Dark Council's side for a good many years now, but he'd had his uses—especially since he was the only Council member who could request an audience with the High Lord and actually be granted one.

But it would seem that Magstrom's usefulness was coming to an end. And he wasn't about to forget that if it hadn't been for Magstrom's interference yesterday afternoon, the Dark Priestess would have had her Black-

Jeweled weapon safely tucked away somewhere where he could be useful.

He was tempted to send someone to take care of Magstrom that night, but the timing might lead certain people—like the High Lord—to look into the service fair a little too closely.

He could wait. Magstrom couldn't have seen *that* much. And if anything was questioned, it was easy enough to dismiss a clerk or two for negligence and offer profuse apologies.

But when the time did come . . .

10 / Kaeleer

Alexandra huddled in the chair in front of the blackwood desk.

The High Lord requests your presence.

Requests? *Demands* was more like it. But the study had been empty when that large, stone-faced butler had opened the door for her and, after fifteen minutes, she was still waiting. Not that she was in any hurry to face the High Lord again.

She strengthened the warming spell she'd put on her shawl and then grimaced at the futility of seeking a little warmth in this place. It wasn't so much the *place*—which was actually quite beautiful if you could get past the oppressive, dark feel of it—it was the *people* who produced a bone-deep chill.

She didn't think it was out of courtesy that she and her entourage had been given dinner in a small dining room located near the guest rooms. He wouldn't have cared that she was too physically and emotionally exhausted to cope with meeting whoever else lived there. He wouldn't have cared that she wouldn't have been able to choke down a mouthful of food if she had to sit at a table with Daemon Sadi.

No, she and her people had dined alone because he hadn't wanted her presence at his table.

And now, when she wanted to do nothing more than retire to her room and get whatever sleep she could after an exhausting day, *he* had requested her presence—and then didn't even have the courtesy to be there when she arrived.

She should leave. She was a Queen, and the insult of keeping her waiting had gone on long enough. If the High Lord wanted to see her, let him come to her.

As she stood up, the door opened and his dark psychic scent flooded the room. She sank back into the chair. It took all her self-control not to cower as he walked past her and settled into the chair behind the blackwood desk.

"When a male asks to speak with a Queen, he doesn't keep her waiting," Alexandra said, trying to keep her voice from quivering.

"And you, being such a stickler about courtesy, have never kept anyone waiting?" Saetan asked mildly after a long pause.

The queer, burning glitter that filled his eyes scared her, but she sensed this was the only chance she would have. If she backed down now, he would never concede anything.

She filled her voice with the cool disdain she used whenever an aristo male needed to be put in his place. "What a Queen does is beside the point."

"Since a Queen can do anything she damn well pleases, no matter how cruel the act, no matter how much harm she causes."

"Don't twist my words," she snapped, forgetting everything else about him except that he was male and shouldn't be allowed to treat a Queen this way.

"My apologies, Lady. Since you twist so much yourself, I'll do my best not to add to it."

She gave herself a moment to think. "You're deliberately trying to provoke me. Why? So you can justify executing me?"

"Oh, I already have all the justification I need for an execution," Saetan said mildly. "No, it's simpler than that. Your being terrified of me gets us nowhere. If you're angry, you'll at least talk."

"In that case, I want my granddaughters returned to me."

"You have no right to either of them."

"I have every right!"

"You're forgetting something very basic, Alexandra. Wilhelmina is twenty-seven. Jaenelle is twenty-five. The age of majority is twenty. You have no say in their lives anymore."

"Then neither do you. *They* should decide to stay or leave."

"They've already decided. And I do have far more say in their lives than you. Wilhelmina signed a contract with the Warlord Prince of Ebon Rih. He, in turn, serves in the Dark Court. I'm the Steward. So court hierarchy gives me the right to make some decisions about her life."

"What about Jaenelle? Does she serve in this Dark Court, too?"

Saetan gave her an odd look. "You really don't understand, do you? Jaenelle doesn't serve, Alexandra. Jaenelle is the Queen."

For a moment, the conviction in his voice almost convinced her.

No. *No.* If Jaenelle were really a Queen, she would have *known.* Like would have recognized like. Oh, there *might* actually be a Queen who ruled this court, but it wasn't, *couldn't be,* Jaenelle.

But his declaration gave her a weapon. "If Jaenelle is the Queen, you have no right to control her life."

"Neither do you."

Alexandra clamped her hands around the arms of the chair and gritted her teeth. "The age of majority acknowledges certain conditions that have to be met. If a child is deemed incapable in some way, her family maintains its right to take care of her mental and physical well being and make decisions on her behalf."

"And who decides if the child is incapable? The family that gets to maintain control of her? How very convenient. And don't forget, you're talking about a Queen who outranks you."

"I forget nothing. And don't you try to take the moral high ground with me—as if you had any concept of what morality means."

Saetan's eyes iced over. "Very well, then. Let's take a look at *your* concept of morality. Tell me, Alexandra. How did you justify it when it was obvious Jaenelle was being starved? How did you justify the rope burns from her being tied down, the bruises from the beatings? Did you just shrug it all off as the discipline needed to control a recalcitrant child?"

"You lie!" Alexandra shouted. "I never saw any evidence of that."

"You just tossed her into Briarwood and didn't bother to see her again until you decided to let her out?"

"Of course I saw her!" Alexandra paused. An ache spread through her chest as she remembered the distant, almost accusing way Jaenelle would look at them sometimes when she and Leland went to visit. The wariness and suspicion in her eyes, directed at them. She remembered how much it had hurt, and how Leland wept silently on the way home, when Dr. Carvay had told them that Jaenelle was too emotionally unstable to have any visitors. And she remembered the times she had felt relieved that Jaenelle was safely tucked away so others wouldn't have firsthand knowledge of the girl's fanciful tales. "I saw her whenever she was emotionally stable enough to have visitors."

Saetan snarled softly.

"You sit there and judge me, but you don't know what it was like trying to deal with a child who—"

"Jaenelle was seven when I met her."

For a moment, Alexandra couldn't breathe. Seven. She could imagine that voice wrapping itself around a child, spinning out lies. "So when she told her stories about unicorns and dragons, you encouraged her."

"I believed her, yes."

"Why?"

His smile was terrible. "Because they exist."

She shook her head, struck mute by the collision of too many thoughts, too many feelings.

"What would it take to convince you, Alexandra? Being impaled on a unicorn's horn? Would you still insist he was a fanciful tale?"

"You could trick anyone into believing anything you choose."

His eyes got that glazed, sleepy look. "I see." He stood up. "I don't give a damn what you think of me. I don't give a damn what you think about anything. But if I sense one flicker of distress from Wilhelmina or Jaenelle because of you, I'll bring everything I am down on you." He looked at her with those cold, cold eyes. "I don't know why Jaenelle ended up with you. I don't know why the Darkness would place such an extraordinary spirit in the care of someone like you. You didn't deserve her. You don't deserve even to know her."

He walked out of the room.

Alexandra sat there for a long time.

Tricks and lies. He'd said Jaenelle had been seven, but how old had she really been when the High Lord first started whispering his sweetly poisoned lies into a child's ear. Perhaps he had even created illusions of unicorns and dragons that looked real enough to be convincing. Maybe the uneasy way Jaenelle had sometimes made her feel had really been an aftertaste of him and not the child herself.

She couldn't deny that horrors had been done at Briarwood. But had those men done those things by choice or had an unseen puppet master been pulling the strings? She had experienced Daemon Sadi's cruelty. Wasn't it likely that her father had refined his taste for it? Had all that pain and suffering been caused in order to make one particular child so vulnerable she became emotionally dependent on these men?

Dorothea had been right. The High Lord was a monster. Sitting there, Alexandra was certain of only one thing: she would do whatever she had to in order to get Wilhelmina and Jaenelle away from him.

He felt Daemon's hands slide up his shoulder blades, then settle on his shoulders a moment before those strong, slender fingers began kneading tight muscles.

"Did you tell her Jaenelle is Witch?" Daemon asked softly.

Saetan took a sip of yarbarah, the blood wine, then closed his eyes to better savor the feel of tension and anger draining away as Daemon coaxed his muscles to relax. "No," he finally said. "I told her Jaenelle was the Queen, which should have been enough, but . . ."

"It wouldn't have mattered," Daemon said. "That last night, at the Winsol party, when I finally understood what Briarwood really was, I had intended to tell Alexandra about Jaenelle. I'd convinced myself that she would help me get Jaenelle away from Chaillot."

"But you didn't tell her."

Daemon's hands paused, then started working on another group of knotted muscles. "I overheard her tell another woman that Witch was only a symbol for the Blood, but if the living myth did appear, she hoped someone would have the courage to strangle it in its cradle."

A bolt of anger flashed through Saetan, but he couldn't tell if it was his or Daemon's. "Mother Night, how I hate that woman."

"Philip and Leland aren't exactly innocent."

"No, they're not, but they only follow Alexandra's lead both as their Queen and the family matriarch. She accused me of spinning lies to ensnare Jaenelle, but how many lies did *they* tell by cloaking them in the conviction of truth?" He made a sound that might have been a bitter laugh. "I can tell you how many. I've had years to observe the emotional scars their words left on her."

"And what happens when she finds out they're here?"

"We'll deal with that when it comes."

Daemon leaned closer, brushed his lips against Saetan's neck. "I can create a grave no one will ever find."

The kiss followed by that statement jolted Saetan enough to remember that this son still needed careful handling. He might indulge in imaginary gravedigging to channel some of his anger, but, just then, Daemon wouldn't hesitate to do it.

He jolted again when he felt the feather-light brush of dark, feminine power across the deepest edge of his inner barriers.

"Saetan?" Daemon said too softly.

Wolf song filled the night.

"No," Saetan replied gently but firmly as he stepped away far enough to turn and face Daemon. "It's too late for that."

"Why?"

"Because that chorus of welcome means Jaenelle is back." When Daemon paled, Saetan ran a hand down his son's arm. "Come to my study and have a drink with me. We'll bring Lucivar with us since he's probably fussed over Marian enough by now to annoy her."

"What about Jaenelle?"

Saetan smiled. "Boyo, after one of these trips, greeting

males, no matter who they are, comes in a poor third on her list of priorities—the first being a very long, hot bath and the second being an enormous meal. Since we can't compete with those, we might as well sit back and relax while we wait for her to get around to us."

11 / Kaeleer

Surreal stormed through the corridors. Each time she came to an intersection, a silent, solemn-faced footman pointed in the right direction. Probably the first one had warned the others after she'd snarled at him, "Where's the High Lord's study?"

It struck her as a little odd that none of the servants had seemed startled by her roaring through the corridors wearing nothing but a nightgown. Well, considering that the witches had to deal with the males who lived in this place, it probably wasn't unusual.

When she finally reached the staircase that led down to the informal receiving room, she hitched her nightgown up to her knees to keep from tripping on the hem, raced down the stairs and into the great hall, and swore because the marble floor was cold against her bare feet. In lieu of a knock, she walloped the study door once and then stomped up to the blackwood desk where Saetan sat watching her, a glass of brandy raised halfway to his lips.

Daemon and Lucivar, comfortably slouched in two chairs in front of the desk, just stared at her.

Now that she was there, she wasn't quite as willing to address the High Lord directly, so she half turned toward Daemon and Lucivar and tossed out the question, "Don't I have the right to decide if I want a male in my bed?"

The air behind the desk instantly chilled, but Lucivar said blandly, "Graysfang?" and the air returned to normal.

The smirk in Lucivar's voice had her turning toward him fully. "I don't know about you, but I'm not used to sleeping with a wolf."

"What's wrong with Graysfang staying with you?" Daemon asked.

The soothing tone he was putting into his voice only

infuriated her. "He farts," she snapped, then waved her hand dismissively. "Well, so do the rest of you."

Someone made a choking sound. She *thought* it was Daemon.

"Do you resent his being there because he's a wolf or because he's interfering with another kind of male warming your bed?" Lucivar asked.

Maybe it hadn't been meant as a slur that she used to be a whore, but she took it as such because then she could vent her temper on him. "Well, sugar, from where I'm standing, there's not much to choose between you. He takes up more than his share of the bed, he snores, and he gives slobbery kisses. But if I had to choose, I'd pick him. At least *he* can lick his *own* balls!"

A glass hit the desk with an ominous *thunk*.

Surreal closed her eyes and bit her lip.

Shit. She'd been so focused on being mad at Lucivar, she'd forgotten about the High Lord.

Before she could turn, Saetan had a firm grip on her arm and was pulling her toward the door.

"If you don't want Graysfang in your room at night, tell him," Saetan said, sounding like he had something stuck in his throat. "If he persists . . . Well, Lady, he wears a Purple Dusk Jewel and you wear a Gray. A shield around your room should take care of the problem."

"I *did* shield the room," Surreal protested. "And I still woke up and found him there. He sounded pleased that I'd shielded the room against the 'strange males,' but when he realized he couldn't get in, he had somebody named Kaelas help him through the shield."

Saetan's hand froze over the doorknob. He straightened up slowly. "Kaelas helped him through the shield," he said, spacing out the words.

She nodded cautiously.

Saetan swiftly opened the door. "In that case, Lady, I strongly suggest you and Graysfang get this settled between you."

The next thing she knew, she was standing in the great hall, staring at a firmly closed door.

"You said you'd help," she muttered. "You said I could come to you if I needed anything."

When the door opened again, she half-expected the High

Lord to call her back. Instead, Daemon and Lucivar got shoved into the hall and the door was slammed shut behind them.

They stared at the door for a moment, then looked at her.

"Congratulations," Lucivar said. "You've been here a little over twenty-four hours and you've already gotten tossed out of his study. Even I was here three days before he tossed me out the first time."

"Why don't you go sit on a spear," Surreal growled.

Lucivar shook his head and tsked. Daemon seemed to be straining a lot of muscles to keep from laughing.

"So why did he toss the two of you out?" Surreal asked.

"For privacy. You'll notice there are very strong shields around that room now, including an aural one." Lucivar looked at the closed study door. "Having witnessed this behavior a number of times, the males in the First Circle have come to the conclusion that he's either sitting there laughing himself silly or he's indulging in a fit of hysterics, and either way, he doesn't want us to know."

"He *said* he would help me," Surreal snarled.

Lucivar's eyes were bright with laughter. "I'm sure he'd intended to explain a few things to Graysfang—right up until you mentioned Kaelas."

"That name keeps coming up," Daemon said. "Just who is Kaelas?"

Lucivar eyed Daemon thoughtfully, then directed the answer to Surreal. "Kaelas is an Arcerian Warlord Prince who wears a Red Jewel. But because of some quirk in his talent or his training, he can get through any kind of shield—including a Black."

"Mother Night," Daemon muttered.

"He's also eight hundred pounds of feline muscle and temper." Lucivar smiled grimly. "We all try not to upset Kaelas."

"Shit," Surreal said weakly.

"Come on," Lucivar said. "We'll escort you to your room."

Walking between two strong males suddenly sounded like a good idea.

After a couple of minutes, Surreal said, "At least, being that big, he'll be easy enough to spot."

Lucivar hesitated. "The Arcerian Blood always use sight shields when they hunt. It makes them very effective predators."

"Oh." Being friends with a wolf was sounding better and better by the minute.

When they reached her room, she said good night and went inside.

Graysfang was standing exactly where she'd left him. Well, she *had* told him to "Stay right there," and he had taken her at her word.

Looking at the sadness in those brown eyes, she sighed.

Puppy love. It was a term whores used to describe clumsy, eager young males during their first few weeks of sexual experience. For a short time, they would try to please so they wouldn't be refused the bed. But after the novelty wore off, they would address those same women with a hardness in their eyes and a sneer in their voices.

"Tomorrow we're going to have to come to an agreement about a few things," Surreal told Graysfang.

His tail went *tock-tock*, just once.

Giving in, she climbed into bed and patted the covers beside her. He jumped up on the bed and lay down, watching her cautiously. She ruffled his fur, turned off the light, and found herself smiling. She had ended up in a place where, when someone spoke of puppy love, they were talking about a real puppy.

12 / Kaeleer

Too edgy to sleep and too restless to find distraction in a book, Daemon wandered through the dimly lit corridors of the Hall.

You're running, he thought, bitterly aware of the doubts and fears that had come swarming up when he had neared his suite of rooms—and had sensed Jaenelle's presence in the adjoining suite.

For most of his 1,700 years, he had believed, without question, that he'd been born to be Witch's lover. Thirteen years ago, faced with a twelve-year-old girl, that conviction hadn't been shaken. His heart had been committed; it was just the physical union that would have been delayed a few more years. But a brutal rape and the years he'd been lost in madness separated them now, and he wasn't sure he could stand to face her and see only a sense of obligation or, worse, pity in her eyes.

He needed to find a place that would help him regain his balance.

Daemon paused, then smiled reluctantly as he realized that he hadn't been running so much as searching. Somewhere on the grounds of the estate, there would be a place dedicated to performing the Blood's formal rituals for the sacred days in each season, but he doubted Saetan would build a home that didn't also contain a place for informal, private meditations.

He closed his eyes and opened his inner senses. A moment later, he was moving again, heading back toward the part of the Hall that contained the family living quarters.

He would have missed the entrance completely if he hadn't caught a glimpse of his reflection in the door's glass.

Stepping outside, he looked down at the sunken garden. Raised flower beds bordered all four sides except where the stone steps led down into the garden. Two statues dominated the space. A few feet in front of them were a raised stone slab and a wooden seat. Carefully positioned candlelights illuminated the statues and the steps.

The statues pulled at him. He went down the steps, hesitated a moment, then stepped onto the grass.

Power filled the air, making it almost too rich to breathe. As he filled his lungs with it, he felt his body absorb the strength and peace contained within this garden. On the stone slab were half a dozen candles in tinted glass containers. Choosing one at random, he used Craft to create a little tongue of witchfire and light it. A hint of lavender reached him before he walked over to the fountain that contained the female statue.

The back of the fountain was a curved wall of rough stone curtained by water that spilled into a stone-enclosed pool. The woman rose halfway out of the pool, her face lifted toward the sky. Her eyes were closed, and there was a slight smile on her lips. Her hands were raised as if she were just about to wipe the water from her hair. Everything about her embodied serene strength and a celebration of life.

He didn't recognize the mature body, but he recognized that face. And he wondered if the sculptor had continued his exquisite detail beneath the hips that rose out of the water, wondered what his fingers would find if he slid his hand past her belly.

Because he wondered, he turned to the other statue—the male.

The beast.

His visceral response to the crouched, blatantly male body that was a blend of human and animal was a gut-deep sense of recognition. It was as if someone had stripped him of his skin to reveal what really lay beneath.

Massive shoulders supported a feline head that had its teeth bared in a snarl of rage. One paw/hand was braced on the ground near the head of a small sleeping woman. The other was raised, the claws unsheathed.

Someone like Alexandra would look at this creature and assume it was about to crush and tear the female, that the only way to control that physical strength and rage would be to keep it chained. Someone like Alexandra would never look beyond that assumption to notice the small details. Like the sleeping woman's hand reaching out, her fingertips just brushing the paw/hand near her head. Like the way the crouching body sheltered her. Like the way the glittering, green stone eyes stared at whoever approached, and the fact that the snarling rage came from the desire, the *need*, to protect.

Daemon took a deep breath, let it out slowly—and then tensed. He hadn't heard any footsteps, but he didn't have to turn around to know who now stood at the foot of the stairs. "What do you think of him?" he asked quietly.

"He's beautiful," Jaenelle replied in her midnight voice.

Daemon slowly turned to face her.

She wore a long black dress. The front lacing ended just below her breasts, revealing enough fair skin to make a man's mouth water. Her golden hair flowed over her shoulders and down her back. Her ancient sapphire eyes didn't look as haunted as he remembered, but he had the painful suspicion that he was the reason for the sadness he saw in them.

As the silence between them lengthened, he couldn't move toward her any more than he could move away.

"Daemon . . ."

"Do you understand what he represents?" he asked quickly, tipping his head just enough to indicate the statue.

Jaenelle's lips curved into just a hint of a dry smile. "Oh, yes, Prince, I understand what he represents."

Daemon swallowed hard. "Then don't insult me by offering regrets. A male is expendable. A Queen is not—especially when she is Witch."

She made an odd sound. "Saetan said almost the same thing once."

"And he was right."

"Well, being a Warlord Prince made from the same mold, you would think that, wouldn't you?" She started to smile. Then her eyes narrowed. Her attention sharpened.

Daemon had the distinct impression there was something about him that didn't please her. When her intense focus ended a moment later, he realized that she had made some decision about him, just as she had done the first time he'd met her. And now, like then, he didn't know what she had decided.

The Consort's ring was a heavy weight on his finger, but, because of it, he could ask for one thing he desperately needed.

"May I hold you for a minute?"

He tried to tell himself that her hesitation came from surprise and not wariness, but he didn't believe it. That didn't stop him from closing his arms around her when she walked up to him. That didn't stop the tears from stinging his eyes when her arms cautiously circled his waist and she rested her head on his shoulder.

"You're taller than I remember," he said, brushing his cheek against her hair.

"I should hope so."

Her voice sounded a bit tart, but he could hear the smile in it.

Oh, how his hands wanted to caress and explore, but he was afraid she would pull away from him, so he kept them still. She was alive, and he was with her. That's all that mattered.

He could have stayed that way for the rest of the night, just holding her, feeling the easy rise and fall of her breathing, but after a few minutes she drew away from him.

"Come on, Daemon," she said, holding out her hand. "You need to get some rest, and my orders were to herd you back to your room so that you'd get some sleep before daylight."

His temper sharpened instantly. "Who would dare give *you* orders?" he snarled.

She gave him a look full of exasperated amusement. "Guess."

He almost said "Saetan," and then thought about it. "Lucivar," he said grimly.

"Lucivar," Jaenelle agreed as she took his hand and pulled him toward the stairs. "And trust me, boyo, having Lucivar haul you out of bed because you weren't on the practice field when he told you to be is not an experience you want to have."

"What's he going to do? Pour a bucket of water over me?" Daemon said as they reached the corridor and headed toward their suites.

"No, because soaking the bed would get Helene mad at him. But he wouldn't hesitate to shove you under a cold shower."

"He hasn't—"

She just looked at him.

His opinion was blunt and explicit. "Why do you put up with that?"

"He's bigger than me," she grumbled.

"Someone should remind him that he serves you."

Jaenelle laughed so hard she staggered into him. "He reminds me of that himself whenever it suits him. And when it doesn't, I end up dealing with my big brother. Either way, most of the time it's easier just to go along with him."

They had reached the door to Jaenelle's suite. He reluctantly let go of her hand.

"He hasn't changed at all, has he?" Daemon said, feeling a stab of anxiety as he remembered how volatile Lucivar had always been in a court.

When he looked at Jaenelle, there was an odd light in her eyes. "No," she said in her midnight voice, "he hasn't changed at all. But then, he, too, understands what that statue represents."

CHAPTER
FOUR

1 / Kaeleer

"Tell me again why I had to miss breakfast," Daemon said, breathing heavily as he wiped his sweaty face and neck with a towel.

"Because no one wants to dance around in it if you miss a block and get hit in the belly," Lucivar replied, sipping his coffee while he watched Palanar and Tamnar go through a warmup routine with the sticks. "And we're getting an earlier start this morning because I want the males finished before the women get here for their first lesson."

Daemon took a sip of Lucivar's coffee, then handed the mug back. "You're really going to teach the women how to use the sticks?"

"By the time I'm done with them, they'll be able to handle sticks, bow, and knife."

A sharp command by Hallevar had the youths stepping back and then going through a move again slowly.

"I'll bet the warriors weren't pleased when you told them," Daemon said, watching the moves.

"They bitched about it. Most of the women didn't look happy about it either. I don't expect them to become warriors, but they'll be able to defend themselves long enough for a warrior to reach them."

Daemon eyed Lucivar thoughtfully. "Is that why you taught Marian?"

Lucivar nodded. "She kept resisting because Eyrien females traditionally didn't touch a warrior's weapons. I told her if a male hurt her because she was too stubborn to learn how to defend herself, I'd beat the shit out of her. And she told me if I ever raised a hand to her, she'd gut me. I figured we were making progress."

Daemon laughed. The laughter backed up into his lungs when he saw Jaenelle striding over the lawn, heading toward them. His senses sharpened to a razor's edge, the heat of desire washed through him, and the smell of other males became a declaration of rivalry.

'Rein it in, old son,' Lucivar murmured, glancing over his shoulder and then at Daemon.

Palanar and Tamnar finished their routine, and Hallevar and Kohlvar stepped into the practice circle.

Palanar shifted his mouth into a sneer. "Here comes a chirpy, trying to grow some balls."

Daemon whipped around, his eyes filmed with the red haze of fury.

Hallevar pivoted and smacked Palanar on the buttocks with his stick hard enough to make the boy jump.

"That's my sister, boyo," Lucivar said too quietly.

Palanar looked sick. Someone else muttered a vicious curse.

"Now, I'm going to forget you said that," Lucivar continued just as quietly, "as long as I never hear it again. But if I do, there will come a morning when you step into the practice circle, and I'll be waiting for you."

"Y-yes, sir," Palanar stammered. "I'm sorry, sir."

Hallevar cuffed the boy on the back of the head. "Go get something to eat," he growled. "Maybe with some food in you, you'll use more of your head than just your mouth."

Palanar slunk away, Tamnar trailing behind him.

Hallevar eyed the distance between them and Jaenelle, figured she was close enough to have heard, and swore softly. "I taught him better than that."

Lucivar rolled a shoulder. "He's old enough to want his cock admired. That makes him stupid." He looked at the older Warlord. "He can't afford to be stupid. What the Queens in this court may be willing to overlook from a youngster, the males in the court won't—at least, not a second time."

"I'll blister his ears to make sure he gets the message," Hallevar promised. "Might as well blister Tamnar's while

I'm at it." He went back to the circle and began the warmup routine with Kohlvar.

Daemon turned toward Jaenelle, Palanar already forgotten. When he saw the feral look in her eyes, his smile died before it formed.

Lucivar simply raised his left arm.

With one wild-shy glance at him and a murmured greeting he could barely hear, Jaenelle ducked under Lucivar's arm.

Lucivar lowered his arm, and the hand that settled at her waist tucked her tight against his side. Her right arm rested against his back, her hand curled over his bare shoulder.

They stand that way often, Daemon thought as he fought to rein in his jealousy—and the hurt—because she had barely spared him a glance.

But he suspected that Lucivar was better prepared to deal with the feral look in her eyes than he was. That hurt, too.

"Do you want the introductions now?" Lucivar asked quietly.

Jaenelle shook her head. "I want to warm up first."

"When you're ready, I'll go a round with you."

She glanced at Lucivar's bare chest. "I would have thought you'd already done your workout."

"I've gone through two of them. Haven't worked up a sweat yet."

"Ah."

Lucivar paused. "Your sister's here."

"I know." She flicked a glance at the empty women's practice circle. "I'm surprised you haven't dragged her out here."

"She's got another thirty minutes to arrive on her own before she gets dragged." Lucivar grinned wickedly. "I promise I'll go easy."

"Uh-huh."

That, Daemon thought sourly, he would like to see.

"We also have company," Lucivar said.

Her eyes iced over. "I know," she said in her midnight voice.

Daemon took a step toward her. He didn't know what he could say or do, but he was certain he—or someone— had to shift the mood she was in.

Lucivar . . . he began.

Just keep things soft and easy, Bastard, Lucivar replied. *The workout will take the edge off her.*

Daemon took another step toward her. Her expression changed to something close to panic—and he realized that, last night when she had let him hold her, the Queen had been doing her duty for one of the males in her First Circle, but the *woman* didn't want to get anywhere near him.

As she darted away from Lucivar—and him—she almost ran into Jazen, who was carrying a tray containing a pot of fresh coffee and clean mugs.

"Who are you?" Jaenelle said a little too softly.

Jazen stared into her eyes, frozen. "Jazen," he finally said. "Prince Sadi's valet."

Her eyes changed from ice to curiosity. "Is it interesting work?"

"It would be more interesting if he wore something besides a black suit and a white shirt all the time," Jazen muttered.

Lucivar choked back a laugh. Daemon felt the blood rush into his face and wasn't sure if it was from temper or embarrassment. Jazen looked horrified.

Then Jaenelle's silvery, velvet-coated laugh rang out. "Well, we'll do our best to rumple him up for you." As she walked past Jazen, she brushed her left hand over his shoulder. "Welcome to Kaeleer, Warlord."

Daemon waited until she had reached the women's practice circle before turning to his valet. "Should I apologize for being boring in my taste in clothes? And why in the name of Hell are you out here doing a footman's work?"

"Beale asked me to bring this tray out." Jazen gulped. "I don't know why I said that other."

"You said what you've been thinking," Lucivar said, amused. "Don't worry about it. By the time we're done with him, you'll have to work hard to keep him looking pristine."

Daemon snarled at his brother, then glared at Jazen.

"I'll take that," said Holt, one of the footmen who had carried out the other trays.

Jazen glanced at Daemon, handed the tray to Holt, and made as quick a retreat as possible without actually running.

"Looks like breakfast is being served out here," Lucivar said as he eyed the various dishes that were being set out on the table.

Daemon took a deep breath and watched Jaenelle go through the warmup movements. "I should talk to her, explain about Jazen before she passes judgment."

Lucivar gave him an odd look. "Old son, she just did. She welcomed him to Kaeleer. That's all anyone needs to know."

"This way," Marian said, making a friendly "come on" gesture to Wilhelmina Benedict while she eyed Surreal's loose-sleeved tunic and trousers. "What are you wearing under the tunic?"

Surreal worked to keep her voice warm. Marian didn't seem the type to be interested in a former whore's underwear. "Why?"

"Lucivar will insist that you strip down for the lesson."

"Strip?" Wilhelmina said. "In front of those men?"

"You don't want your movements restricted by your clothing," Marian said kindly. "And you'll want to put on something dry afterward."

"I take it I'm going to be sweating," Surreal said. She glanced at Wilhelmina and wondered if that kind of exercise was a good idea. The young woman looked as pale as water and scared enough to break.

"I don't think he'll work the beginners that hard, but you . . ." Marian's gold eyes flicked to Surreal's pointed ears. "You're Dea al Mon. He may push you harder, just to find out what you can already do."

"Lucky me," Surrel muttered as they headed across the lawn toward the other women who were already gathered at the practice circle.

Marian smiled. "My first weapon was the skillet."

"Sounds dangerous," Surreal said, returning the smile.

"I'd been working for Lucivar as his housekeeper for about four months. My moon's blood had started that morning, and I wasn't feeling well. Looking back, I realize that he must have gone through the other moontimes with his teeth clenched to keep from saying anything. But that morning, he started fussing at me to take it easy, and I took it as a criticism that I couldn't do my job. I threw a pot at him. Well, not really *at* him. I didn't want to *hit* him, I just felt mad enough that I needed to throw something. It hit the wall about two feet away from where he was standing.

"He looked at the pot for a minute, then picked it up and went outside. I could hear him throwing it, and thought he was doing that instead of using his fists on me the way some Eyrien males would have.

"He came back inside, muttering, took one of the skillets, and went back out. A few minutes later, he dragged me outside. He said a pot didn't have the right balance, but a skillet would work if it was thrown properly. I spent two months practicing slinging a skillet before he declared me proficient enough to suit him." Marian grinned at the memory.

"What does he consider proficient?" Surreal asked.

Marian didn't look amused now. "Being able to break bone nine out of ten times."

Surreal just gaped at her for a moment, and then started thinking hard. She was a damn good assassin. Just how much, under Lucivar's training, could those skills be honed?

When they reached the practice circle, Wilhelmina hung back. Surreal pushed her way to the front. When an Eyrien warrior snarled at her for elbowing him in the ribs, she snarled back, pleased that he was the one to give ground.

She looked around, saw Daemon, and felt her breathing hitch. He looked calm enough, standing there with a mug of coffee in one hand, but his face had that set look that she'd seen when they were in the Coach on the way here. It wasn't as bad as it had been then, but it wasn't good.

Then Lucivar started talking, and she put her concern for Daemon aside for the time being.

"There are reasons why Eyrien males are the warriors," Lucivar said, his eyes skimming over the women as he paced slowly down the line and back again. "We're bigger, stronger, and we have the temperament for killing. You have other strengths and other skills. Most of the time, that works out well. But that's no reason for you to be unable to defend yourselves. And before you give me any shit about not being able to handle a weapon, I'll remind you that most of you don't have any trouble using kitchen knives, and some of them are as big as a hunting knife. They just look different. And some of you will want to wiggle out of this training by telling me that, no matter how much she knows, a woman can't hold her own against a male. Right?" Looking at the other practice circle, he roared, "CAT! Get over here!"

Wondering why he'd want a feline, Surreal looked toward the circle. Her breath came out in a hiss as the woman talking to Karla, Morghann, and Gabrielle turned around. "Jaenelle," she whispered.

She focused on Daemon again. He didn't look shocked to see Jaenelle. Maybe they'd already had a chance to talk. Maybe . . . No, it was probably way too early to think about *those* maybes.

The other women strode toward the practice circle. Jaenelle came more slowly, her eyes fixed on Lucivar while she whipped the stick around her waist with enough force to sting the air.

Lucivar sidestepped to the middle of the circle, always watching her. "Come play with me, Cat," he said, giving her an arrogant smile.

She snarled at him and began to circle.

"Hallevar," Lucivar said as he circled with her. "Call the time."

Surreal felt Falonar tense beside her.

"What's time?" she asked, nudging him when he didn't answer.

"Ten minutes," Falonar replied grimly. "He'll beat her into the ground long before that."

Surreal slashed a look at Daemon and started to sweat. If that happened, what would Sadi do? Easy answer. The hard question was, what could any of them do to stop him from tearing Lucivar apart?

The first clash of the sticks had her heart jumping into her throat. After that she wasn't aware of anything except Jaenelle and Lucivar moving gracefully through a savage dance.

Seconds passed into minutes.

"Mother Night," Falonar whispered. "She's making him work for it."

Lucivar's chest glistened with sweat. Surreal could hear

his deep, harsh breathing. Her own sweat chilled her skin when she saw the wild look in Jaenelle's eyes.

She didn't know how much time had passed when, after half a dozen lightning-fast moves, Jaenelle lost her balance for a split second. Lucivar danced back just long enough to let her get her feet solidly under her before attacking again.

"He could have put her on the ground right then and ended it," Falonar said softly.

"He wants to work her, not get her mad enough to really go after him," Chaosti replied just as softly, stepping up behind Surreal.

Finally, Hallevar yelled, "TIME!"

Lucivar and Jaenelle circled, thrust, clashed.

"DAMN YOU BOTH, I SAID TIME!"

They broke apart, backed away.

Hallevar strode into the circle and took the stick away from Lucivar. He looked at Jaenelle, hesitated, then backed off when Lucivar shook his head.

"Come on, Cat," Lucivar gasped as he moved toward her. "We've got to walk to cool down."

Her head snapped up. She braced her feet in a fighting stance.

Lucivar held up his hands and kept moving forward.

The wild look in her eyes faded. "Water."

"Walk first," he said, taking the stick away from her.

"Prick," she snarled halfheartedly, but she walked with him.

"If you don't give me a hard time about it, you can even have breakfast." Lucivar handed the stick to Falonar as he and Jaenelle walked past. He took a couple of towels from Aaron, draped one over Jaenelle's neck, and began to rub himself down with the other.

Looking around, Surreal noticed that Khardeen was also in the crowd, watching and alert. And she noticed, with a sigh of relief, that Saetan was talking quietly with Daemon.

Turning back to Falonar, she brushed her fingers against the stick. "Do you think I'll ever get half that good with one of these?" She half expected some dismissive comment, but when he didn't answer, she looked up to see him studying her seriously.

"If you can become half as proficient with this as she is, you'll be able to take down any male except an Eyrien warrior," Falonar said slowly. "And you'll be able to take down half of them as well." Then he looked at Marian. "Are you all right, Lady?"

Marian let out a shuddering breath. "I'm fine, thank you, Prince Falonar. It's just . . . sometimes when they're so intense . . ."

Falonar bowed just enough to show respect, then left them to talk with Hallevar.

"Are you really all right?" Surreal asked, drawing Marian a little ways away from the crowd.

Marian's smile was a trifle strained. "Lucivar's always tense after he's been at the service fair, and he's been worried about Daemon."

Looking back, Surreal saw Daemon walking toward the Hall with the High Lord. Well, that was one worry out of the way for the moment.

She also noticed the way Jaenelle kept glancing at Daemon while Lucivar piled food on a plate. She smiled.

"Usually I can help him relieve the tension," Marian continued.

Her self-conscious expression told Surreal exactly how Marian helped relieve the tension. The woman had guts to get into a bed with a man like Lucivar when his temper was already on the edge.

"Since that wasn't an option this time . . ."

No, Surreal thought as Marian gave her a speculative look. If Lucivar had never suggested an alternative to intercourse, *she* certainly wasn't going to supply the information.

After a moment, Marian shrugged. "Usually when Jaenelle is his sparring partner, they just keep working through the moves until he's sweated out the tension. But this morning . . . Jaenelle's relatives showing up like this has put her on edge, too."

"Yeah, seeing her family again isn't a reason to cheer."

Marian stiffened. "Her *family* lives here."

"Yes," Surreal said after a minute, "I guess they do."

2 / Kaeleer

Wilhelmina walked silently beside Lucivar as he escorted her to her room. She wished he would put his arm around her. Maybe then she would stop shivering. Maybe then she wouldn't feel so afraid.

That was funny. A few hours ago, she'd been terrified of him, especially after she'd seen him and Jaenelle attacking each other with the sticks.

Afterward, she'd tried to slip back to the Hall before anyone noticed because she'd been sure her heart would just burst if any of those Eyrien warriors snarled at her when she couldn't do the exercises properly. But Lucivar had noticed her slinking away. He'd grabbed the back of her tunic and hauled her into the practice circle.

And he'd been kind. While other Eyriens instructed the other women, and Marian and some of the coven had demonstrated the moves, he had worked with her and the girl, Jillian. Never in a hurry, never impatient, his hands firm but gentle when he repositioned her body, his voice always calm and encouraging.

She hadn't expected that from him. And she hadn't expected him to stay with her when she went to meet Alexandra, Leland, and Philip.

She should have said "no" when the High Lord told her they were here and wanted to talk to her. But she'd felt an obligation to see them, since they'd come all this way.

They'd been angry when Lucivar refused to let the Province Queens and the escorts into the room and refused to leave himself. Oh, he'd gone out onto the balcony, but no one was going to forget his presence.

She could tell they had been as insulted as she had been relieved, but they *had* been glad to see her. They'd all hugged her and complimented her on how pretty she'd become and how worried they had been about her and how much they'd missed her . . .

And then Alexandra told her not to worry. They would find a way to break the contract and get her out of this place and away from these people. She'd tried to explain that she intended to honor the contract, that the High Lord and Prince Yaslana weren't the monsters Alexandra was trying to make them out to be.

They didn't listen, just as they hadn't listened years ago when her father, Robert Benedict, had tried to force himself on her after Jaenelle disappeared—a few months after he had come down with the illness that had finally killed him. She had run away because she'd been afraid that, one day, no one would hear her screams or, if they did, would ignore them because she was turning into a "difficult" child, just like Jaenelle.

They didn't listen. Because they were so sure they were right, so sure that they knew what was best. Even Philip. He kept telling her that it would be all right now, that Robert was dead so it would be all right. But it wouldn't be, *couldn't be,* all right because they thought of her as being "damaged" somehow—she could see that in their eyes—and anything she thought or felt or wanted would be colored by that conviction. And because she cared for Philip and knew he would be hurt by it, she couldn't tell them why she *really* wanted to stay there.

Her fear that they might actually be able to take her away after she'd struggled so hard to get to Kaeleer had escalated to the point where she had leaped up from the couch, and yelled, "No! I don't want to!"

Lucivar was in the room and hurrying her away from them before anyone else could move.

But she couldn't stop shaking, and the fear was eating her alive.

Lucivar's hand came down on her shoulder, stopping her. A moment later, he called in a flask. He vanished the cap, gripped the back of her head with one hand, and held the flask up to her lips.

"If you keep shaking like that, you're going to rip something," he said, sounding annoyed. "Take a sip of this. It'll settle your nerves."

"I don't want a sedative," Wilhelmina said, trying to pull away as desperation swelled inside her. "There's nothing wrong with me."

"Nothing except you've gone way past scared, and that's not good for you." Lucivar paused, studying her. "It's not a sedative, Wilhelmina," he said quietly. "It's Khary's home brew. It's got a kick to it that will mellow you out—and it'll also keep you from breaking apart. Now, hold your nose and swallow."

She didn't hold her nose. She *did* swallow the sip he gave her.

Golden.

It flowed over her tongue like ripe plums and summer

heat, pooled in her stomach for a moment, and then flowed into her limbs.

When he offered her another swallow, she took it. That glorious heat melted her fear and produced a sensuous warmth inside her. If she had another sip, she might even feel brave—fiercely, wonderfully brave.

But Lucivar wasn't offering another sip. She wasn't aware that he'd released her, but he had the cap in one hand now and the flask in the other, and he was going to take away that delicious heat.

She snatched the flask and ran down the corridor, whipped around a corner, and guzzled as much as she could before he caught up to her and took it away.

She leaned against the wall and smiled at him. She felt enormously pleased when he took a couple of steps back and watched her warily.

Lucivar sniffed the flask, took a small sip, and said, "Shit."

"That would be a rude thing to do in the corridor."

He swore softly while he capped the flask and vanished it, but it sounded more like laughter. "Come on, little witch. Let's get you settled somewhere while you can still walk."

She walked toward him to prove that she could, but the floor suddenly got lumpy, and she tripped and fell against him.

"I am very brave," she told him, leaning against his chest.

"You are very drunk."

"Mmmm not." Then she remembered the important thing she had to do. The most important thing. "I want to see my sister." She smacked her hand as hard as she could against the surface she was leaning on to emphasize her point. She looked at her stinging hand. "It hurts."

"We'll have matching bruises," Lucivar said dryly.

"Okay."

Muttering, he steered her through the corridors.

She felt so wonderful, she wanted to sing, but all the songs she knew seemed so . . . polite. "Do you know any naughty songs?"

"Mother Night," he muttered.

"Don't know that one. How does it go?"

"This way," he said, steering her around a corner.

She got away from him and ran down the corridor, flapping her arms. "I can flyyyyy."

When he caught her again, he wrapped one arm around her waist, knocked once on the door in front of them, and hauled her inside.

"Cat!"

Tears filled Wilhelmina's eyes when Jaenelle walked out of the adjoining room. The warm smile of greeting was all she needed to see.

Slipping out of Lucivar's grip, she stumbled a couple of steps and hugged Jaenelle.

"I've missed you," Wilhelmina said, laughing while tears ran down her face. "I've missed you so much. I'm sorry I wasn't braver. You were my little sister, and I should have looked after you. But you were the one who always looked after me." She leaned back, holding Jaenelle's shoulders for balance. "You're so pretty."

"And you're drunk." Those sapphire eyes stared at Lucivar. "What did you do to her?"

"Her nerves were so strained after meeting your relatives, I was afraid she'd break. So I asked Khary for the strongest brew he had in a flask because I figured she wouldn't take more than a sip." Lucivar winced. "She guzzled half the flask—and it wasn't one of his home brews, it was the concoction you created."

Jaenelle's eyes widened. "You let her drink a 'gravedigger'?"

"No no no," Wilhelmina said, shaking her head. "You shouldn't ever drink a gravedigger until he's had a bath." She smiled placidly when Jaenelle and Lucivar just stared at her.

"Mother Night," Lucivar muttered.

"Do you know that song?" Wilhelmina asked Jaenelle.

"What did you have for breakfast?" Jaenelle demanded.

"Water. I was too nervous to eat. But I'm not nervous anymore. I am very brave and fierce."

Lucivar wrapped one hand around her arm. "Why don't you sit on the couch now?"

She headed straight across the room—more or less. When he started to lead her around the table, she dug in her heels.

"I can go through the table," she announced proudly. "I

studied my Craft. I want to show Jaenelle that I can do that now."

"You want to do something really challenging?" Lucivar asked. "Then let's walk *around* the table. Right now, that will be impressive."

"Okay."

Getting around the table *was* sufficiently challenging, especially since Lucivar kept getting his feet in the way. When she finally reached the couch, she plopped down next to Jaenelle. "I brushed Dejaal, and now he likes me. If I brushed Lucivar, do you think he'd like me, too?"

"He'd promise to like you if you stopped stepping on him," Lucivar growled softly while he pulled off her shoes.

"It's Marian's job to brush Lucivar," Jaenelle said solemnly.

"Okay."

"Why don't I have some coffee and toast sent up?" Lucivar said.

Wilhelmina watched Lucivar until he left the room. "I used to think he was scary. But he's just big."

"Uh-huh. Why don't you lie down for a little while?" Jaenelle said.

Wilhelmina obeyed. When Jaenelle finished tucking a blanket around her, she said, "Everyone said you had died, but when they talked to me, they said we had 'lost' you. But I always knew you weren't lost because you told me where to find you. How could you be lost when you knew where you were?"

She looked into Jaenelle's sapphire eyes. The mind behind those eyes was so vast. But she wasn't afraid of that anymore. "You always knew where you were. Didn't you?"

"Yes," Jaenelle replied softly. "I always knew."

3 / Kaeleer

Alexandra paused, took a deep breath, and opened the door without knocking.

The golden-haired woman grinding herbs with a mortar and pestle didn't turn around, didn't indicate in any way that she knew someone was there. A large bowl floated above the worktable, heated by three tongues of witchfire. A spoon lazily stirred the bowl's contents.

Alexandra waited. After a minute, she said in a tight voice, "Could you stop fiddling with that for a minute and say 'hello' to your grandmother? After all, it's been thirteen years since I've seen you."

"A minute or so won't make any difference to a greeting that's waited for thirteen years," Jaenelle replied, pouring the finely ground herbs into the bowl's bubbling contents. "But it *will* make a difference to this tonic developing the right potency." She half turned, gave Alexandra one slashing glance, then focused her attention on the brew.

Alexandra clenched her teeth, remembering why she had found this granddaughter so different to deal with. Even as a small child, Jaenelle had displayed these gestures of superiority, implying that *she* had no reason to show respect for her elders or yield to a Queen.

Why? For the first time, Alexandra wondered. She'd always assumed, along with everyone else, that those displays were attempts to compensate for not wearing the Jewels, for being less than the other witches in the family. But, perhaps, they had been a result of someone—like the High Lord—whispering sweet lies into a child's ear until the girl truly believed she was superior.

She shook her head. It was hard to believe that the child who had been unable to do the simplest Craft lessons could grow up to become some terrible, powerful threat to the Realm of Terreille as Dorothea claimed. If that were *true,* where was the power? Even now, when she was trying to sense Jaenelle's strength, it felt . . . muted . . . just as it always had. Distant, which was the way a Blood female who didn't have enough psychic strength to wear a Jewel felt.

That meant Jaenelle *was* just a pawn in an elaborate game. The High Lord—or, perhaps, the mysterious Queen who ruled this court—wanted a figurehead to hide behind.

"What are you making?" Alexandra asked.

"A tonic for a young boy who's ill," Jaenelle replied, adding a dark liquid to the brew.

"Shouldn't a Healer be doing that?" *Hell's fire, are they really letting her make tonics for people?*

"I *am* a Healer," Jaenelle replied tartly. "I'm also a Black Widow and a Queen."

Of course you are. With effort, Alexandra bit back the words. She would remain calm; would forge a bond, somehow, with her younger granddaughter; would remember that Jaenelle had already endured some terrible experiences.

Then Jaenelle finished making the tonic and turned around.

Staring into those sapphire eyes, Alexandra forgot about remaining calm or forging a bond. Staggered by the . . . *something* . . . that looked at her out of those eyes, she groped for an explanation that would fit.

When she found it, she wanted to weep.

Jaenelle was insane. Totally, completely insane. And that monster who ruled here indulged that insanity for his own reasons. He let Jaenelle think she was Healer and a Black Widow and a Queen. He would probably let her give that tonic to a sick little boy, regardless of what the stuff would actually do to a child.

"Why are you here, Alexandra?"

Alexandra shivered at the sound of that midnight voice, then gave herself a mental shake. The child had always indulged in theatrics. "I came to take you and Wilhelmina home."

"Why? For the past thirteen years, you thought I was dead. Since that was far more convenient for you than having me alive, why didn't you just continue to pretend I was dead?"

"We weren't pretending," Alexandra said hotly. Jaenelle's words hurt, mostly because they were true. It *had* been easier mourning a dead child than dealing with the difficult girl. But she would never admit *that.* "We thought you *were* dead, that Sadi had killed you."

"Daemon would never have hurt me."

But you would—and did. That was the message underneath the cold, flat reply.

"Leland is your mother. I'm your grandmother. We're your *family,* Jaenelle."

Jaenelle shook her head slowly. "This body can trace its bloodline to you. That makes us related. It doesn't make us family." She moved toward the door. When she was just about to pass Alexandra, she stopped. "You apprenticed with an Hourglass coven for a little while, didn't you? Before you had to make the choice between becoming a Black Widow and becoming Chaillot's Queen."

Alexandra nodded, wondering where this was leading.

"You learned enough to make the simplest tangled webs, the kind that would absorb a focused intent and draw that object to you. Isn't that true?" When she nodded again, Jaenelle's eyes filled with sadness and understanding. "How many times did you sit before one of those webs dreaming that something would help you keep Chaillot safe from Hayll's encroachment?"

Alexandra couldn't speak, could barely breathe.

"Has it ever occurred to you that that may be the answer to the riddle? Saetan was also an intense dreamer. The difference is that when the dream appeared, he recognized it." Jaenelle opened the door. "Go home, Alexandra. There's nothing—and no one—for you here."

"Wilhelmina," Alexandra whispered.

"She'll fulfill the eighteen months of her contract. After that, she can do as she pleases." There was something awful and ironic about Jaenelle's smile. "The Queen commands it."

Alexandra took a deep breath. "I want to see this Queen."

"No, you don't," Jaenelle replied too softly. "You don't want to stand before the Dark Throne." She paused. "Now, if you'll excuse me, I have to finish this tonic. It's simmered long enough."

Dismissed. As casually as that, she was being dismissed.

Alexandra left the workroom, relieved to be away from Jaenelle. She found one of the inner gardens and settled on a bench. Maybe the sun would take away the chill that had seeped into her bones. Maybe then she could believe she was shaking from cold and not because Jaenelle had mentioned something she had never told anyone.

Her paternal grandmother had been a natural Black Widow. That's what had drawn Alexandra to the Hourglass in the first place. But by then, the aristo Blood in Chaillot were already starting to whisper about Black Widows being "unnatural" women, and the other Queens and the Warlord Princes would *never* have chosen a Queen who was also a witch of the Hourglass covens.

So she left her apprenticeship and, a few years later when her maternal grandmother stepped down, became the Queen of Chaillot. But during her first few years as Queen, she *had* secretly woven those simple tangled webs. She *had* dreamed that something or someone would appear in her life that would help her fight against Hayll's undermining of Chaillot society. At the time, she had thought it would be a Consort—a strong male who would support and help her. But no man like that had ever appeared in her life.

Then, when her Black Widow grandmother had been dying, Alexandra had been given what she came to think of as the riddle. *What you dream for will come, but if you're not careful, you'll be blind until it's too late.*

So she had waited. She had watched. The dream hadn't come. And she would not, *could not*, believe that a disturbed, eccentric child had been the answer to the riddle.

4 / Kaeleer

As he stared out the window, he reached inside his shirt and fingered the slim glass vial that hung from a chain around his neck. The High Priestess of Hayll had assured him that she and the Dark Priestess had woven the strongest spells they knew to keep him undetected. So far, they had worked No one sensed he was anything more than another escort Alexandra Angelline had brought with her. He was just a bland man, almost invisible. That suited him perfectly.

It had sounded so easy when he'd been given the assignment. Find the target, drug her so that she would be complacent, and then slip her out of the Hall to the men who would be waiting just beyond the boundaries of the estate. When he'd seen the size of the place, he'd thought it would be even easier.

But, despite its size, the Hall was crawling with aggressive males, from the lowest male servant right up to the High Lord. And the bitches *never* seemed to be alone. He'd lingered in corridors for hours without so much as a sniff of either one of them.

He shuddered as he remembered his one glimpse of the golden-haired bitch. He'd been told, repeatedly, that she was his primary target, but he had no intention of getting anywhere near *her* because something about her spooked him, and he wasn't sure the spells would hold up under that sapphire stare. So he would snatch the other one, the sister. But he would have to do it soon. He could only dodge just so long around so many bristling, suspicious males.

Maybe he would escort Wilhelmina Benedict all the way back to Hayll. Once he got her out, what difference did it make if he was found to be missing?

And it would make no difference to him if Alexandra was left behind to explain her granddaughter's disappearance—or was the one who ended up paying whatever price the High Lord chose to extract.

5 / Terreille

The rage twisted inside Dorothea like a choking vine. The brief report dangled from one hand.

"You're distressed, Sister," Hekatah said as she shuffled into the room and took a seat.

"Kartane was gone to Kaeleer." She couldn't draw a deep enough breath to give her voice any strength.

"Gone to see if any of their Healers can cure him?" Hekatah thought about that for a moment. "But why now? He could have gone anytime in the last few years."

"Perhaps because he thinks he has something to barter now that would be worth more than gold marks."

Hekatah hissed, immediately understanding. "How much does he know?"

"He was at my 'confession' the other day, but that's not much to tell someone."

"It's enough to put Saetan on his guard," Hekatah said ominously. "It's enough to make him start asking questions."

"Then perhaps something should be arranged before Kartane has a chance to talk to anyone outside of Little Terreille," Dorothea said softly, almost absently. She could think of a number of interesting "arrangements" that could be made for a son who wanted to woo her enemy.

Hekatah stood up and paced around the room for a minute. "No. Let's see if we can use Kartane as bait to lure a specific Healer to Little Terreille."

Dorothea snorted. "Do you really think Jaenelle Angelline is going to help *Kartane*?"

"I'll go to Little Terreille tonight and speak to Lord Jorval. He'll know how to phrase a discreet request." When Hekatah reached the door, she paused. "When your little Warlord comes home, perhaps you should give him a lesson in loyalty."

Dorothea waited until Hekatah left before going over to the fire. She dropped the report into it, watched the flames devour the paper.

When the war they were going to start was over, she would build a bonfire and watch the flames devour that desiccated walking corpse. And while she watched Hekatah burn, she would give her son that lesson in loyalty.

6 / Kaeleer

"I need a favor," Karla said abruptly after ten minutes of small talk and discussion about the Eyriens whom Lucivar had brought in.

Jaenelle glanced up from the piece of needlepoint she was working on, her eyes filled with wary amusement. "All right."

"I want a Ring of Honor like you gave the boyos in the First Circle."

"Darling, they wear the Ring of Honor on their cocks. You may be ballsy, but you don't have one of *those*."

"The kindred males don't wear them there. You had small Rings made that attach to the chain holding their Jewels."

"So you want a Ring of Honor," Jaenelle said, still sounding amused, still adding stitches to the needlepoint design.

Karla nodded solemnly. "For everyone in the coven."

Jaenelle looked up, no longer amused.

Karla met that look, recognizing by the subtle change in

the sapphire eyes that she was no longer talking to Jaenelle, her friend and Sister. She was talking to Witch, the Queen of Ebon Askavi. *Her* Queen.

"You have a reason," Jaenelle said in her midnight voice. It wasn't a question.

"Yes." How much would she need to say to convince Jaenelle? And how much of what she'd seen in the tangled web could be left unsaid?

A few minutes passed in silence.

Jaenelle resumed her stitching. "If it's going to be worn on a finger, it should look decorative enough so that it's real purpose isn't obvious," she said quietly. "I assume you're mostly interested in the Ring because of the protection spells I added to it."

"Yes," Karla said quietly. The protection spells, the Ebony shields Jaenelle added to the Rings, were the reason she wanted one.

"Do you want the Rings linked just between the coven or linked to the boyos as well?"

Karla hesitated. A typical Ring of Honor allowed a Queen to monitor the emotions of the males in her First Circle. Because of a quirk in the way Jaenelle had made the first Ring of Honor—the one Lucivar *still* wore—the First Circle males in the Dark Court had the same means of gauging the Queen's mood. Did she, or any of the coven, really want to deal with males who were even more attuned to feminine moods than the boyos already were? Was a little emotional distance worth not having a means of sending a warning that couldn't, in any way, be blocked? "They should be linked with the First Circle males."

"I'll get the Rings made as soon as possible," Jaenelle said quietly.

"Thank you, Lady," Karla replied, acknowledging the Queen rather than the friend.

Another silence filled the room.

"Anything else?" Jaenelle finally asked.

Karla took a deep breath, let it out slowly. "I don't like your relatives."

"*Nobody* here likes my relatives," Jaenelle replied, but there was a sharp edge underneath the amusement—and sorrow. Then she added very quietly, "Saetan formally requested my consent for their executions."

"Did you give it?" Karla asked neutrally. She already knew the answer. She had been in the same position five years ago when she became Queen of Glacia. She had exiled her uncle, Lord Hobart, instead of executing him, even though she strongly suspected he had been behind the death of her parents and Morton's.

Jaenelle, if pushed, would choose the same.

"If it's any consolation, I do like your sister," Karla said when Jaenelle didn't answer the question. "She'll adjust to living in Kaeleer just fine if she can stop being scared long enough to catch her breath."

Jaenelle looked a little pained. "Lucivar got her drunk. She offered to brush him."

"Oh, Mother Night." When the laughter finally fizzled out, Karla groaned her way off the couch, said good night to Jaenelle, and headed for her own suite.

In the privacy of her bedroom, she indulged in a few grunts and moans as she got ready for bed. No matter how much she exercised when she was home, it always took her a few days to adjust to the workouts Lucivar put her through. But she wasn't about to miss a chance to get a little extra training from him. Especially now.

Later, as she was drifting off to sleep, it occurred to her that Jaenelle, who was a strong and very gifted Black Widow, might have had her own reasons for agreeing to the favor.

7 / Kaeleer

With exaggerated care, Daemon tied the robe's belt. The hot bath had warmed and loosened his tight, tired muscles. A large quantity of brandy would blur the mental sharp edges. Neither of those things would ease a bruised, bleeding heart.

Jaenelle didn't want him. That was becoming painfully clear.

When she had come looking for him last night, he had thought she had been pleased to see him, had hoped that they could begin again. But today she had shied away from him whenever he tried to approach her, using Lucivar or Chaosti or the whole coven as a buffer. It had forced him to realize that she had given him the title of Consort out of some sense of obligation, but she didn't want *him*.

How long, he wondered as he walked into his bedroom, could he stand watching her interact with the other males in her court while he was being shut out of her life? How long could his sanity hold together when, day after day, he was close enough to touch her but wasn't allowed to? How long . . .

Seeing the mound in the dim light, he thought someone had come in and dumped a white fur cover over his bed without smoothing it out.

Then a head lifted off his pillows and muscles rippled under the white fur as the huge cat shifted position.

The front paws, dangling over the side of the bed, flexed, displaying impressive claws. Gray eyes stared at him as if daring him to do more than breathe.

Even if he hadn't seen the Red Jewel lying against the white fur, Daemon would have had no doubts about who was sprawled on his bed.

We all try not to upset Kaelas, Lucivar had said.

Hell's fire, Mother Night, and may the Darkness be merciful.

With his heart pounding in his throat, Daemon cautiously backed toward the door. Saetan's suite was right across from his. He could . . .

Something large thumped against the other side of the door just as his hand touched the knob.

Kaelas curled his lips in a silent snarl.

There was only one escape open to him.

Never taking his eyes off Kaelas, Daemon sidled over to the door that separated his bedroom from Jaenelle's. He opened the door only as much as necessary, slipped into her bedroom, Black-locked the door, and added a Black shield. If what Lucivar had said about Kaelas being able to get through any shield was true, the lock and shield were useless, but they made him feel a little better.

As he backed farther into Jaenelle's room, he began to shake. It wasn't because of Kaelas, exactly. Any man with a healthy survival instinct would be cautiously afraid of a cat that size—especially when that cat was also a Red-Jeweled Warlord Prince. But he knew that, before he had shattered his mind the first time that night at Cassandra's Altar, he wouldn't have felt this kind of overwhelming fear. He would have had enough confidence in himself to match that feline arrogance even while being prudent enough to yield. Now . . .

"Daemon?"

He twisted around, suddenly finding it impossible to breathe.

Jaenelle stood in the doorway that led to the rest of her suite, dressed in sapphire-blue pajamas.

Seeing her, he lost his balance in too many ways.

She ran to him, wrapped her arms around his waist to keep him from falling. "What's wrong? Are you ill?"

"I—" He was sweating from the effort to take a deep enough breath.

"Can you walk far enough to sit on the bed?"

Unable to speak, he nodded.

"Sit down," Jaenelle said. "Put your head between your knees."

When he obeyed, his robe parted. He leaned over farther, hoping, since she was crouched in front of him, that he wasn't revealing anything she didn't want to see.

"Can you tell me what's wrong?" Jaenelle asked as her fingers brushed through his hair.

You don't love me. "On my bed," he gasped.

Jaenelle swiveled to look at the door adjoining their rooms. Her eyes narrowed. "What's Kaelas doing in your room?"

"Sleeping. On my bed."

"It's your room. Why didn't you tell him to get off?"

Why? Because he didn't want to die tonight.

But she sounded so baffled, he raised his head to look at her. She was serious. She wouldn't think twice about hauling eight hundred pounds of snarling feline off a bed.

Jaenelle stood up. "I'll get him—"

Daemon grabbed her hand. "No. It's all right. I'll find another bed. A couch. Hell's fire, I'll sleep on the floor."

Those ancient eyes studied him. Something odd flickered at the back of them for a moment. "Do you want to sleep here tonight?" she asked quietly.

Yes. No. He didn't want to come to her as a frightened, needy male. But he also wouldn't refuse the only invitation to her bed he might ever receive. "Please."

She pulled the covers back as far as she could with him still sitting on the bed. "Get in."

"I—" His face heated.

"I gather you wear the same thing to bed as every other male here," Jaenelle said dryly.

Which meant "nothing."

She moved to the other side of the room, her back politely turned.

Daemon quickly slipped out of the robe and slipped into the massive bed. No wonder she had offered to let him stay there. The bed was so big she would never notice another occupant.

A minute later, she got into bed, keeping well to her side of it. As she turned off the candle-light, she murmured, "Good night, Daemon."

He lay in the dark a long time listening to her breathe, certain that, like him, she wasn't asleep.

Eventually, the warm bed, the murmur of the fountain in the garden below, and the scent of whatever soap or perfume she used lulled him into a deep sleep.

The quiet, almost furtive sounds roused him.

Daemon opened his eyes.

Darkness. Swirling mist.

Propping himself up on one elbow, he looked around and saw her standing next to the altar. The golden mane that wasn't quite hair and wasn't quite fur. The delicately pointed ears. The thin stripe of fur that ran down her spine to the fawn tail that flicked over her buttocks. The human legs that ended in hooves. The hands that had sheathed claws.

Witch. The living myth. Dreams made flesh.

He was back in the misty place, deep in the abyss. The place where . . .

He rose slowly. Moving carefully so that he wouldn't startle her, he walked around the altar until he was standing across from her.

On the altar was a crystal chalice laced with hairline cracks. As he silently watched, she picked up a sliver of crystal and slipped it into place.

Something shifted inside him. Looking more intently at the chalice, he realized it was his own shattered mind.

He noticed three other tiny fragments. As he reached for one, she slapped his hand.

"Do you have any idea how much searching I had to do to find these?" she snarled at him.

She turned the chalice, slipped another tiny sliver into place.

The mist swirled, danced, spun.

Falling, falling, falling into the abyss. His mind shattering. Waking up in the misty place. Seeing Jaenelle as Witch for the first time as she pieced his crystal chalice back together.

Another sliver slipped into place.

A narrow bed with straps to bind hands and feet—the bed from Briarwood. A sumptuous bed with silk sheets. A seductive trap made of love and lies and truth—a trap to save a child. The Sadist whispering that she would take the bait because he, in all his male sexual glory, was the bait.

The last sliver was slipped into place.

Re-forming the psychic link with Saetan after he had persuaded Jaenelle to ascend to the level of the Red Jewels. The two of them forcing her to heal her own torn, bleeding body. Jaenelle's panic when the males from Briarwood started fighting the defenses Surreal had created in the corridors leading to the Altar. Cassandra opening the Gate between the Realms and taking Jaenelle away.

His crystal chalice glowed, heated as Witch's dark power covered all the cracks and sealed them.

Now that the gaps were filled in, the memories reformed, and, finally, he knew *exactly* what had happened at Cassandra's Altar thirteen years ago. Finally, he knew *exactly* what he had done—and not done.

He took a deep breath, let it out slowly.

She glanced at him, nerves warring with the sharp, feral intelligence that filled her ancient eyes. "The missing pieces made weak spots that kept the chalice fragile. You should be fine now."

"Thank you."

"I don't want your gratitude," she snapped.

Studying her, Daemon opened his inner barriers just enough to taste her emotions. The hurt inside her surprised him.

"What *do* you want?" he asked quietly.

She nervously caressed the stem of the chalice. He wondered if she realized he could feel those caresses. And he wondered if she had any idea what those caresses were doing to him. He started to move around the altar, his fingers lightly brushing the stone.

"Nothing," she said in a small voice as she shifted a half step away from him. Then she added, "You lied to me. You didn't want Witch."

The fire of anger washed through him, waking the part of him the Blood in Terreille had called the Sadist. When the anger cooled, another kind of fire took its place.

His voice shifted into a sexual purr. "I love you. And I've waited a lifetime to be your lover. But you were too young, Lady."

She raised her head, her body stiff with dignity. "I wasn't too young here, in the abyss."

Slowly, he continued moving around the altar. "Your body had been violated. Your mind had shattered. But even if that hadn't been the case, you were still too young—even here in the abyss."

He came up behind her. His fingers lightly brushed her hips, her waist. Moving upward, he spread his hands across her ribs, his fingers just brushing the undersides of her breasts. He moved closer, smiling with savage pleasure as the fawn tail's nervous flicking teased and aroused him.

He kissed the spot where her neck and shoulder joined. The first kiss was light and chaste. With the second kiss, he used his teeth to hold her still while the tip of his tongue caressed and tasted her skin.

He could feel her heart pounding, feel each breathy pant.

Leaving a trail of soft kisses up her neck, he finally whispered in her ear, "You're not too young anymore."

She let out a breathless squeak when he gently rubbed himself against her.

Suddenly his hands were empty, and he was alone.

Hungry desire roared through him. He turned in a slow circle, searching, probing—the predator seeking his prey.

The last thing he was fully aware of was the mist thickening and swirling up around him until there was nothing else.

He struggled to get past the thick fog of sleep when something grabbed his arm and dragged him out of bed.

Groggy, he tried to wake up enough to wonder why he was being pushed and prodded across the room.

He didn't have any trouble waking up after Lucivar shoved him into the shower cubicle and turned on the cold water full blast.

Daemon clawed at the dial until he managed to shut off the water. Bracing one hand against the wall, he tried to convince his cold-tightened muscles to let go of his lungs long enough for him to take a breath. Then he glared at Lucivar.

"Jaenelle woke up in a similar mood," Lucivar said mildly. "Must have been an interesting night."

"Nothing happened," Daemon growled as he swiped his hair back.

"Nothing physical," Lucivar said. "But I've danced with the Sadist enough times to recognize him when I see him."

Daemon just waited.

Lucivar's lips curled into that lazy, arrogant smile. "Welcome to Kaeleer, brother," he said softly. "It's good to have you back." He paused at the bathroom door. "I'll bring you a cup of coffee. That and a hot shower ought to wake you up enough."

"Enough for what?" Daemon asked warily.

Lucivar's smile turned wicked. "You're late for practice, old son. But, all things considered, I'll give you another fifteen minutes to get to the field before I come looking for you again."

"And if you have to come looking again?" Daemon asked too softly.

"Trust me. If I have to come looking for you again, you're not going to like it."

He already didn't like it. But he sipped the coffee Lucivar brought him while the hot water pounded his neck and back—and the Sadist began planning the quiet, gentle seduction of Jaenelle Angelline.

CHAPTER
FIVE

1 / Kaeleer

Alexandra walked through the corridors, Philip beside her. She would have preferred Leland's company rather than an unavailable male, but the way Philip had quickly offered to accompany her meant he wanted to discuss something with her in private without making it obvious.

Irritated by his presence, she snapped, "We've been here for over a week and nothing's happened. How long does that 'escort' expect us to be able to remain guests?"

Philip didn't have to point out that Osvald, the escort Dorothea had provided, hadn't been able to get close to either Wilhelmina or Jaenelle without having to deal with at least one male chaperon, let alone get close enough to slip the women away from the Hall. He also didn't have to point out that they would be "guests" until the High Lord—or the *real* Queen who ruled this court—decided otherwise.

"Lucivar came to see me this morning," Philip said abruptly.

Hearing the tightness in his voice, Alexandra glanced at him, then took a closer look at the flush darkening Philip's face. Was that anger or embarrassment? "And?"

"He strongly suggested that you tighten your hold on Vania's leash before she gets hurt. It seems she's too aggressive in her efforts to coax a Kaeleer male into her bed. He said if she's that itchy for a male, she should invite her Consort, since that's why he's here."

Personally, Alexandra thought Vania acted like a slut. But Vania was also generous about sharing the use of her males with visiting Queens—a generosity Alexandra never refused whenever she visited that Province. She had kept no steady lover in her own court for more than twenty-five years—ever since she had asked Philip to see Leland through her Virgin Night. It wouldn't have been fair to any of them if she had asked him to warm her bed after that when he really wanted to be her daughter's lover, and the other men she had considered since then had been far more interested in the power they might wield as her Consort than in giving her pleasure.

But remembering Vania's generosity—and the fact that no male currently warmed *her* bed, either—made Alexandra defensive. "She wouldn't have to be 'aggressive' if this court remembered to provide visiting Queens with the basic amenities."

"I mentioned that," Philip said through gritted teeth. "And was told that there are no males in this court whose service requirements include that duty."

"I find that hard to believe. Not every Queen who comes here would necessarily have a Consort at that moment or have brought him. There must be *some* arrangement—" She stopped, shaken by the depth of the insult. "It's because we're from Terreille, isn't it?"

"Yes," Philip said flatly. "He said there are a few males in the Second and Third Circles who would normally be willing to accommodate a guest of the court if asked, but because Terreillean Queens don't know how to enjoy a male without mistreating him, no Kaeleer male would willingly offer himself." He hesitated. "He also said there are no pleasure slaves in Kaeleer."

That verbal slap hurt as much as a blow because it was a reminder that, for a few months, Daemon Sadi had been a pleasure slave in her court.

"I see," she said tightly.

"Despite his anger over the situation, Lucivar actually seemed concerned," Philip said, sounding baffled. "Mostly because Vania's fixed her efforts on Prince Aaron."

"Aaron *is* a very handsome man, and—"

"He's married."

There wasn't much she could say to that, not when she

could feel waves of anxiety rolling off of Philip. Vania's marked attention toward a married man would be a sharp reminder of his own vulnerability.

While more and more aristo marriage contracts in Terreille were being made for social or political reasons, most Blood males still cherished the idea of marriage because it was the one relationship where the genders met on common ground as partners. Or as close to being partners as was possible—or reasonable. It also meant that male fidelity was a marriage requirement, and any man who looked beyond his wife's bed could swiftly find himself without home or family, could even lose his children.

"There's another reason to curb Vania," Philip said. "If the males here get any more riled . . ."

"I know," Alexandra replied sharply. They would never get Wilhelmina and Jaenelle away from the Hall if the males became more hostile than they already were. "I know," she said again, softening her voice. "I'll talk to her."

"Soon?"

She disliked herself for thinking less of him because of the anxiety in his voice.

"Yes, Philip," she said gently, "I'll talk to her soon."

2 / Kaeleer

An interesting gathering, Daemon thought as he slipped his hands into his trouser pockets and wondered what it meant when the Steward of the Court summoned the Master of the Guard, the Consort, and the First Escort to his study in order to "discuss something."

He'd spent the past couple of days studying the book of Protocol Saetan had given him and had been surprised by the differences between these rules and the ones he had been taught in Terreille. *This* Protocol, while reinforcing the matriarchal nature of the Blood, gave males some rights and privileges that helped balance the power. Which explained the refreshing lack of fear and subservience in these males. They understood the boundaries that defined acceptable male behavior, and within those boundaries, they stood on solid ground, never having to wonder what would happen to them if they were no longer in a particular Lady's favor.

He'd also been surprised by the section of Protocol that involved First Circle males since he'd never even seen the vaguest mention of it in Terreille.

There was a phrase that summed up a male's surrender into formal service: Your will is my life. It gave the Queen the right to do anything she pleased with a male, including kill him. That wasn't new, and, in Terreille, it was a serious risk. What *was* different was the tacit agreement on the Queen's part that, by accepting the male, she was also accepting his right to have a say in her decisions and *her* life. If a Queen gave an order and the majority of males in her First Circle opposed it, she could yield to their decision or dismiss them from her court. *But she couldn't hurt them for opposing her.*

If the males in Terreille had known about that part of Protocol, they might have been able to keep the behavior of Dorothea's pet Queens in check, might have been able to keep the younger strong witches safe and whole, might have found a way to fight the threats of slavery and castration that had made most of the males too afraid to challenge the witches in power.

But something—or someone—must have purged the sections about male power from the books of Protocol in Terreille so long ago that no one had remembered they existed.

No wonder Terreilleans found living in Kaeleer such a shock. And now it finally made sense why immigrants from Terreille were required to serve in a court. They would need that time to absorb the new rules and understand how those rules applied to day-to-day living.

Which made him even more curious to observe the formal give-and-take between a Queen and the male triangle.

Assuming, of course, the Queen was going to show up.

"Did anyone tell Cat she's supposed to be here?" Lucivar asked, echoing Daemon's thought.

Saetan gave Lucivar a bland look. "I told her. However, Lord Ladvarian had already cornered her to discuss a couple of things. I expect she'll be along as soon as she can talk herself around whatever he and Kaelas have in mind." That bland look was then aimed at Daemon.

Daemon met that look with one equally bland while his

heart rate kicked up to a gallop—because he had the distinct feeling that whatever Ladvarian and Kaelas wanted to discuss with Jaenelle had to do with him.

He was trying to think of a reasonable excuse to drag Lucivar into the great hall for a minute to ask him why the kindred were so interested in the Consort when Jaenelle rushed into the room.

"Sorry I'm—" She checked when she saw them, and her rush suddenly became cautious. "Is this family or court?" she asked warily.

"Court," Saetan replied.

Fascinated, Daemon watched the subtle shift from woman to Queen.

"And what is the court's pleasure?" Jaenelle asked quietly.

No hint of a sneer or sarcasm in her voice, Daemon decided as he recognized one of the ritual openings for discussion.

"I received a message from Lord Jorval," Saetan said with equal calm, although his eyes seemed a little too carefully blank. "A person from a prestigious aristo family has come to Kaeleer seeking the assistance of a Healer for an illness that has baffled all the Healers in Terreille. Since you're known to be the best Healer in the Realm, he urgently requests that you come to Goth to offer your opinion."

Lucivar snarled quietly but viciously. A small, but sharp, hand gesture from Andulvar silenced him.

"Jorval also says that, while he's been assured that the illness is not contagious, it does seem to afflict only males. And since he doesn't want any harm to come to the males of your court—"

This time Andulvar snorted.

"—he has offered to provide you with an escort while you're in Little Terreille."

"NO!" Lucivar exploded into movement, pacing furiously. "You are *not* going into Little Terreille to do a healing without a full escort of your own males. Not again. Never again. If this person wants to see you so badly, why doesn't he come here?"

"I can think of a few reasons," Jaenelle said with dry amusement as she watched Lucivar.

Daemon's blood sang when her eyes met his for a moment. Then it chilled when he glanced at Saetan and saw something flicker at the back of those golden eyes. What was the High Lord trying to hide behind that deliberately blank gaze—and what would happen if the leash holding it back snapped?

"Did Jorval mention where this person is from? Or anything else that might be useful?" Jaenelle asked, turning back to Saetan while Lucivar paced and swore.

"Only that the short-lived races seem most affected," Saetan said.

Jaenelle's lips softened in a hint of a dreamy smile that was malevolent enough to make Daemon shiver. "The races from the western part of Terreille?" she asked in her midnight voice.

"He didn't say, Lady."

Jaenelle nodded thoughtfully. "I'll think about it."

"There's nothing to think about," Lucivar snarled. "You're not going. You may not remember much of what happened seven years ago, *but I do*. We're not going through that again, especially you."

Daemon studied Lucivar. Behind the fury was fear bordering on panic. He suppressed a sigh, not happy that his first official act as the Consort might be opposing his Queen. But anything that spooked Lucivar so badly wasn't something Daemon was going to easily agree to.

Then he noticed Jaenelle's face as she turned toward Lucivar—and wondered how any man would dare oppose Witch now that she had reached maturity and had come into her full power.

Lucivar froze in midstride as those sapphire eyes fixed on him. His body trembled, but he met her gaze, and his voice was steady as he said quietly, "The only way you're going into Little Terreille is by going through me."

Then he walked out of the study.

Jaenelle's shoulders slumped for a moment, then straightened again as she turned to face Daemon. "Please go with him."

"Why?" Daemon asked too softly.

The Queen stare melted a little into exasperation. "Because you're strong enough to hold him back, and I don't want him getting the boyos riled about something I haven't even decided to do yet."

It was the first thing she had asked of him, and he wasn't sure he could do it. "What happened seven years ago?"

Her face went death pale, and it took her a moment to answer. "Why don't you ask Lucivar? As he said, he remembers it better than I do."

He waited a few heartbeats. Then, "How long do you need?"

Now she looked at Saetan. "Would an hour be convenient?"

"It would be our pleasure to reconvene in an hour," Saetan said.

"All right," Daemon said. "I can hold him for an hour."

Nodding to acknowledge that she heard him, she hurried out of the room.

Daemon stared at the closed door, fully aware that Andulvar and Saetan were waiting for some indication of what he was going to do. "I am going to ask him," he said quietly. "And if I don't like the answer, she's going to have to go through me, too." He would sacrifice any chance of being her lover if that's what it took to protect her.

"You're not going to like the answer," Saetan said, "but I wouldn't worry about having to take a stand. If Jaenelle decides she's going into Little Terreille, she's going to have to go through the whole First Circle to do it. Since it isn't likely that she'll fight the court that hard over this particular healing, it's only respectful to allow the Lady the time to reach that conclusion on her own."

"In that case, if you'll excuse me, I'd better see what I can do about restraining Lucivar's temper."

3 / Kaeleer

Lucivar is unhappy, Ladvarian said as he watched Jaenelle stare at the waterfall and tiered pools she had built in this inner garden several years ago.

"I want to think, Warlord," Jaenelle said quietly. "Alone."

The Sceltie shifted his feet, thought a moment, then stood firm. *He's snarly and upset and he won't talk to any of us.* This particular smell of anger and fear on Lucivar only happened when Jaenelle or Marian did something to upset the Eyrien. Since Marian hadn't done anything un-usual—he'd already checked—that meant Jaenelle had done something. Or was going to do something.

His lips pulled back in a silent snarl. *Jaenelle.*

As she turned to face him, he saw the large blackwood hourglass resting on her hand. Saying nothing, she turned it over, set it on the stone lip of the lowest pool, and walked to the other end of the garden.

Ladvarian growled softly at the hourglass.

The kindred had trouble understanding the way humans carved up a day into these little chunks called hours and minutes. They had understood easily enough that sometimes human females wanted to be left alone, but, for a while, they had come back too soon and had gotten snarled at. So the High Lord and the Lady had made these hourglasses because they were easy to understand. If the sand was all at the bottom, the female was ready to play again. If it wasn't, the kindred would go away without disturbing her.

Jaenelle had two sets of hourglasses. Each set had an hourglass sized for one hour, a half hour, and a quarter hour. Jaenelle used the set made of light-colored wood as a request for private time and could be interrupted if necessary. Witch, the Queen, used the set made from blackwood, and those hourglasses were a silent command.

Ladvarian trotted out of the garden, accepting the dismissal.

He wouldn't challenge his Queen, but he had learned that, if nipped sharply enough, Lucivar would lash out. And then Ladvarian and the other males would find out what the Lady was planning to do.

4 / Kaeleer

Using Craft, any of the Jeweled Blood would be able to send an ax cleanly through a chunk of wood. Lucivar, Dae-mon decided as he watched the ax come down and split the wood in half, wasn't using anything but muscle and temper.

And that, more than anything else he'd observed since arriving in Kaeleer, told him how different serving in a court was here. In Terreille, Lucivar would have picked a fight with another strong male, and the resulting violence would have triggered a vicious brawl that could tear a court apart. Here he was venting his temper by chopping wood that would warm the Hall in the winter days ahead.

"She send you out here to keep me hobbled?" Lucivar snarled as he swung the ax again.

"What happened seven years ago, Lucivar?" Daemon asked quietly. "Why are you so against Jaenelle doing a healing in Little Terreille?"

"You're not going to talk me around this, Bastard."

"I'm not interested in talking you around this. I just want to know why I'm about to draw the line that puts me on the opposing side of my Queen's wishes."

The ax came down just hard enough to set the blade into the chopping block.

Lucivar called in a towel and wiped the sweat off his face. "Seven years ago she had been in Little Terreille, making one of those visits that had been a concession to the Dark Council. A child had been badly injured, and she was asked to do the healing. Whoever set it up did it well. The injury was extensive enough that the healing would have left her physically and mentally exhausted but not enough that she might have called in other Healers than the ones in Little Terreille. Because if she'd called Gabrielle or Karla for help, a male escort would have come with them.

"When the healing was done, someone gave her food or drink that was drugged, and she was too tired to detect it. It made her complacent enough to do what she was told—and she was told to sign a marriage contract."

The cold slipped through Daemon's veins, sweet and deadly. *You weren't here. You can't think of it as a betrayal since you weren't here.* It didn't matter. A Consort could be nothing more than a physical accommodation. But a husband . . . "Then where is he?" he asked too softly.

Lucivar twisted the towel. "He didn't survive the consummation."

"You took care of that? Thank you."

"He was dead when I got there." Lucivar closed his eyes and swallowed hard. "Hell's fire, Daemon, she splattered him all over the room." He opened his eyes. The bleakness in them made Daemon shiver. "They gave her a large dose of *safframate* on top of the other drug."

Daemon's body went completely numb for a moment.

He knew all too well what *safframate* could do to a person. "You took care of her?" Meaning, *you gave her the sex she needed?* There was no room in him now to feel jealousy or betrayal, just the desperate hope that Lucivar had done what was needed.

Lucivar looked away. "I took her hunting in Askavi."

Daemon just stared at his brother, letting the magnitude of those words ripen. "You went out with her as *bait?*"

"What was I supposed to do?" Lucivar snapped. "Let her stay locked up in Ebon Askavi suffering? Bloodletting relieves the pain of *safframate* as well as sex does." He paused to take a deep breath and regain control. "It wasn't easy, but we survived it."

And that, Daemon realized, was all Lucivar intended to say about a period of time that must have been a nightmare for him.

"She's only been back to Little Terreille a couple of times since then, and then only with a full, armed escort that included me," Lucivar said. "She hasn't been back at all since she formally set up her court."

"I see," Daemon said quietly. "It's almost time to hear her decision. Do you want to get cleaned up?"

"What for?" Lucivar asked with a grim smile. "Once I hear it, I'll probably be back out here anyway."

5 / Kaeleer

"May I help you?"

Osvald, the escort, clenched his teeth, then made an effort to smile as he turned to face the footman. Hell's fire, wasn't there *one* male in this whole damn place who wasn't spoiling for a fight? "I seem to have gotten turned around, so I thought I'd admire the pictures in this part of the Hall."

"I would be happy to show you the way back to your room," Holt said with frigid courtesy.

In Terreille, he could have had the footman whipped for no better reason than sufficient lack of subservience. In Terreille, servants wouldn't wear their Jewels so blatantly that it forced their social superiors to acknowledge that strength. It galled him that he, who was favored by the High Priestess of Hayll, had to acknowledge that a *footman* was also an Opal-Jeweled Warlord.

"This way," Holt said just as Wilhelmina stepped out of her room.

Osvald swore silently. If Holt had shown up a few minutes later, he could have had the bitch and gotten out of this place.

Then the large striped cat stepped out of the room and immediately fixed those unblinking eyes on him, making him glad of Holt's presence. When the cat's lips began to lift into a snarl, he didn't need any more urging. He offered Wilhelmina a polite greeting—and felt intensely relieved when she returned it so automatically it sounded like casual familiarity, the kind of automatic response the other bitches in this place only gave to males they knew fairly well. With every other male, there was that slight pause that practically screamed "stranger."

That could work to his advantage, he thought as he followed Holt back to the wing where Alexandra and her entourage had been quartered. It wouldn't seem odd for an escort to deliver a message from one Lady to another—especially if it was assumed he'd been working for that family for a number of years.

Yes, that could work very well.

6 / Kaeleer

When they work in tandem, they're dangerous, Andulvar said to Saetan, using an Ebon-gray communication thread.

Looking at Lucivar and Daemon, Saetan understood the distinction Andulvar was making. All Warlord Princes were dangerous, but when two men with complementary strengths became a team . . . *So were we at their age,* he replied dryly. *We still are.*

If it ever came down to a fight, I wouldn't want to go up against those two, Andulvar said thoughtfully.

Any amusement Saetan felt fled with that statement. His heart wanted to shout, *They'll never be enemies. They're my children, my sons.* But another part of him—the part that had to assess the potential danger of another strong male—couldn't be sure. He *had* been sure when it had been Lucivar alone. But Daemon . . .

Lucivar had endured a brutal childhood, but in some ways, it had been a clean brutality. He hadn't gotten entangled in a court until he was a youth. But Daemon had been raised in Dorothea's court, and he had taken the twisted lessons taught there into himself, had made them a part of himself, and then used them as a weapon.

While he might fight individuals, Lucivar had been able to embrace loyalty to family and court. Saetan strongly suspected that Daemon's loyalty would always be superficial, that the only loyalty the rest of them could count on was his commitment to Jaenelle. Which meant Daemon was capable of doing *anything* in the name of that loyalty. Which meant this son had to be handled very, very carefully.

It didn't help that Jaenelle was acting like a rabbit to Daemon's fox. With any other man, Saetan might have found this chase amusing. He knew the boyos certainly did, and he understood why they were delighted by her reaction to Daemon. But he didn't think Daemon found it the least bit amusing, and he wondered what would happen when his son's temper finally snapped—and who would suffer because of it.

When Jaenelle entered the study, Saetan put aside the problem that hadn't arrived yet in order to deal with the one already at the door.

"High Lord," Jaenelle said formally.

"Lady," Saetan replied, equally formal.

She took a deep breath and turned to Lucivar. "Prince Yaslana, as First Escort, I want you to arrange for accommodations somewhere along the border of Little Terreille for myself and a limited escort. Not an inn. A private house or a guard station. Somewhere that ensures discretion. In can be in whichever Territory you choose. You can decide the time of the meeting—although not within the next three days."

He wasn't standing close enough to her to catch the scent, but he could tell by the sudden blaze in Daemon's eyes and the sharpness in Lucivar's that her moon's blood had started. He wanted to sigh. Hell's fire, how was he supposed to channel Daemon's instinctive aggression while fighting to control his own? Witches were vulnerable during the first three days of their moontimes because they couldn't wear their Jewels or do more than basic Craft without causing themselves physical pain. And when it was his Queen who was vulnerable, a Warlord Prince's temper rode the killing edge during those days.

"You don't have to tell anyone about the arrangements

you've made," Jaenelle continued. "Although, out of courtesy, you should inform the Steward, the Master of the Guard, and the Consort. The Steward will contact Lord Jorval to confirm the meeting place in Little Terreille."

"What's the point of setting up a secure place if you're going to go to Little Terreille?" Lucivar asked, but Saetan noticed he was keeping his tone carefully respectful.

"Because I'm going to go to Little Terreille without *going* to Little Terreille. That will satisfy the court's concerns about my well-being and still allow me to meet with this person."

Lucivar narrowed his eyes, considering. "You could just refuse."

"I have my own reasons for doing this," Jaenelle replied in her midnight voice.

And that, Saetan knew, would decide the matter for Lucivar.

Except Lucivar was still studying her. "If I agree to this, do we get to fuss for the next three days without getting snarled at?"

That's all it took to change the Queen back into a stuttering, snarling younger sister. "Who is 'we'?" she asked ominously.

"The family."

Saetan wondered if anyone else had noticed that the look Daemon gave his brother should have left Lucivar bleeding. And he wondered if Lucivar even realized that, whether he had included or excluded Daemon under the term "family," it wasn't sitting well with the Queen's Consort.

"Papa!" Jaenelle said, whirling around to face him.

"Witch-child?" he replied mildly, but he could feel beads of sweat forming on his forehead as Daemon's face shifted into a cold, unreadable mask.

She stared at him for a moment, then whirled back to Lucivar. "Within reason," she snapped. "And I get to decide what's reasonable."

When Lucivar just grinned at her, she stomped out of the study. The grin faded when he looked at Andulvar. "Since you're the Master of the Guard, she should have asked you to make the arrangements."

Andulvar shrugged. "My ego's not bruised, puppy. She's too good a Queen not to understand the needs of the males who serve her. Right now, you need to make the arrangements more than I do." His smile had sharp edges. "But if you don't inform me of your arrangements, I *will* be insulted."

"If you have time now, we could take a look at a map," Lucivar said.

"You're learning, puppy," Andulvar said as he draped an arm over Lucivar's shoulders and led him out of the study. "You're learning."

When Daemon made no move to leave, Saetan leaned against the blackwood desk. "Something on your mind, Prince?"

"I don't give a damn what familial ties you and Lucivar claim to have with her, I am *not* her brother," Daemon said too quietly.

"No one said you were. The fact that I'm her adopted father and you happen to be my son is irrelevant. You've never thought of her as a sister, and she's never thought of you as a brother. That hasn't changed."

The chill in Daemon's eyes thawed to bleakness. "She may not think of me as a brother, but she also doesn't want me to be anything else."

Saetan snapped to attention. "That isn't true."

Daemon's soft laugh held bitterness and grief. "It usually takes me less than an hour to seduce a woman when I'm trying. And usually not more than two when I'm not. I can't even get close enough to talk to her most of the time."

Daemon's acknowledged ability to seduce chilled Saetan. Because the people telling the tales didn't know they were talking about his son, he'd heard enough stories about the Sadist to feel uneasy. Those bedroom skills, like the man who wielded them, were a double-edged sword.

If Daemon felt driven enough to use those skills prematurely . . .

Saetan crossed his arms to hide the slight tremor in his hands. "The boys find this little chase between you and Jaenelle amusing."

"Do they?" Daemon asked too softly.

"And, I confess, so do I." *Or would, if I could be certain you weren't going to go for my throat before I finish this.*

Daemon's gold eyes held a bored, sleepy look Saetan knew too well—because there had been times when he had looked into a mirror and seen it in his own eyes.

"Do you?" Daemon asked.

"A couple of days ago, Jaenelle asked for my opinion about the dress she was wearing for dinner."

"I remember it. It's a lovely gown."

"I'm delighted that you appreciated it." Saetan paused. "Can you also appreciate that, in the thirteen years she's lived here, Jaenelle has never been concerned enough about clothes to ask for my opinion about something she was wearing. And can you appreciate that she wasn't asking for my opinion as her Steward or her father but as a man. And I admit that, considering the way that dress fit her, my opinion of it as a father would have differed considerably from my opinion as a man."

Daemon almost smiled.

"She sees you as a man, Daemon. A *man,* not a male friend. For the first time in her life, she's trying to deal with her own lust. So she's running."

"She's not the only one trying to deal with it," Daemon muttered, but the sleepy look had changed to sharp interest. "I *am* her Consort. She could just—"

Saetan shook his head. "Do you really think Jaenelle would demand that from you?"

"No." Daemon raked his fingers through his hair. "What can I do?"

"You don't need to do anything more than you're already doing." Saetan thought for a moment. "Do you know how to make a brew to ease moontime discomfort?"

"I know how to make a few of them."

Saetan smiled. "In that case, I suggest that the Consort prepare one for his Lady. I don't think even Jaenelle would disagree about that falling into the category of 'reasonable fussing.' "

7 / Kaeleer

Surreal paused in the dining room doorway and swore under her breath. The only people in the room were Alexandra and her entourage.

Hell's fire. Why couldn't Jaenelle have left well enough alone? The meals had certainly been more relaxed and the conversation more interesting when Alexandra and her people had been taking their meals separately. When she had pointed that out to Saetan, he had informed her it had been Jaenelle's idea to have Alexandra and the others join the rest of them for meals, in the hope that they might acquire some understanding about Kaeleer.

The intention might have been good, Surreal thought crossly as she strode to the table, but the reality was a miserable failure. Not one of them, from Alexandra right down to the least-ranking escort, wanted to understand *anything* about the Blood in Kaeleer. And the midday meals were the worst since Saetan didn't preside over them.

As she reached the table, the two Province Queens, Vania and Nyselle, gave her looks that mingled smug superiority with disgust. She might have taken it personally if she hadn't known that they looked at *all* the witches there in exactly the same way—including the Queens who far outranked them.

Then Vania looked at the doorway, and her expression changed to predatory delight.

Glancing over, Surreal saw Aaron pause in the doorway—and decided that a man who had been told the date of his execution looked pretty much the same way. Figuring that he didn't need another woman staring at him, she turned her attention to the table.

The first point of interest was the way this group had split. Alexandra, Philip, and Leland were sitting at one end of the table. Nyselle was sitting at the other end, her Consort and the escorts ranged around her. Vania's Consort sat on his Lady's left, looking unhappy. The chair on Vania's right was empty, as were the ones across from her.

The second point of interest was the serving dishes on the table. Breakfast and the midday meal were usually set out on the huge sideboard so that everyone could fill a plate and take a seat as they pleased. Dinner was the only meal that had a set starting time, and was the only meal where the footmen served the food. *This* midday meal had been set out family-style, as if only a small number of people were expected.

That was fine, Surreal thought as she began filling her plate from the closest serving dishes. That was just *fine*— as long as everyone else was going hungry to avoid eating with the guests. But if she found out that another midday

meal was being quietly served elsewhere, she was going to
have a few things to say to *someone* about not being told.

"May I sit with you?" Aaron asked ˙ quietly as he
joined her.

She was about to make a tart reply about there being
plenty of chairs when she saw the hunted look in his eyes.

As if her noticing him had given him some kind of permission, he shifted closer to her. Close enough for her to
feel the way his muscles quivered with the strain of keeping
strong emotions tightly leashed.

"Why don't you sit over here, Aaron?" Vania said, giving him a coy smile while she patted the chair on her right.

Well, that more than explained the hunted look.

During the time Surreal had been at the Hall, she'd observed that the males—from the most menial male servant
right up to the High Lord—had some very particular ideas
about what was considered acceptable physical distance,
and the cold courtesy they could all turn on a woman was
usually an effective determent when that distance wasn't
respected. The males in the First Circle not only tolerated
being approached and touched by all of the witches in the
First Circle, they welcomed that friendly intimacy. But they
didn't welcome it from anyone else.

He considers me one of them, she realized, feeling a jolt
of pleasure at the acceptance. *He considers me safe.* Because of that, her "Of course," in reply to his question was
as soothing as she could make it. Which, for some reason,
distressed him.

I was a good whore, she thought as she picked up the
serving fork and the carving knife from the platter holding
the roasted turkey. *A* damned *good whore. So why is it
that, all of a sudden, males are impossible to figure out?*

"Would—"

Surreal turned her head to look at Aaron, the carving
knife poised over the turkey. "You weren't going to suggest
that I don't know how to handle a knife, were you, sugar?"

Aaron's eyes widened. "I would never be so foolish as
to suggest that a Dea al Mon witch didn't know how to
handle a knife," he said, sounding suspiciously meek. "I
was going to ask if you would mind cutting a slice for me."

"Of course you were," she replied tartly. She felt something in him relax and swore silently about perverse male

behavior. Then again, she mused as she cut the turkey breast, maybe the males were just so used to that blend of tart and sweet in a witch's personality, they could relax around it. It could be an acquired taste, like pickleberries.

The thought made her chuckle.

After placing the serving fork and carving knife back on the platter, she settled down to eat. There wasn't much conversation, which suited her just fine—especially since all of Vania's remarks were aimed at Aaron and his replies had become curt to the point of rudeness.

Hoping to break, or at least change, the tension that was getting thicker by the minute, Surreal looked up, intending to ask Alexandra when she and her party were going to leave. But she didn't say anything because she found herself looking straight at Vania. There was a nasty kind of anger in the woman's eyes directed right at Aaron.

After toying with her food for a minute, Vania pushed her plate away and smiled coyly. "I declare, I'm just too tired to eat right now. Aaron was *so* stimulating this morning."

It took Surreal a moment too long to understand that remark.

With a howl of rage, Aaron lunged across the table, grabbed Vania by the hair, and yanked her forward. His left hand closed on the carving knife and swung it toward her throat.

Surreal grabbed Aaron's left wrist with both hands and pulled back as hard as she could. He gave her a couple of inches before his muscles bunched and his arm surged forward.

The knife's point jabbed Vania's neck. She screamed as blood began flowing from the wound.

Surreal poured the power of her Gray Jewels into her hands to give her added strength, but there was some kind of tight shield around Aaron that just absorbed the power.

All right. Muscle against muscle. She could hold him off for the few seconds needed for the other men at the table to help her.

Except no one moved.

Then she got a glimpse of Aaron's face and knew none of the other people in the room were going to approach a Warlord Prince who looked that cold and merciless.

She fought harder, used every bit of leverage she could find. She didn't give a damn if Vania got her throat slit, but she didn't want Aaron to get into trouble because the bitch had pushed him too far.

Surreal? Graysfang said anxiously.

Help me!

The wolf must have been nearby because he was in the dining room seconds after she called.

*Surreal . . . *

Don't just stand there. Do something!

Aaron is First Circle, Graysfang whined. *I can't bite Aaron.*

Then find someone who can!

Graysfang rushed out of the room.

If she could have, she would have used Craft to vanish the knife, but Aaron had extended that damned shield to include the weapon. She couldn't get the knife, couldn't even break his wrist to stop him.

Her grip on his wrist slipped for an instant—long enough for the knife to slice Vania's neck again.

Then Chaosti was there, his hands clamped on Aaron's right wrist. Lucivar's hands closed over hers, adding more force and strength.

Aaron fought against them mindlessly, intent only on the kill.

"Damn it, Aaron," Lucivar snarled. "Don't force me to break your wrist."

Good luck, Surreal thought sourly as Lucivar's hands tightened on hers. She just hoped he remembered her hands were in the way before he started breaking bones.

Aaron seemed far past the ability to hear them, but he reacted when an icy midnight voice said, "Prince Aaron, *attend.*"

Aaron began shivering uncontrollably. Lucivar quickly took the carving knife away from him and vanished it. Chaosti pried Aaron's right hand open, releasing Vania's hair.

Vania kept screaming—had been screaming, Surreal realized, since the first jab.

"*SILENCE.*"

Ice instantly coated all the glasses on the table. Vania glanced in Jaenelle's direction and stopped screaming.

"Prince Aaron," Jaenelle said too calmly. "*Attend.*"

Flinching, Aaron slowly straightened up. Chaosti and Lucivar released him and stepped aside.

Deathly pale, Aaron walked over to where Jaenelle stood and sank to his knees.

"Wait for me in the High Lord's study," Jaenelle said.

With effort, Aaron got to his feet and left the dining room.

Surreal looked at those frozen sapphire eyes, felt the lightest brush of immense, barely controlled rage, and started to shake. Her legs gave out. She sat on the table.

Jaenelle slowly approached the table and turned her eyes on Lucivar. "You knew about this."

Lucivar took several shallow breaths before answering. "I knew."

"And you did nothing."

He swallowed hard. "I had hoped it would be taken care of quietly."

Jaenelle just stared at him. Then, "I'll see you in the High Lord's study in thirty minutes, Prince Yaslana."

"Yes, Lady."

Those sapphire eyes pinned Chaosti next. "And you after him."

"It will be my pleasure, Lady," Chaosti replied, his voice husky.

Oh, I doubt that very much, Surreal thought, still shaking.

Then Jaenelle looked at Vania—and the cold began to burn.

"If you ever again cause one of my males any physical, mental, or emotional distress, I will hang you by your heels and skin you alive."

No one spoke, no one moved until Jaenelle walked out of the room.

Could she do that? Surreal wondered. She didn't realize she had spoken out loud until Lucivar made a sound that was a cross between a laugh and a whimper.

"In the mood she's in right now? Not only could she do it, she wouldn't bother using a knife."

Surreal looked at her own hands, thought about it for a moment, and then wondered if anyone would be upset if she threw up on the floor.

"Surreal?" Lucivar's hand shook as he lifted her head up.

He's scared shitless. Hell's fire, Mother Night, and may the Darkness be merciful.

"Surreal? Are you injured?"

The sharp concern in Lucivar's voice made her focus her attention. "Hurt? No, I don't think—"

"There's blood on your face and neck."

"Oh." Her gorge rose. "I must have gotten splashed when . . ." Keeping her mouth shut seemed like a very good idea right now.

Lucivar looked over his shoulder. "Falonar?"

"Prince Yaslana," Falonar replied quietly.

"Your sole duty this afternoon is to take care of Lady Surreal."

"It will be my pleasure."

"Lady Vania needs a Healer," one of the escorts said frantically.

"Well, shit," Surreal said, suddenly feeling a bit drunk, "they really are alive. They can talk and they can move. The way they were sitting on their thumbs a few minutes ago, I'd doubted it. I really had."

"Shut up, bitch," an escort yelled.

Lucivar, Chaosti, and Falonar snarled at the man.

"I suggest you ask Lord Beale to send for the Healer in Halaway," Lucivar said coldly.

"Surely the Hall keeps a Healer," Alexandra said, sounding outraged.

"There's Lady Gabrielle and Lady Karla," Lucivar replied. "If I were you, I wouldn't ask either of them right now."

"You could always ask Jaenelle," Surreal said with a venomous smile.

Frightened silence met that statement.

With Vania supported by two of the escorts, Alexandra and her entourage quickly left the room. Lucivar and Chaosti gave Falonar a hard look before leaving.

Falonar approached Surreal cautiously. "This must have been . . . distressing . . . for you." He looked like he was about to bite down on a toad. "Do you need smelling salts or something?"

Surreal narrowed her eyes. "Sugar, I'm an assassin. I've done worse than this at a dinner table."

"I wasn't talking about . . ." He looked at the blood-splashed table.

"Oh." At least he was smart enough to realize it wasn't *Aaron* who had scared her.

He paused, then added, "I meant no insult."

"None taken," she replied. It was her turn to pause. "On any other day, I'd be willing to find out what the rules are for inviting a man to have a sweaty afternoon of sex, just to get my mind off this for a few hours. But I don't think sex of any kind would be a good idea today."

Surprise and interest flickered in Falonar's eyes, and his voice held regret. "No, I don't think it would be a good idea . . . today."

"So why don't we go through another practice round with the sticks? I'd like to get out of this building for a while."

Falonar nodded thoughtfully. "You can handle a knife?"

Surreal smiled. "I can handle a knife." She glanced at his groin. "I can also handle spears quite well."

He actually blushed a little. "A bow?"

Still smiling, she shook her head.

"A new skill requires concentration."

"So do some old skills . . . if you want to do them right."

His blush deepened while his interest sharpened.

Surreal stood up. "Let's go concentrate on a new skill."

"And discuss the possibility of practicing old skills?"

"Oh, definitely."

In charity with each other, they hurried to escape the growing fury that filled the Hall.

8 / Kaeleer

Daemon paused outside Jaenelle's sitting room. He took a deep breath, straightened his shoulders, and knocked on the door.

No answer.

She was there. He could feel the fury swirling in the room. And he could feel the cold.

He knocked again, then went into the room, ignoring the fact that he hadn't been invited.

Jaenelle prowled the sitting room, her arms wrapped

around her middle. She glared at him, and snarled, "Go away, Daemon."

She should have been resting today, Daemon thought as his temper sharpened. Probably had been before that scene in the dining room.

"Since I'm the only male in the First Circle who isn't the recipient of your displeasure, I thought I'd check and see if you needed anything. Why is that, by the way?" Despite his efforts to keep his tone mild, his voice had an edge to it. Rationally, he knew he should be grateful to have escaped the verbal lashing the others had received. Instead, he resented the exclusion—until he got the full thrust of that frozen sapphire stare.

"Did you know you should have reported Vania's stalking of Aaron?" Jaenelle asked too quietly.

"No, I didn't. Even if I had known, I wouldn't have reported it."

"Why in the name of Hell not?" Jaenelle shouted.

Heat. Daemon felt his legs weaken as relief washed through him. Thank the Darkness, this was no longer cold rage but hot anger. He could work around hot anger. "Because she *was* stalking him. Aaron wasn't casting any lures or making any unspoken invitations. She was trying to push him into her bed because she wanted the conquest. She didn't give a damn what it would do to him."

"Exactly."

She still didn't understand. Daemon raked his fingers through his hair. "Hell's fire, woman, the man has a wife and an infant daughter. If he had said anything, would Kalush really believe he was innocent?"

"Of course she would!" Jaenelle shouted. "But if he didn't feel he could tell Kalush, he could have told me or Karla or Gabrielle."

"How would that have helped?" Daemon shouted back. "You would have told Kalush, and he'd still be under suspicion for something he didn't do, didn't even *want* to do."

"Why do you keep harping about suspicion? This—"

"I am not harping."

"—has nothing to do with suspicion."

"Then why are you so furious with him?" Daemon roared.

"BECAUSE HE GOT HURT AND HE SHOULDN'T HAVE!" Jaenelle's eyes suddenly filled with tears. "I'm mad at him because he got hurt. Don't you think I know how ecstatic and terrified he's been since Kalush got pregnant? How much she and Arianna mean to him? How vulnerable he feels about another woman showing interest in him?" She swiped at a tear that rolled down her face. "But you all hid it so well, we weren't picking up anything but the edginess the boyos have felt since those . . . people . . . came to the Hall. If we'd known, the coven would have done something before now."

Hearing something underneath the words, Daemon narrowed his gold eyes. "What else?"

Jaenelle hesitated. "Alexandra is my grandmother."

He advanced on her so fast, she took a quick step back and tripped on the train of her gown. Catching her by the arms, he pulled her up against him. "You are *not* going to wallow in guilt, Jaenelle," he said fiercely. "Do you hear me? You're not going to do it. She's your *grandmother*. A grown woman. As an adult, she's responsible for her own actions. As a Queen, she's responsible for controlling her own court. If anyone should share the blame with Vania, it's Alexandra. She was warned about this and did nothing." When she started to argue, he gave her enough of a shake to make her bare her teeth and snarl at him. "If you want to shoulder guilt and blame because they're here, then Wilhelmina is equally guilty and equally to blame."

Oh, the protective fierceness in those eyes.

Daemon ran his hands soothingly up and down her arms. "If one granddaughter shouldn't be blamed for Vania's actions or Alexandra's lack of action, how can you, in all fairness, blame the other?"

"Because I'm the Queen, and a Queen not only controls her court, she protects it."

Daemon snarled in frustration and muttered a few uncomplimentary things about female stubbornness.

"It's not stubbornness when you're right," Jaenelle snapped.

He couldn't win this fight if that was the stand she was going to take, so he tried to shift them to different ground. "All right. We should have reported it." Or taken care of it themselves better than they had.

She stared at him suspiciously. "Why are you agreeing with me all of a sudden?"

Daemon raised one eyebrow. "I would think you would prefer having males agree with you," he said mildly. "Should I keep arguing?"

"When any of you gives up this quickly, it's only because another of you has gotten into position to continue the argument from another angle."

"You make the First Circle sound like a hunting pack," Daemon said, trying hard to suppress a chuckle.

"I think they learned that tactic from the wolves," Jaenelle replied sourly.

Daemon began massaging her neck and shoulders.

She closed her eyes. "Did you know you and Lucivar were the only living human males in the First Circle that Vania didn't try to bed?"

"She wouldn't have dared try with me," Daemon said too softly.

"And she was smart not to try with Lucivar. When someone puts him in that position, he has a tendency to hit first and discuss after."

"Sounds like a successful deterrent."

"Mmm. Oh, right there."

Daemon obligingly focused on a knot of tight muscle. As he caressed and massaged, he subtly coaxed her to lean against him until her arms were around his waist and her head rested on his shoulder. "Lucivar's very hurt over your being so angry with him," he said quietly. "All the boyos are."

"I know." She sighed. "I'm too tired to think of a task for each of them. I guess I'll have to stub my toe."

"I beg your pardon?" His hands stopped caressing for a moment.

"I'll stub my toe, and then I'll let them all fuss and fetch and carry, and they'll know I'm not angry with them anymore."

"They'll actually believe a stubbed toe is a serious injury?"

Jaenelle snorted softly. "Of course not. It's more like a ritual."

"I see. The Queen can't apologize for the discipline but has to give a clear signal that it's done."

"Exactly. If it had been just one of them, I would have asked his assistance with something that I could just as easily do myself, and he would have understood. With so many, I'll have to let them fuss." Her voice took on a bit of a growl. "They'll plump pillows and tuck blankets around me that I don't want. They'll make me take naps."

"So it's not just forgiveness, but a little revenge thrown in."

"The revenge isn't so little. Usually, one of the coven will sneak a book in so I can read during my 'naps.' Once, when Papa came in to check on me, I stuffed the book under a pillow, but not quite well enough. He didn't say anything. When Khary and Aaron came in, he even poked the book farther under the pillow to hide it better. Then Saetan had the balls to say I looked flush so that they could fuss even more."

Daemon paused for a moment, sorting through the distinction she made between "Papa" and "Saetan." "Sweetheart," he said carefully, "if Saetan has balls, then so does Papa."

"It sounds disrespectful somehow to say that about Papa."

"I see," Daemon said in a tone of voice that indicated he didn't see at all.

"Papa," Jaenelle explained, "is charming and intelligent, a well-rounded companion."

Thinking of Saetan and Sylvia, Daemon said dryly, "I don't think Saetan is the companion who's well-rounded."

A long pause. Then, "You would call Sylvia's figure well-rounded?"

Daemon bit his tongue. Was she asking about Sylvia because she had picked up a stray thought of his or through an obvious connection of topics? And how in the name of Hell was a Consort supposed to safely answer that? "Her figure is more well-rounded than his," he hedged—and then threw Saetan into the verbal pit without a qualm. "They do seem fond of each other, even if Sylvia *won't* lend him that book."

When Jaenelle raised her head, there was nothing cold about the gleam in her eyes. "What book?"

*　*　*

"You mentioned *what*?"

Daemon rubbed the back of his neck as he warily studied his father. He had felt some obligation, male to male, to give Saetan fair warning—and now sincerely wished he hadn't.

Saetan stared at him. "Whatever possessed you to tell her about it in the first place?"

Oh, no. He was not going to repeat anything that had led up to that comment. "Jaenelle's in a much better mood now."

"I'm sure she is." Saetan rubbed his hands over his face. "What's she doing now?"

"Resting," Daemon said. "I'm going to talk to Beale about having a tray brought to her sitting room. We'll have dinner there and then play cards for a while."

The way Saetan's eyes suddenly glittered made him nervous.

"You're going to play cards with Jaenelle?" Saetan asked.

"Yes," Daemon replied cautiously.

"In that case, Prince, I'd say you've more than made up for mentioning that book."

9 / Kaeleer

Osvald lingered in the corridor.

At first, he'd thought Vania's greedy lust was going to spoil all their plans. But after the pale bitch-Queen had ripped into the males of the court because of it, they'd all gone off to lick their emotional wounds and hadn't been seen for the rest of the day.

Jaenelle's fury would have been a gift that had fallen into his hands if Wilhelmina Benedict had been in her room. But she wasn't, and he had no idea where to look for her. If she was with the other bitches, he couldn't approach her. He didn't want any of them taking special notice of him before he was ready to disappear.

Soon, he thought as he returned to his own room. Soon.

10 / Kaeleer

And they call me *the Sadist,* Daemon thought as he eyed the game board and cards—and did his best not to snarl in frustration.

"You almost won that round," Jaenelle offered, trying not to look too gleeful as she tallied up the scores.

Daemon bared his teeth in a poor imitation of a smile. "My deal?"

Nodding, Jaenelle busily turned the paper over, drew a line down the middle, and wrote their names at the top.

Daemon picked up the cards and began shuffling the deck.

Hell's fire, he shouldn't be having *this* much trouble with a card game. It was just a variation of the game "cradle" that Jaenelle had played as a child. All right, it was *twenty-six* variations of "cradle." He still shouldn't be having this much trouble winning a round. But there was something a little *off* about this game, something that defied rational thinking. *Male* thinking.

A game board with colored stones and bone discs with symbols etched on one side. A hand of cards. And the convoluted interaction between them. He could picture the coven sitting around on a stormy winter afternoon, putting this game together piece by piece, building one variation off another, adding bits from other games distinct to their own cultures, until they had created something that was pure torture for the male brain. He particularly despised the wild card game because the player in control of the board when the wild card turned up could call for a different variation—which could turn a good hand and game plan into garbage.

There had to be a way to turn that to his advantage. Had to . . .

Continuing to shuffle the cards, Daemon studied the game board carefully, studied the stones and the bone discs. Thought about how each piece *could* interact with the other pieces—and the cards.

Yes, that would work. That would work quite well.

"Which variation do you want to play?" Jaenelle asked as she placed the stones and discs in their starting positions.

Daemon gave her the smile that used to terrify the Queens in Terreille. "Variation twenty-seven."

Jaenelle just frowned at him. "Daemon, there is no variation twenty-seven."

He dealt the cards and purred, "There is now."

11 / Kaeleer

She was so young, Surreal thought as she studied her mother. *I had thought of her as being so big, so strong. But she's smaller than me . . . and she was so young when she died.*

Titian tucked her feet up on the window seat and wrapped her arms around her knees. "It's good you've come to Kaeleer."

Surreal stared out the window. But the night-darkened glass didn't show her anything but her own reflection—and that made her think of the questions that had gone unanswered for too long. "Why didn't we come here before?" she asked quietly. "Why didn't you go home after you got away from Kartane?" She hesitated. "Was it because of me?"

"No," Titian said sharply. "I chose to keep you, Surreal. I had to fight against my body's instinctive rejection of a child conceived by force, and *I chose you.*" Now Titian hesitated. "There were other reasons not to go home then. If I had, your life would have been easier, but . . ."

"But what?" Surreal snapped. "If you had gone home, you wouldn't have had to whore for food and shelter. If you had gotten out of Terreille, you wouldn't have died so damn young. What reason is good enough to balance those things?"

"I loved my father," Titian said softly. "And I loved my brothers. Rape is punishable by execution, Surreal. If I had gone home as soon as I escaped from Kartane, my father and brothers would have gone to Hayll to kill him."

Surreal stared at her. "How in the name of Hell did they expect to get past all of Dorothea's guards in order to get to Kartane?"

"They would have died," Titian said simply. "And I

didn't want my father and brothers to die. Can you understand that?"

"Not really, since I've spent most of my life preparing for the day when I can kill Kartane. Now, if it had been your mother . . ." Surreal tried to smile and couldn't. "What do you think your father would have said about your choice?"

Titian's smile was rueful. "I *know* what he said. He was in the Dark Realm for a little while before he returned to the Darkness. But he lived the full span of his years, Surreal, and my brothers raised children who never would have been born." She paused. "And if I had chosen differently, you wouldn't have been in Chaillot thirteen years ago, and we would have lost the greatest Queen the Blood has ever known."

"And if you hadn't ended up in Terreille, under Kartane, you would have been a Queen and a Black Widow."

"I still *am* a Queen and a Black Widow," Titian snapped. "When Kartane broke me, he severed me from the strength that would have been mine, but he couldn't take away what I am."

"I'm sorry," Surreal said, not sure how to express regret without giving insult.

"Don't shoulder regrets, little witch," Titian said gently as she got to her feet. "And don't shoulder the burden of anyone's actions but your own." She held out her hand. "Come on. You'll need your wits about you if you're sparring with Lucivar tomorrow."

Surreal rose wearily and followed Titian. Between that scene with Vania at midday, the extra workout with Falonar, and coping with the aftermath of Jaenelle's fury, she was more than ready to crawl into bed. She had hugged more distressed males that day than she had in her entire life. Which reminded her of something else. "How *do* I deal with the male relatives I've suddenly acquired?"

"You set your boundaries," Titian replied as they reached the corridor near Surreal's room. "You decide what you're willing to let them do for you and what you have to do for yourself. Then you tell them—gently. This is Kaeleer, Surreal. You have to handle the males—" Titian froze. Her nostrils flared.

"Titian?" Surreal asked, startled by the awful expression on her mother's face. "What's wrong?"

"Where's the High Lord?" Titian snarled. Not waiting for an answer, she ran for the nearest staircase.

Surreal raced after her, catching up to her when Titian jerked to a halt in front of a door.

Titian banged the door once with her fist, then flung it open. "High Lord!"

A muffled sound came from the adjoining room.

Titian flung that door open and rushed into the room. Surreal rushed in behind her, then stopped abruptly.

Saetan froze in the act of reaching for the dressing robe that was on his bed. He slowly straightened up and turned to face them.

Surreal couldn't stop herself from giving him one quick, professional—and approving—glance.

Titian didn't seem to notice that she had walked in on a naked, and now irritated, man.

"There's a tainted male in the Hall," Titian said abruptly.

Saetan stared at her for a moment. Then he grabbed the robe, said tersely, "Where?" and was out the door, with Titian at his heels, before Surreal could gather her wits.

By the time she caught up to them, Titian was questing back and forth in the corridor like a hound searching for a scent while Saetan prowled more slowly. Neither of them paid any attention to her arrival.

"It was here," Titian said as she searched. "It was *here*."

"Can you still sense it?" Saetan asked too quietly.

Titian's shoulders tensed. "No. But it *was* here."

"I'm not doubting you, Lady."

"But you sense nothing."

"No. Which only means that whoever created the spells designed to hide him knew exactly who and what to hide him from."

"Hekatah did this," Titian said.

Saetan nodded. "Or Dorothea. Or both. Whoever he is, they made sure he would blend in so there would be no reason to give him a closer look. The only thing they couldn't anticipate was a Harpy catching a trace of his true psychic scent. But why was he lingering here?" He turned to study the doors. "Surreal's room. And Wilhelmina's room."

Surprised by her own discomfort, Surreal cleared her throat. "It could just be a man who hasn't heard that I retired from the Red Moon houses."

Saetan gave her a long, assessing look, then turned to Titian, who shook her head. "I agree," he said cryptically. He knocked sharply on Wilhelmina's door. When he got no answer, he went in. He came out a minute later. "She's in the garden with Dejaal. He'll stay with her."

It took Surreal a moment to connect the name with the young tiger she had frequently seen with Wilhelmina.

"Graysfang is on his way," Saetan said, giving Surreal a hard look. "He's not to leave your side tonight."

It took her another moment to fit the pieces together. She bristled. "Wait just a minute, High Lord. I can take care of myself."

"He's a Warlord," Saetan snapped. "He defends and protects."

"He wears Purple Dusk to my Gray. You can't assume that this other male wears a lighter Jewel than he does."

"I'm assuming nothing. *He defends and protects.*"

Furious, Surreal strode up to Saetan and grabbed two fistfuls of his robe. "He's not fodder," she snarled. "It's not right for him to die when I'm perfectly capable of defending myself."

Dry amusement slowly filled Saetan's eyes. "You will not wound his pride by telling him he isn't capable of protecting you. However, since the Queens share your opinion, it *is* considered acceptable for you to provide the protective shields for both of you and to guard his back."

"Oh." Releasing him, Surreal tried to smooth the wrinkles in his robe that her fists had made. When she noticed Saetan's amusement growing, she gave up and stepped back.

"Will you station guards tonight?" Titian asked.

Saetan thought for a moment, then shook his head. "No. Nothing that obvious tonight. The Ladies in the court will be protected. The rest we'll deal with in the morning." He looked at Surreal. "I'd like you to stay in your room tonight, or the inner garden your room overlooks. No one will be coming at you or Wilhelmina from that direction."

All of Surreal's instincts sharpened as she considered all the ways an assassin could gain access. "Are all these rooms occupied?" she asked thoughtfully. Slip into an empty room, slip through the garden, enter the victim's room through the glass doors that opened onto the garden . . .

"A couple of the guest rooms are empty," Saetan said, "but no one will be coming at you through the garden. Kaelas will be there."

Daemon took one look at Saetan and Titian, stepped into the corridor, and closed Jaenelle's sitting room door. "Lady Titian," he said respectfully, masking his surprise at seeing her. He knew she was demon-dead, but he hadn't expected to see her at the Hall—and he didn't like her tense stance any more than he liked Saetan's controlled neutrality.

"As Steward of the Court, I'm formally requesting that you remain with the Queen tonight," Saetan said quietly. "*All night.*"

Daemon tensed. This evening was the first time since Jaenelle had finished healing his mind that she'd been willing to spend time with him, and he'd hoped playing a few hands of cards would remind her that he was a friend, which was the first step toward her accepting him as her lover. But if he told her he was going to spend the night in her bed, she'd start running from him again. Didn't Saetan understand that?

Yes, he realized as he studied that controlled neutrality, Saetan understood. But the Steward of the Court, while sympathizing with the Consort's hesitation and feelings, felt compelled to dismiss them.

"I'm making this request to all the Consorts and First Escorts," Saetan added.

Daemon nodded as he considered that bit of information. A formal request like that, in this court, was equal to a call to battle. Every Warlord Prince at the Hall would be riding the killing edge that night. "Will Lucivar be with Marian?"

"No," Saetan said, "Prothvar will stay with Marian and Daemonar. Lucivar will . . . tour . . . the Hall tonight."

"Where will Kaelas be?" Daemon asked. Suddenly that feline strength and temper were a comfort.

"Kaelas will be in the garden. It will give him more flexibility."

"Then I'll wish you a good night—and good hunting," Daemon added too softly. "High Lord. Lady."

"Is there a problem?" Jaenelle asked when he returned to the sitting room.

Daemon hesitated but couldn't think of any other way to say it. "The Steward has formally requested that I remain with you tonight."

The flicker of panic in her eyes hurt him, but it was the knife-edged way she focused on the sitting room door that made him wary—especially when that focus shifted to him.

"Is that request being made of all the Consorts and First Escorts?" Witch asked in her midnight voice.

"Yes, Lady, it is."

A long silence. Then Jaenelle wrinkled her nose. "A *formal* request seems a bit much just to get the boyos off the couches tonight."

Daemon suppressed a sigh of relief. She was willing to pretend that that's all the request meant. Most likely, she just wanted a few more hours before admitting that Alexandra or one of her entourage had done something serious that would have to be dealt with.

"Would you like to play another round?" he asked, taking his seat.

She narrowed her eyes. "Whose deal is it?"

He smiled at her. "Mine."

"Why didn't you tell him about the tainted male?" Titian asked.

"I can't count on Daemon's control right now," Saetan replied after a long pause. "A Warlord Prince who's focused on being accepted as a Consort has an extremely volatile temper."

After a moment, Titian shook her head. "Even if everyone else didn't sense the spells Dorothea and Hekatah created, I don't understand why Jaenelle didn't notice them."

"Nor do I. But as I said, Dorothea and Hekatah knew exactly who they had to hide him from," Saetan replied, feeling his heartbeat thicken until he could feel each thump like a blow.

"Even so, Jaenelle always takes a careful look at the people who intend to stay in Kaeleer."

"But she would have no reason to look that closely at

someone who *wasn't* intending to stay, especially if emotional and personal issues were being used as a blind to hide a different purpose."

Titian frowned. "Who else is staying at the Hall?"

"Jaenelle's Chaillot relatives and their companions." He saw his own hatred reflected in Titian's face.

"And you haven't done anything about them?"

"My formal request for execution was denied," Saetan replied, doing his best not to respond to the accusation in her voice. "I'll choke on it, but I'll abide by it. Besides, there will be another time and another place to settle those debts," he added softly.

Titian nodded. "If I slip into their rooms, maybe I can sense something. Then we could quietly take care of the tainted male tonight."

Saetan snarled in frustration. "Except for that bitch Vania, no one has *done* anything yet that justifies an execution." He shook his head. "We've made sure nothing will happen tonight. After breakfast, I'll talk to Jaenelle about getting those . . . *people* . . . out of the Hall and out of Kaeleer."

"I suppose that's best." They walked in silence for a while. "Are *all* of Jaenelle's relatives here?"

"Except for Robert Benedict. He died a few years ago—and was in the Dark Realm for a very brief time."

Titian stopped walking. Saetan turned to face her. She lifted her hand and pressed it lightly against his face.

"And, during that time, did he have a private conversation with the High Lord of Hell?" she asked with malevolent sweetness.

"Yes," Saetan replied too softly, "he did."

CHAPTER
SIX

1 / Kaeleer

Daemon's nerves were raw when he and Jaenelle walked into the dining room the next morning, and the speculative looks from the other males in the First Circle didn't help. The fact that it was Jaenelle's moontime and he couldn't have done more than warm the bed didn't matter. He knew what was expected of a Consort, and he knew the other men were aware that he wasn't fulfilling those duties.

He tried to push those thoughts aside. There were reasons to be alert that day.

Lucivar stood near the sideboard, sipping a mug of coffee, while Khardeen and Aaron filled their plates. Leland and Philip, the only members of Alexandra's entourage who were present, were eating breakfast at one end of the table. Surreal and Karla were at the other end.

A greedy look filled Jaenelle's eyes when she focused on the mug in Lucivar's hand. "Are you going to share that?"

Lucivar bared his teeth in a smile. "No."

She gave him a frigid look but kissed his cheek anyway.

Daemon could have cheerfully killed Lucivar for being given that kiss. It was a grumpy, habitual kiss, but still a kiss—which was more than *he'd* gotten that morning. Since killing Lucivar wasn't an option—at that moment, anyway—he watched Jaenelle select two slices of pear and a spoonful of scrambled eggs.

As she turned away from the sideboard, Lucivar reached over, jabbed a fork into a hunk of steak, and dumped it on her plate. "You need the meat today. Eat it."

She snarled at him. Lucivar just sipped his coffee.

"Long night?" Daemon quietly asked Lucivar.

"I've had longer," Lucivar replied with a smile that turned sharp as he flicked a glance at Philip and Leland, then raised his voice just enough to carry. "What about you, old son? You look like you put in a long night yourself."

"It was interesting," Daemon said cautiously. He wasn't about to admit that he and Jaenelle had played cards until, bleary-eyed, they had fallen into bed for a few hours of restless, broken sleep.

Jaenelle snorted. "There's something a bit sneaky about the positions in variation twenty-seven that give a male so much of an advantage, but I haven't worked it out . . . yet."

Daemon noticed Philip's white-lipped anger—and he noticed the way Khardeen and Aaron snapped to attention.

"You know twenty-seven variations?" Khardeen asked slowly.

Daemon said nothing.

"Yes, he does," Jaenelle grumbled. "And that variation is brilliant. Sneaky, but brilliant." She studied the platter of steaks, selected two more pieces, and headed for the table.

Before Daemon could reach for a plate, Khardeen was holding one arm and Aaron had the other, and they were hustling him out of the dining room.

"We'll get breakfast later," Khary said as he and Aaron led Daemon to the nearest empty room. "First, we need to have a little talk."

"It's not what you think," Daemon said. "It's really nothing."

"Nothing?" Aaron sputtered, while Khary said, "If you've figured out a new variation of 'cradle' that gives a man the advantage, it's your duty as a Brother of the First Circle to share it with the rest of us before the coven figures out how to beat it."

He just stared at them, not sure he had heard them correctly.

Aaron smiled. "Well, what did you *think* Consorts do at night?"

Daemon burst out laughing.

2 / Kaeleer

Osvald knocked on Wilhelmina's door, then stepped back and firmly gripped the carved wooden box with both hands.

It hadn't taken much persuasion to convince Alexandra to keep most of her people in their rooms. It had taken more to convince her to send Leland and Philip down to breakfast in order to give the appearance that everyone else was merely late. With so many absent, no one would be sure exactly who was missing until he was long gone from the Hall.

Assuming, of course, that the spells Dorothea and the Dark Priestess had prepared to cut a "door" in the High Lord's defensive shields actually worked.

No. He wouldn't doubt. The spells that had kept him from being detected were proof enough that Dorothea and the Dark Priestess knew how to deal with the bastard who ruled this place. He would escape with the lesser of the two prizes, true, but that lesser prize, sufficiently squeezed, might be enough bait to in turn capture Jaenelle Angelline.

Everything was in place. The three men Dorothea had arranged to help him were waiting at the bridge. There *was* a Dark Altar beside the Hall, but she had warned him that the detection spells around that Altar would immediately alert the High Lord, and he would never get the Gate open in time to escape. So he would take Wilhelmina to Goth, where Lord Jorval would help him reach another of the Gates.

By this evening, he would be back in Terreille with his prize, and Alexandra and the fools who were with her would still be explaining Wilhelmina's disappearance to the High Lord . . . or dying.

Smiling, Osvald knocked on Wilhelmina's door again. A moment later, impatient, he knocked harder. She was in there. He'd made sure of it this time. What was taking her so long to open a damn door?

It was tempting to use one of the simple compulsion spells Dorothea had prepared for him, but he only had two of them and didn't want to waste one for this. Still, every minute's delay increased the chance of someone noticing him.

He was just about to give in and trigger one of the compulsion spells when the door finally opened. "Good morning, Lady Wilhelmina." Smiling, he lifted the box just enough to draw it to her attention. "Lady Alexandra asked me to bring this to you."

"What is it?" Wilhelmina asked, sounding anything but eager.

"A token of her regard for you—and a gesture of goodwill. She's planning to leave soon and has felt distressed that her concern for you may have been misunderstood. She hopes that, by accepting this little memento, you'll be able to remember her fondly in the days to come."

Wilhelmina still looked wary. "Why didn't she bring it herself?"

Osvald looked at her sadly. "She feared you might refuse the gift and didn't want to face that rejection in person."

"Oh," Wilhelmina said quietly, her wariness slowly changing to sympathy. "I hold no ill feelings toward her."

He held the box out, both to entice and to keep his face as far away from it as possible. When she opened the lid, a drugged mist would burst out of the box. Startled, she would gasp and inhale enough of the highly potent drug to make her sufficiently compliant so that he could get her away from the room and this corridor before forcing the second, liquid dose down her throat.

Inside the room, something thumped to the floor.

That damned striped cat.

Osvald triggered the first compulsion spell and shaped the command. *Step into the corridor and close the door. Step into the corridor and close the door. Step into . . .*

He smiled when, looking slightly confused, Wilhelmina obeyed.

"I was told to report your reaction to the gift," he said, sounding apologetic about putting her to the extra bother.

She stayed close to the door, her hand still gripping the knob.

Cursing silently, he triggered the second compulsion spell. *Step close to the box and raise the lid. Step close to the box . . .*

Moving as if her muscles fought against the effort, Wilhelmina stepped close to the box and slowly lifted the lid.

3 / Kaeleer

With Graysfang beside her, Surreal wandered around one of the inner gardens. The cryptic remarks Jaenelle and Karla had made at breakfast about a new variation intrigued and worried her.

There were plenty of sexual variations that gave the male an advantage, so she didn't think they were talking about *that* . . . unfortunately. Daemon was getting burned by his own sexual energy, and the strain of trying to keep it leashed sufficiently in order not to scare Jaenelle was starting to show. She wasn't sure how much longer he could endure the easy affection Jaenelle gave to the other males in the First Circle before he lashed out. Maybe she should talk to the High Lord . . .

Graysfang snarled. Before she could ask what was wrong, he took off, heading straight for the wall. As he approached, he leaped and climbed air as if he were climbing a steep hill, scrambled over the roof, and was gone.

"Graysfang!" Surreal shouted.

Dejaal is being attacked, he replied. *I'm going to help him.*

Surreal swore viciously as she ran for the nearest door.

"Surreal!"

She spun around.

Falonar strode toward her from the other side of the garden. "Lucivar sent me to find you since you didn't show up for—"

"Can you get me over this roof?" Surreal said with enough fury in her voice to make him check his stride. "Graysfang said Dejaal is under attack, and the son of a bitch took off without me!"

In the two strides it took him to reach her, he made the shift from cautious male to warrior. "Hold on to me," he ordered.

Surreal hesitated a moment, trying to decide what she could hold on to without impeding his wings. She hooked one arm around his neck and snugged the fingers of her other hand under his wide leather belt.

It wasn't until she felt his wings pumping that she wondered if he could carry an extra person's weight. "I'm going to learn to do that air walking so I won't have to be carted around," she growled.

"I don't mind carrying you," Falonar snapped, setting her none too gently on the roof.

Surreal clenched her teeth. One male at a time. And it was the furry gray one who had first dibs on her temper. "Do you see him?" she asked as she scanned the courtyard below.

"No. He could have—"

A blast of Jeweled power came from the next courtyard, followed by a woman's scream.

Falonar launched them off the roof with enough force that Surreal wrapped her legs around one of his to give herself another way to hold on. She gritted her teeth as her body, with appalling timing, expressed its approval of the hard male thigh riding between her legs. Which did nothing for her temper.

"If he gets hurt because he didn't wait for me, I'm going to smack him so hard he'll have to lift his tail to see the world," she snarled.

"Wait here," Falonar said as he looked down into the courtyard.

"Do you like having balls?" Surreal snapped, twisting to look around. But she pulled her fingers out from under his belt so that he wouldn't worry that she'd meant the threat.

She caught her breath and swore. The young tiger, Dejaal, was lying in the courtyard, not moving. A footman writhed in agony. Graysfang was dashing back and forth, not actively engaging in an attack but still holding the attention of the man who had a firm grip on Wilhelmina, who was struggling ineffectively.

She swore again when she recognized the man. Osvald. One of Alexandra's escorts. Mother Night.

"Can you keep your balance?" Falonar asked a moment before he let go and stepped away from her.

At least he asked, Surreal thought as she used Craft to prevent a fast slide off the roof.

Graysfang dashed in low, as if he were trying to hamstring Osvald.

Surreal saw the flash of Osvald's Opal Jewel. She threw a Gray shield around Graysfang, fast enough to prevent him from receiving a killing blast of power but not in time to keep him from being knocked over by the clash of Gray and Opal strength.

Seeing the wolf go down, Wilhelmina screamed and clawed at the hand clamped around her arm. Osvald swung around and hit her with enough force to send her to the ground, stunned. Then he turned to make another attack on Graysfang, who had gotten shakily to his feet.

"Tell the wolf to back off," Falonar said as he called in his Eyrien longbow and nocked an arrow.

Surreal quickly obeyed—and felt relief when Graysfang responded. As kindred howls and roars alerted everyone in the Hall, she could sense the flood of furious male strength coming toward them from all directions. And she sensed the cold feminine power coming in its wake.

Falonar took aim.

"Put it through the bastard," Surreal whispered.

"We don't know what's going on down there," Falonar replied.

Don't we? Surreal thought viciously. *What more do you need to see?*

As Osvald turned back toward Wilhelmina, Falonar loosed the arrow, sending it through the man's left knee.

Osvald went down, screaming.

Grabbing Surreal's left arm, Falonar dropped them off the roof—a jump barely slowed by his spread wings.

"Guard the woman," Falonar said as he ran toward Osvald, the Eyrien bow now replaced by a bladed stick.

"I can—"

"Do as you're told."

No time to argue. Calling in her meanest knife, Surreal ran toward Wilhelmina. She saw Osvald grasp Wilhelmina's ankle with his left hand and cursed his cleverness. Maybe someone else would know how to do it, but as long as he had physical contact with Wilhelmina, she couldn't throw a protective shield around the young woman. Then she saw sunlight flash on the short knife in his right hand—and knew by the mixture of rage and triumph on his face that the poison on that knife would be quick and lethal.

Another flash in the sunlight. As Osvald's hand arced down to drive the knife into Wilhelmina's leg, Falonar sliced through the wristbones as easily as if they were soft butter, then turned the blade of his stick in order to catch the severed hand and the knife it still held and flip it away from Wilhelmina.

The bladed stick flashed down again, severing the hand that grasped Wilhelmina's ankle.

A moment later, Surreal reached Wilhelmina—and Lucivar and most of the First Circle males poured into the courtyard. So did Karla and Gabrielle.

So did Alexandra and her entourage.

It didn't turn out quite like you'd planned, did it? Surreal thought as she watched Alexandra scan the courtyard and turn sickly pale. Vanishing her knife, she placed one hand on Wilhelmina's back, the other hand on Graysfang as soon as he wobbled up to her, and created a Gray shield around the three of them. It probably wasn't necessary, but there was no reason to take chances. She looked at Falonar, who had positioned himself so that, the next time, the bladed stick would come down on the bastard's neck. She put a shield around him, too. She felt his surprise and pleasure when her shield settled around him—and wondered why he was afraid.

Gabrielle rushed over to help the footman while Karla, without actually touching Osvald, used healing Craft to seal the severed blood vessels.

"What's going on here?" Alexandra demanded, the sharp edge in her voice sounding more frightened than angry. "Why are you attacking one of my escorts?"

"Did you send him?" Lucivar asked, an odd note in his voice.

"I sent him to bring a gift to Wilhelmina," Alexandra said.

There was something queer and bitter about Lucivar's laugh. "And the bastard delivered it, didn't he?"

"When I went to deliver the gift, Lady Wilhelmina wasn't feeling well," Osvald whimpered. "I offered to walk with her so that she could get some fresh air. Then that *creature* attacked us."

Lucivar looked at Osvald, then at Falonar. "If that bastard says anything else, cut his tongue out."

Falonar looked shocked, but nodded.

"How dare you?" Alexandra said. "You're so quick to make demands to *me* about controlling my court, yet you allow this—"

"Shut up," Lucivar snapped. "Things are bad enough right now. Don't make it worse."

Surreal gave Lucivar a sharp look. What was going on here?

Shivering, Graysfang moved closer to her. *Queen's rage is bad, Surreal. Males fear Queen's rage. Even Kaelas.*

Following the wolf's gaze, Surreal saw the huge white cat standing on the roof next to a tiger. That was Kaelas? *Mother Night!*

Who's the tiger? she asked.

That is Jaal. He is Dejaal's sire.

Surreal swallowed hard. The tiger was dwarfed by Kaelas, but he was still twice as large as the young tiger lying in the courtyard. *Dejaal is dead, isn't he?*

He has returned to the Darkness, Graysfang said sadly.

How were they going to explain this to Jaenelle?

As if the thought had conjured the woman, Jaenelle walked into the courtyard, flanked by Daemon and Saetan.

Surreal might have taken some comfort in their presence if the High Lord's face hadn't turned gray at the sight of Dejaal's body.

Alexandra started to speak, but before she could make a sound, her hands flew up to her throat and her eyes became wide and terrified.

Surreal wasn't sure which one of the males had acted, but she would have bet it was Daemon who had created the phantom hand that was now choking Alexandra into silence.

Everyone moved out of the way as Jaenelle walked over and knelt beside Dejaal. The hand that caressed the fur was gentle and loving, but the eyes that finally looked up and focused on Wilhelmina . . .

What Surreal saw in those sapphire eyes went so far beyond cold rage there were no words for it.

Yes, there were, she realized as Graysfang whimpered softly. *This* was what the wolf had meant by Queen's rage.

Hell's fire, Mother Night, and may the Darkness be merciful.

She said the only thing she could think of, the only thing that, she hoped, would release her from those eyes. "She's alive."

Jaenelle looked at Karla, who bowed formally before walking over to examine Wilhelmina.

"You said the right thing," Karla whispered to Surreal as she examined Wilhelmina. Then she swore and added, "Whatever else you do, follow Protocol to the letter." Taking a deep breath, she stood up and faced Jaenelle. "Wilhelmina has some bruises from the struggle—and she's been heavily drugged."

"Can you counteract it?" Jaenelle asked too calmly.

"I need more time to determine the exact nature of the drug that was used," Karla answered quietly. "But I'm sensing nothing that will cause permanent harm. My recommendation is closely supervised isolation and rest. With your permission, I'll take her to her room now and look after her."

"Thank you, Sister."

Responding to Karla's slight gesture, her cousin, Morton, picked up Wilhelmina and followed Karla out of the courtyard.

Surreal remained crouched beside Graysfang, unwilling to make a movement that would draw those sapphire eyes back in her direction.

"What about me?" Osvald whimpered.

Falonar glanced at Lucivar, silently asking if he should carry out his order and cut out the man's tongue. Lucivar shook his head, the barest of movements.

Jaenelle crossed the courtyard, looked down at Osvald, and smiled. "I'm going to take care of you personally."

Lucivar leaped forward. "Lady, with respect, Dejaal was our Brother, and it's the males' right—"

Jaenelle silenced him by simply raising her hand. For a moment, she just stood there, but Surreal felt the flick of power that burst from her as a quickly expanding psychic probe—and realized that no one wearing a Jewel lighter than the Gray would have sensed anything at all.

"There are three men waiting by the bridge that leads to Halaway," Jaenelle said. A terrible glitter filled her eyes as she looked at Osvald. "Three strangers. I don't care what you do with them."

Osvald floated to an upright position. When Jaenelle turned and walked out of the courtyard, he floated after her, protesting his innocence.

"Kalush and Morghann are coming," Gabrielle said, her eyes filling with tears. "We'll stay with Dejaal until . . ."

Pointing at Alexandra, Lucivar looked at Falonar. "You and Surreal escort these . . . people . . . to their rooms." He paused. "If *any* of them give you any trouble, kill them."

"My pleasure," Surreal said. Falonar just nodded.

Lucivar left the courtyard, followed by the other Warlord Princes in the First Circle. When Daemon turned to follow them, Saetan said, "No. You stay with me."

Quickly rounding up her prisoners, Surreal hurried them—and Falonar and Graysfang—out of the courtyard. She didn't know what the High Lord had in mind, but she'd rather not be around while they discussed it.

Daemon stepped aside as Morghann and Kalush rushed into the courtyard.

"Let's get out of here," Saetan said, his voice rough with suppressed grief—and something that might have been fear.

It was that fear—and his concern for the man—that made Daemon follow his father. But even those things weren't sufficient for him to swallow his own anger.

As they slowly headed away from the courtyard, Daemon said, "I may not have Lucivar's talent with weapons, but I can deal with an enemy quite effectively."

Saetan stopped walking. "Remember who you're talking to, Prince. If anyone can appreciate how effective you are as a predator, it's me."

"Then why did you stop me?"

"Lucivar doesn't need your help to handle whoever is waiting at the bridge for that bastard—especially not with the males who went with him. But I *do* need you. Right now, I need every drop of strength and every grain of skill you've got in order to handle Jaenelle. Hell's fire, Daemon. Don't you realize what happened here?"

With enormous effort, Daemon held on to his temper. "Alexandra played the bitch and arranged to have her own granddaughter abducted."

Saetan slowly shook his head. "Alexandra was working with Dorothea and Hekatah in order to abduct her own granddaughter."

Daemon absorbed the impact of the words—and realized

what might happen once Jaenelle learned *that.* "Mother Night."

"And may the Darkness be merciful," Saetan added. "We have an enraged Queen who, by now, has gone so deep into the abyss we have no chance of reaching her that way—and no way at all to deflect whatever she might unleash in her present emotional state."

"What can I do?" Daemon asked, knowing with dread certainty where the conversation was leading.

"It's what *we* can do as Steward and Consort, what Protocol gives us the *right* to do in situations like this."

"Protocol didn't take into account dealing with a Queen who's twice as strong as a Black-Jeweled Warlord Prince!"

Saetan's hand shook a little as he smoothed his hair back. "More like six times our combined strength."

"What?" Daemon said weakly. He braced a hand against the wall.

"There's no real way to measure Jaenelle's strength. But considering the number of Birthright Black Jewels that were transformed into Ebony when she made the Offering to the Darkness, my best guess is that, at her full strength, she's six times more powerful than our full strength combined."

"Mother Night." Daemon concentrated on breathing for a minute. "Just when were you going to mention this to me? Or weren't you?"

Saetan winced. "I wanted you to be . . . comfortable . . . with each other before I told you. But now—"

A blast of power shook the Hall, tossing them to the floor.

Daemon felt as if he were desperately holding on to a crumbling bank inches from a raging flood that would not only sweep him away but crush him in the process.

He felt Saetan grab him, dig in, hold on.

That rush of power vanished as quickly as it had struck—and that scared him more than the blast. For Jaenelle to unleash and reabsorb that much power that quickly . . .

"Jaenelle," Daemon said, springing to his feet. He sent out a psychic probe, a quick, casting search for her, and brushed against a spot in the Hall that was burning cold. Despite his pulling back quickly, the lancing pain almost drove him to his knees. And that drove him forward.

"Daemon, no!" Saetan said, struggling to get to his feet.

Daemon ran through the corridors. He didn't need to search anymore. The corridors got colder and colder the closer he got to the room where she had unleashed that power.

"Daemon!"

He heard Saetan running to catch up to him, but by then he'd reached the door to the room. Using Craft, he opened the door, then stepped into the room.

The cold had a jagged edge that was physically painful, but he barely noticed it because, as he looked around, he couldn't quite understand what he was seeing. It wasn't until he realized that the odd red speckles on the windows were frozen drops of blood that his mind identified the rest . . .

"Daemon."

. . . and he understood what Lucivar had been telling him about Jaenelle's forced marriage. *She splattered him all over the room.*

"*Daemon.*"

He heard the plea in Saetan's voice, but couldn't respond to it. A peculiar numbness had settled over his emotions . . . and without being able to feel, he could think.

He knew why Saetan hadn't wanted him to see this room. By the very nature of his duties, a Consort couldn't be inhibited when dealing with his Queen. A Consort knowingly and willingly made himself physically vulnerable to her in ways no other male in the court had to. A Consort who feared his Queen couldn't function in the bed.

But he'd seen this side of her before. Oh, it had been only a faint glimpse, but he'd known that this was another facet of Witch.

And this was the side of her that would be drawn to the surface by intense arousal as well as intense rage. Could he live with that? Could he lead the sexual dance once he brought out this side of her?

The heat of the sexual hunger inside him, the driving need to mate with Witch that suddenly engulfed him, burned away the emotional numbness. And left in its place a chilling approval of what he saw.

He stepped out of the room and closed the door.

"Daemon," Saetan said softly, watching him.

Daemon smiled. "It's a pity about the wallpaper. It was a lovely design."

4 / Kaeleer

"Well," Surreal said as she pushed her hair away from her face, "I don't think any of the 'guests' are going to be eager to leave their rooms right now, do you?"

"No," Falonar replied, sounding a bit queasy, "I don't."

"Yeah." Surreal leaned against the wall and closed her eyes. "Shit."

"Were you hurt by . . . *that*?" Falonar asked, meaning the blast of power that had shaken the Hall. He briefly touched her shoulder before stepping back.

Surreal shook her head. *Hurt? No. Scared shitless? Oh, yes.*

But the people who lived with Jaenelle *didn't* live in constant fear. In fact, thinking about how Karla and Lucivar had acted in the courtyard, she would have called their behavior cautious rather than fearful—and that caution wasn't usually in evidence either.

Putting those thoughts aside for the moment, she scowled at Falonar and decided to tackle something easier—like the arrogant way he had been tossing out orders after they reached the courtyard. "I could have handled that bastard."

Falonar looked insulted. "It's a male's right to defend and protect."

Surreal bared her teeth. "I've heard that song before, and—"

"Then you should heed that song, Lady—and respect it."

"Why? Because poor little me isn't capable of handling myself in a fight?" she said with venom-laced sweetness.

"Because you're deadlier," he snarled. He paced a few steps away from her, swore, paced back. "*That's* why males defend, Lady Surreal. Because you females are deadlier when you're roused—and you're merciless when you're riding the killing edge. At least if I go down first in a fight, I don't have to deal with you afterward."

Not sure if she'd just been complimented or insulted, Surreal said nothing. She was about to concede that he *might* have a point when he growled at her, "You've picked a lousy time to play the bitch. It's going to be hard enough facing Yaslana without having to dance with you right now."

Now that *was* an insult. "Since you feel like that, sugar, I'll just get out of your way." She pushed away from the wall.

Falonar reached out, touched her arm. "Surreal . . . You were right. I should have killed that bastard. Now I'll have to accept the consequences for that error." He hesitated, and added quietly, "He could have killed you or Lady Benedict with that poisoned knife."

She shrugged. "You couldn't have known about the knife, and he didn't kill either one of us, so—"

"What difference does that make?" Falonar said harshly. "My error gave him the chance."

Surreal studied him. "You think you're going to be punished?"

"That's a certainty. The only question is how severe it will be."

"Well, I have a few things to say about that. When Lucivar gets around to discussing this—"

"There is no discussion," Falonar snapped. "He's the Warlord Prince of Ebon Rih. I serve him. He'll do as he pleases." He looked away. "I'd rather be tied to the whipping posts than be sent back to Terreille."

"There's no reason for you to be punished at all!"

Falonar smiled grimly. "That's the way it is, Lady Surreal."

We'll just see about that, Surreal thought.

5 / Kaeleer

Daemon watched Saetan pour a large brandy. "Can you drink that?" he asked, keeping his voice mildly curious.

"It gives me vicious headaches," Saetan replied, pouring a second glass for Daemon. "But I doubt it's going to make the one I've already got any worse, so . . ." He raised his glass in a salute, then swallowed half the brandy. "Dejaal was Prince Jaal's son."

Mentioning the tiger Warlord Prince seemed an abrupt change of subject. "Lucivar found the men?"

"And got the information we wanted before they were executed."

Daemon studied his father. Something wasn't quite right here. Since he didn't know what questions to ask, he voiced his own concern. "Jaenelle isn't here, is she?"

Saetan shook his head. "She's gone to Ebon Askavi—and has asked to be left alone for the time being."

"Are you going to abide by her wishes?" Daemon asked carefully.

Saetan's look was steady and far too knowing. "*We* are going to abide by her wishes. If she needs to remain cold in order to make the decisions that have to be made, forcing her to feel before she's ready would be cruel."

Daemon nodded. He didn't like it, but he could accept it. His thoughts went back to the three men who had been waiting to help Osvald abduct Wilhelmina. "Those men served Hekatah and Dorothea?"

"They worked for them."

He felt Saetan retreat, so he pressed. "Lucivar executed the men?" It wouldn't have been Lucivar's first kill, so *that* couldn't be bothering Saetan. Was there something different about a formal execution?

"The other males in the First Circle withdrew their right to collect any part of the debt that was owed them for the death of a Brother," Saetan said.

"What does that mean?" Daemon asked slowly.

Saetan hesitated, then finished the brandy before replying. "It means they gave those men to Jaal . . . and to Kaelas."

6 / Kaeleer

Fuming silently, Surreal glared at the four men in the High Lord's study. She had snarled her way into this little discussion, only to be bluntly told that they would tolerate her presence as long as she didn't interfere. Her opinion wasn't requested or required.

If it had been any other men, she would have given them her opinion of *that*, probably delivered on the end of her stiletto. But Lucivar looked like he'd been pushed hard enough and wouldn't hesitate to throw her out—*through* the door. And Saetan and Andulvar Yaslana weren't the kind of men who would allow anyone to step on their authority as Steward and Master of the Guard.

What really bit her was that Falonar hadn't looked at her once since she'd managed to win enough of the argument to stay in the room. She would have thought that he'd be grateful to have someone speak in his defense. But he . . .

Well, that was fine. That was *just fine*. She didn't need to be there, wasting her time on a thick-skinned, hard-headed male who didn't want her there in the first place.

She looked at Lucivar at that moment, saw the sharp amusement in his gold eyes, and knew that, now, if she tried to leave, she would be ordered to stay. So instead of cursing herself for her own stubbornness, she cursed Lucivar instead. And seeing his amusement deepen, realized he knew it—the prick.

Saetan leaned against his blackwood desk and crossed his arms. "Prince Falonar, please explain your actions this morning."

His voice sounded polite, only mildly curious. Surreal wondered if that was a bad sign.

Falonar responded. In Surreal's opinion, the dry recitation of actions fell far short of an explanation, but the other men didn't seem to notice that.

When Falonar finished speaking, Saetan looked at Andulvar and Lucivar, then back at Falonar. "You erred on the side of caution," Saetan said quietly. "That's understandable—and, in a Warlord Prince, also unacceptable. You can't afford the luxury of caution."

Falonar swallowed hard. "Yes, sir."

"You do understand that discipline is required?"

"Yes, sir."

Saetan nodded, appearing satisfied. He looked at Lucivar. "This is your decision."

Falonar turned to face Lucivar.

Lucivar studied him for a moment. "Five days of extra guard duty, beginning tomorrow."

Instead of looking relieved, Falonar looked as if he'd been slapped.

"Anything else we need to discuss?" Saetan asked.

Lucivar looked at her, then at Saetan, who, after a pause, dipped his head in the barest of nods.

Lucivar opened the study door and waited.

After bowing to Saetan and Andulvar, Falonar walked out. Since it seemed the proper thing to do, Surreal also bowed to the two men, then followed Falonar out of the study so fast she stepped on his heels.

Swearing, he lengthened his stride, finally stopping when he reached the center of the great hall.

Surreal caught up to him. "Well, that wasn't—" The dislike and anger in his face as he watched Lucivar approach them stopped her.

"Five days of extra guard duty is an insult," Falonar said.

Surreal grabbed two fistfuls of her long tunic to keep from belting him. Fool. Idiot. He should be grateful it wasn't worse.

"It's not an insult," Lucivar replied mildly. "It's fair. You made a mistake, Falonar. Some reparation has to be made for it. You acted, but you also hamstrung yourself by being too cautious."

"I realize what my caution could have cost."

"Yes, you do. Which is why the discipline is fair." Lucivar's mouth curved in a lazy, arrogant smile. "Don't worry about it. You'll stand extra guard duty plenty more times before you've been here a year. I certainly did."

Falonar stared at him. "You?"

The smile sharpened. "Hard to believe that I would err on the side of caution, isn't it? But I wanted to stay in Kaeleer, and I wanted to serve my Queen, so I kept my temper leashed as much as possible—for me. And ended up in that study, facing those two, more times than I care to count." Lucivar paused. "This is Kaeleer. Here, a Warlord Prince's temper is considered an asset to a court."

Falonar took a moment to digest this. Then, courteously, "Extra guard duty doesn't seem like much when a witch could have died."

"Well, there is another part to your . . . discipline," Lucivar said. He tipped his head toward Surreal. "You get to cope with her until sunrise. Since she looks like she's going to break her teeth unless she gets to yell at a male, it might as well be you." The smile got even sharper. "Of course, you could always offer to warm her bed and see if that buys you any leniency."

Falonar choked. Surreal made a sound like a teakettle ready to boil over.

"You consider spending a night with me a form of *discipline*?" Surreal shouted. "You prick. You . . . *I* would call it a reward!"

Lucivar shrugged. "Please yourself. Just keep in mind that, if you both decide to extend this 'discipline' past tonight, you have to have formal permission from the Steward of the Court. He agreed to overlook that formality until sunrise, but not after that. And this is an area where it isn't wise to push Saetan's temper."

After he left them, Surreal and Falonar eyed each other.

"It would seem that I didn't keep my . . . interest . . . in being with you as . . . restrained . . . as I had thought since Lucivar noticed it," Falonar said.

Or the High Lord did, Surreal thought. As family patriarch and sexual chaperon, she didn't think much got past that man.

"So," Falonar said warily. "Are you going to yell at me?"

Surreal smiled at him. "Well, sugar, I may not yell *at* you. With the right incentive, I may just yell."

CHAPTER SEVEN

1 / Kaeleer

Lord Jorval settled into a chair in Kartane SaDiablo's sitting room. "Your meeting with the Healer has been delayed."

"Why?" Kartane said sharply. "I had thought it was all arranged."

"It was," Jorval soothed. "But there was an . . . incident . . . at the Healer's residence, so it will be a few more days before she can meet with you."

"You could insist," Kartane said. "Perhaps she doesn't realize how important I—"

"It would do no good to insist," Jorval interrupted. "When she comes here, you want her attention on you, not on some domestic trivia."

"Then I suppose I have no choice but to wait."

Jorval rose. "No choice at all."

An incident has occurred that requires postponing . . .

An incident, Jorval thought as he walked back to his own home. That was how the High Lord had so carefully, so courteously phrased it. Since the men who had been in Halaway to assist the escort had suddenly disappeared, and there was no word from or sign of the escort, he had a good idea what sort of "incident" was delaying Jaenelle Angelline's trip to Little Terreille.

Which meant he had to inform the Dark Priestess that, in all probability, Alexandra was no longer a useful tool.

Hekatah wouldn't be pleased about that, would probably

come to Little Terreille in a foul temper—which she would take out on him.

But, perhaps, he could redirect that temper. Perhaps now would be a good time to take care of that other little problem.

Reaching his home, he rushed into his study and penned a quick note to Lord Magstrom.

2 / Kaeleer

"Where is my escort?" Alexandra demanded as soon as she took a seat in the High Lord's study. After being confined for two days, she felt relieved to be out of her room, but she felt no relief at being in *this* room—or being with *him.*

Saetan leaned back in his chair and steepled his fingers, resting the long, black-tinted nails against his chin. His gold eyes looked sleepy—just as they had when he'd first seen her.

Conscious of the chill in the room, she pulled her shawl more tightly around herself.

"It's interesting that Osvald is the first person you ask about," Saetan said too mildly.

"Who *should* I have asked about?" Alexandra snapped, fear making her voice sharp.

"Your granddaughter, Wilhelmina. She is recovering from the drugs that bastard gave her. There will be no permanent damage."

"Of course there's no damage. He only gave her a mild sedative."

"What he gave her was a great deal more than a *mild* sedative, Lady," Saetan replied, his own voice turning sharp.

Alexandra hesitated. He was lying. Of course he was lying.

Saetan looked at her, curious. "I keep wondering what sort of payment Dorothea and Hekatah offered you that was worth your granddaughter's life."

She shot out of the chair. "You're insulting!"

"Am I?" he replied, his voice returning to that infuriating—and frightening—mildness.

"I wasn't selling Wilhelmina to Dorothea, I was just trying to get her away from *you!*"

A queer look came over his face. "Yes, that always seems sufficient justification, doesn't it? Just get the child away from me and be damned to what happens to the child. A lifetime of pain, of humiliation and torture, is certainly better than being with me."

Alexandra settled back in the chair and watched him. He had turned inward, following some private thought—and she didn't think he was talking about Wilhelmina anymore.

"What did you think was going to happen to Wilhelmina?" he asked.

"Osvald was going to get her out of Kaeleer, and then we would take her home."

As Saetan studied her, a deep sadness filled his eyes. "Not a payment then," he said softly, "but a bargaining chip."

"What are you talking about?"

"How were you planning to get Wilhelmina out of Hayll?"

Alexandra stared at him. "She wasn't going to Hayll."

"Yes, she was. Those were the orders, Alexandra. Wilhelmina would have been Dorothea's 'guest' for as long as you were willing to make concessions. How many concessions could you have made to Hayll before your people choked on them and refused to accept you as their Queen any longer? What could you have bargained with then to keep her safe?"

"No," Alexandra said. "*No.* Dorothea agreed to help me because—" Because Dorothea was preparing to go to war with this man and had wanted Jaenelle's alleged dark power away from his control. But she couldn't let him know that. "Wilhelmina wasn't a bargaining chip." But wouldn't Jaenelle have become exactly that? A bargaining chip in the game of war? That was different. Jaenelle was obviously already permanently warped by the High Lord's attentions, and if *Jaenelle* had ended up as Dorothea's "guest" . . .

With brutal honesty, Alexandra knew that she would never have made any concessions to Hayll to ensure Jaenelle's well-being. She would have told her court about a family sacrifice made for the good of her people. And in truth, she wouldn't have felt more than a twinge of guilt over that sacrifice. Always such a difficult child, always . . .

"Wilhelmina wasn't a bargaining chip," she said again lamely.

Saetan snorted softly. "Think what you choose."

That casual dismissal, as if it no longer mattered, disturbed her. "What happened to Osvald? Were his wounds at least treated?"

Something queer filled Saetan's eyes. "He was executed. So were the three men who had been waiting for him."

Alexandra stared at him. "What right do you have—"

"He tried to abduct one member of the court and killed another. Did you really expect us to just sit back and swallow that?"

"He wasn't abducting her!" Alexandra shouted. "He was helping her leave this place. That animal attacked him. He had to defend himself."

"He was taking her against her will. That's abduction."

"He was carrying out the wishes of her family."

"She's a grown woman," Saetan snarled. "You have no right to make decisions on her behalf."

"She's mentally fragile. She doesn't have the ability to make—"

"Is that how you deal with anyone who doesn't agree with you?" Saetan's voice rose to a roar. "You declare them mentally incompetent so you can justify locking them away in a place that revels in violating and torturing them?"

"*How dare you!*"

"Knowing what I know about Briarwood, I dare a great deal."

The air whooshed out of her lungs. His eyes were filled with the hatred he no longer bothered to mask.

With effort, she gathered her strength and sat up straight to face him. "I am a Queen—"

"You're a naive, snotty little bitch," Saetan replied in a singsong croon that made the words feel like a violent—and violating—caress. "Live a long life, Alexandra. Live a long life and burn yourself out at the end of it so that you return straight to the Darkness. If you don't, if you end up making the transition to demon-dead, I'll be waiting for you."

It took her a moment to understand him. The High Lord *of Hell.*

"Robert Benedict made the transition," Saetan crooned, "and he paid his part of the debt that is owed to me for what was done to the daughter of my soul."

"I owe you nothing." Alexandra tried to sound firm, but she couldn't stop her voice from shaking.

Saetan smiled a gentle, terrible smile.

She had to get out of there, had to get away from him. "Since this is supposed to be a court, I think it's time I talked to this mysterious Queen of yours. The *real Queen.* In fact, I demand to talk to her."

He went absolutely still. "It seems she wants to talk to you, too," he said in an odd voice. "You've been summoned to Ebon Askavi to stand before the Dark Throne."

3 / Kaeleer

With her heart pounding in her throat, Alexandra followed the High Lord down the dark stone stairs. The huge double doors at the bottom of the stairs swung open silently, revealing intense darkness.

She had protested when she had learned that Leland, Philip, and the rest of her entourage had also been summoned to the Keep. Not that it had made any difference. No one had made the slightest indication that they had even heard her protests, let alone might comply with them.

She had also protested when Daemon and Lucivar had joined the High Lord as "escorts." Now she felt pathetically grateful for the male strength that was guarding her. She had found the Hall frightening, but compared to the Keep, the Hall was just a pleasant manor house.

As Saetan walked forward, torches began to light until only the back of the room was still too dark to see at all.

Another torch lit. She stared at the huge dragon head coming out of the back wall. Its silver-gold scales gleamed. Its eyes were as dark as midnight. On a dais beside the head was a simple blackwood chair. The woman who sat in it was still too much in shadow for Alexandra to make out more than the shape.

So this was the Queen of Ebon Askavi.

The light in the room shifted somehow, softly illuminating the unicorn's horn that was part of the scepter the woman held in her hands.

As Alexandra stared at the rings on those hands, a shiver of fear ran down her spine. At first glance, she would have said the rings held pieces of a Black Jewel, but the Jewels in those rings felt darker than the Black. Which was impossible—wasn't it?

The light continued to grow, and as it grew, the power in the room swelled. The woman's face was still in shadow, but now Alexandra could make out the black gown and another Black-but-not-Black Jewel that was set in a necklace that looked like a spiderweb of gold and silver threads.

The light grew. Alexandra looked up and found herself staring into Jaenelle's frozen sapphire eyes.

Long seconds passed before those eyes shifted to look at Leland and Philip, Vania and Nyselle, and the Consorts and escorts who had come with them.

Released from that frozen stare, Alexandra pressed a hand to her stomach, desperately trying not to double over. In this formal setting, she finally understood what Jaenelle had said at their first meeting at the Hall. *The difference is that when the dream appeared, he recognized it.*

The dark power that flowed from Jaenelle could have kept Chaillot free of Dorothea's influence. But how could she have been expected to recognize *this* in a difficult, eccentric *child*?

. . . he recognized it.

She dared a quick glance at Daemon. He had recognized it, too. Had recognized it and . . .

But wasn't that what Dorothea had said? The Sadist and the High Lord had recognized the potential of all that dark power and had set out to seduce and shape it. It was clear now why Dorothea had wanted control of Jaenelle, but that didn't alter the possible truth of what she had said about Daemon and the High Lord.

The thoughts kept spinning, twisting—until those sapphire eyes pinned her again.

"You conspired with Dorothea SaDiablo and Hekatah SaDiablo, who are known enemies, with the intent of handing over to them a member of my court, my sister." The voice, while quiet, filled the immense room. "In attempting to carry out that plan, you killed another member of my court, a young Warlord Prince."

Leland stirred, shrugging off Philip's attempt to restrain her. "It was just an animal."

Something vicious and terrible filled Jaenelle's face. "He was Blood . . . and he was a Brother. His life was worth as much as yours."

"I didn't kill him," Alexandra said, her voice muted.

Underneath the ice in those sapphire eyes was deadly rage bordering on madness. "You didn't strike the killing blow," Jaenelle agreed. "Because of that, I have decided not to execute you."

Alexandra would have fallen if Philip hadn't reached out to steady her. *Execute her?*

"However," Jaenelle continued, "everything has a price, and a price will be paid for Dejaal's life."

Desperation began to well up in Alexandra. "There is no law against murder."

"No, there isn't," Jaenelle replied too softly. "But a Queen can demand a price for the life that was lost."

Vania or Nyselle whimpered. She wasn't sure which one.

"You are no longer welcome in Kaeleer. You will never again be welcome in Kaeleer. If any of you return for any reason, you will be executed. There will be no reprieve."

"Can she do that?" Nyselle whispered.

Jaenelle's eyes flicked to the Province Queens before returning to Alexandra. "I am the Queen. My will is the law."

And no one, Alexandra realized, *no one* would defy that will.

"You will be taken to Cassandra's Altar and sent back through that Gate to Terreille," Jaenelle said. "High Lord, you will see to the arrangements."

"It will be my pleasure, Lady," Saetan replied solemnly.

"You're dismissed." The scepter swung until the unicorn's horn pointed right at Alexandra's breast. "Except you."

Leland made a wordless protest, but didn't argue when Philip, looking pale and sick, took her arm and led her from the room. The other members of the entourage hurried after them, followed more slowly by Saetan, Daemon, and Lucivar.

When the double doors had closed and they were the

only people left in the room, Jaenelle lowered the scepter. "You should have gone when I first told you to. Now . . ."

It took Alexandra a minute to speak. "And now?"

Jaenelle didn't answer.

Alexandra swayed, then took a half step to catch her balance as the room began to spiral and everything went dark.

What in the name of Hell just happened? Alexandra wondered as she caught her balance. Then she looked around.

She stood alone in the center of a large stone circle. The floor was perfectly smooth. Surrounding the circle was a solid wall of sharp, jagged rock that soared high above her head. Beyond that wall . . .

She felt the enormous pressure pushing against those walls, as if something was trying to break in and crush this space.

Where . . . ?

We're deep in the abyss, said a midnight voice.

Alexandra turned toward Jaenelle's voice—and stared at the creature who now stood a few feet away. Stared at the slender, naked human body; at the human legs that ended in delicate hooves; at the human hands that had unsheathed claws instead of fingernails; at the delicately pointed ears; at the gold mane that wasn't quite hair and wasn't quite fur; at the tiny spiral horn in the middle of its forehead; at the frozen sapphire eyes.

What are you? Alexandra whispered.

I am dreams made flesh, the other answered. *I am Witch.*

Jaenelle's voice. Jaenelle's strange eyes. But . . .

Alexandra backed away. No. *No.* *You're* what's inside . . . *

She couldn't say it. Revulsion choked her. This is what her daughter Leland had birthed? *This?*

What did you do with my granddaughter? Alexandra demanded.

I did nothing to her.

You must have! What did you do? Devour the spirit in order to use the flesh?

If you mean the husk you call Jaenelle, that flesh was always mine. I was born within that skin.

*Never! *Never!* You couldn't have come from Leland.*

Why? Witch asked.

Because you're monstrous.

A painful silence. Then Witch said coldly, *I am what I am.*

And whatever that is, it didn't come from my daughter. It didn't come from me.

Your dreams—

NO! THERE IS NO PART OF ME IN YOU!

Another long silence. Beyond the wall of rocks, it sounded like a fierce storm was gathering.

Have you anything else to say? Witch asked quietly.

*I will never have anything to say to *you,** Alexandra replied.

Very well.

The rock walls vanished. The power in the abyss rushed in to fill the empty space—and tried to fill the vessel inside that space.

Alexandra felt that rushing flood of power start to crush her, then felt another source of dark power balance and control that flood, to keep her mind from shattering. Something inside her snapped and, for a fleeting second, she felt intense pain and agonizing grief.

And then she felt nothing at all.

Alexandra woke slowly. She was lying in a bed, covered up and comfortably warm, but it only took a moment for her to realize something was wrong. Her head had an odd stuffed-with-wool feeling, and her body ached as if she had a fever.

She opened her eyes, saw Saetan sitting in a chair near the bed, and said hoarsely, "I don't want you."

"I don't want you either," he replied dryly as he reached for a mug sitting on the bedside table. "Here. This will help clear your head."

With a grunt, she propped herself up on one elbow—and saw her Opal Jewels, the pendant and ring, lying on the table. They were empty, completely drained of the reservoir of stored power.

Instinctively, desperately, she turned inward, reaching for the depth of her Opal strength. She couldn't even reach the depth of the White. She was sealed off from the abyss, and her mind felt as if it had been encased in stone.

"You still have basic Craft," Saetan said quietly.

Alexandra stared at him in horror. "Basic Craft?"

"Yes."

She continued to stare as she remembered that crushing flood of power and the fleeting moment of pain. "She broke me," Alexandra whispered. "That bitch *broke me.*"

"Take care what you say about my Queen," Saetan snarled.

"What are you going to do?" she snapped. "Rip my tongue out?"

He didn't have to answer. She saw it in his eyes.

"Drink this," he said too quietly as he handed her the mug.

Not daring to do otherwise, she drank the brew and handed the mug back to him.

"I'm not even a witch anymore," she said as tears filled her eyes.

"A witch is still a witch, even if she's broken and can no longer wear the Jewels. A Queen is still a Queen."

Alexandra laughed bitterly. "Oh, that's so easy to say, isn't it? What kind of Queen can I be? Do you really think I can hold a court around me?"

"Other Queens have. Psychic strength is only one factor that attracts strong males and entices them to serve. You don't need that kind of strength if you have the use of theirs."

"And do you think I can hold on to a strong-enough court to remain the Queen of Chaillot?"

"No," Saetan replied quietly after a long pause. "But that has nothing to do with your ability to wear Jewels."

She choked on the insult, not daring to do anything else. "Do you realize what's going to happen to Chaillot now?"

"Your people will, in all probability, choose another Queen."

"There *isn't* another Queen strong enough to be accepted as the Territory Queen. That's why—" —*I still rule.* No, she couldn't say that to him.

She pushed herself into a sitting position, then waited for her head to clear. That odd, muffled feeling would go away eventually, but the sense of loss *never* would. The bitch who had masqueraded as her granddaughter had done this to her. "She's monstrous," she muttered.

"She is the living myth, dreams made flesh," Saetan said coldly.

"Well, she wasn't *my* dream," Alexandra snapped. "How that repulsive, distorted creature could be *anyone's* dream—"

"Don't cross that line again, Alexandra," Saetan warned.

Hearing the edge in his voice, she hunched to make herself smaller. She could grit her teeth and hold her tongue because she had no choice, but she couldn't stop thinking about that creature. It had lived in her house. She shuddered. *Every year at Winsol, we dance for the glory of Witch. Every year, we celebrate* that.

She didn't realize she had spoken out loud until the room turned to ice. "I want to go home," she said in a small voice. "Can you arrange that?"

"It would be my pleasure," Saetan crooned.

4 / Kaeleer

Daemon stared with intense dislike at the blackwood hour-glass floating outside Jaenelle's door. When he'd noticed it the first time he'd tried to check on Jaenelle, Ladvarian, the Sceltie Warlord, had explained what it meant. So he had accepted Ladvarian's offer to act as guide and had done a little exploring of the Keep. Returning an hour later, he'd discovered that the hourglass had been turned, the sand trickling into the base to mark another hour of solitude. This was the third time the sand had almost run out, and *this* time he was going to be waiting at the door when the last grain of sand dropped.

"You are impatient?" asked a sibilant voice.

Daemon turned toward Draca, the Keep's Seneschal. When they had first arrived at the Keep, Lucivar had given him a cryptic warning: *Draca is a dragon in human form.* The moment he'd seen the Seneschal, he'd understood what Lucivar meant. Her looks, combined with the feel of great age and old, deep power, had fascinated him.

"I'm worried," he replied, meeting the dark eyes that

stared right through him. "She shouldn't be alone right now."

"Yet you sstand outsside the door."

Daemon gave the floating hourglass a killing look.

Draca made a sound that might have been muted laughter. "Are you alwayss sso obedient?"

"Almost never," Daemon muttered—and then remembered who he was talking to.

But Draca nodded, as if pleased to have something confirmed. "It iss wisse for maless to know when to yield and obey. But the Conssort iss permitted to bend many ruless."

Daemon considered the words carefully. It was hard to catch inflections in that sibilant voice, but he thought he understood her. "You know more of the finer points of Protocol than I do," he said, watching her closely. "I appreciate the instruction."

Her face didn't alter, but he would have sworn she smiled at him. As she turned away, she added, "The glasss iss almosst empty."

His hand was on the doorknob, quietly turning it as the last grains of sand trickled into the hourglass's base. As he opened the door, he saw the hourglass turning to declare another hour of solitude. He slipped quickly into the room and closed the door behind him.

Jaenelle stood by a window, looking out at the night, still dressed in the black gown. As a man, that gown appealed to him in every way a woman's garment could, and he hoped she didn't just wear it for formal occasions.

He stepped away from those thoughts. Not only were they useless tonight, they teased his body into wanting to respond to her in a way that wouldn't be acceptable.

"Are they gone?" Jaenelle asked quietly, still staring out the window.

Daemon studied her, trying to decide if it was meant as small talk or if she had withdrawn so deep within herself she really didn't know. "They're gone." He moved toward her slowly, cautiously, until he was only a few feet away and at an angle where he could see her profile.

"It was the appropriate punishment," Jaenelle said as another tear rolled down her face. "It's the appropriate punishment when one Queen violates another's court to do harm."

"You could have asked one of us to do it," Daemon said quietly.

Jaenelle shook her head. "I'm the Queen. It was mine to do."

Not if you're going to eat your heart out because of it.

"There's a traditional way to break one of the Blood, to strip away the power without doing any other harm. It's quick and clean." She hesitated. "I took her deep into the abyss."

"You took her to the misty place?"

"No," Jaenelle said too sharply, too quickly. "That's a special place. I didn't want it tainted—" She bit her lip.

He didn't want to examine the relief he felt at knowing Alexandra hadn't fouled the misty place with her presence.

As he continued to study her, it struck him with the force of a blow: she hadn't withdrawn so far into herself because she grieved over having to break another witch; she had withdrawn in order to deal with some kind of personal pain.

"Sweetheart," he said quietly, "what's wrong? Please tell me. Let me help."

When she turned to look at him, he didn't see a grown woman or a Queen or Witch. He saw a child in agony.

"Leland . . . Leland cared, I think, but I never expected much from her. Philip cared, but there was nothing he could really do. Alexandra was the m-mother in the family. She was the one who had the strength. She was the one we all wanted to please. And I could never please her, could never be . . . I loved all of them—Leland and Alexandra and Philip and Wilhelmina." Jaenelle's breathing hitched on a suppressed sob. "I loved *her*—and she s-said I was m-monstrous."

Daemon just stared at her, the sudden rage that engulfed him making it impossible to speak for a moment. "The bitch said *what*?"

Startled by the venom in his voice, she gave him a clear-eyed look before she crumbled again. "She said I was monstrous."

He could almost see all the deep childhood scars re-opening, bleeding. This was the final rejection, the final pain. The child had defied that rejection, had tried to justify the sparse love given only with conditions placed on it. The child had tried to justify being sent to that horror, Briarwood. But the child was no longer a child, and the agony of having to face a bitter truth was ripping her apart.

He also realized that, faced with this emotional battering, she was now clinging to the one solid wall of her childhood: Saetan's love and acceptance.

Well, he could give her another wall to cling to. He opened his arms enough to invite but not enough to demand. "Come here," he said softly. "Come to me."

It broke his heart the way she crept toward him without looking at him, the way her body was braced for rejection.

His arms closed around her, comforting and protecting.

"She was a good Queen, wasn't she?" Jaenelle asked in a pleading voice a few minutes later.

Daemon felt a stab of pain. At another time, the lie would have been easy enough to say, but not tonight. Knowing he was going to rip away her last justification for Alexandra's behavior, he gave her the truth as gently as he could. "Compared to the other Queens in Terreille, she was a good Queen. Compared to any of the Queens I've met since I've been in Kaeleer . . . No, sweetheart, she was not a good Queen."

Pain flowed with the tears as Jaenelle finally gave up the people she had once tried to love.

He held her, saying nothing. Just held her while he let all of his love surround her.

The door opened quietly. Ladvarian walked in, followed by Kaelas.

Daemon watched them, and wondered if they had decided on their own to defy the command for solitude or if they had equated his presence with permission to enter.

After a minute, the tip of Ladvarian's tail waved once. *We will come back later.*

They left as quietly as they had come.

CHAPTER
EIGHT

1 / Kaeleer

Lord Magstrom nervously wandered around the room where the records from the service fair were stored. He'd only been home a couple of days and was still catching up on the official business of his own village. But Lord Jorval had urgently requested him to return to Little Terreille's capital to discuss something of the "utmost importance."

He'd spent several days with his eldest granddaughter and her husband—days that had been filled with excitement and apprehension instead of the rest he so badly needed. His granddaughter was pregnant with her first child, and, though delighted, she was also quite ill. So he'd spent most of his time reassuring her husband that his granddaughter wouldn't divorce a man she loved just because she couldn't keep her breakfast down for a few weeks.

He shouldn't have said "a few weeks." The younger man had looked ready to faint when he'd said that.

He *had* written a hurried letter to the High Lord about the discrepancies he had found in the service fair records but then had hesitated over sending it, wondering if his own exhaustion had made something sinister out of what was really just sloppy clerical work.

No matter. As soon as he was home again, he would write a more thoughtful, carefully worded letter, one that expressed concern rather than alarm.

He had just reached this decision when the door swung open and Lord Jorval entered the room.

"I'm glad you came, Magstrom," Jorval said a little breathlessly. "I wasn't sure who else I could trust. But anyone who's worked with you knows you couldn't be involved in *this*."

"And just what is 'this'?" Magstrom asked cautiously.

Jorval went to the shelves holding the records and pulled out a thick folder.

Magstrom's stomach tightened. It was the Hayllian folder—the same one he had examined before his hasty departure from Goth.

Jorval's hands trembled as he leafed through the papers, then put several on the large table. "Look. There are discrepancies in these lists." Hurrying to the shelves, he pulled out several folders and dumped them on the table. "And not only in the Hayllian lists. At first I thought it was a clerical error, but . . ." Taking a sheet of paper from one of the folders, he pointed. "Do you remember this man? He was most unsuitable to immigrate to Kaeleer. *Most* unsuitable."

"I remember him," Magstrom said faintly. A brute of a man whose psychic scent had made his skin crawl. "He was accepted into a court?"

"Yes," Jorval said grimly. "This one."

Magstrom squinted at the scrawled writing. The Queen's name and the territory she ruled were almost illegible. The only thing he could definitely make out was that the territory was in Little Terreille. "Who is this . . . Hektek?"

"I don't know. There is no Queen named Hektek who rules so much as a village in Little Terreille. But thirty Terreilleans were accepted into this alleged court. *Thirty*."

"Then where are these people going?"

Jorval hesitated. "I think someone is secretly creating an army right under our noses, using the service fair to cover the tracks."

Magstrom swallowed hard. "Do you know who?" he asked, half expecting Jorval to accuse the High Lord— which was ridiculous.

"I think so," Jorval replied, an odd glitter appearing in his eyes. "If what I suspect is true, the Territory Queens in Kaeleer must be warned immediately. That's why I asked you to come. I'm to meet someone tonight who claims to have information about the people missing from the lists. I wanted another member of the Council to come with me as a witness to confirm what was said. I wanted you because, if we *are* in danger, the High Lord will listen to you."

That decided Magstrom. "Since there may be some risk in revealing this information, we shouldn't keep this person waiting."

"No," Jorval replied, sounding queer, "we shouldn't."

They found an available horse-drawn cab almost as soon as they left the building. A heavy silence filled the cab until, a few minutes later, it pulled up.

Magstrom stepped out, looked around, and felt a jagged-edged fear. They were at the edge of Goth's slums, not a place for the unwary—or for an older man at any time.

"I know," Jorval said hurriedly as he took Magstrom's arm and began leading him through narrow, dirty streets. "It seems an unlikely meeting place, but I think that's why it was chosen. Even if someone recognized us, they would think they were mistaken."

Breathing heavily, Magstrom struggled to keep up with Jorval. He could feel eyes watching them from shadowed doorways—and he could sense the flickers of power coming from the ones who watched. There were many reasons why a dark-Jeweled male could end up in a place like this.

Finally, they slipped into the back door of a large building and silently climbed the stairs. At a second floor door, Jorval fumbled with a key, then stepped aside to allow Magstrom to enter the suite.

The furnishings in the sitting room were secondhand and shabby. The room itself looked as if even minimal cleaning hadn't been done in a long time. And it stank of decay.

"Something wrong?" Jorval asked in an oddly gleeful voice.

Magstrom moved toward the narrow windows. A little air might help relieve the smell. "I think a mouse or a rat must have died behind the walls, so—"

Jorval made a queer sound—a sharp, high-pitched giggle—at the same time the bedroom door opened and a hooded figure stepped into the sitting room.

Magstrom turned—and couldn't say a word.

Knucklebones peeked out of the split skin as brown hands pushed the hood back.

Magstrom stared at the hate-filled gold eyes in the ravaged, decaying face. She took a step toward him. He took a step back. Then he took another . . . and another . . . until there was nowhere to go.

Jorval smiled at him. "I thought it was time you met the Dark Priestess."

2 / Kaeleer

"Is something wrong?" Daemon asked Saetan. He glanced at Lucivar, who was intently studying their father.

Saetan finally looked up from the sheet of paper lying in the middle of his desk. "I received a letter from Lord Jorval, informing me that Lord Magstrom was brutally killed last night."

Daemon let his breath out slowly while Lucivar swore. "I met Magstrom briefly at the service fair. He seemed to be a decent man."

"He was," Saetan replied. "And he was the only member of the Dark Council Jaenelle was willing to deal with."

"How did he die?" Lucivar asked bluntly.

Saetan hesitated. "He was found in an alleyway in the Goth slums. The body was so torn up that speculation is running wild that Magstrom was killed by kindred."

Daemon said, "Why would they suspect the kindred?" at the same time Lucivar snarled, "It was a full death?"

"Yes, it was a full death," Saetan said grimly, answering Lucivar's question first. "So there's not even a chance of Magstrom being a ghost in the Dark Realm long enough to tell someone what really happened to him. There are feral dog packs, and they *can* be a danger, but a Craft shield would have protected Magstrom from them. Only a pack of kindred, or one who wore darker Jewels than Magstrom, could have drained his psychic power to finish the kill."

"Is that likely?" Daemon asked.

"If an unknown human wanders into one of the kindred Territories, it's almost a given. But in Goth? No."

"So he was mutilated in order to hide the real death wounds."

"So it would seem."

"Does Jorval want to postpone the healing?" Lucivar asked.

Saetan shook his head. "The meeting is still set for late this afternoon. Is everything ready?"

Lucivar nodded. "We'll be leaving within the hour."

"The place you're taking Jaenelle to is secure?" Saetan asked.

"It's a guardhouse in Dea al Mon," Lucivar said. "Chaosti will come with us, and the Dea al Mon guards will supply the added physical protection. Cat said she has a few errands to run in Amdarh, so we'll go directly there afterward, and probably stay for a day or two. Chaosti will return here and report."

With effort, Daemon caged the jealousy that was chewing him up inside. There was no reason for Lucivar to think twice about making plans to spend a couple of days with Jaenelle, despite the Eyriens still waiting to be settled in Askavi before winter set in, despite his having a wife and child. Jaenelle was not only his sister but his Queen. There was no question that he would go with her whenever or wherever she needed him.

Putting those thoughts aside, Daemon concentrated on the timetable. He hadn't really been aware of the journey from Goth to the Hall, but it had to have taken a couple of hours at the least. Going to this secret location in Dea al Mon would probably take even more time. If Lucivar was planning to leave within the hour to reach the guardhouse, he was planning to arrive so that there would be just enough time for Jaenelle to rest and eat a late midday meal before doing whatever she was going to do. Just enough time . . .

The Sadist in him woke up. He looked at Saetan and saw his own suspicions reflected in his father's eyes. "When was the body found?" he asked too softly.

Lucivar jerked to attention, then swore viciously.

Saetan returned his stare for a moment. "If Jorval had been informed immediately, there would have been just enough time to pen a hasty note and send it here by courier."

"*Was* it hastily written?"

"No, I wouldn't say so."

Which meant Jorval had known about Magstrom's death

before the body had been found. And Jorval was the one who had made these arrangements for Jaenelle to come to Little Terreille.

As soon as he and Lucivar were away from Saetan's study, Daemon settled one hand on Lucivar's shoulder, his long, black-tinted nails providing just enough bite to ensure that he had his brother's undivided attention. "You will do anything you have to in order to keep her safe and take care of her, won't you?"

"I'll keep her safe, Bastard. You can count on that." Then Lucivar smiled that lazy, arrogant smile. "But you're the one who's going to take care of her. You've got less than an hour to get packed, old son. Bring enough to get you through a couple of days in Amdarh as well."

Daemon stared at Lucivar, then stepped back and slipped his hands into his trouser pockets. "She's not comfortable with me, Prick." Not even to Lucivar would he admit how Jaenelle had practically fled her own rooms in order to get away from him after he had spent the night with her. "My being there would only distress her."

"You're her Consort," Lucivar said sharply. "Stand your ground."

"But . . ."

"She isn't going to pay attention to either of us before this meeting, and I'll be with you when you go to Amdarh. While she's swearing about tripping over me, she isn't going to have time to feel nervous about being around *you*." Lucivar rode over another, more feeble protest. "I want you at that guardhouse, Daemon."

He finally understood. Lucivar didn't want him there because he was the Consort, but because he was the Sadist.

Daemon nodded. "I'll be ready to leave when you are."

3 / Kaeleer

Seeing the contained grief in Jaenelle's eyes, Lucivar didn't need to ask if she'd been told about Lord Magstrom's death. He almost asked if she wanted to postpone the meeting, but didn't bother. There was something else in her eyes that told him she would see this meeting through, for her own reasons.

He eyed the large flat case that stood near her traveling
bag. She had several cases like that of different sizes that
contained the wooden frames she used to weave her various webs.

"You're expecting to weave a healing web that size?"
he asked.

"It's not for a healing web; it's for the shadow."

He eyed the case again. A "shadow" was an elaborate
illusion that could fool the eye into believing a person
was really there. Jaenelle could create one that was so
realistic, the only difference between it and her real body
was that, while the shadow could pick up or touch anything, it couldn't *be* touched. She had made that kind of
shadow eight years ago, when she had begun her search
for Daemon to bring him out of the Twisted Kingdom,
and he still clearly remembered the kind of physical toll it
had taken.

"Do you feel well enough to channel that much power
through your body to make the shadow capable of doing
an extensive healing?"

"There won't be much healing required," Jaenelle replied calmly.

That wasn't the impression he or Saetan had gotten from
Jorval's urgent letters, but he knew better than to say anything. Serving Jaenelle in the past few years had taught him
when to yield.

She vanished the case and traveling bag, then picked up
a hooded, full-length black cape. "Shall we go?"

4 / Kaeleer

Kartane SaDiablo restlessly paced the sitting room of his
suite.

The bitch was late. If he'd been home, the bitch wouldn't
have dared keep Dorothea's son waiting. Hell's fire, he'd
almost be glad to get back to Hayll.

Working himself up to insulted outrage, he almost missed
the quiet knock on the door. He pulled himself together.
He needed this bitch, who, Jorval assured him, was the best
Healer in Kaeleer. If he was uncivil, nothing and no one
could stop her from walking out the door again.

He walked over to the windows and looked out. There was no reason for her to know he had been waiting anxiously, no reason to give her even that little bit of power over him. "Come in," he said when the knock sounded again.

He didn't hear the door open, but when he turned around, a figure shrouded in a hooded black cape stood inside the room.

At first he thought it was that witch Dorothea called the Dark Priestess, but there was something slimy about the Dark Priestess's psychic scent and this one's scent . . .

Kartane frowned. He couldn't detect a psychic scent at all. "You're the Healer?" he asked doubtfully.

"Yes."

Kartane shivered at the sound of that midnight voice. Trying to ignore his uneasiness, he reached up to unbutton his shirt. "I suppose you want to examine me."

"That won't be necessary. I know what's wrong with you."

His fingers froze around the button. "You've seen this before?"

"No."

"But you know what it is?"

"Yes."

Annoyed by the terse answers, he tossed aside any effort at civility. "Then what in the name of Hell is it?"

"It's called Briarwood," replied the midnight voice.

The blood drained out of Kartane's head, leaving him dizzy.

"Briarwood is the pretty poison," the voice continued as fair-skinned hands reached up and pushed the hood back. "There is no cure for Briarwood."

Kartane stared at her. The last time he'd seen her, thirteen years ago, she had been more like a drugged puppet than a child—a plaything locked in one of Briarwood's cubicles, waiting to be used. But he'd never forgotten those sapphire eyes, or the terror he'd felt after he'd tried to touch her mind.

"You." The word came out as nothing more than exhaled breath. "I thought Greer destroyed you."

"He tried."

It hit him then. He pointed an accusing finger at her. "You did this to me. *You* did this!"

"I created the tangled web, yes. As far as what's happened to you, Kartane, you did this to yourself."

"No!"

"Yes. To each is given what he gave. That was the only command I spun into the web."

"Since you did this, you can damn well undo it!"

She shook her head. "Many of the children who were the threads of that tangled web have returned to the Darkness. They're out of reach, even for me, and there's no way to undo the web without them."

"You lie," Kartane shouted. "If I hand you enough gold, you'd find a way fast enough."

"There is no cure for Briarwood. But there *is* an end to this, if that's any consolation. To each is given what he gave."

"WHAT DOES THAT MEAN?"

"Every blow, every wound, every rape, every moment of fear that you ever inflicted on another is coming back to you. You're taking back what you gave, Kartane. When you've taken it all back, the debt will be paid, and the web will release you as it did the other males who amused themselves in Briarwood."

"They're all dead, you stupid bitch! I'm the last one left. No one survived this web of yours."

"The web only set the terms. If none of the others survived . . . How many of the children who were sent to Briarwood survived any of you?"

"Since you didn't come here to heal me, why *did* you bother to come? Just to gloat?"

"No. I came to stand as witness for those who are gone."

Kartane studied her, then shook his head. "You can end this."

"I've already told you, I can't."

"You can end this. You can stop this pain. And you're damn well going to!"

With a howl of rage, Kartane rushed her—and went right through her. He hit the door, unable to stop himself.

When he turned around, there was no one else in the room.

5 / Kaeleer

Daemon approached Jaenelle cautiously, reluctant to disturb her solitude and not sure what to think about the odd blend of sadness and satisfaction on her face. The solitude was an illusion, of course. When she had left her room in the guardhouse and gone out to sit near the creek, Lucivar, Chaosti, and half a dozen Dea al Mon guards had followed her, swiftly disappearing into the woods. He couldn't see any of them, but he knew they were nearby, watching and listening.

"Here," he said quietly, handing her a mug. "It's just herbal tea. Nothing fancy." When she thanked him, he slipped his hands into his trouser pockets, feeling self-conscious. "Is everything all right?"

Jaenelle hesitated. "I did what I went to do." She took a sip of the tea, peered into the cup, then looked at him. "What's in this?"

"A little of this and that."

"Uh-huh."

If that doubtful tone had come from any other woman, he would have felt insulted. But the concentration—and hint of frustration—in her eyes as she took another sip indicated that her doubt was caused by his dismissive "nothing fancy" rather than the brew itself.

She eyed him speculatively. "I don't suppose you would be willing to exchange the recipe for this brew for one of mine?"

Since she liked it that much, it was tempting to refuse so that he would be the only one who could make it for her, but he quickly realized that the time spent with her over a table full of herbs would serve him far better.

Daemon smiled. "I know a couple of brews you might find interesting."

Jaenelle returned the smile, then drained the mug and stood up. "I'd like to head out to Amdarh soon," she said as they walked back to the guardhouse. "That way, we can get settled in tonight."

Despite Lucivar's and Chaosti's firm warnings, Daemon had to bite his tongue to keep from suggesting that she eat something first. They had told him her resistance against

any attempt to get some food into her would be in direct
proportion to her mood when she returned from this meeting. He'd only needed one glance at her face when she
came out of her room to know any suggestion would have
been pointless.

"I think you'll like Amdarh," Jaenelle said. "It's a beautiful—" She stopped walking, then sniffed the air. "Is
that stew?"

"I believe it is," Daemon replied mildly. "Lucivar and
Chaosti made it. It should be just about done."

"They made wildwood stew?"

"I believe that's what it's called."

Jaenelle eyed him. "I suppose you're hungry."

Even if he had never picked up a cue before in his life,
he couldn't have missed that one. "Actually, I am. Do you
think we could wait until after dinner before heading to
Amdarh?"

Jaenelle turned her head away from him, but not enough
that he couldn't see her lick her lips. "It wouldn't take that
long to have a bowl of stew. Or two," she added as she
hurried toward the guardhouse.

Daemon lengthened his stride to keep up, and wondered
how much of a tussle the males were going to have in order
to get their fair share.

6 / Kaeleer

Kartane burst into Jorval's dining room. "Is that bitch
alive?" he demanded.

Jorval hurried toward him while a man Kartane had
never seen before sat at the table and just stared.

"Lord Kartane," Jorval said anxiously. "If I'd known the
healing would be done so soon, we would have waited
din—"

"Damn you, just answer the question! Is she alive?"

"Lady Angelline? Yes, of course she's alive. Why do you
ask? Didn't she arrive?"

"She arrived," Kartane snarled.

"I don't understand," Jorval said, almost wailing. "She's
the best Healer in the Realm. If she—"

"SHE'S THE ONE WHO DID THIS TO ME!"

Jorval's shocked look was quickly replaced by a sly one. "I see. Please, come and join us. I can see you've had a distressing afternoon. Perhaps some food and company will help."

"Nothing will help until that bitch is made to heel," Kartane snapped, accepting a chair at the table and a quickly filled glass of wine. He glared at the other man, who continued to stare at him.

"Lord Kartane," Jorval said smoothly, "may I present Lord Hobart? He, too, has reasons to want to see Jaenelle Angelline subdued."

"Not just Jaenelle Angelline," Hobart growled.

"Oh?" Kartane said, pushing his anger aside as his interest in Hobart sharpened.

"Lord Hobart had controlled the Territory of Glacia for several years," Jorval said. "When his niece became the Territory Queen—"

"The ungrateful bitch EXILED me!" Hobart shouted.

"And you want to regain control," Kartane said, starting to lose interest.

Then Jorval added, "Lady Karla is a close friend of Jaenelle's."

Kartane randomly selected food from the dishes offered as he nibbled on that bit of information. There was nothing he would have liked better right then than to hurt a close friend of the bitch. "I may be able to help. My mother is the High Priestess of Hayll."

Not only didn't Hobart look sufficiently impressed, he looked distinctly uneasy. He cleared his throat. "It's a generous offer, Lord Kartane. A very generous offer, but . . ."

"But you're already receiving some assistance from the Dark Priestess," Kartane guessed. When Hobart paled, he crossed two fingers and held them up. "Perhaps you're not aware that my mother and the Dark Priestess are like that."

Hobart swallowed hard. Jorval merely drank his wine and watched them out of dark eyes filled with sly glee.

"I see," Hobart finally said. "In that case, your help is most welcome."

CHAPTER
NINE

1 / Kaeleer

Andulvar settled into a chair in front of Saetan's black-wood desk. "Karla says you've been in here sulking for the past two hours, ever since you got a message from Lady Zhara."

Saetan gave his longtime friend his iciest stare. "I. Am. Not. Sulking."

"All right." Andulvar waited. "Then what *are* you doing?"

Saetan leaned back in his chair. "Answer me this: if I were to run away from home, is there anywhere in any of the Realms I could go and not be found?"

Andulvar scratched his chin. "Well, if you wanted to hide from the Dhemlan Queens or the coven, there are quite a few places you could go to ground. If you wanted to hide from your male offspring, there are a few places in the Dark Realm that would take even Mephis a while to think of. But if *Jaenelle* was looking for you . . ."

"Which is precisely why I'm still sitting here." Saetan rubbed his forehead and sighed. "Zhara has summoned me to Amdarh to take care of a problem for her."

Andulvar frowned. "Lucivar's in Amdarh, isn't he? If Zhara needs help from a male stronger than the ones who serve in her court, why didn't she ask him?"

Saetan narrowed his golden eyes and let the words fall like precisely dropped stones. "Lucivar is in Amdarh with Jaenelle."

The silence thickened into a solid curtain.

"Ah," Andulvar finally said. "Well, Daemon—"

"Is in Amdarh with Lucivar and Jaenelle."

"Mother Night," Andulvar muttered, then added warily, "What did Zhara say?"

Saetan picked up the message and read in a funereal voice, " 'Your children are having a wonderful time. Come and get them.' "

2 / Kaeleer

Daemon braced his head in his hands and closed his eyes.

"Mother Night," Lucivar said, enunciating very carefully.

"I've never been this drunk," Daemon moaned quietly.

Lucivar stared at him with bloodshot eyes. "Sure you have."

"Maybe a couple of times in the stupid phase of my youth, but not since I've worn the Black. My body burns it up too fast to get drunk."

"Not this time," Lucivar said, then added after a long, possibly thoughtful, pause, "I've been this drunk."

"Really? When?"

"Last time I went on a crawl with Jaenelle. Big mistake. Should have remembered it. Would have, too, if I'd been sober when I *did* remember it."

After a minute's painful effort, Daemon gave up trying to decipher that comment and found something else to think about. "I've never been thrown out of a city before."

"Sure you have," Lucivar said in a hearty voice that made them both whimper.

Daemon shook his head and realized his error a bit too late. Even when he managed to stop, the room continued moving back and forth, and what was left of his brain sloshed noisily inside his skull. He swallowed carefully. "I've been thrown out of courts and wasn't allowed back into the city because that was the Queen's territory, but that's different."

"Iz all right," Lucivar said. "In a few weeks, Zhara will welcome you with open arms."

"She didn't seem like a foolish woman. Why would she do that?"

"Because we provide a restraining influence on Jaenelle."

"We do?"

They just stared at each other until the dining room door opened.

Daemon braced himself, absolutely certain that hearing the door slam would kill him.

"Mother Night," Surreal said, choking back laughter. "They're pathetic."

"Aren't they?" There was no laughter in Saetan's reply. The soft footsteps approaching the table made the room vibrate.

"Please don't yell," Daemon whimpered.

"I wouldn't dream of yelling," Saetan replied in a voice that, nonetheless, rattled Daemon's bones. "There would be no point in yelling. You'd both be on the floor, insensible, after the first word. So I'll save the lecture until you're sober enough to listen to it, because I intend to deliver it with considerable volume. The only question I want answered right now is what in the name of Hell did you two pour down your throats to get in this condition?"

"Gravediggers," Lucivar mumbled.

"How many?" Saetan asked ominously.

Lucivar took a couple of careful breaths. "Not sure. Things got a bit blurry after the seventh one."

"After the—" Long pause. "Are either of you capable of walking to your rooms?"

"Sure," Lucivar said. It took him a couple of tries, but he got to his feet.

Not to be outdone, Daemon stood up, too—and regretted it.

"You take Lucivar," Saetan said to Surreal. "He isn't listing quite as much."

"That's because I didn't finish the drinks." Lucivar pointed at Daemon, tipped, and almost flattened Surreal against the table. "That's why *you're* so drunk. I *told* you not to finish them."

Daemon tried to make a rude noise and ended up spitting on Saetan.

Without further comment, he was hauled out of the room and up a terrifyingly steep set of stairs. Once he reached his bed, he tried to lie down, but was hauled upright and undressed while his father's ire made the room pulse.

"Do you need a basin?" Saetan asked with no sympathy whatsoever.

"No," Daemon replied meekly.

Finally, he was allowed to lie down. The last thing he was aware of was Saetan's hand brushing his hair back in a gentle caress.

Surreal closed the door of Lucivar's room at the same moment Saetan stepped out of Daemon's room.

"I appreciate your assistance," Saetan said when they met at the top of the stairs.

Surreal grinned. "I wouldn't have missed this for anything."

They started down the stairs together. "You got Lucivar settled?"

"He snarled a lot and kept telling me to keep my hands off him since he's a married man. He didn't want to get undressed, but I pointed out that, since he was married, he should know better than to try to get into a bed wearing boots in that condition. While we wrestled with the boots, we pondered how that little fish got wedged under the laces."

Saetan stopped at the foot of the stairs. "How *did* it get under the laces?"

"He has no idea. So I gave the fish a proper burial at sea, so to speak, managed to convince Lucivar that stripping to the waist was not improper since I'm family, and let what was left of him fall into bed." Surreal looked around. "Say, aren't you going to tuck Jaenelle in?"

"At this moment," Saetan said dryly, "Jaenelle is in the kitchen, tucking into a very large breakfast."

"Oh, dear," Surreal said, then started to laugh.

3 / Kaeleer

Karla removed the ring from the jeweler's box and slipped it on the second finger of her right hand. It was a simple ring of yellow and white gold, with a small oval sapphire. A tasteful design, but nothing that would really catch the eye, yet feminine enough that no one would wonder about a woman wearing it. An everyday ring rather than flash and glitter. "It's perfect."

"I had asked Banard to have that one done first," Jaenelle said, "but he'd gotten all the rings for the coven done since the designs are simple." She paused, then added, "I also ordered rings made for Surreal and Wilhelmina. They'll be ready next week."

Karla nodded as she studied the ring. "How do I activate the shield inside it?"

"You would deliberately activate it through your Gray Jewel. Otherwise, it's keyed in the same way the boyos' Rings of Honor are and will respond to fear, rage, and pain caused by a serious wound. It's set for fairly intense emotions because, when it activates, everyone else within range who wears a Ring that's connected to this one is going to act as if it was a call to battle. Which it is."

"How much range does it have?" Karla asked. "If it gets activated, would Morton sense it even if he's not in the same city?"

Jaenelle gave her an odd look. "Karla, if something wakes the shield in that ring, not only will you have Morton pounding on your door, you're going to have Sceron, Jonah, Kaelas, Mistral, and Khary showing up on your doorstep—along with our Sisters in that part of the Realm."

"Mother Night!" Karla frowned at the ring. "But . . . I know the boyos have used this shield on occasion and it didn't make the rest of them go berserk."

"I wouldn't count on their responding to a signal picked up from a ring worn by a Queen in the same way they respond to a signal from another Brother in the court," Jaenelle said dryly. "Besides, at this point, the males are all attuned to each other. They can tell when to remain on alert but to wait for another signal and when to drop everything and head for the person in trouble with all possible speed."

"And you don't think they'll wait?"

"Not a chance."

Karla sighed. That was a little more male attention than she'd anticipated, and she was glad of the warning.

"I'll link it to your Gray Jewel now," Jaenelle said, holding out her right hand.

"Won't the boyos pick that up?" Karla asked, placing her right hand in Jaenelle's.

"Yes, and it will take them under two minutes to figure out that someone in the coven is wearing a ring they can connect with now."

Well, there's safety in numbers, Karla thought. *With all of us wearing a ring like this—*

"And it will take them about another minute to figure out the distinctive feel of this particular ring and recognize it as you."

"Hell's fire."

Jaenelle's smile was sympathetic but amused. "Wait until Lucivar shows up the first time. It's an experience."

"I'm sure it is," Karla mumbled.

A moment later, she felt a flash of cold followed by heat. The ring throbbed against her finger. The sensations faded, but she could sense the deep reservoir of power waiting just out of reach.

"The other thing to be aware of is that, when the shield wakes, the only people who will be able to reach you if you physically need help are the rest of the First Circle," Jaenelle said.

Karla nodded. "In that case, I'd better always wear it. It wouldn't do to have someone else slip it on and have that kind of protection."

"No one else can wear this ring. It was made for you. If anyone else tried to activate the shield, the results would be . . . unpleasant."

"I see." She didn't ask Jaenelle to define "unpleasant."

Jaenelle studied Karla for a moment. "Wear it well, Sister."

"Thank you. I will."

"I'd better see that the rest of the coven gets their rings." Jaenelle picked up the bag that held the other ring boxes, then hesitated. "Do you really have to leave tomorrow?" she asked a little plaintively.

"Duty calls," Karla said with a smile. She waited until Jaenelle left the room before adding, "And Uncle Saetan made it quite clear that no excuse for staying would be considered acceptable."

All the Queens were returning to their home Territories. So were the First Circle males. Lucivar was taking his family and the other Eyriens to Ebon Rih. Surreal and Wilhelmina would go with him as well. Andulvar and Prothvar were already on their way to Askavi, and Mephis had left for his town house in Amdarh.

She understood why Saetan was clearing the Hall. They all did. By tomorrow afternoon, all the friends Jaenelle had used as buffers would be gone. Her only human companions would be the High Lord, who, Karla was sure, was going to make himself scarce, and Daemon. The Consort would have a clear field in which to woo his Lady.

"May the Darkness help us," Karla muttered as she strode to the door and threw it open. Then she stood in the doorway and stared.

Lucivar, Aaron, Chaosti, Khardeen, and Morton smiled at her.

"Well, well, well," Lucivar crooned. "Look who we found."

Trying to return the smile, Karla said weakly, "Kiss kiss," and sincerely hoped it wouldn't take Jaenelle long to activate the other rings.

CHAPTER
TEN

1 / Kaeleer

After spending two weeks in Ebon Rih, Surreal returned to the Hall, took one look at Daemon, and went hunting for Jaenelle.

She finally tracked Jaenelle down—actually, Graysfang tracked down Ladvarian, who was with Jaenelle—in a part of the Hall so far away from the family's living quarters that it practically guaranteed no one would think to look there.

Jaenelle stepped out of a room and noticed Surreal striding down the corridor. Her face lit up with pleasure. "Surreal! I didn't expect you back so—"

Surreal grabbed Jaenelle's arm and hauled the younger woman back into the room. "This is girl talk," she growled at Graysfang and Ladvarian. "Go water some bushes." Then she slammed the door on two startled, furry faces.

"Surreal," Jaenelle said, shaking free of the hard grip, "did something happen in—"

"What in the name of Hell are you doing?" Surreal shouted.

Jaenelle looked wary and baffled. "I was reading."

"I'm not talking about what you were doing five minutes ago. I'm talking about Daemon. Why are you doing this to him?"

Jaenelle flinched and said defensively, "I'm not doing anything to him."

"That's exactly the point. Damn it, Jaenelle, he's your *Consort.* Why *aren't* you using him?"

In the flick of a moment, she saw a defensive young woman change into an angry Queen.

"He's been used enough, don't you think?" Jaenelle said quietly in her midnight voice. "And I am *not* going to be the next in a long list of women who have forced him into physical intimacy."

"But—" Surreal took a mental step back. She hadn't expected this to be the reason for Jaenelle's resistance—and she was sure Daemon had no idea this was why he was getting locked out of the bedroom. *Ah, sugar,* she thought sadly. *You made all the wrong moves for all the right reasons.* "That was different. He was a pleasure slave then, not a Consort."

"*Is* there that much difference, Surreal?"

Remember who you're talking to. Remember what she must have seen in Briarwood—and what sort of conclusions a twelve-year-old girl who knew about that side of sex would come to about the time Daemon had spent as a pleasure slave.

"The boyos who are Consorts don't seem to mind performing their duties. Quite the opposite, in fact."

"They've never been pleasure slaves. They've never been forced. All right, yes, sometimes a Consort is asked to give more than he feels like giving at that moment, but when a man accepts the Consort's ring, he goes into that kind of service willingly and by his own choice."

"Daemon made that choice," Surreal pointed out quietly. "Not because he wants the status of being the Consort and is willing to put up with the duties that go along with it, but because he wants to be your lover." She studied Jaenelle. "You do care about him, don't you?"

"I love him."

Surreal heard such a deep river of feelings in those simple words.

"Besides," Jaenelle said, shifting back into a nervous young woman, "I'm not sure he really does want to do . . . *that.* He hasn't even tried to kiss me," she added sadly.

Surreal hooked her hair behind her pointed ears. Damn, damn, damn. How had the ground gotten so boggy so fast? "If I understand the rules a Consort is supposed to play by, isn't the Queen supposed to initiate the first kiss so that the Consort knows his attentions will be welcome?"

"Yes," Jaenelle said reluctantly.

"But you haven't kissed him either?"

Jaenelle snarled in frustration and started pacing. "I'm not twelve anymore."

Surreal braced her hands on her hips. "Sugar, from where I'm standing, that's all to the good."

Jaenelle threw up her hands and shouted, "Don't you understand? I don't know how to do any of this!"

Surreal just stared. "You've never been kissed? Family kisses and friendly kisses don't count," she quickly amended.

A disgusted look filled Jaenelle's face. "Teeth, tongues, and drool."

"Wolves and dogs don't count either."

Jaenelle let out a huff of laughter, and said dryly, "I wasn't referring to the kindred."

Shit. "Haven't you received even *one* kiss you liked?"

Jaenelle hesitated. "Well, Daemon kissed me once."

"Well, there you—"

"When I was twelve."

Surreal bristled automatically at the thought of a grown man kissing a child, then took a moment to consider the man. There were kisses and there were *kisses*. And Daemon would know exactly how to kiss a young girl without crossing the line—especially when that girl had been Jaenelle. "He kissed you when you were twelve," she said carefully.

Jaenelle shrugged and looked uncomfortable. "It was at Winsol, just before . . . everything happened. He had given me a silver bracelet, and I thought a kiss was a more grown-up way of saying thank you."

"Okay," Surreal said, nodding. "So you kissed him, and then he kissed you."

"Yes."

"And he didn't drool on you?"

Jaenelle's lips twitched. "No, he didn't drool."

"So why can't you kiss him now?"

"Because I'm not twelve anymore!" Jaenelle shouted.

"What's that got to do with it?" Surreal shouted back.

"I don't want him to laugh at me!"

"I doubt laughing would be his first response. As a matter of fact, I don't think it would even occur to him." Surreal paused. *Hell's fire, this is as bad as talking to an adolescent girl.*

She let that thought sink in and settle. If she put age aside and only considered experience, *wasn't* she talking to an adolescent girl? There had to be some key she could turn, some way to make it seem like Daemon desperately needed help. If he needed help, Jaenelle would . . .

"You know, sugar, Daemon is as nervous as you are."

"Why would Daemon be nervous?" Jaenelle asked warily. "He *knows* how to kiss, and he's—"

"A virgin."

Jaenelle's mouth fell open. "But . . . But he's—"

"A virgin. Granted, he may know a bit about kissing, but there's a whole lot he only knows in theory."

"But . . . Surreal, he *can't* be."

"Trust me, he is."

"Oh."

"So you can see why he'd be nervous," Surreal said, feeling a little nervous herself. If Daemon ever found out about this little chat, she could end up the main ingredient in a carnivore's stew. "Frankly, sugar, if push comes to shove, all you have to do is lie there. But if *he's* nervous about his ability to perform well . . ." Cocking her elbow, Surreal stiffened her hand and fingers, then let them droop.

Jaenelle studied the drooping hand long enough for Surreal to start to sweat before saying, "Oh." Her eyes widened. "Oooh." Then she shook her head. "No, that wouldn't happen to Daemon."

That naive assurance of Daemon's ability was touching. Scary, but touching. And not something she was going to introduce to reality.

"Let's sit down," Surreal said, heading for a couch. "Thirty minutes ought to be enough, but we might as well be comfortable."

"Enough for what?" Jaenelle said, settling on the other end of the couch.

"I'm going to explain the basics of kissing." There was a slight edge to Surreal's smile. "You would agree that I know a few things about kissing?"

"All right," Jaenelle replied cautiously.

"And you never thought to ask me about it in the month that I've been in Kaeleer?" And *that* rankled.

"I thought about it," Jaenelle muttered. "It didn't seem polite."

Oh, Mother Night. Well, *that* would explain the glazed look she sometimes noticed in the High Lord's eyes. How many nights had he sat in his study totally flummoxed by dealing with a Queen this powerful who still worried about being polite?

"I thank you for your concern, but, since we're family, I wouldn't have been offended by a little girl talk."

There was speculation in Jaenelle's eyes. Surreal could almost see the questions piling up.

"For today, let's just stick to basic kissing."

"Should I take notes?" Jaenelle asked earnestly.

"No," Surreal replied slowly, "but I think you should try some hands-on practice as soon as possible."

Surreal quietly closed the door and hurried down the corridor. She wasn't sure that look of intense concentration that had been on Jaenelle's face boded well for the man on the receiving end of that attention, but she'd done her best. Any further instructions would have to come from Daemon—and good luck to him. For a woman who had grown up around some of the most sensual males Surreal had ever met, Jaenelle was appallingly dense about sex. Maybe it had taken Daemon's arrival to wake her up sexually, but you would think she would have picked up *some* clues.

How in the name of Hell did two inexperienced lovers ever figure out how to do anything? Surreal wondered. Which made her think about how many things could go wrong once Daemon and Jaenelle got past kissing.

Which made her think that, maybe, she should tell the High Lord about this little chat. Maybe she should. Just in case.

She turned a corner and almost ran into the very last person she wanted to see right now.

"What's wrong?" Daemon asked.

"Wrong?" Surreal said, taking a step back. "Why should anything be wrong?"

"You look pale."

Oh, shit. "Um." Maybe she should tell *him* about that little chat, just to give him a little warning. *Daemon, Jae-*

nelle and I had a little talk about sex. I think you'll enjoy the results.

Maybe not.

"Surreal?" Daemon said, an edge coming into his voice.

Surreal took a deep breath. "Act nervous. It will help."

Then she was past him, running through the corridors. A few minutes later, breathless, she burst into Saetan's study.

Saetan froze, his pen poised above the papers on his desk. "Surreal," he said cautiously.

She sat down in the chair in front of his desk and smiled a bit desperately. "Hi. I thought I would keep you company for a while."

"Why?"

"Do I need a reason?"

Apparently that question meant something different to him because he carefully put the pen back in its holder, set his half-moon glasses on the desk, leaned back in his chair, and stared at the study door before fixing that stare on her.

"If you're intending to watch me do paperwork, would you like to move that chair behind the desk?" he asked mildly.

That would put him between her and any irate male—namely Daemon—who might come through the door. "What a marvelous idea," Surreal said. She picked up the chair and brought it around the desk.

Before she could sit down, Saetan picked the chair up again and moved it closer to the bookcases that filled the back of the alcove. "Sit down," he said as he walked his fingers over the titles on one shelf. Selecting a book, he handed it to her. "This is a history of the Dea al Mon. You should learn a bit more about your mother's people. And it will be a reasonable excuse for why you're sitting there should anyone come in and wonder about it." He paused. Waited. "*Are* you expecting anyone?"

"No, I'm not expecting anyone."

"I see. In that case, I'll do a bit more paperwork while you catch your breath. Then we'll have a little chat."

Surreal gave him a weak smile. "It seems to be my day for little chats."

Fortunately, his response to that was muttered softly enough that she could pretend she didn't hear it.

2 / Kaeleer

Daemon stared at the empty corridor, shook his head, then kept walking. He'd spent the day walking, first on the grounds of the estate and now along the corridors of the Hall.

In the month that he'd been in Kaeleer, he'd come to love the place. Loved the feel of it, the sprawling mass of it, the furnishings in it.

And he was going to have to leave it.

He'd come to that conclusion after another long, sleepless night. Oh, the boyos had tried to help with their stories about pursuing their Ladies, but it was becoming painfully clear that there was no hope for him. Maybe if he wasn't wearing the Consort's ring, wasn't reminded every minute of the relationship it implied, he could accept being just a friend or—may the Darkness help him—another older brother. Maybe he could get past desire that had become painful and just . . .

Just what? Watch Jaenelle accept another man one day? Pretend he could quench the fire raging inside him?

A month wasn't long, was no time at all in the courtship dance. But he had already waited so long for Witch to appear. Then, when she'd offered him the Consort's ring, he had hoped . . .

He would talk to Saetan, give back the ring, see if there was a remote court somewhere in the Realm where he could serve out the required time in order to remain in Kaeleer. He would . . .

A door opened. Jaenelle stepped into the corridor. Her face turned pale at the sight of him.

He stopped walking. He might have to give up everything else, but he wouldn't give up loving her.

"Um. Daemon," Jaenelle said in an odd voice. "Do you have a minute?"

"Of course." It cost him, but he gave her a warm, reassuring smile and followed her into the room.

Standing out of reach, she stared at the floor, looking uneasy and intense—as if she was trying to find the right way to break bad news.

She's going to ask me to return the Consort's ring. As

soon as that thought formed, Daemon ruthlessly buried any ideas about noble sacrifices. He wasn't going to give up that easily. And he wasn't going to return the Consort's ring without a fight.

"How hard can it be?" Jaenelle muttered.

Daemon just waited.

Letting out a big sigh, Jaenelle walked up to him, braced her hands on his shoulders, rose up on her toes a little, mashed her lips against his, then scampered back out of reach and eyed him warily.

Daemon wasn't sure what to say about this unexpected move. As a kiss, it left a lot to be desired. As a kiss from Jaenelle . . .

It took effort not to lick his lips.

"Are you nervous?" Jaenelle asked, still eyeing him warily.

He was going to have a little chat with Surreal about the uselessness of cryptic advice. But at least he had some idea what the right answer should be.

"Actually, I'm terrified that I may say or do something stupid and you won't want to kiss me again."

Maybe that was too much of the right answer. Now she looked worried. Then she threw up her hands in a gesture of exasperated helplessness.

"I don't know what I'm doing," she almost wailed. And then added under her breath, "Surreal should have let me take notes."

Daemon clamped his tongue between his teeth. Yes, he really needed to have a little chat with Surreal.

Jaenelle began pacing. "It always sounds so easy in love stories."

"Kissing isn't difficult," Daemon said carefully.

She glared at him as she paced past him. "Lucivar said the same thing about cooking," she growled. "The wolves didn't even wait for it to come out of the oven before they were digging the hole to bury it."

That sounded like an interesting story. He'd have a little chat with Lucivar, too.

"Kissing isn't difficult," Daemon said firmly. "You just kissed me."

"Not very well," she grumbled.

Knowing better than to answer that, Daemon studied

her. Frustration. Embarrassment. And an emotion that knocked the wind out of him—longing. "Why did you ask Surreal about kissing?"

"*She told you that?*"

"No, I guessed." And between overhearing Jaenelle's remark about taking notes and receiving Surreal's succinct instructions, it wasn't difficult to reach the correct conclusion.

Jaenelle grumbled and snarled a few comments in a language he thankfully didn't understand. Then, "I wanted to impress you, and I didn't want you to laugh."

"Laughing isn't what comes to mind at the moment," Daemon said dryly. He raked his fingers through his hair. "Sweetheart, if it's any comfort, I want to impress you, too."

"You do?" She sounded astonished.

He started to wonder what had happened in the past thirteen years that would make her so stunned by that idea—but he already knew. She had told him the first time he'd ended up in the misty place, when he'd tried to bring Witch back to heal her wounded body. When it came to physical pleasure, the males wanted to indulge themselves in the body without having to deal with the one who lived inside it. And Jaenelle, with the horrors of Briarwood in her past, would never yield that way.

"Yes, I do," he said.

She pondered this. "Kaelas is annoyed with you."

It seemed like an abrupt shift in topic—and not a welcome one. "Why?" he asked cautiously.

"Because I haven't been sleeping well lately and I keep kicking him. He's decided it's your fault."

Oh, wonderful. "I haven't been sleeping well either."

She turned away, looking distressed.

Enough, Daemon thought. It was more his fault than hers that they had struggled through the past month. Saetan had told him she'd never had a lover, and yet he'd expected an open-armed welcome to her bed. He had acted as if she were an experienced woman who would take advantage of his availability.

That had been his biggest mistake. Jaenelle didn't have it in her to take advantage of anyone who served in her court. Well, she had made the first stumbling move. Now it was his turn.

He loosened the choke-hold control on his sexuality just enough to produce a subtle feel in the air, without it being strong enough for her to recognize it.

"Come here," he said quietly.

Looking baffled, she obeyed.

Setting his hands lightly on her waist, he drew her close to him. "Kiss me again. Like this." He brushed his lips against hers, softly, delicately. "And this." He kissed the corner of her mouth. "And this." He kissed her throat.

She imitated each move—until she kissed his throat. When the tip of her tongue licked his skin, he tilted her head up, lightly fastened his mouth on hers, and kissed her in earnest. Kissed her with all the hunger that had been building inside him during the past month, during a lifetime. Kissed her while his hands roamed over her back and hips and delicately explored her breasts. Kissed her until she moaned. Kissed her until she opened for him and let his tongue dance with hers. Kissed her until her hands slid up his back and clamped on his shoulders. Kissed her until the moan turned into a hungry snarl and he felt her nails prick his skin through the shirt and jacket.

And then realized he had taken them farther than he had meant to right now. Returning his hands to her waist, he eased back to the light, easy kisses.

Sensing his withdrawal, she snarled again—and there was anger as well as hunger in the sound. "You don't want me?" she asked in her midnight voice.

He nudged her hips toward him just enough to prove his answer. "Yes, I want you." He gave in for one more moment, fastened his mouth on her neck and sucked hard enough to leave a love bite. Tearing his mouth away, he gave her little butterfly kisses from jaw to temple. "But this is just playtime, just an appetizer."

"Playtime?" Witch said suspiciously.

"Mmm," he replied, licking the spot on her forehead where the tiny spiral horn would be if they were in the abyss. "This isn't the right place for more than playtime."

"Why?"

"Because I'd like my first time to be in a bed."

Her anger vanished instantly. "Oh. Yes, that would be more comfortable," Jaenelle said.

Will you invite me to your bed tonight? He knew better than to ask so bluntly, but he also knew he *had* to ask. "May I come to you tonight?" Feeling her tense, he quickly pressed a finger against her lips. "No words. Just a kiss will be answer enough."

Her answer was everything he had hoped it would be.

3 / Kaeleer

Daemon braced his hands on the dresser and closed his eyes.

Breathe, damn you, he thought fiercely. *Just breathe.*

How in the name of Hell did men *do* this the first time? Maybe, for a youth, the thrill was enough to push him past the doubts. Maybe it was easier the first time when the woman wasn't quite so special—or when the next hour wouldn't determine whether the woman you desperately wanted would have you.

He knew dozens upon dozens of ways to kiss, to caress, to arouse a woman and make her crave having him in her bed.

He couldn't remember a single one.

Daemon straightened up, retied the belt on the robe he wore over silk pajama bottoms . . . and swore with heartfelt intensity.

He should have just followed where those kisses had been leading them this afternoon, should have given in to the hunger he had awakened in Jaenelle, should have acted instead of stepping back and giving himself the past several hours to think himself into a panic.

But, wanting more than sex for his own sake as well as hers, he *had* stepped back—and now sincerely hoped that when he walked into her bedroom . . .

He smiled at the bitter irony of it, that the one thing he had never done with a woman, the one thing he had never wanted to do and now wanted more than anything, was the one thing he might not be *able* to do.

What got him moving was the concern that if he delayed

much longer, Jaenelle might perceive it as a kind of rejection.

When he tapped on the door between their bedrooms, he took the muffled sound for an invitation and went in.

The only light in the room came from the fire burning in the hearth and scented candles grouped here and there throughout the room. The covers of the huge bed were turned down. Covered dishes, two glasses, and a bottle of sparkling wine filled a table near the hearth.

Jaenelle stood in the middle of the room, twisting her laced fingers. The edge of what looked like a sheer night-gown made of black spidersilk peeked beneath the hem of a thick, shabby robe—one he imagined she wore on rainy evenings when she snuggled up in her room to read. She looked like a lost waif rather than a sex-hungry woman.

She studied him a moment. "You look like I feel."

"Sick and terrified?" He winced, wished he hadn't said that.

She nodded. "I thought . . . some food . . ." She glanced at the covered dishes and turned pale. Then she glanced at the bed and turned paler. "What are we going to do?" she whispered.

He hadn't done either of them any favors by giving them time to think. "Basics," he said. "We'll start with something extremely simple." He took a step forward and opened his arms. "A hug."

She considered this a moment. "That sounds easy enough," she said, and stepped into his embrace.

He closed his eyes and held her lightly. Just held her. Breathed in the scent of her.

After a while, his fingers flexed. There was a comforting appeal to the texture of her shabby robe, to the way her hair brushed against his hand.

His arms tightened, drew her closer as his hand stroked up and down her back, just for the simple pleasure of it.

She sighed. The tension in her muscles eased a bit, and she rested against him more fully.

He wasn't thinking of seduction when his hands began to wander over her—or when her hands hesitantly stroked him.

He wasn't thinking of seduction when his body delighted in how different the silky skin of her neck felt under his mouth compared to the robe beneath his hands.

He wasn't thinking of sex when he opened his robe and then hers so that only that film of spidersilk separated skin from skin. Or when even the spidersilk no longer separated them.

He wasn't thinking of sex when his mouth settled over hers and he sent them both sliding into dark, hot desire.

And by the time he found himself in bed, listening to her purr with pleasure while he moved inside her, he wasn't able to think at all.

4 / Terreille

Dorothea held up a letter. "It seems Kartane has become acquainted with Lord Jorval and Lord Hobart."

Hekatah's lips curved in an awful grin. "Such useful males. One gathers Kartane got no satisfaction from the High Lord."

"It appears not," Dorothea replied, striving to sound indifferent while the fury of Kartane's betrayal singed her blood. "He suggests that Lord Hobart would welcome any assistance Hayll can provide to wrest Glacia away from the bitch-Queen niece. He will remain in Little Terreille to act as a liaison."

"It sounds as if your son finally understands to whom he owes his loyalty."

Dorothea crushed the letter. "He's not my son. Not anymore. He's just a tool like any other."

5 / Kaeleer

Lucivar walked to the far end of the low-walled garden that bordered one side of his home. Marian was reading a bedtime story to Daemonar, and the wolves had gathered in the room to listen, too, so he knew whatever Prothvar wanted to tell him wouldn't be overheard.

Two weeks ago, Saetan had sent Surreal back to Ebon Rih with a terse—and oddly harried—note, bluntly telling him to stay away from the Hall. The only reason he had obeyed was because Saetan had signed it as the Steward of the Court. After two weeks of silence, Andulvar, as Master of the Guard, had sent Prothvar to the Hall to request more information from the Steward. Now Prothvar was here, wanting to see him away from anyone. "Problem?" Lucivar asked quietly.

Prothvar's teeth gleamed as his mouth curved in a feral smile. "Not as long as you stay away from the Hall. I gathered it's rather uncomfortable living there right now if you wear Jewels darker than the Red."

"Mother Night," Lucivar muttered, rubbing the back of his neck. What in the name of Hell had happened? "Maybe the High Lord should send Daemon here for a while."

"Oh, I don't think it would be wise to try to shift Daemon away from the Hall."

Lucivar just stared at Prothvar for a moment. Then he grinned. "Well, it's about time."

"For both of them."

"So why does Saetan have his back up?"

"Because, despite Daemon's efforts to shield the bedroom, the . . . um . . . revelry tends to leak through the shields and makes the darker-Jeweled residents itchy. And neither of them wants to broach the subject with Jaenelle to ask *her* to create the shields since she's happily oblivious to anything but her Consort at the moment—and Saetan, not to mention Daemon, wants to keep it that way."

"Well," Lucivar said blandly, "if Saetan needs a respite from the frolic going on in the Hall, he could always spend an evening—or two—with Sylvia."

"Now, Lucivar," Prothvar scolded, "you know they're just friends."

"Of course they are." Noticing the moon, Lucivar did a quick mental tally, then gave Prothvar a sharp look. "Has anyone talked to Daemon about drinking a contraceptive brew?"

"That was taken care of. I had the impression that Daemon would welcome a child in the future, but, right now, he wants to enjoy his Lady's bed."

"In that case, Saetan should have a few days' reprieve fairly soon." Lucivar glanced back at the lights shining from the windows of his home and thought about enjoying his own Lady's bed as soon as Daemonar was asleep. But he asked politely, "Do you want to come in? I have some yarbarah."

"Thanks, but no," Prothvar replied. "I still have to report

to Andulvar." He said good night, spread his dark wings, and vaulted into the night sky.

As Lucivar walked back to his home, a lone wolf howled. He grinned. Since the sound was coming from the direction of Falonar's eyrie, he didn't have to ask where Surreal was spending the night.

So Surreal was snuggled up with Falonar, Jaenelle was snuggled up with Daemon, and Marian . . .

When he entered the eyrie, she was standing in the kitchen doorway. She smiled in that quiet way that always excited his body and thrilled his heart.

"I was going to make some tea," she said. "It's cold tonight."

He returned the smile, then gave her a long, very thorough kiss. "I have a better way to warm you up."

6 / Kaeleer

The Arachnian Queen floated in the air in front of her tangled web of dreams and visions—the web she had linked to the web Witch had spun. The cold season was almost upon them. It was time for the Dream Weavers to settle into the caves and burrows, but she needed to see this web once more . . . just to be sure.

She studied Witch's tangled web first.

One small thread was dark, dark, dark. The first death. There would be more. Many more.

Then she studied her own tangled web.

But not until the warming earth season. Even humans tended to remain in their lairs during the cold season.

So then. She could settle into her own lair in the sacred cave where she would rest and dream the soft dreams. When the seasons turned again, she would speak to the brown dog, Ladvarian. He was the link between kindred and human Blood. The kindred obeyed him and humans listened to him. And she needed him for what had to be done.

Because when the earth warmed next time, she would need all her strength and skill—and all the strength and skill the brown dog would gather for her—in order to save Kaeleer's Heart.

PART 2

CHAPTER
ELEVEN

1 / Kaeleer

After tucking the note in the center drawer, Morton locked his desk and frowned. It troubled him that the Sanctuary Priestess hinted at deep concerns but said nothing to the point—especially since that Sanctuary contained a Dark Altar, one of the thirteen Gates that linked the Realms of Terreille, Kaeleer, and Hell.

There had been several troubled—and troubling—messages from the Priestess over the winter months. Supplies missing. Voices late at night. Indications that the Gate had been opened without the Priestess's knowledge or consent.

Of course, the woman had reached an age where insignificant memories might slip away without being noticed. There were reasonable explanations for all the concerns. The supplies might have simply gotten used up but weren't replaced. The young Priestess-in-training might have taken a lover and the late-night voices were an assignation. The Gates . . .

That was the item that troubled him—and troubled Karla, too. Were some Terreilleans using the Gate in Glacia to slip into Kaeleer instead of enduring the service fairs? There had always been a few who, by luck or some instinct, had managed to light the black candles in the right order and speak the right spell to open a Gate between the Realms. It was even said in stories that the power contained in those ancient places would sometimes recognize a spirit's need to go home and open the Gate into the right Realm whether the person knew the spell or not. More likely, that person had found the key in some old Craft text. But the other made a better story for the telling during the long winter nights.

So he would go to that little village near the Arcerian border and talk to the Priestess.

Morton checked his pockets to make sure he had a clean handkerchief and a few silver marks so that he could buy a bit of dinner and a round at the tavern. Last, he used the lightest touch of Craft to make sure his Opal Jewel was linked to the Ring of Honor around his organ.

He smiled. Ever since Jaenelle had given the coven similar Rings, the males in the First Circle, by unspoken consensus, had begun wearing theirs all the time. That extra way of being able to decipher feminine moods had annoyed the witches as much as it had pleased the males.

Morton paused at his door, then shook his head. There was no reason to bother Karla. He would go to the village, talk to the Priestess, and then report to his cousin.

Besides, he thought as he left the mansion that was the Queen's residence, Karla's moontime was giving her more discomfort than usual this month. And she'd had minor illnesses on and off all winter—sniffles, a "weather ache" in her joints, light touches of flu. The two Healers who served in Karla's court couldn't find anything wrong that would account for this sudden vulnerability. They had suggested that, perhaps, she had been working too hard and was just worn down. She had dismissed that, saying caustically that she, too, was a Healer, and a Gray-Jeweled one at that. If something was wrong, wouldn't she know it?

Of course she would. But ruling a Territory that had people who still supported Lord Hobart and his ideas of how Blood society *should* be, Karla might ignore a great deal in order to appear invulnerable. But if it was a more serious illness, she would tell *him,* wouldn't she? She wouldn't use Craft to hide an illness from other Healers instead of getting help, would she?

Knowing the answer to *that,* Morton swore. Well, Jaenelle was making her spring tour of the Territories and would be in Scelt in a couple of days. He would send a message to her through Khardeen, formally requesting her services as a Healer on Karla's behalf.

Having made that decision, he caught one of the Winds

and rode that psychic path through the Darkness to the Priestess's village.

2 / Kaeleer

Despite his kitten's grumble-growl impatience, Kaelas kept to an easy trot. After all, the kitten was only half his size and had half the stride. Even at this easy pace, KaeAskavi had to run every few steps in order to keep up with him.

This journey pleased him because he had never known his own sire. That had not been the Arcerian way. A small coven of Arcerian witches might den near each other for protection and for the different Craft skills each one knew. But the males had been on the outside, viewed as a threat once the kittens were born.

It was true that the Arcerian males who weren't kindred had been known to kill their own kittens, and being kindred didn't eliminate feline instinct or behavior. But the kindred males had resented this exclusion—especially the Warlord Princes. They were allowed to leave meat near their mates' dens, and they could watch their kittens from a distance, but they had never been allowed to play with them or even be the ones to teach them about hunting and Craft.

Having been raised by the Lady and having lived among her human kin, he had resented the exclusion even more. Other kindred males weren't excluded. And human males certainly weren't. They were allowed to play with their kittens and groom them and teach them.

So he had brought his mate to the Hall shortly after Lucivar's kitten had been born. She had recognized another predator, even if he did have wings and only two legs. She had watched Lucivar handle his young one. She had watched the High Lord. And she had observed the human she-cat's—and the Lady's—approval of having the human kitten handled by these full-grown males.

Because of that visit, and because she had felt honored that the Lady had done the naming of her kitten—a name that, in the Old Tongue, meant White Mountain—his mate had warily allowed him into the den soon after KaeAskavi had been born.

So his kitten was learning the Arcerian way of hunting,

and the human ways that Lucivar had quietly taught *him*. That much exposure to humans had whetted KaeAskavi's curiosity about humans—which brought them to the reason for this journey.

While on a solitary prowl, KaeAskavi had wandered too close to a human village in Glacia and had met a human she-kitten. Instead of being afraid of a large predator, she had been delighted with him, and they became friends. After many secret meetings throughout the summer and early winter, the she-cats, both human and feline, had found out about the friendship—and neither had been pleased.

So KaeAskavi had turned to him, wanting his approval of the friendship to this young human female.

In a way that his mate never would, Kaelas could understand his kitten's fascination with the human she-kitten. KaeAskavi was a Warlord Prince, and Warlord Princes found it harder to do without female companionship. It would be many many seasons before KaeAskavi or the little female would look for a mate. If the she-kitten was a suitable friend, why not let them have each other for companions?

Not that he particularly liked humans. He had never forgotten the hunters who had killed his own dam. But some humans were capable of being more than just meat. The ones who belonged to the Lady, for instance. And the Lady's mate. Despite having only two legs and small fangs, there was much that was feline in that one, and he approved.

So he would look at this little female, and, if he thought she could be accepted by the kindred, he would ask the Lady to look at her, too. The Lady would know if this was a proper friend for his kitten.

Suddenly, the wind shifted so that it was coming from the village, still a mile away.

Kaelas froze. Blood and death scented the air.

Della! KaeAskavi lunged forward.

With one swipe, Kaelas bowled the kitten over.

When blood and death are in the air, you do not run toward it, Kaelas said sternly.

Della's village!

Using Craft, Kaelas probed the area around them. The season humans called spring had already come to other lands, but here winter still had fangs—and deep snow.

Make a den. Stay hidden, Kaelas ordered.

KaeAskavi snarled, but immediately rolled to a submissive posture when Kaelas stepped toward him.

I can fight, KaeAskavi said defiantly.

You will hide until I call you. Kaelas waited a moment. *What does the kitten's den look like?*

From KaeAskavi's mind, he received an image of a small human den, open ground, and then a thick stand of trees where KaeAskavi had waited for his friend.

Stay here, Kaelas said. *Make the den.*

Kaelas didn't wait to see if KaeAskavi would obey him. Wrapping himself in a sight shield and air walking so that he left no prints in the snow, he headed for the village, his full, ground-eating stride covering the distance within minutes.

The air near the village smelled of fear and desperation as well as blood and death. His sharp ears picked up the sounds of fighting, the clash of human weapons.

He cautiously used Craft to probe the village and bared his fangs in a silent snarl as he detected a Green-Jeweled Warlord Prince. Something about that one's scent . . .

Reaching a spot in the trees that looked directly on the back of the she-kitten's den, he heard a female scream and a male's roar. Then a window opened. A young human female climbed out the window and jumped into the snow. But when she tried to rise, she fell again, lame.

Kaelas burst out of the trees, charging toward the spot where the she-kitten lay at the same time an Eyrien Warlord came around the corner of the house. Spotting the she-kitten, the Eyrien raised his bloody weapon and moved forward for the kill.

The human male sensed no danger until eight hundred pounds of hatred slammed into him.

Kaelas bit off the arm that held the weapon while his claws tore open the belly. One blast of psychic power burned out the human's mind, finishing the kill.

He paused to bite some clean snow. Like its psychic scent, there was something about this human that tasted like bad meat.

He shook his head, then turned toward the girl, who was staring at the dead male. *Little one,* he growled.

She pushed herself up and looked around desperately. "KaeAskavi?"

Kaelas, he said. With the same gentleness he used with his own kitten, he seized her by the middle and loped off with her, heading for the shelter of the trees.

She made no sound. She didn't struggle. He approved of her courage. And now she was an orphan, as he had once been.

Choosing a spot where the snow had drifted deep, he set the girl down on air, quickly dug a small den, set the girl inside it, then covered up most of the entrance. *Stay,* he ordered.

She curled up in a small, shivering ball.

He loped back to the human den and passed through the wall next to the window the girl had come from. The room smelled of her—and other things, bad things.

The door leading into the rest of the den was open. He could see a bloody female arm. Sensing no life, he didn't bother to go over and sniff her to be sure.

He wished Ladvarian was there with him. Despite living almost all of his life among humans, he didn't understand them as well as the dog did. The dog would have known what the little female needed most.

He thought for a moment. She would need human fur. Using Craft, he opened the drawers and wardrobe, and vanished everything inside them.

What else would Ladvarian bring? Looking around the room, he vanished the puffy bedcovering that smelled of feathers. The kitten could be wrapped in that and kept warm. The urgent need to leave this place pushed at him, but he thought for a moment more.

Kindred had little use for things, but . . .

He saw it, lying next to the bed. At first, he felt blind hatred, but when he went over to sniff the white toy cat, he realized it had been made from fluffy cloth and not Arcerian fur as he'd first thought. It smelled strongly of the she-kitten—and, fainter, the she-cat's smell was there, too. And there was a psychic smell on it, a smell he associated with the Lady. The High Lord had called it love.

Vanishing the toy, he moved cautiously toward the open door. The dead female had a knife still clutched in one hand. She had fought a stronger male in order to save her kitten—as his own dam had fought against the hunters so that he could escape.

He thought, looking at her, that if she could know her kitten was safe and protected, she wouldn't mind the little female being among the Arcerian cats now.

Passing through the back wall of the house, he stopped near the dead Eyrien male. Using Craft, he passed the remains through the first few inches of snow, then pushed them down deep. The snow was stained with blood and gore, but he didn't think anyone would be looking for this one right away. And until they dug up the body, they wouldn't know that the human hadn't been killed by one of his own kind.

Hurrying back to the trees, Kaelas summoned KaeAskavi. *Come quickly . . . and silently.*

Reaching the makeshift den, he dug out the entrance. Calling in the puffy bedcovering, he laid it on the snow, using two spells he had learned from the Lady—a warming spell on the inside and a spell to keep the covering dry on the outside. Lifting out the she-kitten, he awkwardly wrapped her in the covering.

She just stared.

Feeling uneasy, he sniffed her carefully. She wasn't dead, but he knew those staring, unseeing eyes weren't good.

Sensing KaeAskavi's approach, he lifted his head. He could detect the faint shadowing of the lighter-Jeweled sight shield, and softly growled approval.

Della! KaeAskavi sniffed the bundled female.

Take the she-kitten to my mate, Kaelas said. *Use the Winds as soon as you reach a thread you can ride. The little one needs help quickly.*

My dam will not accept a human kitten in her den, KaeAskavi protested.

Tell her the human she-cat fought against hunters to save the kitten—and died.

KaeAskavi stood perfectly still for a moment, then said sadly, *I will tell her.* Carefully gripping the covering with his teeth, he trotted off with the she-kitten.

Kaelas waited, keeping track of them through a psychic thread. When he felt KaeAskavi catch the Wind that would take the young cat closest to the home den, he turned back to the village.

3 / Kaeleer

The Green-Jeweled Eyrien Warlord Prince looked upon the carnage with satisfaction. This Gate was now secured for the Dark Priestess's use. She had already selected the sixty pale-skinned, fair-haired people who would replace the ones he and his men had just slaughtered—people she had acquired at the last couple of service fairs. As long as the village looked inhabited and the people appeared to be going about their usual business, he doubted anyone would give any of them a second look. And if a visitor *should* know the village well enough to realize that the people were all strangers, what was one more corpse?

He turned as the Warlord who was his second-in-command approached. "Did that old bitch Priestess send the message?"

The Warlord nodded. "Sent to Lord Morton, the Glacian Queen's cousin and First Escort."

"And he usually responds to those messages?"

"Yes. And he usually comes alone."

"Then we'd better figure on having company soon. Assign five men with longbows to take up a position behind the landing web."

The Warlord studied the carnage. "If Morton sees this, he might just catch the Winds again and go back to report."

"Then I'll just have to make sure I provide a strong enough lure to get him off the landing web but still within easy range of the bowmen," the Warlord Prince said. "The old Priestess is dead?"

"Yes, Prince."

He heard a faint, pain-filled cry. "And the young Priestess?"

The Warlord smiled viciously. "She's getting the appropriate reward for betraying her own people."

4 / Kaeleer

Daemon followed Khardeen into the house. "It was kind of you to invite me to dinner."

"Kindness has nothing to do with it," Khary replied.

"There's no sense having you rattle around by yourself while you're waiting for Jaenelle."

He'd accompanied her for much of the Spring visit to the Kaeleer Territories, but when it came time to visit the kindred, she had gently but firmly suggested that he go on to Scelt, where she would meet him. They would spend a few days here before visiting the rest of the Territories on this side of the Realm. "Well, you didn't have to give up an afternoon to show me around Maghre. I could have wandered about the village by myself."

"That wasn't kindness either," Khary said after requesting coffee and cakes. He settled into a comfortable chair by the fire. "It got me out of the house. As for dinner, it'll be a pleasure talking to someone who isn't going to snarl at me because of a queasy stomach."

"Is Morghann feeling all right otherwise?" Daemon asked, taking the other chair.

"Oh, she's doing fine for a dark-Jeweled witch in the early stages of pregnancy. Or so Maeve tells me often enough." Khary's smile was a bit rueful.

"But a Territory Queen who's suddenly restricted to basic Craft while she carries a babe is not a Lady with a smooth temper."

"Since you both had to stop drinking the contraceptive brew for this to happen, you're not entirely to blame," Daemon said with a smile.

"Ah, but I'm not the one who loses my breakfast. That seems to make a difference. And there are other—frustrations—for her at the moment. You didn't hear the tussle this morning? I'm surprised since your house is barely a half mile from ours. I was sure all of Maghre heard her shouting this morning."

"At you?"

"No, thank the Darkness. At Sundancer." After thanking the maid who brought the tray, Khary poured the coffee. "Morghann wanted to go riding this morning. Maeve, who's the Healer in Maghre, had said it was fine. *Jaenelle* had said it was fine as long as Morghann felt well enough."

"But?" Daemon said, the coffee cup halfway to his lips.

"Sundancer didn't think it was fine. He said that since mares in foal weren't ridden, he didn't think a human mare in foal should ride."

"Oh, dear," Daemon said—and then laughed. "No wonder you wanted to get out of the house."

The door opened. Morghann scowled at the tray, then at Khary. But she smiled at Daemon.

Setting his cup down, he rose to give her a kiss. In the months since he'd come to Kaeleer, he'd learned the value of these little gestures of affection—and he'd learned to take pleasure in them.

Khary, he noticed with some amusement and a good dollop of sympathy, had also risen but had wisely not tried to approach his wife.

A maid appeared at the door. "Would you be wanting a cup of that herbal tea Maeve made up for you, Lady Morghann?"

"I suppose," Morghann growled.

Giving Khary a quick glance, Daemon put on his best smile. "Darling," he said to Morghann, "I'm so glad you joined us."

"Why?" Morghann said darkly as she took a seat.

"Because Jaenelle's birthday is in a couple of months, and I wanted your advice about a gift."

As they discussed ideas, Morghann became involved enough not to notice she was drinking a Healer's tea instead of coffee. She even nibbled a little piece of nutcake—which meant the men could have some without having the tray dumped over their heads.

At the end of an hour, Morghann rose. "I have some correspondence to take care of. I'll see you at dinner?"

"I look forward to it," Daemon replied.

She kissed his cheek—and then gave Khary a more generous kiss.

Khary waited a minute after the door had closed behind her. He lifted his coffee cup in a salute. "That was very well done, Prince Sadi. My thanks."

Daemon lifted his cup in response. "It was my pleasure, Lord Khardeen."

5 / Kaeleer

Morton took a couple of steps away from the landing web and froze, unable to take his eyes off the bodies lying in the snow.

What in the name of Hell had happened?

He felt a mild hum from his Ring of Honor, almost like a question. That snapped him out of his shock enough to create an Opal shield. He almost activated the shield in the Ring, then hesitated. That would summon the other boyos—and alarm Karla. He didn't want to do either of those things. Not yet.

He tried probing the area, but didn't pick up anything that would lead him to believe he was in danger. But he *did* sense the presence of several living people.

His first reaction was to rush forward to help the survivors. Then his training kicked in. Whatever had happened here was more than he could handle alone. And now that he'd been here for a minute, something more than the slaughter felt *wrong* about this place.

He took a step back, intending to catch the Winds, head for the nearest village, and bring back help.

As he took another step back, an Eyrien came around the corner of a building and saw him.

"Lord Morton?" the Eyrien called.

Morton didn't recognize the Green-Jeweled Warlord Prince. He tensed, ready to catch the Winds and run.

"Lord Morton!" The Eyrien raised a hand and hurried toward him. "Thank the Darkness, you got Yaslana's message!"

That name was enough to catapult Morton a few feet toward the Eyrien. "What happened here?"

"We're not sure," the Eyrien answered, stopping a few feet away. "Yaslana found tracks heading away from the Dark Altar. He took some of the men and followed them." He looked over Morton's shoulder, his face stamped with concern. "Didn't you bring any Healers?"

"No, I—"

It happened too fast. A blast of the Eyrien's Green-Jeweled power shattered his Opal shield at the same moment three arrows pierced his body. The Ebony shield in Jaenelle's Ring of Honor snapped up around him. Two more arrows hit the shield and turned to dust.

He used Craft to remain standing and cursed himself for a thrice-times fool for not activating the shield in the first place. But there was nothing they could do to him now, not even stop him from walking or crawling back to the landing web and riding the Winds away from there. And the wounds, while painful, weren't that serious. He had an arrow in each leg and one in the left shoulder, but it was high enough . . .

He felt a deadly cold filling his limbs and knew what it had to be. Poison on the arrow tips. But how virulent a poison?

He saw the answer in the Eyrien's cruel smile.

He fell to his knees. No time to give all the warnings he needed to give. No time. So he focused on sending a warning to the person who had always mattered the most to him.

As the body's death closed in on him, he gathered his strength and sent one word. *KARLA!*

6 / Kaeleer

Karla sat at her dressing table, one hand braced on the table, the other pressed against her abdomen. The cramps didn't usually last this long, and they weren't usually this painful.

"Here you are," Ulka said sympathetically, setting a steaming mug on the dressing table. "This moontime brew will make you feel different in no time."

"Thanks, Ulka," Karla murmured. She had accepted Ulka into her Third Circle for the same reason she had accepted other witches from Glacia's aristo families—to placate them after she had exiled her uncle, Hobart. And while she didn't personally like Ulka, she had to admit the woman had been a solicitous companion this winter, fussing a little too much over the minor illnesses but having a good instinct of when to gossip and when to stay quiet.

As soon as the brew cooled enough, Karla took a large swallow. Making a disgusted face, she set the mug down. The brew had an odd, rancid taste. Hell's fire, had some of the herbs gotten moldy or gone bad somehow? Then again, a lot of things hadn't tasted quite right to her all winter. Or maybe she'd just gotten spoiled by the delicious-tasting brews Jaenelle made. It didn't matter how it tasted. It wasn't going to ease the pain if it sat in the cup.

As she reached for the mug again, she looked in the mirror. A chill ran through her when she saw the watchful anticipation in Ulka's eyes. "You poisoned it, didn't you?" Karla said flatly.

"Yes," Ulka said, sounding smug and pleased.

Karla felt her body sluggishly gathering itself to fight off the poison. Because she was a Black Widow, she had a stronger tolerance for poisons than other people would have, but even a Black Widow could succumb to a poison her body couldn't recognize or tolerate.

As she stared at the other woman's reflection, she finally knew. All the minor illnesses, all the foods that had tasted a little off. And Ulka always there, being so helpful, acting so concerned. "You've slipped mild poisons into a lot of things this winter."

"Yes."

Poisons which had weakened her body but never made her ill enough to become suspicious—despite having been warned of her own death in the tangled web she'd created last fall. Oh, she'd been careful. She knew too much about poisons not to be. The fact that she hadn't been able to detect the poisons meant that whatever plants had been used weren't native to Glacia. She would have recognized one of *those* instantly, no matter how it was disguised.

With effort, Karla got to her feet. One moment her legs were full of fiery spikes, the next they were numb. She flooded her body with her Gray strength, accepting the pain her own power caused during her moontime in order to fight the poison.

As one staggering wave of pain ripped through her, she felt the Ebony shield in the ring Jaenelle had given her surround her.

"Why?" Karla asked. How could she have misjudged this bitch so badly? What had she missed?

Ulka pouted. "I thought I would be an important Lady in your court. I should have been in your First Circle, not the *Third*."

"A witch who would poison her Queen isn't suitable to serve in the First Circle," Karla said dryly. "It's a question of loyalty."

"I *was* loyal," Ulka snapped. "But being loyal to you didn't get me anywhere. And then I got a better offer. Once you're gone and Lord Hobart controls Glacia again, I *will* be an important Lady."

"All you'll be is some man's whore," Karla said flatly.

Ulka's face became ugly. "And you'll be dead! And don't think they won't finish the kill to make sure they're rid of *all* of you!"

The ring Jaenelle had given her produced a sharp, warning tingle seconds before Morton's warning cry filled her mind.

KARLA!

Morton? Morton!

Nothing. An emptiness where someone had been for as long as she could remember.

Another kind of cold filled Karla—a cold that fed her body, gave her strength. "You killed Morton," she said too quietly.

"*I* didn't," Ulka replied. "But he's dead by now."

The bladed Eyrien stick Lucivar had given her was in her hands and whistling through the air before Ulka had time to realize the danger. The blades, honed to a killing edge, swept through Ulka's leg bones as easily as they swept through the woman's wool dress.

Blood gushed. Ulka fell, screaming.

Karla staggered, braced herself. She couldn't use her body this way and fight the poison long enough for . . .

For what? With Morton dead, who would be able to reach her fast enough? No matter. She would fight to live for as long as she could. And she had more power at her disposal than her enemies had imagined since she didn't have to use her Gray Jewels to shield herself.

Looking down at Ulka, Karla raised the bladed stick. "Well, bitch, I may not be able to finish the kill, but I can make damn sure you're of no use to anyone when you become demon-dead."

She cut off Ulka's hands, then her head. The last stroke tore through the belly and severed the spine.

Karla staggered back a few steps, away from the growing pool of blood. Sinking to the floor, she carefully stretched out, her right arm wrapped around her belly, her left hand clamped around the bladed stick.

She had seen her own death in her tangled web, and she'd done what she could to change that part of the vision. But if she had to die now, she would accept it.

Dark power washed over her, warming icy limbs. She felt

a tendril of power wrap around her and recognized a healing thread helping her fight against the poison.

Cradled by Jaenelle's strength, she turned inward to concentrate on the battlefield her body had become.

7 / Kaeleer

Daemon snarled in frustration when he felt the tingling
coming from Jaenelle's Ring of Honor. He hadn't yet
learned how to interpret all the information that could be
absorbed from the Ring. He recognized this particular sensation as a call for help, but had no idea where the call
was coming from. "Do you—" he said, turning toward
Khardeen.

The intense blankness in Khary's eyes, the sense of focused listening, stopped him from saying anything more.

"Morton," Khary said quietly. "And *Karla.*" He lunged
for the door.

Daemon grabbed him. "No. You're needed here."

"That's not the way it works," Khary said sharply.
"When one of us needs help—"

"You all take the bait?" Daemon asked just as sharply.
"You have a pregnant Queen who can't defend herself
without risking a miscarriage. Your place is here. I'll take
care of Karla—and Morton." He studied Khary. "Who else
will have heard that call for help?"

"Everyone in the First Circle who lives in the western
part of Kaeleer. The Ring has more of a range than if we
were trying to reach someone on our own, but the alert
wouldn't be felt beyond that. However, every male who
felt that call for help will relay a warning through a communication thread to the First Circle within *his* range."

"Then relay this message to the First Circle as fast as
you can: 'Stay put. Stand guard.' " Daemon paused. "And
locate Jaenelle."

"Yes," Khary said grimly. "The Queens need to be protected. Especially her."

Satisfied, Daemon rushed out of the house and swore.
He couldn't reach any of the Winds from here.

He started to run down the drive, then turned toward

the sound of pounding hooves. Sundancer slid to a stop beside him.

I heard the call, Sundancer said. *You must ride the Winds?*

"Yes."

I can run faster. Mount.

Grabbing a fistful of Sundancer's mane, he swung up on the Warlord Prince's bare back.

It was a short but harrowing ride. The stallion chose the fastest route to reach the nearest Winds without regard for what lay in his path, and Daemon's legs were shaking when he slid off Sundancer's back. Before he could say anything, the stallion pivoted and was gone.

Fight well! Sundancer said as he raced back to Khary and Morghann's house.

"You can count on it," Daemon replied too softly. Catching the Black Wind, he headed for Glacia.

8 / Kaeleer

Kaelas made an effortless leap to the roof of a human den in time to see Morton fall. He snarled silently, the desire to attack warring with the instinct for caution. Slipping down to the depth of his Red Jewel, where he couldn't be detected by the winged males who were there, he opened his mind and carefully let a psychic tendril drift toward Morton.

The first thing he sensed was the Lady's shield. That wasn't a problem. The Lady had made a Ring of Honor for the kindred males, too. So he had the same protection and, more important right now, he had the means to safely slip past that shield.

The moment he did, he knew Morton's body was dead, but he could still sense Morton, very faintly, inside it. Morton was a Brother in the Lady's court, and the Brothers looked after each other. That was important. So he would get his Brother away from the enemy and then decide what to do next.

Looking in the opposite direction, he saw the Sanctuary that held the Dark Altar. Near it was a large, old tree that wouldn't wake again. The pale humans would have cut it down and burned it in their fires. They wouldn't need it now.

Using Craft, he opened the Sanctuary door, letting it swing as if it hadn't been latched properly.

Leaping from the roof, he circled around the backs of the human dens, air walking so that he would leave no tracks. Just because the sight shield made him invisible was no reason to be careless. Playing "stalk and pounce" with Lucivar had taught him that.

Thinking of Lucivar, he remembered something else: never show your full strength to an enemy until it was needed.

His Birthright Jewel was the Opal. Morton's Jewel of rank was the Opal. Yes, *that* might confuse the winged males.

Baring his teeth in what might have been a feline smile, Kaelas unleashed a burst of Opal strength at the dead tree. It exploded. Flaming branches soared through the air in all directions. Another burst of power shattered windows in the dens near the Sanctuary. Another burst of power sent enough snow into the air to form a small blizzard. The last controlled burst of power slammed the Sanctuary door.

The Green-Jeweled Eyrien Warlord Prince had spun around at the first blast, his face twisted with fury. Other males were shouting. When the Sanctuary door slammed, the Eyrien started running, shouting orders.

"What about that bastard?" one of the other men called out.

The Warlord Prince hesitated for a moment. "Leave him. He's not going anywhere. We'll finish the kill after we take care of our new guests."

Kaelas moved forward in stalk position, using all of his senses to keep track of the winged humans. Then, a burst of speed brought him to Morton.

One sniff of the body had him backing away, confused. Morton smelled like poisoned meat. He did not want to set his teeth in poisoned meat. But he had to get Morton away from the winged males.

Moving forward again, he brushed against the Lady's shield, felt it recognize itself in the Ring of Honor he wore and let him in. He put a snug Opal shield around Morton's left arm. When he took that arm between his teeth, the Opal shield was between him and the poisoned meat. Satisfied, he used Craft to float Morton on the air, expanded his sight shield to cover both of them, then raced for the trees.

When he was among the trees, he slowed slightly, but

didn't stop until he reached the hiding den KaeAskavi had
dug. Releasing Morton's arm, he studied the den. The
human would fit easily enough without the pointed sticks—
the arrows—poking out. But the Healer would need the
stick part to remove the arrow. Wouldn't she?

After a little thought, he used Craft to shear the shafts
in half. He tucked Morton into the den and placed the
sheared-off shafts next to him. Then he paused again.

He had never seen human Blood become demon-dead.
He didn't know how long it would take for Morton to wake
and reclaim the dead flesh. But he *did* know that when
Morton woke and found himself in a strange place, he
would wonder if the enemy had put him there.

Kaelas pressed a forepaw into the snow near Morton's
head, leaving a deep imprint, then put a shield over the
print, so that it couldn't be brushed away carelessly. Morton
would see the print and understand.

Pleased that he had worked out the complicated thinking
required to deal with humans, he covered up the den, leaving a small airhole. A dead human didn't need air, but the
freshness would show Morton the easiest place to dig free.

Now to take care of the bad winged males.

After sending out a summons for the dark-Jeweled Arcerian Warlords and Warlord Princes to join him, Kaelas
headed back to the village.

9 / Kaeleer

Ignoring the official landing web, Daemon dropped from
the Winds as close as he could get to Karla's home. The
moment he appeared on a street, he wrapped a Black sight
shield, psychic shield, and protective shield around himself.
He ran a couple of blocks, turned a corner, and stopped.

The street was full of struggling, fighting men. Blasts of
Jeweled power made the air smell like lightning. Those who
had already drained their Jewels, or had never worn them,
were fighting with mundane weapons. He spotted some
women, fighting desperately but ineffectively.

So familiar. He didn't need the whiff of rot present in
some of the psychic scents to recognize Dorothea's hand in
this. He'd seen it too many times in Terreille. Those whose

ambition far outstripped their ability would sell their own people for Hayll's "assistance." The fighting would eliminate the strongest males and females, the ones best able to oppose Dorothea, and the ones who were left . . .

This time he didn't have to be subtle. This time he didn't have to dance around the agony Dorothea would inflict on him if she suspected his interference. But being subtle had become ingrained in him. Besides, a silent predator was the most feared.

Smiling a cold, cruel smile, Daemon slipped his hands into his trouser pockets and glided between clumps of fighters—invisible, undetectable—and left devastation in his wake.

He entered Karla's mansion. The fighting must have started here and spread into the street. He stepped over corpses, homed in on the psychic scents that had a flavor he associated with Dorothea, and killed those fighters so swiftly, so cleanly their opponents froze for a moment, stunned and confused.

A Warlord Prince wearing the badge of the Master of the Guard was fighting off other males near the staircase, using the last of his Jeweled strength to shield himself against three men who were still fresh.

Three flicks of Black power. Three men fell.

As he started up the stairs, Daemon saw the sharp hunter's look in the other Warlord Prince's eyes, saw the moment the man guessed something dangerous was climbing the stairs.

A White-Jeweled Warlord rushed at the Warlord Prince, forcing him to turn toward the enemy who was attacking.

Daemon climbed the stairs. Even exhausted, the Warlord Prince would have no trouble with the Warlord, and it would keep him occupied a little while longer.

No need to hunt for Karla's room. The Ring of Honor led him unerringly, the throbbing against his organ irritating him enough to hone a temper that had already risen to the killing edge.

The door stood open. He saw a hacked-up woman lying on a blood-soaked carpet. He saw five men sending blast after blast of power against the shield surrounding another woman. Karla.

He didn't know who the men were—and didn't care.

Reaching up from the depth of the Black, he slipped under the men's inner barriers and unleashed iced rage, turning their brains into gray dust and consuming their psychic strength, finishing the kill.

He was across the room before they fell. Kneeling beside Karla, he dropped the sight shield and reached out cautiously.

The shield around her held a feral, deadly hunger.

Not sure how to get through the shield, and wondering what he might unleash if he did it incorrectly, Daemon took a deep breath and brought his hand a little closer.

A flick of power against his palm. A tasting. An acceptance.

His hand passed, unharmed, through the shield.

"Karla," he said as his hand closed on her arm. "*Karla.*" Her rasping effort to breathe told him she was still alive. But if she'd gone so deep into a healing sleep that she couldn't hear him . . .

"Kiss kiss," Karla rasped.

Relief washed through him. He leaned over her so that she could see him without trying to move her head. "Kiss kiss."

"Poisoned," she said. "Can't identify. Bad."

Pushing her robe aside, Daemon laid his left hand on her chest and sent out a careful psychic probe. His knowledge of healing Craft was limited, but he knew about poisons. And he recognized at least part of this one.

"Get your hand . . . off my . . . tit," Karla said.

"Don't be bitchy," Daemon replied mildly, probing a little more. Her body was fighting it far better than he would have thought possible, but she wouldn't survive without more help than he could give her. He hesitated. "Karla . . ."

"About . . . three hours left. Body . . . can't fight more . . ."

Riding the Black Winds, it had taken him almost two hours to get there from Scelt. Pandar and Centauran were closer, but he didn't know Jonah or Sceron as well as he knew Khardeen, and he didn't know if the satyr or centaur Healers could deal with this poison.

Besides, Jaenelle would most likely head for Scelt. And that decided him.

"I'm getting you out of here," he said as he started to

lift her. Then he realized her hand was still clamped around the bladed stick. "Sweetheart, let go of the stick."

"Have to clean . . . the blades. Can't . . . put a weapon away . . . without cleaning the blades. Lucivar . . . would skin me."

Daemon almost gave her his succinct opinion about that, but glancing over his shoulder at the hacked-up woman, he swallowed any criticism he might have had about Lucivar's training methods. "I'll clean the blades. And I promise I'll never tell Lucivar you didn't do it yourself."

Karla's lips curved in the barest of smiles. "You'd be likable if . . . you weren't so *male*."

"My Queen likes me that way," Daemon said dryly. He vanished the bladed stick, carefully lifted Karla, and turned.

Her Master of the Guard blocked the doorway. "What are you doing with my Queen?"

"Taking her away from here," Daemon answered quietly. "She's been poisoned. She needs help."

"We have Healers."

"Would you trust them?" Daemon saw the moment's hesitation. "I have no quarrel with you, Prince. Don't force me to go through you."

The other man studied him, focused on the Black-Jeweled Ring. "You're Lady Angelline's Consort."

"Yes."

The man stepped aside. As Daemon passed him, he said quietly, "Please take care of her."

"I will." Daemon paused. "Have you seen Morton?"

The Master of the Guard shook his head.

There was no time to think about Morton or what might have happened to him. "If you see him, tell him I'm taking Karla to Scelt. Don't tell anyone *but* Morton."

The man nodded. "Come this way. There's a Craft-powered carriage out back. It'll get you to the Winds faster."

The Master of the Guard drove the carriage while Daemon held Karla, using those precious minutes to wrap Black shields around her to protect her during the ride on the Winds. They stopped a few feet from where he had landed.

"May the Darkness embrace you, Prince," the man said.

"And you." Wrapping his arms around Karla, Daemon caught the Black Wind and rode hard toward Scelt.

He stopped once, halfway there, to send a message to Khary. *I'm on my way back with Karla. She's been poisoned. We'll need a Healer and a Black Widow. The best you have.*

Jaenelle's on her way here, Khary replied.

That was all he needed to know. He caught the Black Wind again and continued the journey, knowing the sand in the hourglass was trickling away far too fast.

10 / Kaeleer

Sight shielded, Kaelas and twenty Arcerian males crouched on the roofs of the human dens, watching the bad winged males move around the village. Some of the dens had lights now that night had closed around them, and he could smell food cooking.

Meat? one of the Arcerian Warlords asked.

No, Kaelas replied. He felt a ripple of anger run through the other males. *The meat tastes bad.*

We have come for the hunt but will have no meat to bring back to the home dens? another male asked irritably.

We promised the Lady we wouldn't hunt human meat, a younger male said tentatively.

These males killed a male who belonged to the Lady, Kaelas said firmly. *They killed the pale humans who belonged to Lady Karla.*

Another ripple of anger, this time directed at the bad winged males. Arcerians didn't have much use for humans, but they liked Lady Karla and adored the Lady. For them, they would hunt and return to the dens without meat.

The wind shifted slightly, brought a different scent.

We will take the animals that belonged to the pale humans, Kaelas said. *The humans do not need them now. It will be payment for work.* He was pleased that he remembered that peculiar human idea. If the Lady snarled at him for taking animals from a human village, he could use those words.

Payment for work? a couple of males echoed. Then one of them asked, *This is a human thing?*

Yes. We kill these bad males, then we can take good meat back to the dens.

Satisfied, the Arcerians settled down to study their prey.

Kaelas watched the winged males for a minute. *We must hunt fast . . . and silent.*

Fast kills, the others agreed.

Kaelas watched the Green-Jeweled Warlord Prince walk to a den near the Sanctuary. *But not for that one.*

11 / Kaeleer

Jaenelle was waiting for him by the time Daemon reached Khary and Morghann's house.

"She's bleeding too much for this just to be moon's blood," he said abruptly as he rushed into the guest room, followed by Morghann, Khary, and Maeve, the village Healer. "And there's not much time left."

Jaenelle placed a hand on Karla's chest, her eyes focusing on something only she could see. "There's enough," she said too calmly.

Morghann laid a padding of towels on the bed.

Daemon gave her a cold stare as he laid Karla on the bed. Was the woman more worried about her precious linens than about a friend who had been poisoned?

"It'll disturb her less to change a towel than to change the linens," Morghann said quietly, her eyes clearly telling him she knew what he'd been thinking—and had been hurt by it.

There was no time for an apology. Morghann and Maeve stripped off the bloody nightgown and robe, and quickly wiped the blood off Karla's skin. Jaenelle paid no attention to the physical ministrations, remaining focused on the healing.

Daemon was about to tell her what he knew about the poison when he looked down at his blood-soaked sleeve. Memories of being soaked in Jaenelle's blood rushed at him. He ripped off the jacket, then the shirt. Khary took them and handed him a wet cloth.

As he scrubbed the blood off his skin, Jaenelle said, "There were two poisons used. I don't know one of them."

Handing the cloth back to Khary, Daemon moved to the

bed. "One of them comes from a plant that only grows in southern Hayll."

Jaenelle looked up, her eyes blank and iced. "Do you know an antidote?" she asked with an odd calm that scared him.

"Yes. But the herbs I have are several years old. I don't know if they'll still be potent enough."

"I can make them potent enough. Make the antidote, Daemon."

"What about the other poison?" he asked as he started clearing a work space on the bedside table.

"It's witchblood."

A chill went through him. Witchblood only grew where a witch had been violently killed—or where she had been buried. Used as a poison, it was virulent and deadly—and usually undetectable.

"You can detect it?" Daemon asked cautiously.

"I can recognize witchblood in any of its forms," Jaenelle replied in her midnight voice.

Another memory rushed at him. Jaenelle staring at the bed of witchblood she had planted in an alcove on the Angelline estate. *Did you know that if you sing to them correctly, they'll tell you the names of the ones who have gone?*

Even dried into a poison, did the plants tell Witch the names of the ones who were gone?

Locking away the memories, along with his heart, Daemon concentrated on making the antidote.

"Maeve," Jaenelle said, "get some basic plasters ready. We'll have to draw out some of the poison. Morghann, I want you to leave the room. Don't come back for any reason until I tell you."

"But—"

Jaenelle just looked at her.

Morghann hurried out of the room.

"May I stay?" Khary asked quietly. "You three will be involved in the healing. You'll need a free pair of hands to fetch things."

"This won't be easy, Lord Khardeen," Jaenelle said.

Khary paled a little. "She's my Sister, too."

Jaenelle nodded her consent, then leaned over the bed

and said so softly Daemon was sure he was the only one
close enough to hear, "Arms or legs, Karla?"

The answer, if she got one, was private—Sister to Sister.
But it began a healing so gruesome he desperately hoped
he would never witness anything like it again.

12 / Kaeleer

Kaelas listened to the sounds coming from the room and
snarled silently. The Green-Jeweled Eyrien Warlord Prince
was mating with the pale female, the young Priestess. Her
cries disturbed him. They were not like the sounds the Lady
made with Daemon. There was fear and pain in *these*
sounds.

He almost slipped through the Green shield the male
had placed around the room, almost decided to repay Morton's death with a fast kill instead of the kind of death that
was owed when the female cried, "But I helped you. *I
helped you!*"

Remembering KaeAskavi's she-kitten, who was now an
orphan, and all the other pale humans that had belonged
to Lady Karla and were now dead, Kaelas took a step back.
The female had fouled her own den, had brought in poisoned meat. She deserved this winged male for a mate.

Careful not to disturb the Green shield and alert the
male, he placed a Red shield around the room, caging the
humans. He added a Red psychic shield so that when the male
noticed he was trapped, he wouldn't be able to warn the
other winged males.

Slipping out of the building, Kaelas paused, listened.
There were more winged males than cats, but that didn't
matter. The Green-Jeweled Warlord Prince was the only
one of the winged males who wore one of the dark Jewels,
and he was already caged. Among the cats here, Kaelas
was the only one who wore a Red Jewel, but the shields
from the Opal, Green, and Sapphire Jewels the others wore
would protect them while they attacked with teeth and
claws.

Now, Kaelas said.

Silent, invisible, the cats spread out and went hunting.

CHAPTER
TWELVE

1 / Kaeleer

Lucivar and Falonar stood back at a prudent distance and watched the women at archery practice. Hallevar stood a few feet behind the women, giving instructions that could be heard in the still morning air as clearly as the smack of sticks coming from the arms practice field.

The weather had turned overnight, bringing the warm promise of spring. It wouldn't last, but while it did, Lucivar intended to have the women on the practice field for a couple of hours every morning. This was the first day they were actually aiming an arrow at a target. Watching them would have been amusing if he hadn't felt so edgy.

A day and a half had passed since Daemon's order to "stay put and stand guard" had been relayed through the First Circle—an order which, a couple of hours later, had been reinforced by Jaenelle. The only other message he had received had been equally brief: Karla had been poisoned and Morton was missing.

He would have disregarded the order if Daemon hadn't been with Jaenelle, but he knew that if anyone could protect the Queen better than he could, it was the Sadist.

So he'd stayed . . . and watched . . . and waited.

Falonar huffed out a breath as a spattering of arrows made a pathetic attempt to reach the targets. "Do you really think they can do this?" he asked doubtfully.

Lucivar snorted. "During your first six months in the hunting camps, you couldn't hit anything smaller than the side of a mountain."

Falonar just looked at him. "But I didn't whine about taking up time that could be used to air out the bedding. What's the point of pretending they can use a—*shit*." That when a woman with a bow fully drawn started to turn toward Hallevar as he added instructions. Hallevar leaped forward and shoved her so that the arrow skittered along the grass instead of into the woman next to her.

Lucivar and Falonar both winced at the language Hallevar used to explain that little error.

"Do you see?" Falonar demanded.

"Hallevar didn't learn to leap like that because this was the first time someone had done something so stupid," Lucivar replied. He paused, then added, "What's really biting your ass about this?"

Falonar scuffed a boot over the ground. "If we aren't the warriors and protectors, we don't have much to offer—until a woman is looking for a stud. And that's not easy to stomach."

"Can you cook?" Lucivar asked mildly.

Falonar glared at him. "Of course I can cook. Any Eyrien who's been in the hunting camps knows how to do rough-and-ready cooking."

Lucivar nodded. "Then relax. Just because a woman knows how to catch her own dinner doesn't mean she's going to grow balls any more than you're going to grow tits just because you know how to cook it." He watched Surreal put an arrow into the outer ring of the target and smiled. "Do you want to go over and tell *her* you don't think she's capable of handling a bow?"

"Not while she's got a weapon in her hand," Falonar muttered.

They jumped when one of the women let out a loud yelp.

Lucivar relaxed when he noticed the way Hallevar was rubbing one hand over his mouth and the woman was surreptitiously rubbing her forearm against her right breast.

"Five minutes of free practice," Hallevar called before hurrying toward the other two men.

"What happened?" Falonar demanded.

"Damnedest thing," Hallevar said, breaking into a wide grin. "Didn't think to warn them about it 'cause . . . well, Hell's fire, I've never *had* to consider it before. How was I supposed to know you could catch a tit with a bowstring?"

"Catch a—" Falonar looked at the women—who had all turned to glare at the men. He looked at the ground and cleared his throat—several times. "Bet it stings."

Lucivar felt his jaw muscles cramp with the effort to keep from laughing. "Yes, I'm sure it does. I didn't think to warn Marian when I taught her, and I'd already worked with Jaenelle. But Marian's got . . . a bit more chest."

Falonar choked.

Hallevar just nodded solemnly. "That's a fine, respectful way to phrase it—especially when there's a handful of women out there who might just get mad enough to actually hit something if you phrased it any other way."

"Precisely," Lucivar said dryly. "Work them through one more quiver and—"

He was running toward the arms practice field before the first panicked scream could be drowned out by furious shouts. He leaped up on the low stone wall that separated the two fields. Ice formed around his heart when he saw Kaelas give a Green-Jeweled Eyrien Warlord Prince a casual swat that opened up the back of one thigh. The ice became a painful cage when he saw Rothvar and Zaranar running toward the stranger with weapons drawn.

NO! he shouted on a spear thread. *I'll gut any man who raises a weapon!*

They skidded to a stop, their shock at his order rivaling their fury. But they, and the other men on the practice field, obeyed.

"Help me!" the stranger yelled as he swung his war blade at Kaelas, trying to keep the cat in front of him while he limped backward toward the other men. "Damn you all to the bowels of Hell, *help me!*"

Lucivar turned, looked back at the women. *Marian, take all the women up to our eyrie. Close the shutters.*

Lucivar, what—

Do it!

He strode toward the loose circle of men, Falonar and Hallevar right behind him. A gut-sick satisfaction filled him as he watched how easily Kaelas dodged the stranger's attempts to counterattack—and he wondered what the other men would say if they knew *he* had been the one who had taught the cat how to move with and against human weapons.

As soon as the Eyrien shifted into a fighting stance, Kaelas charged. The speed and the sheer weight behind the charge knocked the man back several feet. The claws ripped open the Eyrien's shoulders and followed through down the arms, leaving them useless. The cat leaped away and began lazily circling a man barely able to get to his feet.

Falonar looked behind them and cursed softly, viciously. Turning and opening his wings to hide the practice field, he snarled, "Go back with the other women."

"Don't give me any of that—oh, shit," Surreal said as she dodged Falonar and got a good look at the man and cat.

Kaelas continued the light, almost playful swats, inflicting surface wounds that would slowly bleed out his prey. He continued until the Eyrien stranger spread his torn wings and tried to fly. The cat leaped with the man, then landed lightly. The man, with his back ripped open, fell heavily.

"Mother Night," Surreal whispered, "he's *playing* with that man."

"He's playing," Lucivar said grimly as nerves twisted his belly, "but it's not a game. This is an Arcerian execution."

Surreal understood before Falonar did. Lucivar saw her face tighten—and he saw her eyes fill with cool professional interest.

"Yaslana," Falonar warned.

Lucivar sensed the growing tension in the other men and knew it wouldn't be long before one of them disobeyed his order and joined the "fight." He started to move closer.

Kaelas must have sensed it, too, because the playfulness ended. The Eyrien stranger screamed as the claws ripped his chest open, ripped his thighs to the bone.

"Kaelas," Lucivar said firmly, "that's—" He felt the crackle of Red-Jeweled power as the paw lashed out again. The object flew at him so fast, he instinctively caught it before it slammed into his chest. For a second or two, Lucivar stared at the head that had been severed at the base of the neck. Then he dropped it.

"Mother Night," Surreal said softly.

The Eyrien's right hand, with its Green-Jeweled ring, sailed through the air and plopped on the ground next to the head.

With a full-throated snarl of rage, Kaelas gutted the man, then defecated in the open belly before moving away from the corpse. Finally, he looked at Lucivar. *That one is still inside . . . for the High Lord.*

Lucivar tried to swallow. Kaelas had deliberately not finished the kill. *Why?*

He killed Morton, Kaelas replied, making the effort to use a communication thread that could be heard by all the humans present. *And he killed the pale humans that belonged to Lady Karla.*

Fury washed through Lucivar, a cleansing fire. *Where?* An image appeared in his mind, oddly focused but clear enough for him to identify the place. *My thanks, Brother,* he said, using a spear thread directed specifically at the cat.

Kaelas leaped, caught the Winds, and disappeared.

"I've done a lot of things as an assassin," Surreal said, hooking her hair behind her ears, "but I've never shit on the body. Is that some kind of feline quirk?"

"It's the way Arcerians show contempt for an enemy," Lucivar said. He looked at Falonar, who seemed to be fighting not to be sick. A quick glance was enough to confirm that most of the men were doing the same, despite their experience on battlefields. "I don't recognize him. Do you?"

Falonar shook his head.

"I do," Rothvar said heavily as he approached them. "When he found out I was immigrating to Kaeleer, he offered me a place in his company. Said he wasn't going to have to lick any bitch's boots, that he'd be ruling a fine piece of land before a year was out. I never liked him, so I said no. But . . ." He glanced at the head, then away. "I heard . . . thought I heard . . . Did the cat speak true?"

"He wouldn't lie." Lucivar took a deep breath. "Falonar, select four men to go with us." Looking around, he realized Surreal was no longer with them.

Falonar turned, too, and swore. "Damn it, she's probably off someplace puking her guts—"

Surreal leaped over the low stone wall and trotted toward them, a large, dented metal bucket in one hand. When they just looked at her, she huffed and said tartly to Lucivar, "Were you planning to tuck that thing under your arm to take it to the High Lord?"

Lucivar smiled reluctantly. "Thanks, Surreal." He hesitated. His hands were already bloody, but he still hesitated. She didn't. With another huff, she dumped the head and hand into the bucket, then covered the bucket with a piece of dark cloth.

The men winced. She snarled at them.

Seeing the wariness in Falonar's eyes, Lucivar said, "You have your orders, Prince."

Falonar and Rothvar left with more speed than discretion.

"Tell me he hasn't done as much on a battlefield," Surreal said with a hint of bitterness. "I suppose everything would have been just fine if I'd clung to his arm and begged for smelling salts."

"Don't condemn him out of hand," Lucivar said quietly. "He isn't used to a woman like you."

Surreal turned on him. "And what kind of woman is that?"

"A Dea al Mon witch."

Her smile came slowly, but it was genuine. "I suppose I should have been more tactful." She waved a hand at the bucket, then hesitated. "I'd like to go with you."

"No. I want you to stay here with the other women."

Her eyes frosted. "Why?"

Abruptly impatient, he snarled, "Because you wear the Gray, and I trust you." He waited until he knew she understood. "My eyrie has Ebon-gray shields, but Marian can key them. Don't let anyone in that she doesn't know—for any reason. I'll be back as soon as I can."

Surreal nodded. "All right. But you be careful. If you get hurt, I'll smack you."

Lucivar waited until she was out of earshot before he waved Hallevar over to him. "Send Palanar to my mother's house. He's to escort Lady Luthvian to my eyrie without delay."

Hallevar shifted uneasily. "She'll take a strip out of the boy."

"Tell her it's an order from the Warlord Prince of Ebon Rih," Lucivar said. "Then I want you to keep an eye open around here. If you see anything, hear anything, sense anything you don't like, you send one of the boys to the Keep and the other to the Hall for help. The wolf pack will also keep watch. If you see anyone who doesn't live right here, whether you knew them well in Terreille or not, treat them as an enemy. Understand?"

Nodding, Hallevar went off to attend his duties.

A short time later, Lucivar and five of his men were flying toward the Keep.

2 / Kaeleer

Lucivar set the metal bucket on the opposite end of the worktable and watched Saetan pour fresh blood into a bowl of simmering liquid. "I thought you would be at the Hall, waiting for the reports to come in."

"Draca sent for me," Saetan replied, lightly stirring the bowl's contents. "What brings you here?"

"Morton is dead."

Saetan's hand hesitated a moment, then resumed stirring. "I know."

Lucivar tensed, then said cautiously, "He's in the Dark Realm?"

"No, he's here. That's why Draca sent for me. He came to report."

Lucivar paced restlessly. "Good. I'll talk to him before—"

"No."

The implacable tone in Saetan's voice stopped him—for a moment. "I don't care if he's demon-dead now."

"He does." Saetan's voice gentled. "He doesn't want to see you, Lucivar. Not any of you."

"Why in the name of Hell not?" Lucivar shouted.

Saetan snarled. "Do you think it's easy making the transition? Do you think anything will be the same for him? He's *dead*, Lucivar. He's a young man who will never do a great many things now, who is no longer who and what he used to be. There are reasons why the dead remain, for the most part, among the dead."

Lucivar resumed his pacing. "It's not like the First Circle isn't used to being around the demon-dead."

"You didn't know them when they walked among the living," Saetan said softly. "There were no ties with them that needed to be cut. Yes, the ties *do* need to be cut," he said, overriding Lucivar's protest. "The living have to move on—and so do the dead. If you can't respect that, at least respect the fact that he needs time to adjust before he has to deal with the rest of you."

Lucivar swore softly. "How bad . . . ?"

Saetan set the spoon down and moved to the other end of the table. "The wounds aren't visible when he's dressed. In fact, they wouldn't have been fatal if the arrows hadn't been poisoned."

"Poisoned," Lucivar said flatly as he stared down at the bucket.

"There's not much Morton could tell you, and without more information, even what he knows doesn't help us much."

Lucivar pointed at the bucket. "You may find your answers in there."

Saetan lifted the dark cloth, looked inside the bucket, then let the cloth drop.

"Kaelas," Lucivar said, answering the unspoken question.

"I see," Saetan said quietly. "You're returning to Ebon Rih?"

Lucivar shook his head. "I'm taking a few men to the Dark Altar in Glacia to look around, see if there are any answers there."

"Our Queen's order was quite direct," Saetan said mildly.

"I'll risk her anger."

Saetan nodded. "Then, as Steward of the Court, I formally request that you go to the Dark Altar in Glacia to determine what happened."

"I don't need to hide behind your title," Lucivar snapped.

Saetan smiled dryly. "I'm doing this as much for Jaenelle as for you. This way, she can gracefully back away from having to confront you about disobeying a direct order."

"Oh. In that case . . ."

"Get going, boyo. Report to me at the Hall. And Prince Yaslana," Saetan added when Lucivar reached the door, "remember Glacia isn't your territory. You're not the law there."

"Yes, sir, I'll remember. We just witness and report."

3 / Kaeleer

Seeing the guarded look in Marian's eyes and the way Luthvian managed to convey silently her disapproval of her son's choice of a wife, Surreal wondered how pissed off Lucivar would be if they took his mother into the garden and used her for target practice.

"How did you manage to bake anything this morning?" Nurian, the journeymaid Healer, asked as she accepted a nutcake from the plate Marian was passing around. "And how do you get anything else done after these morning workouts?"

"Oh," Marian said with a shy smile, "I'm used to it by now, and—"

"You're a Healer," Luthvian interrupted, giving Nurian a cool stare. "*Your* finding it difficult to practice a demanding Craft after these workouts is understandable. But they're hardly an excuse for neglecting one's duties when you're talking about *hearth Craft.* After all—"

"If you'll excuse us," Surreal said, hauling Luthvian to her feet. "There's something Lady Luthvian and I need to discuss."

"Let go of me," Luthvian snarled as Surreal dragged her out of the room. "You don't treat a Black Widow Healer like she was—"

"A hearth-witch?" Surreal said with venomous sweetness as she shoved Luthvian into the garden.

"Exactly," Luthvian replied darkly. "But I don't suppose a *whore*—"

"Shut up, bitch," Surreal said too quietly.

Luthvian sucked in air. "You forget your place!"

"No, sugar, that's exactly what I'm not forgetting. You may belong to a higher caste, but my Jewels outrank yours. I figure that evens things out—at least within the family. You don't like me, and that suits me just fine because I don't like you either."

"Crossing a Black Widow isn't wise," Luthvian said softly.

"Crossing an assassin isn't wise either." Surreal smiled when Luthvian's eyes widened. "So let's make this simple. If you make one more disparaging remark about Marian, I'm going to bang your face against the wall until some sense gets knocked into you."

"What do you think Lucivar would say about *that*?" Luthvian's voice sounded certain, but there was doubt in her eyes.

"Oh," Surreal replied, "I don't think Lucivar would say anything to *me*." Watching the verbal thrust hit the mark, she felt a brief moment of pity for Luthvian. The woman drove people away, and then seemed bewildered to find herself alone.

"He could have done better," Luthvian grumbled. "He didn't have to settle for a Purple Dusk hearth-witch."

Surreal studied Luthvian. "This doesn't have anything to do with Lucivar, does it? You're embarrassed because *your* son married a *hearth-witch*. Marian is just a gentle, caring woman who loves him and whose presence makes him happy. If he had married a Black Widow Healer and was miserable, well, that would have been all right because he had married a woman worthy of a Warlord Prince. Right?" *Besides,* she added silently, *the High Lord approves of his son's choice.* Which, she suspected, was the major reason Luthvian never would. "Remember what I said, Luthvian." She started to walk away.

"Just because the High Lord tolerates your using the SaDiablo name doesn't change what you were—and still are," Luthvian said nastily.

Surreal looked over her shoulder. "No," she said, "it doesn't. You would do well to remember that, too."

4 / Kaeleer

Lucivar felt the tingle of residual power the moment he stepped off the landing web. While the other Eyriens stared at the dead bodies and muttered uneasily, he kept his eyes on the pressed-down snow a few feet in front of him. He moved toward it, then skirted around it.

"What?" Falonar asked as he avoided the spot, too.

"Morton died there," Lucivar said quietly.

"He's not the only one who died," Rothvar said grimly, looking at the savaged Eyrien corpses.

"No, he's not the only one," Lucivar replied. *But he's the one I watched grow from a decent youth into a fine man.* "Rothvar, you and Endar—"

If he hadn't spent the past eight years living around kindred, he never would have picked up that particular psychic scent—and wouldn't have known the Arcerian cats were there until it was far too late.

He scanned the village roofs with a seemingly casual eye while he quietly sank to the depth of his Ebon-gray Jewel and probed the area. Eight Arcerians. Two of them Warlord Princes. All of them wearing darker Jewels.

"Keep your hands away from your weapons," Lucivar said, keeping his voice low and even. "We've got company." Moving slowly, he unbelted the short wool cape and opened it to expose his chest and the Ebon-gray Jewel that hung from the chain around his neck. He held his arms out, away from his weapons. "I am Lucivar Yaslana," he said in a loud voice. "I belong to the Lady. And these males belong to me."

I'm not sensing anything, Falonar said on a Sapphire spear thread.

Kindred don't usually announce their presence, Lucivar said dryly. *Especially the Arcerians.*

Mother Night! Falonar looked at the savaged Eyrien bodies. *Those cats are still here? How many?*

Eight of them. Let's hope they decide we're friends, or this is going to turn into a mess.

Lucivar waited until his arms began to ache. Finally there was a wary psychic touch. *You are Kaelas's Brother,* said a growling voice.

And he is my Brother, Lucivar replied. He lowered his arms.

Why are you here? the cat demanded.

To stand witness for the Lady.

A long pause. *Kaelas told us to guard this place so that no more bad meat comes through the Gate.*

Lucivar hoped the cats watching him thought the shiver was due to the cold and not the reference to Eyriens being "bad meat." *Kaelas is wise.*

You look and then go. That wasn't a question.

Lucivar turned toward his men. He raised his voice to make sure the nearest Arcerian cat would hear the orders. "Raise basic shields."

Five men gave him blank looks followed by swift comprehension. Protective shields snapped up around them.

Will these shields protect us? Falonar asked Lucivar, using a Sapphire thread so that the other men couldn't hear him.

No, Lucivar replied shortly. "Weapons to hand." He called in his Eyrien war blade, then nodded when the others followed his example. "Kohlvar, you and Endar keep watch at the landing web. Rothvar and Zaranar, take the left side of the village. Falonar, with me." *And if one of the Arcerians actually shows himself, give him the same courtesy you would give any other warrior,* he added on a general spear thread.

They moved slowly, carefully, fully aware that the cats watched every movement, every gesture.

"How did those cats manage to kill this many Eyriens without anyone sounding an alarm?" Falonar asked quietly when they had checked half the houses on their side of the village. It was obvious that a number of the men hadn't suspected a thing before the attack.

"When an Arcerian is hunting, you don't usually know he's there until he kills you," Lucivar replied absently as he quickly checked through another house. There was evidence of at least minimal fighting in all the houses, but that had been Glacian against Eyrien. "That makes them very efficient."

When they reached the living quarters in the Sanctuary, they both stared at the young Priestess—or what was left of her.

"Hell's fire," Falonar said, disgust filling his voice as he backed away from the door. "Well, I guess gang rape *is* a kind of slow execution. But why keep just this one? And why beat her to death when they'd probably already done enough to kill her?"

"Because the other women fought, while this one expected a different kind of reward," Lucivar replied. When Falonar stared at him with horror-filled eyes, he laughed, a low, nasty sound. "You spent enough time in the Terreillean courts to know how to get dirty, Prince Falonar. *Someone* had to help that Green-Jeweled bastard go through the Gate to get back to Terreille—or at least keep the old Priestess from realizing the Gate was being used without her knowledge or consent. As for the beating . . . I guess when the bastard realized he was trapped in here, he needed to take it out on someone."

"The cat didn't kill him slow enough," Falonar muttered, turning away from the room. "Not nearly slow enough."

I imagine the High Lord will know how to extract the final payment for the debt, Lucivar thought, but he didn't tell Falonar *that.*

As they left the Sanctuary, Zaranar made a "come here" gesture.

"Rothvar's at the back door," Zaranar said uneasily. "I think you should handle this. All we've done is keep an eye on the doors," he added quickly.

Before Lucivar could move, Kohlvar sent an urgent message. *Prince, there's a Glacian at the landing web who says he's Lady Karla's Master of the Guard. He's got forty guards with him.*

Tell him to stay put, Lucivar replied sharply as he and Falonar headed for the back of the house. *I'll talk to him in a few minutes.*

Before he reached the back door, he could hear the nervous snarls coming from inside the house. Rothvar stepped aside. Lucivar started to go in, then stopped abruptly.

The Arcerian Warlord was almost full-grown, so there wasn't much room in the small kitchen for a cat his size to pace. On the table was an odd assortment of food. On the floor was a goat, neatly killed.

When Lucivar took a step toward the goat, the cat pounced on it and snarled.

Mine, the cat said.

"All right," Lucivar replied mildly.

The cat seemed puzzled by his easy agreement. *Payment for work.*

Interesting, Lucivar thought. Was this a kindred testing of a human idea? "Since you're guarding this place instead of hunting, it's fair that you be paid with meat."

Relaxing a little, the cat looked at the table. So did Lucivar. There wasn't anything on it he thought a cat would want to eat. "Is that also payment for work?"

Human food. The cat made it sound more like a hopeful question.

"Yes, it is."

A she-kitten would like this food?

Lucivar rubbed his chin. "I don't know."

The cat growled, but the sound was filled with discouragement. *We burned some meat for her, but she would not eat.* He wrinkled his lips to indicate what he thought of ruining good meat by cooking it. *I promised to bring human food.*

A chill whispered down Lucivar's spine. "A child survived this place?"

Yes. The she-kitten. KaeAskavi's friend. The cat studied him, then asked hesitantly, *You will help?*

Lucivar blinked away tears that would only confuse the cat. "Yes, I will help."

5 / Kaeleer

"Did we do the right thing?" Daemon asked as he and Lucivar air walked above the deep snow toward the place that was designated as an official landing web. They weren't making that effort just to avoid floundering in waist-high snow; tracks might have shown an enemy where the Arcerian dens were located.

"What else could we do?" Lucivar replied wearily. "The girl has lost her mother, her village, everyone she knew. KaeAskavi's the only friend she has left. There are pockets of fighting going on throughout Glacia, so placing her in another village . . . There's no guarantee she would survive the next time a place is attacked. Marian and I would take her to live with us, but . . ."

Daemon shook his head. "You were right about that. She wouldn't be able to handle being around Eyriens right now." Which was why Lucivar had insisted that Daemon come with him to Arceria in the first place.

"And we can't take her anywhere else," Lucivar added grimly. "Not until we know if this attack was part of Hobart's attempt to regain control of Glacia or if it's something more. You said the girl was physically all right."

"She sprained an ankle, but the Arcerian Healers have the Craft to take care of injured limbs. Other than that, she was . . . unharmed." He couldn't say the word "rape." He would never forget the fear that had jolted through him when he had crawled into that den and seen Della—fair-haired, blue-eyed, ten-year-old Della. She didn't look anything like Jaenelle, except in coloring, but that had been enough to cause the memories of what had happened in Chaillot thirteen years ago to come rushing back at him. His hands had trembled as he'd cautiously examined her for injuries, as he had used a delicate psychic probe to answer that particular question. His hands had also trembled because she had been gripping a stuffed toy cat in one hand and a fistful of KaeAskavi's fur in the other—which meant the cat had been literally breathing down his neck. It was the way she had held on to KaeAskavi that had forced him to leave her there. She needed to feel safe in order to heal—and snuggling up to four hundred pounds of muscle and fur obviously made her feel very safe.

Lucivar rested a hand on Daemon's shoulder. "A few weeks among the Arcerians won't hurt her. At least this way she can be 'mothered' without feeling like she's letting someone take her mother's place."

Daemon nodded. "Are you going back to Ebon Rih?" He had been planning to go to the Keep since Jaenelle was on her way there with Karla and Morghann.

Lucivar shook his head. "The High Lord asked me to report to him at the Hall. This side trip has delayed that report for a couple of days, so I'd better get my ass there before he decides to take a piece out of it."

"Then I'll go with you."

When they reached the place where they could catch the Winds, Lucivar hesitated. "How is Karla? I didn't get to see her before they left for the Keep."

Daemon stared at the unbroken snow. "She'll live. Jaenelle thinks she can heal the legs enough for Karla to walk again."

"Jaenelle *thinks* she can?" Lucivar paled. "Mother Night, Daemon, if *Jaenelle* isn't sure, what was done—"

"Don't ask," Daemon said too sharply. He made an effort to soften his voice. "Don't ask. I . . . don't want to talk about it." But this was Lucivar who was asking, so he tried. "There's no antidote for witchblood. The poison had to be drawn into some part of the body in order to save the internal organs and then drawn out. It . . . killed a lot of the muscle, and that muscle had to be . . ." His gorge rose as he thought of the withered limbs that had been healthy legs.

"Let it go," Lucivar said gently. "Let it go."

They both took a couple of unsteady breaths before Daemon said, "The sooner we make our reports, the sooner we can go home." For him, home wasn't a place, it was a person—and right then, he needed to know that Jaenelle was safe.

6 / Terreille

"Kartane sent a report." Dorothea carefully selected a piece of sugared fruit, took a bite, and chewed slowly just to make Hekatah wait.

"And?" Hekatah finally asked. "Has the Gate in Glacia been secured for our use? Is the village ready for our hand-picked immigrants?"

Dorothea selected another piece of fruit. This time she gave it a couple of delicate licks before answering. "The villagers were eliminated. So were the Eyriens."

"*What?* How?"

"The messenger who met with Kartane couldn't find out what happened to the Eyriens, only that they had killed the villagers and had, in turn, been killed." She paused. "Lord Hobart's dead as well."

Hekatah stood perfectly still. "And the bitch-Queen, Karla? Was that, at least, successful?"

Dorothea shrugged. "She disappeared during the fighting. But since Ulka died rather . . . dramatically . . . one would assume she consumed the poison."

"Then that's the end of her," Hekatah said with a little smile of satisfaction. "Even if someone manages to figure out an antidote for the Hayllian poison in time, the witch-blood will finish things."

"Our plans for Glacia are also finished. Or hasn't that occurred to you?"

Hekatah waved that away. "Considering what we *have* achieved, that's a minor inconvenience."

Dorothea dropped the fruit back into the bowl. "We've achieved *nothing!*"

"You're becoming inflexible, Dorothea," Hekatah said with venomous sweetness. "You're starting to act as old as you look."

Dorothea's blood pounded in her temples, and she wanted—oh, how she wanted—to unleash just a little of the feelings that had been growing more virulent. She hated Hekatah, but she also needed the bitch. So she sat back and inflicted a wound that would hurt much deeper than any physical blow. "At least I still have all my hair. That bald patch is starting to ooze, dearest."

Hekatah automatically lifted a hand to cover the spot. With effort, she lowered it before it reached her head.

The impotent hatred in Hekatah's dull gold eyes scared Dorothea a little but also produced a sense of vicious satisfaction.

"We can make do with sneaking through the other Gates," Hekatah said. "We have something better now."

"And what is that?" Dorothea asked politely.

"The excuse we needed to start the war." Hekatah's smile was pure malevolence.

"I see," Dorothea said, returning the smile.

"The immigrants we had picked to replace the villagers will go to Glacia—just as they would have if Hobart had given us that village as payment for our assistance. We'll also add a few immigrants from other Terreillean Territories. The escorts will be males who don't know where the original village was located. Only the Coach drivers will be told where to drop off the happy families—and that won't be anywhere near a settled area, so there won't be any chance of detection. The escorts will, of course, be dismayed to see no sign of a village waiting for inhabitants." A dreamy look filled Hekatah's eyes. "The company of Eyrien warriors who will be waiting for them will take care of things. The slaughter will be . . . horrible. But there will be a couple of survivors who will manage to escape. They'll live long enough to get back to Little Terreille and tell a few people about how Terreilleans are being butchered in Kaeleer. And they'll live long enough to say that two men had been giving the orders—a Hayllian and an Eyrien."

"No one in Terreille will think it's anyone but Sadi and Yaslana," Dorothea said gleefully. "They'll think the High Lord ordered the attack and sent his sons to oversee it."

"Exactly."

"Which will prove that all my warnings were justified. And once people start wondering why there has been no word from friends or loved ones . . ." Dorothea sank back in her chair with a sigh of pleasure. Then she straightened up reluctantly. "We still have to find a way to contain Jaenelle Angelline."

"Oh, with the proper incentive, she'll willingly place herself in our hands."

Dorothea snorted. "What kind of incentive would make her do that?"

"Using someone she loves as bait."

7 / Kaeleer

Chilled to the bone, Saetan listened to Lucivar's and Daemon's reports. He would have liked to believe Lord Hobart

had hired a company of Eyriens to help him seize control
of Glacia, would have liked to believe Morton's death and
the attack on Karla were strictly a Glacian concern. But
he'd had other reports in the past twenty-four hours. Two
District Queens in Dharo had been killed, along with their
escorts. A mob of landens had attacked a kindred wolf pack
that had recently formed around a young Queen. While
the males were dealing with that threat, some Blood had
outflanked them, killed the Queen, and vanished, leaving
the landens behind to be slaughtered by the enraged males.
In Scelt, a Warlord Prince, a youth still not quite old
enough to make the Offering to the Darkness, had been
found behind the tavern in his home village. His throat had
been slit.

Even more troubling, Kalush had been attacked while
walking through a park in Tajrana, her own capital city.
The only reason neither she nor her infant daughter had
been harmed was because her attackers couldn't break
through the protective shield around her—the Ebony shield
that was in the ring Jaenelle had given her—and because
Aaron, alerted by the link through the Ring of Honor he
wore, had arrived riding the killing edge and had destroyed
the attackers with a savagery that bordered on insanity.

It didn't take any effort to see the pattern, especially
since he recognized it. Fifty thousand years slipped away
as if they had never existed. It might have been Andulvar
and Mephis sitting there, voicing their concerns about swift,
seemingly random attacks to a man who had insisted that,
as a Guardian, he could no longer interfere with the affairs
of the living. He was still a Guardian, but he was too entangled in the affairs of the living to obey the rules Guardians
abided by.

They were going to war.

He wondered if Daemon and Lucivar realized it yet.

And he wondered how many loved ones he would have
to assist through the transition to becoming demon-dead
this time—and how many would disappear without a trace.
Like Andulvar's son, Ravenar. Like his own son, his second
son, Peyton.

"Father?" Daemon said quietly.

He realized they were both watching him intently, but it
was Daemon he focused on. The son who was a mirror,

who was his true heir. The son he understood the best—
and the least.

Before he could start to tell them about the other attacks,
Beale knocked on the study door and walked in.

"Forgive the intrusion, High Lord," Beale said, "but
there's a Warlord here to see you. He has a letter."

"Then take the letter. I don't want to be disturbed at
the moment."

"I suggested that, High Lord. He said he needs to deliver
it in person."

Saetan waited a moment. "Very well."

Lucivar sprang out of his chair and positioned himself so
that he would flank anyone standing near the desk. Daemon rose and resettled himself on a corner of the desk.

The intense warrior and the indolent male. Saetan imagined they had played these roles before—and played them
well. With Lucivar's temper so close to the surface, the
attention would be on him—but the death blow would
come from Daemon.

The Warlord who entered the study was pale, nervous,
and sweating. He paled even more when he saw Lucivar
and Daemon.

Saetan walked around the desk. "You have a letter for
me?"

The Warlord swallowed hard. "Yes, sir." He extended
an envelope, the ink a little smeared from his hands.

Saetan probed the envelope. Found nothing. No trace
of a spell. No trace of poison. He took it and looked at
the Warlord.

"I found that in the guest room desk this morning," the
man said hurriedly. "I didn't know it was there."

Saetan looked at the envelope. There was nothing on it
except his name. "So you found it this morning. Is that
significant?"

"I hope not. I mean—" The man took a deep breath,
made an effort to steady himself. "Lord Magstrom is—
was—my wife's grandfather. He came to visit us last fall,
just before . . . Well, before. He seemed disturbed about
something, but we weren't paying much attention. My
wife . . . We had just found out for sure that she was
pregnant. She'd had a miscarriage the year before, and we

were concerned that it might happen again. The Healer says she has to be careful."

Why was the man pleading with him? "Is your wife well?"

"Yes, thank you, she is, but she's had to be careful. Grandfather Magstrom didn't mention the letter. At least, I don't remember him mentioning it, and then, after he . . . was killed . . ." The man's hands trembled. "I hope it wasn't something urgent. As soon as I found it, I knew I had to come right away. I hope it wasn't urgent."

"I'm sure it's not," Saetan replied gently. "I expect it's just the usual information Lord Magstrom sent me after a service fair—a confirmation more than anything else."

The man's relief was visible.

Saetan glanced at the Warlord's Yellow Jewel. "May I offer you the use of a Coach to take you home?"

"Oh, I don't want to put you through any bother."

"It's no bother—and with a driver who can ride the darker Winds, you'll be home in time to have dinner with your Lady."

The Warlord hesitated a moment longer. "Thank you. I—don't like to be away from her too long." He looked a little sheepish. "She says I fuss."

Saetan smiled. "You're going to become a father. You're entitled to fuss." He led the man out of the study, gave Beale instructions about the Coach, and returned to Daemon and Lucivar. Using the letter opener on his desk, he carefully slit the envelope. He called in his half-moon glasses, opened the letter, and began to read.

"You got reports from Magstrom about the service fair?" Lucivar asked, accepting the glass of brandy Daemon poured for him.

"No." And the more he read, the less he liked receiving this one. As he read the letter a second time, he barely listened to Daemon's and Lucivar's conversation—until Daemon said something that caught his attention. "What did you say?"

"I said Lord Magstrom had indicated that he was going to send letters to some of the Queens outside of Little Terreille," Daemon repeated, swirling the brandy in his glass. "But after Jorval took over handling my immigration,

I was told that the Queens outside of Little Terreille wouldn't consider a Black-Jeweled Warlord Prince."

Lucivar snorted. "Jorval probably arranged for the letters not to be sent. Hell's fire, Daemon, you've met the other Territory Queens. They're the coven. If a letter had reached any one of them, she would have had her Steward at the service fair to sign the contract as fast as he could travel."

"Read this," Saetan said, handing the letter to Daemon.

"I don't understand," Daemon said when he'd read half the letter. "Aren't the lists supposed to indicate every immigrant at the service fair?"

"Yes, they are," Lucivar said grimly, reading over Daemon's shoulder. "And you weren't on any of them." He looked at Saetan. "I did mention that at the time."

"Yes, you did," Saetan replied, "but, since Daemon *did* end up in the Dark Court, I failed to appreciate the significance of that remark."

Daemon handed the letter back to Saetan. "There must have been a list somewhere. Otherwise, how would the Queens in Little Terreille have known I was available?"

Saetan kept his voice mild. "What Queens were those?"

"There were four Queens in Little Terreille who were willing to have me," Daemon said slowly. "Jorval insisted they were the only ones."

"So, if you hadn't met Lucivar by chance . . ."

Daemon froze. "I would have signed a contract with one of them."

Swearing quietly, Lucivar started to pace.

Saetan just nodded. "You would have signed a contract with one of Jorval's handpicked Queens, and you would have ended up tucked away somewhere in Little Terreille—with no one else aware that you *were* there."

"What would have been the point of that?" Daemon said irritably.

"In Little Terreille they use the Ring of Obedience on immigrating males," Lucivar snapped. "*That's* the point. It would have been Terreille all over again."

"Not necessarily," Saetan said, still keeping his voice mild. "If Daemon was well treated, was handled with care—which I'm sure was part of the agreement—he would have had no reason *not* to use the strength of his Jewels against an enemy who was threatening the Queen he served. And after the first unleashing of the Black, there would have been no turning back. The lines would have been drawn."

Daemon stared at him.

"What does it matter?" Lucivar said, looking at the two of them uneasily. "Daemon's with us."

"Yes," Saetan said softly, "he is. But where are the other men whose names disappeared from those lists?"

8 / Kaeleer

The golden spider studied the two tangled webs of dreams and visions.

More deaths. Many deaths.

It was time.

Remember this web. Remember every strand, every thread.

Throughout the cold season, she had been pulled away from her own dreaming, compelled to study the web that had shaped this living myth, the Queen who was Witch. And she had realized it would not be enough, because living inside the flesh had changed this dream. It was *more* now. And, somehow, she needed to add that "more" to the web. Without it, Kaeleer's Heart would be gone for too many seasons—and would not be quite the same when the dream returned.

She continued to study the webs.

The brown dog, Ladvarian, was the key. He would be able to bring her the "more" she needed.

Yes. It was time.

She returned to the chamber within the sacred caves, and began to weave the web for dreams that were already made flesh.

CHAPTER
THIRTEEN

1 / Kaeleer

The First Circle of the Dark Court gathered at the Keep. At least, the humans in the First Circle had gathered, Saetan amended as he listened to Khardeen's grim report about the attacks that had taken place in Scelt during the past three weeks. There had been attacks *everywhere* in the last three weeks. Maybe that was why the kindred hadn't answered Jaenelle's summons to come to the Keep. Maybe the kindred Queens and Warlord Princes didn't dare withdraw their strength away from their own lands. Or maybe it was the beginning of a rift between humans and kindred. Maybe they were withdrawing from what they considered a human conflict in order to save themselves.

But he would have thought Ladvarian, at the very least, would have come so that he could explain things to the rest of the kindred. *He* would have realized the conflict wouldn't be confined to humans. Hell's fire, kindred had *already* been attacked.

But Ladvarian wasn't there—and it worried him.

Two other things worried him: the flickers of grief and resignation he was picking up from Andulvar, Prothvar, and Mephis—who had all fought, and died, in the last war between Terreille and Kaeleer—and the fact that Jaenelle had been sitting there for the past two hours with such blankness in her eyes he started to wonder if she hadn't created a simple shadow to fill a space at the table.

"Just defending against these attacks isn't going to save our lands or our people," Aaron said. "There are Terreillean armies gathering against us. If the enemy who's already *in* Kaeleer gains control of a Gate and opens it for those armies . . . We need to do something *now.*"

"Yes, you do need to do something," Jaenelle said in a hollow voice. "You need to retreat."

Protests from all sides rose up in a wave of sound.

"You need to retreat," Jaenelle repeated. "And you will send all of the Queens and Warlord Princes in your Territories to the Keep."

Stunned silence met that statement.

"But, Jaenelle," Morghann said after a moment, "the Warlord Princes are needed to lead the fighting. And asking Queens to leave their lands while their people are under attack . . ."

"They won't be needed if the people retreat."

"Just how far are we supposed to retreat?" Gabrielle snapped.

"As far as necessary."

Aaron shook his head. "We need to gather our warriors into armies to fight against the Terreilleans and—"

"Kaeleer *will not* go to war with Terreille," Jaenelle said in her midnight voice.

Chaosti sprang up from his seat. "We're already at war!"

"No, we are not."

"So we're at war with Little Terreille, since that's where these attackers have been hiding," Lucivar growled. "It's the same thing."

Jaenelle's eyes turned to ice. "We're not at war with anyone."

"Cat, you're not thinking—"

"Remember to whom you speak."

Lucivar looked into her eyes and paled. Finally, reluctantly, he said, "My apologies, Lady."

Jaenelle rose. "If there's time to retreat before the attack, do it. If not, keep the fighting to a minimum. *Defend* for as long as it takes to retreat, but don't attack. And get the Queens and Warlord Princes to the Keep. There will be no exceptions, and I'll accept no excuses."

A long silence filled the room after Jaenelle left.

"She's not thinking clearly," Kalush said reluctantly.

"She's been acting strange since the first attack," Gabrielle snapped, then looked apologetically at Karla.

"It's all right," Karla said slowly, with obvious effort. "She *has* been acting strange. I've wondered if healing me affected her somehow."

"What's affected her is her aversion to killing," Lucivar snarled. "But she's usually clear-sighted enough to be able to see the obvious. We're at war. Dancing around the word isn't going to change the fact."

"You would defy your Queen?" Daemon asked mildly, almost lazily.

Lucivar's instant, razor-edged tension startled all of them.

What's happening between them? Saetan wondered as Daemon and Lucivar just stared at each other. Seeing the sleepy look in Daemon's eyes, he felt ice wrap around his spine.

"I don't think the Lady understands the repercussions of her order," Lucivar said carefully.

"Oh," Daemon purred, "I think she understands them quite well. You just don't agree with her. That's not sufficient reason to disobey her."

"Considering what you've done in other courts, you're not exactly a model of obedience," Lucivar said with a little heat.

"That's irrelevant. We're talking about you and this court. And I'm telling you, Yaslana, that you will not distress her with defiance or disobedience. If you do . . ." Daemon merely smiled.

Lucivar shuddered.

After Daemon glided out of the room, Saetan asked, "Is he bluffing?" He became uneasy when Lucivar just stared at the table. "Lucivar?"

"The Sadist doesn't bluff," Lucivar said roughly. "He doesn't need to." He strode out of the room.

"It would seem there's nothing more to discuss," Saetan said, rising from the table. A flick of a glance brought Andulvar, Prothvar, and Mephis to their feet.

Letting the other men precede him, he had almost shut the door when he heard Aaron say, "What do we really know about Daemon Sadi?"

He closed the door silently. When he turned toward the other men, he saw the same question in Andulvar's eyes—and he was no longer sure he had an answer.

2 / Kaeleer

"What do we really know about Daemon Sadi?" Aaron said.

Karla let the murmurs of opinion and conversation become a wash of sound as she sank deeper into her own thoughts.

What did they really know about Daemon Sadi?

He was a Black-Jeweled Warlord Prince and a natural Black Widow—an explosively dangerous, beautiful-looking man.

He was the High Lord's mirror, but not a perfect reflection.

He was a man who, for most of his life, had been chained in one way or another to Dorothea SaDiablo, Kaeleer's enemy.

He was a man who understood women. Unable to stand the pity in the servants' eyes when they had helped her into the bath the first few days after the healing, she had insisted that she didn't need help. Using Craft, she was able to undress and get herself into the tub but wasn't able to wash herself well enough, especially because the reaction to the poisons was causing her skin to slough off at a grotesque rate. One evening, Daemon had shown up to assist her. She had snapped at him, had told him to go away. His answer, spoken in such a pleasant voice it had taken her a few seconds to comprehend the words, was so creatively obscene she was in the tub being gently, but thoroughly, washed before she could think again. His touch hadn't been impersonal, nor had it been sexual, but by the time he'd started massaging her scalp, she'd been awash in sensual pleasure like she'd never experienced before.

So she understood why the others were worried. A woman could easily become addicted to that touch, would be willing to do a great many things in order to prevent it from being withdrawn. And Jaenelle *had* been acting strange since the first attack. But she didn't think it had anything to do with Daemon.

There was one other thing she knew about Daemon Sadi, something she had seen in the tangled web that had warned her about her own death: he was the friend who would become an enemy in order to remain a friend.

3 / Kaeleer

"What is it about Daemon that scares the shit out of Lucivar?" Andulvar asked as soon as the four men entered a small sitting room in the Keep.

"I don't know," Saetan replied, avoiding their stares by warming a glass of yarbarah over a tongue of witchfire.

He *didn't* know. Lucivar had always evaded talking about the times he and Daemon had tangled when they'd come together in Terreillean courts. Lucivar had said once that if he had a choice of going up against the Sadist or the High Lord, he would choose the High Lord because he would have some chance of winning.

What was it about that smile of Daemon's that could shake Lucivar so badly? What was it about the Sadist that could make a man as aggressive as Lucivar back down? And what might Daemon's presence in the Keep mean to the rest of them?

"High Lord!" Prothvar jerked Saetan's hand away from the tongue of witchfire just before the yarbarah began to boil.

Saetan put the glass down. The yarbarah wouldn't be drinkable.

"SaDiablo," Andulvar said quietly, "should we be watching our backs?"

It didn't occur to him to offer a reassuring lie. "I don't know."

4 / Kaeleer

Ladvarian wearily trotted toward Halaway, responding to a gentle but insistent summons. Every so often, he snarled to vent his frustration and growing anger.

How could a place as big as the Hall not have what he needed? Oh, he'd found plenty of things that were *almost* right but nothing that *was* right. That accounted for his frustration. The anger . . .

The kindred had waited so long for this living myth to come. *This* one. This special one. And now it was going to be spoiled by humans.

No. It *wouldn't* be spoiled. The kindred were gathering.

As soon as the Weaver of Dreams told them what to do, they would act.

When he reached the neat cottage in Halaway, he went to the back door and barked once, politely.

Tersa opened an upstairs window. "Come inside, little Brother."

Using Craft, he floated upward to the window and went in. Most of the kindred referred to Tersa as "the Strange One." They meant no disrespect. They recognized that she was a Black Widow who wandered roads most of the Blood would never see. She was special. She had that in common with the Lady.

Even knowing all that didn't prevent his hackles from rising when he stepped into the room.

A low, narrow bed—*exactly* the kind he had searched for at the Hall. He approached it cautiously and opened his inner and outer senses. It had no smells. There should be human smells as well as a residual psychic scent from the humans who had made the bed, mattress, and bedcovers.

"It has all been cleansed," Tersa said calmly. "There are no psychic scents to interfere with the weaving of dreams."

The weaving of dreams? Ladvarian said cautiously.

"That trunk will provide storage and can be used as a bedside table as well. Remember to bring clothing for warm weather as well as clothing for the spring. Favorite things. Clothes that will be strong with her scent, even if they've been cleaned."

Ladvarian backed away. *Why should I bring clothing?*

Tersa smiled and said gently, "Because Witch does not have fur." Her eyes looked into an inner distance, became unfocused and farseeing. "It is almost time for the debts to be paid. Those who survive will serve, but few will survive. The howling . . . Full of joy and pain, rage and celebration. She is coming." Her eyes focused on him again. "And the kindred will anchor the dream in flesh."

Yes, Lady, Ladvarian said respectfully.

Tersa picked up a cobalt-blue bowl from a nearby dresser. Using Craft, she rested the bowl on the air. "When you next see the Weaver of Dreams, tell her this is how to get the 'more' she needs."

Ladvarian shifted his weight restlessly from one paw to

the other. The Arachnian Queen had not mentioned Tersa.
Why did Tersa know so much about the Arachnian Queen?

Tersa dipped one finger into the bowl. As she raised her
hand, a drop of water clung to her finger. Instead of falling,
the drop began to expand, like a little bubble of blown
glass, a pearl of water. Using her thumbnail, Tersa jabbed
a finger on her other hand. A drop of blood welled up on
the finger. "And the Blood shall sing to the Blood."

Ladvarian felt the power flowing into that drop of blood.

"Let blood be memory's river." Turning her hand, she
brushed the drop of blood against the drop of water. The
blood flowed through the water bubble until it was contained inside it.

After placing a protective shield around it, Tersa tucked
the water bubble into a small padded box and extended it
toward Ladvarian. "Look."

He opened his mind, sent out a tentative psychic probe.

Images, memories flowed past him. Memories of a young
girl leading an exhausted woman out of the Twisted Kingdom. Memories of Jaenelle, older, promising to find Daemon. Memories of conversations, laughter, delight in the
world. Tersa's memories.

"You will tell the Weaver?" Tersa asked.

Ladvarian vanished the box. *I will tell her.*

"One other thing, little Brother. Don't refuse Lorn's gift.
The Weaver will need that, too."

5 / Kaeleer

Leaving the door open, Daemon walked into Jaenelle's
workroom. She had been spending hours there every day
since she'd brought Karla to the Keep to continue the healing, but he didn't think her distraction or the controlled
frenzy of her activities had anything to do with Karla. In
fact, he was certain he was the only one who had been
allowed a glimpse of that frenzy. Something was eating at
her, and after the little scene in the meeting room, he was
determined to find out what.

"Jaenelle, we need to talk."

She glanced up from the mound of books that filled one

table. "I don't have time to talk now, Daemon," she said dismissively.

With a flick of a thought, he slammed the door so hard all the objects in the room jumped—including her.

"Make time," he said too softly. When she started to protest, he cut her off. "I'll do anything for you. *Anything.* But before I pit myself against the rest of the First Circle, I want to know why."

"Kaeleer cannot go to war with Terreille." Her voice trembled.

"Why?"

Hot, angry tears filled her eyes. "Because if we go to war, every person who was in that room will die."

"You don't know that," he snapped.

The tears spilled over, slicing his heart. "Yes, I do."

Daemon rocked back on his heels. She was a very strong, very gifted Black Widow. If she'd seen their deaths in a tangled web of dreams and visions, there was no room for doubt. *That* explained her resistance.

He took a deep breath to steady himself. "Sweetheart . . . sometimes killing is necessary. Sometimes it's the only path to take in order to save what is good."

"I know that." Jaenelle slammed a book on the table. "I've spent the past three weeks searching for an answer. No, I've spent longer than that, but time is running out. I can feel it."

"Jaenelle," he said carefully, "you have the strength . . ." The look in her eyes was almost hateful, but he pushed on. "A portion of your strength would eliminate a Terreillean army."

"And while I was eliminating that one, six more would be killing the Kaeleer Blood in other Territories. Even if I do destroy them, one army at a time, it won't make any difference."

"You wouldn't be the only one fighting," Daemon insisted, bracing one hand on the table to lean toward her. "Hell's fire, woman, look at the strength of the males in this Realm. Look at the Jewels. The Blacks. The Ebongrays. The Grays. We have the dominant strength."

"Kaeleer had the dominant strength in the last war, too," Jaenelle replied quietly. "And Kaeleer won—barely, but Kaeleer won. But all those males died. And it didn't make

any difference. The taint that fed that war is still in the
Blood, even stronger now."

"Hekatah and Dorothea can be destroyed."

Jaenelle moved around the table in order to pace. "It
wouldn't do any good at this point. Even if they're destroyed, even if Kaeleer wins the initial war, the Shadow
Realm won't win. The taint's too widespread now. Terreille
will keep sending armies. Will keep sending them and sending them, and the fighting will go on and on, in Terreille
as well as in Kaeleer, until the Blood can't remember who
they are or that they were supposed to be the caretakers
of the Realms."

"We're at war, Jaenelle," Daemon said earnestly. "It
doesn't matter if it's been formally declared or not. We *are*
at war."

"No."

"You have the strength to make the difference. If you
unleash—"

"I can't."

"You can."

"*I can't.*"

"WHY NOT?"

She turned on him. "BECAUSE, DAMN YOU, I'M TOO
STRONG! If I unleash my strength, it will destroy the Blood.
All the Blood. In Terreille. In Kaeleer. In Hell."

Daemon's legs turned to water. Weakly, he pushed aside
some books so that he could sit on the table. *You had said
she was six times stronger than our combined strength. Oh,
Father, you were so wrong. Six times? Six hundred times?
Six thousand times?*

Enough power to wipe the Blood out of existence.

With her arms wrapped around herself, Jaenelle paced.
"The Keep is the Sanctuary. It wouldn't be affected. But
how many could it hold? A few thousand at most? Who
chooses, Daemon? What if the wrong choices are made and
the taint is still there, hidden because someone is so damn
sure she's right?"

She was thinking of Alexandra. Would anyone have considered Alexandra tainted? Misguided, certainly, but unless
they were obviously twisted, the Queens would definitely
be among the chosen. And what about someone like
Vania? Not tainted the way Jaenelle was talking about, but

the kind of woman who could sour the males around her and eventually ruin a land. Exactly the kind of woman Dorothea cultivated.

"The Blood are the Blood," Jaenelle continued. "Two feet, four feet, it doesn't matter. The Blood are the Blood. The gift of Craft came from one source, and it binds all of us."

So not even the kindred could be spared. No wonder this had been ripping her apart.

"Does Kaeleer win?" Daemon asked quietly.

A full minute passed before Jaenelle answered. "Yes. But the price for winning will be all the Kaeleer Queens and all the Warlord Princes."

Daemon thought about the decent people he had met since he'd come to Kaeleer. He thought about the kindred. He thought about the children. Most of all, he thought about Daemonar, Lucivar's son. If, for some reason, they didn't destroy Dorothea and Hekatah, and those two got their hands on Daemonar . . . "Do it," he said. "Unleash your strength. Destroy the Blood."

Jaenelle's mouth fell open. She stared at him.

"Do it," he repeated. "If that's the only way to get rid of the taint Dorothea and Hekatah have spread in the Blood, then, by the Darkness, Jaenelle, show some mercy for those you love and do it."

She began pacing again. "There has to be a way to separate Blood from Blood. There *has* to be."

A memory teased him, but he couldn't catch hold of it while her frenzied movement seemed to put everything in motion. "Stand still," he snapped.

She came to an abrupt halt and huffed.

He raised a hand, commanding silence. The memory continued to tease, but he caught the tail of it. "I think there's a way."

Her eyes widened but she obeyed the command for silence.

"A few centuries ago, there was a Queen called the Gray Lady. When a village she was staying in was about to be attacked by Hayllian warriors, she found a way to separate the villagers from the Hayllians so that when she unleashed her strength, the villagers were spared."

"How did she do it?" Jaenelle asked very quietly.

"I don't know." He hesitated—and wondered why he hesitated. "A man I knew was with her at the time. A few years before his death, he sent a message to me that he had made a written account of the 'adventure' and had left it for me in a safe place. She was a good Queen, the last Queen to hold Dorothea at bay. He wanted her remembered."

Jaenelle leaped at him, grabbed him. "Then you *do* know how she did it!"

"No, I *don't* know. I never picked up the written account. I decided to leave it where it was, out of Dorothea's reach."

"Do you think you could find it?" Jaenelle asked anxiously.

"That shouldn't be difficult," Daemon replied dryly as he wrapped his arms around her, suddenly needing to touch her. "He left it with the Keep's librarian."

"I retrieved it from the Terreillean Keep the first time you came to Ebon Askavi with Jaenelle," Geoffrey said as he handed Daemon a carefully wrapped parcel. "I wondered at the time why you didn't ask for it. What made you think of it now?"

The question sounded innocently curious, but there wasn't anything innocent about it.

Looking straight into Geoffrey's black eyes, Daemon smiled. "I just remembered it."

He didn't unwrap it, didn't look at it. He probed it just enough to make sure there weren't any spells hidden in it that would be triggered if someone besides him handled it. Then he gave it to Jaenelle and spent the next several hours denying access to the Queen to just about every member of the First Circle. That had caused hard feelings but was easy enough. No one but the Steward, the Master of the Guard, and the Consort were permitted free access to the Queen's chambers. Lucivar had taken one look at him and had retreated. Stalling Saetan and Andulvar had been much more difficult, and he sensed it wouldn't take many more polite confrontations to erode their trust in him. Considering Jaenelle's behavior lately, he could appreciate their concern. It still hurt.

When he finally returned to her, he found her in her

sitting room, her arms wrapped around herself, staring bleakly out the window.

"It didn't help?" he asked softly, resting a hand lightly on her shoulder.

"Actually, it did. I found the answer. I can't do the same thing they did, but I can use it as the foundation for what I need to do."

She turned and kissed him with a desperation that frightened him, but he gave her what she needed. For hours, he gave her what she needed.

When she was finally content just to lie wrapped in his arms, she said, "I love you." And fell asleep.

Despite being physically and emotionally exhausted, Daemon lay awake a long time—and wondered why "I love you" sounded so much like "good-bye."

6 / Kaeleer

"The Lady changed her mind," Saetan said formally to the Territory Queens who made up the coven. "You and the males in the First Circle are to remain at the Keep, but the other Queens in your Territories may stay where they are."

"Why are *we* required to stay?" Chaosti demanded. "Our people are *dying*. We should be home, preparing to fight."

"Why did she change her mind?" Morghann asked. "What did she say when you asked her?"

Saetan hesitated. "The instructions were relayed by the Consort."

He felt their flickers of anger and their growing suspicion about Daemon. Worse, he had those same feelings.

"The Queen commands," he said, knowing how inadequate that sounded when they were all receiving reports of fighting in their homelands.

"That's fine, High Lord," Aaron said coolly. "The Queen commands. But, obviously, no one has informed the kindred of that fact. None of *them* who are members of the First Circle have to stay at the Keep."

They all looked at each other as that realization sank in. But it was Karla who finally asked, "Where *are* the kindred?"

* * *

Saetan watched the drops of rain trickle down the window.

When Jaenelle had given the order for all the Queens to come to the Keep, he hadn't protested for one reason: Sylvia. He had wanted her in the Keep where she would be safe.

But now that Jaenelle had changed her mind—or had had it changed for her—he would issue his own orders as the Warlord Prince of Dhemlan and summon all the Dhemlan Queens to the Hall. It was a risk. The Hall didn't have the defenses the Keep had. *No place* had the defenses the Keep had. But it had been designed to withstand attack, and its defenses were better than anywhere else the Queens might be forced to retreat if the fighting escalated. And it was big enough that the Queens could bring their families with them, bring their children.

He wanted her safe. And her boys, too, Mikal and Beron.

Sassy, opinionated, lovely Sylvia. Mother Night, he loved her.

Even after he realized that the potency of Jaenelle's tonic after she had made the Offering to the Darkness had brought back the hunger of a man—and the ability to satisfy it—he might have resisted becoming Sylvia's lover, might have found the strength to remain just a friend if he hadn't sensed the hurt in her that her last Consort had inflicted. She had shut herself away from sexual pleasure, hadn't been intrigued enough by any man to try again—until she had become friends with him.

They weren't acknowledged lovers. At his insistence, they maintained the illusion in public of being just friends. Oh, his reasons had been very logical, very considerate. He knew Luthvian would be enraged if he openly became another woman's lover, and he hadn't wanted her to take her anger out on the rest of the family—or on Sylvia. And he hadn't wanted people backing away from her because she had chosen a Guardian for a lover.

At first, she had gone along with him, mostly because she was rediscovering the pleasures of the bed, and had been able to accept that he was a lover in the bedroom and a friend outside of it. But gradually, over the past year, she had become more and more unhappy with the secrecy, had wanted an acknowledged relationship.

He had expected her to leave him. Instead, one night during the Winsol celebrations a few months ago, she had asked him to marry her. And, may the Darkness help him, he had wanted to say yes. Had wanted to share a bed with her, a *life* with her.

But he didn't say yes. Not because of Luthvian or because he was a Guardian, but because of a vague uneasiness that had warned him to take care, to wait. So he had smiled and said, "Ask me next Winsol."

He had understood why, for a few weeks after that, there were no invitations to her bed. He had understood why she was always "busy" when he stopped at her home to spend a little time with the boys.

He had missed the friend far more than he'd missed the lover, but he *had* missed those hours in her bed.

Then, just a few days before the attack in Glacia, they had gone to Amdarh for a couple of days to spend time together away from everyone else, to try to rebuild their relationship. And they had made love, but he had known as soon as he touched her that, despite wanting him, she was trying to keep her distance from him emotionally, that she was trying to protect herself from being hurt again. Even when she was caught up in her climax, he had known.

Now, staring at the rain, he almost wished he had said "yes" at Winsol, almost wished he had asked her to stand with him before a Priestess when they had arrived in Amdarh. And he wished he could make love with her one more time to erase the unhappiness that had been in the bed with them that last time.

But the conviction had been growing in him for days now that there wouldn't be another chance.

There were things he should have said that night in Amdarh. He'd never really told her how much she meant to him, how much he loved her. He should have. Now he could give her nothing but words, but at least he could give her that much.

Turning away from the window, he sat at the desk and began to write.

CHAPTER
FOURTEEN

1 / Kaeleer

"**I** need a favor," Jaenelle said as she moved stiffly to her worktable and picked up two small glass jars.

"You have only to ask," Titian replied. *She's been channeling too much power without giving her body time to recover. What is she planning that demands so much?*

"A discreet favor."

"Understood."

"I need blood from two people who have been tainted by Dorothea or Hekatah. Preferably one of each."

Titian thought for a very brief moment. "Lord Jorval lives in the capital of Little Terreille, does he not?"

Jaenelle swallowed. Even that seemed to take effort. "Yes, Jorval is in Goth. And so, at the moment, is Kartane SaDiablo."

"Ah." Looking at the exhausted woman, Titian remembered the child Jaenelle had been. And she remembered other things. "Will it matter if neither of them sees the next sunrise?"

A deadly cold filled Jaenelle's sapphire eyes. "No."

Titian smiled. "In that case, with your permission, I'll take Surreal with me. It's time to pay some debts."

2 / Kaeleer

In the enormous chamber where the Dark Throne resided, Ladvarian trembled as he looked at Lorn. It wasn't that he was afraid of Lorn—at least, not usually. It was just that Lorn was the Prince of the Dragons, the legendary race who had created the Blood. Lorn was very, *very* old, and very wise, and very *big*. Ladvarian was smaller than one of Lorn's midnight eyes. Just then, that made him feel *very* small.

And then there was Draca, the Keep's Seneschal, who had been Lorn's mate and the Dragon Queen before she had sacrificed her true form in order to give other creatures the Craft.

Sacrifices. No, he would *not* think about sacrifices. There was not going to be a sacrifice. The kindred would not allow it.

But being summoned here by Lorn and Draca when the Arachnian Queen was so close to finishing that special web of dreams . . . It frightened him. If they forbade the kindred from doing this . . . The kindred would do it anyway, whatever the cost.

Little Brother, Lorn said in his deep, quiet, thundering voice.

Prince Lorn. Ladvarian was trembling enough for them to see it.

I have a gift for you, little Brother. Give thiss to the Weaver of Dreamss.

A flat, beautifully carved box appeared in the air before Ladvarian. When it opened, he saw a simply designed pendant made of white and yellow gold and an equally simple ring. But it was the Jewel in those pieces that made his hackles rise and his ears flatten tight to his head.

It had no color, and yet it wasn't colorless. Restless, it shimmered, hungry to complete its transformation. It tugged at him, seeking a bond with his mind.

He took a step back. As he looked up at Lorn, angry and confused enough to issue a challenge that would have been foolish as well as futile, he realized Lorn's scales had that same translucent shimmer. Knowledge crashed in on him. He took another step back and whined.

Do not fear, little Brother. It iss a gift. The Weaver will need it for her web.

Gathering his courage, Ladvarian approached the box. *I have never seen a Jewel like this.*

And you never will again, Lorn replied gently. *There will never be another one like it.*

Still cautious, Ladvarian said, *It has no rank. It does not know what it is.*

It doess not yet know what it iss, Lorn agreed. *But it doess have a name: Twilight'ss Dawn.*

When Ladvarian was on his way back to Arachna with the box, Draca and Lorn stared at each other.

"You rissk much giving him a Jewel like that," Draca said.

There iss reasson to rissk much, Lorn replied. *Witch hass almosst completed her web?*

"Yess." For the first time since she had met Jaenelle, she felt the weight of her years.

We cannot heal the taint, Draca, Lorn said softly. *Sshe can.*

"I know. When I gave the gift of magic, I gave it freely, knowing I could never alter what wass done with it." Draca hesitated. "If sshe doess thiss, sshe will be desstroyed."

Sshe iss Kaeleer'ss Heart. Sshe musst not be dessstroyed. Lorn paused and added softly, *The kindred have alwayss been sstrong dreamerss.*

"Will they be sstrong enough?"

The question neither could answer hung between them.

3 / Kaeleer

A stealthy movement and the sudden glow of a small ball of witchlight woke Jorval from an uneasy sleep. "Priestess?"

A hand grabbed his hair, yanked his head up. "No," said the silver-haired woman as her knife cut his throat. "I am vengeance."

4 / Kaeleer

"Enough," Daemon said, leading Jaenelle into her sitting room. "You need to rest."

"The web's almost complete. I need to—"

"*Rest.* If you make an error because you're too exhausted to think clearly, this will all be for nothing."

Making a weak attempt to snarl, she collapsed into a chair.

Daemon wanted to rage at her but knew it wouldn't do any good. She had dropped weight she couldn't afford to lose at a frightening speed. Putting obstacles in her path would only force her to waste energy she couldn't spare, so he took the other path.

"You told me a few minutes ago that you still needed a couple of things to complete the web."

"Those things will take time," she protested.

He bent down and kissed her softly, persuasively. When he felt her yield, he murmured against her lips, "We'll have a quiet dinner. Then we'll play a couple of hands of 'cradle.' I'll even let you win."

Her huff of laughter provoked another hunger. His kiss deepened as his hand caressed her breast.

"I think I am hungry," Jaenelle said breathlessly when he finally gave her a chance to speak.

After they had thoroughly satisfied one hunger, they finally sat down to dinner.

5 / Hell

Pain woke him.

Kartane opened his eyes. Two fading balls of witchlight provided enough light for him to clearly see that he was outside. Then he realized he was upside down. *Someone had tied him upside down.*

Something rustled the bushes nearby.

Turning his head a little, he stared at an odd pile of brown clothing, neatly folded.

Suddenly, his heart pounded. Suddenly, it was hard to breathe.

The surrounding shadows shifted just enough for him to see that the odd pile wasn't clothing, it was brown skin.

As he drew in a breath to scream, glowing red eyes appeared in the darkness around him.

Even with her head under the water, Surreal heard Kartane scream.

She popped up out of the water, then immediately lowered herself to her neck. The pool, fed by a hot spring, was delightfully warm, but the air was cool enough to bite.

She heard snarls, a howl, a terrified shriek.

The air wasn't the only thing around there that had a bite.

"So this is Hell," she said, looking around. It was too dark to see much, but the area around the pool had a kind of stark beauty.

"This is Hell," Titian replied, a blissful smile on her face. She straightened up and gave Surreal a searching look. "Has the debt been paid to your satisfaction, Surreal?"

The snarls and shrieks stopped for a moment, then started again.

"Yes," Surreal said, leaning back with a sigh, "I'm satisfied."

6 / Kaeleer

"Sometimes the heart reveals more than panes of glass can."

Saetan turned away from the window, tensed, took a step forward, stopped. "Tersa, why are you at the Keep?"

Smiling, Tersa walked across the room and held out a thick envelope. "I came to give you this."

Even before he took the envelope, he knew who it was from. Sylvia always added a drop of lavender oil to her wax seal.

Laying one hand on his shoulder, Tersa kissed him on the lips—a lingering kiss that surprised him. Worried him.

She stepped back. "That was the other part of the message." She was almost at the door before he gathered his wits.

"Tersa, this can't be the only reason you traveled to the Keep."

"No?" she said, looking puzzled. Then, "No, it wasn't."

He waited. She said nothing.

"Darling," he prodded gently, "why are you here?"

Her eyes cleared, and he felt certain that, for the first time in all the centuries he had known her, he was seeing a glimpse of Tersa as she had been before she was broken. She was formidable—and a bit dazzling.

"I'm needed here," she said quietly, then walked out of the room.

He stood there for several minutes, staring at the envelope in his hands. "Show some balls, SaDiablo," he finally muttered as he carefully opened the envelope. "No matter what the letter says, it isn't the end of the world."

It was a long letter. He read it twice before he tucked it away.

He hadn't been able to give Sylvia more than words, but apparently, thankfully, that had been enough.

7 / Terreille

Dorothea prowled around the room. "Armies are gathering all over Terreille, the Territories in the Shadow Realm have been attacked for weeks now by the people we had hidden in Little Terreille, and Kaeleer *still* hasn't formally declared war."

"That's because Jaenelle Angelline doesn't have the backbone to go along with her power," Hekatah said as she carefully arranged her full-length cape. "She's just a mouse scurrying around in her hidey-hole while the cats gather for the feast."

"Even a mouse will bite," Dorothea snapped.

"This mouse won't bite," Hekatah replied calmly. "She's too emotionally squeamish to take the step that would begin a full-scale slaughter."

Dorothea wasn't as sure of that as Hekatah seemed to be, but Jaenelle's sparing Alexandra's life after the abduction failed certainly seemed to indicate a lack of the proper temperament. *She* certainly wouldn't have spared the bitch. That lack in Jaenelle was in their favor, but . . . "You seem to be forgetting that the High Lord has fangs and isn't the least bit squeamish about using them."

"I forget nothing where Saetan is concerned," Hekatah snarled. "His honor hobbles him, just as it always has, and his own emotional failings will muzzle him. With the right persuasion, he'll tuck his tail between his legs and submit to whatever we require of him."

She hoped that rotting sack of bones was right. They *had* to eliminate Saetan, Lucivar, and Daemon. When those three were gone, the Terreillean armies would be able to destroy the Kaeleer Queens and Warlord Princes. Entire armies would be slaughtered in the process, but they *would* win the war. And then she would rule the Realms—after she hurried the Dark Priestess to a well-deserved, and permanent, rest.

Pleased by that thought, Dorothea stopped prowling long enough to notice that Hekatah was preparing to go out. "Where are you going?"

Hekatah smiled malevolently. "To Kaeleer. It's time to collect the first part of the bait that will give us control of Jaenelle Angelline."

8 / Kaeleer

Finally admitted to Jaenelle's sitting room, Andulvar studied her and thought of several things he'd like to do to Daemon Sadi. Damn it, the man was her Consort and should have been taking care of her. She was far too thin, and the skin under her eyes was faintly bruised from exhaustion. And there was a queer, almost desperate glitter in her eyes.

"Prince Yaslana," Jaenelle said quietly.

So. It was going to be formal.

"Lady," Andulvar replied stiffly. "Since I'm obviously not here as your uncle, am I here as your Master of the Guard?" When she flinched, he regretted the harshness of his words. She didn't look like she could endure too many more emotional blows.

"I—There's something I need to tell you. And I need your help."

He did his best to soften his tone. "Because I'm your Master of the Guard?"

She shook her head. "Because you're the Demon Prince. After Saetan, you have the most authority in Hell. The demon-dead will listen to you—and follow you."

He went to her and hugged her gently, afraid that if he held on to her the way he wanted to she would shatter. "What is it, waif?"

She eased back just enough to look him in the eyes. "I've found a way to get rid of Dorothea and Hekatah and the taint they've left in the Blood. But the rest of the Blood will be at risk unless the demon-dead are willing to help me."

*   *   *

Thirty minutes later, Andulvar closed the sitting room door, took a couple of steps, then sagged against the wall.

Mother Night.

He didn't doubt the plan would work. Jaenelle wouldn't have said she could do it if she had any doubts. But . . . *Mother Night.*

He had fought in the last war between Terreille and Kaeleer. That war had devastated both Realms, and millions had died. And it had made no difference. They were standing on the edge of that same cliff, fighting against a greed and ambition that would simply go to ground again if it wasn't finally, completely eliminated.

Like Mephis and Prothvar, he had known it would be futile to fight another war in the same way. Like them, he had looked around the table when the First Circle argued for a formal declaration of war and had wondered how many would still be among the living when it was over.

Jaenelle hadn't wondered. She had *known* none of them would survive. Hell's fire, no wonder she had been doing anything she could to keep them in the one place where they would be safe.

And now she had a *plan* that . . . Mother Night.

Even after she had told him, there was something about it that hadn't felt quite *right*—as if she had glossed over something. Saetan would have known what it was, but Saetan . . .

She *was* right about that. The coven and the boyos would need Saetan's wisdom and experience to mend the wounds already inflicted on Kaeleer. So he couldn't tell his friend what Jaenelle intended to do, couldn't take the chance that Saetan might choose to throw his strength in with the rest of them instead of staying behind. He couldn't do that because, after everything was over, the High Lord would be needed by the living.

Ladvarian waited in the shadows until he was sure Andulvar was really gone. Then he slipped into Jaenelle's sitting room.

She was staring out the window. He wanted to tell her it would be all right, even though he wasn't sure it would be. Yes, he was. It *would* be all right. The kindred would not doubt. The kindred would be strong. But he couldn't

tell her that because this was a time for fangs and claws.
This was a time for killing. And they weren't sure she
would be able to kill if they told her what was going to
happen afterward.

But there was something else he *had* to tell her.

Jaenelle?

There was as much sadness as pleasure in her eyes when
she turned and saw him. "What is it, little Brother?"

I have a message for you—from the Weaver of Dreams.

She went absolutely still, and he was afraid Witch might
look right into him and see what he wanted to hide.

"What is the message?"

*She said the triangle must stay together in order to sur-
vive. The mirror can keep the others safe, but only if
they're together.* He hesitated when she just stared at him.
Who is the mirror?

"Daemon," she replied absently. "He's his father's mirror."

She seemed lost for a moment, long enough to make him
nervous. *Do you understand the message?*

"No," she said, looking very pale. "But I'm sure I will."

9 / Kaeleer

Luthvian heard her bedroom door open, but she continued
stuffing clothes into a travel bag and didn't turn around.
Damn Eyrien pup, coming up to her room without permission. And damn Lucivar for insisting that she come to the
Keep and insisting that she have an escort. She didn't need
an escort—especially not Palanar, who was barely old
enough to wipe his own nose.

As she started to turn around to tell him just that, a
caped figure rushed at her. Instantly, instinctively, she
threw up a Red shield. A blast of Red power struck her at
the same moment, preventing the shield from forming, and
the figure was on her. They tumbled to the floor.

Luthvian didn't realize she'd been knifed until the enemy
yanked the blade out of her body.

Being a Healer, she knew it was bad—a killing wound.

Furious, knowing she didn't have long, she ripped the
hood off her enemy and then stared for a moment, frozen. "You."

Hekatah rammed the knife into Luthvian's belly. "Bitch," she hissed. "I could have made something of you. Now I'll just turn you into carrion."

Luthvian tried to fight, tried to scratch and claw, but her arms felt too heavy to lift. She couldn't do anything even when Hekatah's teeth sank into her throat and her blood fed the vile bitch.

Nothing to be done for the body, but the Self . . .

Gathering her strength and her rage, she channeled it into her inner barriers.

Hekatah pounded against them as she fed, pounded and pounded, trying to blast them open to finish the kill. But Luthvian hung on, letting rage form the bridge between life and death as she poured her strength into her inner barriers. Poured and poured until there was nothing left. Nothing.

At some point, the pounding stopped, and Luthvian felt a grim satisfaction that the bitch hadn't been able to break through.

Far, far away, she felt Hekatah roll off her. Somewhere in the vague, misty distance she saw sharp nails descending toward her face.

The hand stopped before the nails touched her eyes.

"No," Hekatah said. "If you manage to make the transition to demon-dead, I want you to see what I do to your boy."

Movement. The bedroom door closed. Silence.

Luthvian felt herself fading. With effort, she flexed her fingers—just a little.

Her rage had burned through the transition without her being aware of it, without Hekatah being able to sense it. She was demon-dead, but she didn't have the strength to hold on. Her Self would soon become a whisper in the Darkness. Perhaps, someday, when it had rested and regained some strength, the Self would leave the Darkness and return to the living Realms. Perhaps.

How many times had Lucivar told her to set up warning shields around the house? And every time he'd tried, she had dismissed it with a sneer. But she'd been secretly pleased that he had tried.

It had been a test, but she had been the only one who had known that. Every time he had mentioned the shields again after she had dismissed the idea, every time he had endured her sharp tongue while he helped her in some way had been a test to prove that he cared about her.

Oh, there were times when, seeing the tightness in his face and the coolness in his eyes, she had told herself it would be the last time, the last test. The next time he mentioned the shields, she would do what he wanted so that he would know she cared about him, too.

Then the next time would come and she would want, would *need,* just one more test. One more. And one more. Always one more.

Now there would be no more tests, but her son, her fine Eyrien Warlord Prince, would never know she had loved him.

All she would have needed was an hour as one of the demon-dead. An hour to tell him. She couldn't even leave him a message. Nothing.

No. Wait. Maybe she *could* say the most important thing, the thing that had been chewing at her ever since Surreal had lashed out at her.

She gathered everything that was left of her strength, shaped it into a bubble to hold one thought, then pushed it upward, upward, upward until it rested just outside her inner barriers.

Lucivar would find it. She knew he would.

No anchor. Nothing to hold on to. Filled with regrets tempered by one bubble of acknowledged love, she faded away and returned to the Darkness.

10 / Kaeleer

Palanar knocked reluctantly on the kitchen door. He supposed being asked to escort Lady Luthvian to the Keep was an honor, but she had made it very clear that she didn't like Eyrien males. So he wasn't really sure if this was Hallevar's way of showing confidence in him or a subtle punishment for something he'd done.

He opened the door and cautiously poked his head into the kitchen. "Lady Luthvian?"

She was there, standing near the table, staring at him. Then she smiled and said, "No balls, little warrior?"

Stung, he stepped into the kitchen. "Are you ready?" he

asked, striving to put the same arrogance into his voice that Falonar or Lucivar would have had.

She looked at the traveling bag next to her, then at him.

Since when did Luthvian expect a male to carry anything? The last time he'd tried, she'd almost dented his head. Hallevar had been right when he'd said, "Best resign yourself to the fact that a female can change her mind faster than you can fart."

He took a couple of steps toward her, then stopped again.

"What's wrong?" she asked suspiciously.

She stank. That's what was wrong. Really *stank*. But he wasn't about to say *that*. Then he noticed she looked a little . . . strange.

"What's wrong?" she asked again, taking a step toward him.

He took two steps back.

Her face shifted, wavered. For a moment, he thought he saw someone else. Someone he didn't know—and didn't *want* to know.

And he remembered something else Hallevar had told him: sometimes running was the smartest thing an inexperienced warrior could do.

He ran for the door.

He didn't reach it. Power blasted through his inner barriers. Needles stabbed into his mind, grew hooks and dug deeper, tore out little bits of his Self. His body vibrated from the fierce tug-of-war as he tried to get out the door while she drew him back into the room.

Helpless, he felt himself turn around—and saw the witch who held him captive. He screamed.

"You will go exactly where I tell you to go," she said. "Say exactly what I tell you to say."

"N-n-no."

Gold eyes glittered in her decayed face, and pain seared him.

"It's a small task, puppy. And when it's done, I'll set you free."

She held out a small crystal. It floated through the air. His left hand reached out and took it.

She told him exactly where to go, exactly what to say, exactly what to do with the spell in the crystal. Then he was turned around again, like a marionette with knotted strings. He walked out the door.

A warrior would not do this, no matter the price. A warrior would not do this.

He tried to bring his right hand up to reach his knife. He could cut his throat, cut his wrists, do *something* to get away from her.

His hand closed on the hilt.

Dying won't save you, little warrior, the witch said. *I am the Dark Priestess. You can't escape me that way.*

His hand dropped to his side, empty.

Now go!

Palanar spread his wings and flew as fast as he could to do what a warrior would not do.

It wasn't the wind in his face that made him weep.

11 / Kaeleer

Lucivar landed at his eyrie, and shouted, "Marian!" Where in the name of Hell was the woman? he thought as he strode toward the door. She should have arrived at the Keep hours ago.

He walked through the door, saw the neat pile of traveling bags. His heart stopped for a moment. By the time he felt it beat again, he had risen to the killing edge. *"Marian!"*

The eyrie was a big place, but it didn't take him long to give it a thorough search. Marian and Daemonar weren't there. But she had packed, so what had prevented her from leaving? Maybe Daemonar was ill? Had she taken him over to Nurian's eyrie to have the Healer look at him?

As the Warlord Prince of Ebon Rih, his eyrie was set a little apart from the other eyries nestled in the mountain, but it was only a couple of minutes before he landed in front of Nurian's home. Before his feet touched the ground, he knew they weren't there.

"Lucivar!"

Lucivar turned as Hallevar hurried up to him. He noticed Falonar and Kohlvar as they walked out of the communal eyrie that was as close as Eyriens came to having inns and taverns. Both men, hearing the agitation in Hallevar's voice, moved toward him.

"Have you seen that pup, Palanar?" Hallevar asked.

Before Lucivar could respond, Falonar jumped in. "Didn't you send him to escort Lady Luthvian to the Keep?"

"I did," Hallevar said grimly. "And told him to get his ass right back here." He looked at Lucivar. "I wondered if he might be dawdling at the Keep to dodge some chores."

"Palanar didn't arrive at the Keep. Neither did Luthvian. Neither did Marian and Daemonar," Lucivar added too quietly.

The other men stiffened.

"I sent him first thing this morning," Hallevar said.

"Any sign of trouble at your eyrie?" Falonar asked sharply.

"No," Lucivar said. "The bags were packed and set near the door." He swore softly, viciously. "Where in the name of Hell did she go?"

"She went to Lady Luthvian's," said a young female voice.

They all turned and stared at Jillian, Nurian's young sister. She hunched her shoulders and looked ready to bolt back into the eyrie.

Hallevar pointed a finger at the ground a few feet away from him. "Here, little warrior," he said sternly.

Scared now, Jillian crept to the spot, glanced at the large warriors surrounding her, then stared at her feet.

"Make your report," Hallevar said in that tone that, although encouraging, had made every young male who had trained under him snap to attention.

It had the same effect on Jillian. She stood upright and focused on Hallevar. "I was doing my stamina run this morning." She waited until she got Hallevar's approving nod. "And I thought I would take the path to Prince Yaslana's eyrie because I thought, well, maybe Lady Marian would want a little help with Daemonar, that I could look after him for a bit so she could get some of her chores done. It wasn't like I was shirking the rest of my workout or anything, 'cause looking after Daemonar *is* work."

Despite being worried, Lucivar's lips twitched as he fought not to smile.

"I was almost there when I saw Marian standing at the door talking to Palanar. He looked . . . sick. He was sweating hard, and . . . I don't know. I've never seen anyone look like that. And then Marian jerked like someone had hit her, but Palanar didn't touch her. He said, 'Bring the boy.' She went inside and came back out with Daemonar.

Daemonar took one look at Palanar and started howling.
You know, that sound Daemonar makes when he doesn't
like something?"

Lucivar nodded. He felt a cold sweat forming on his skin.

"Palanar grabbed one of Marian's arms. He kept saying,
'I'm sorry, I'm sorry.' "

"Did he see you?" Lucivar asked too quietly.

Jillian shook her head. "But Marian did. She looked right
at me, and her face had the same sick look that Palanar's
did, and she said, 'Luthvian's.' Then they left." Having finished her report, her confidence faded as she looked up at
the grim-faced men.

"You didn't report this to anyone?" Lucivar asked.

Pale now, Jillian shook her head again. "I—Nurian
wasn't home when I got back, and . . . I didn't know I was
supposed to report," she finished in a barely audible voice.

And would have been reluctant to go to one of the warriors and be casually dismissed because she was female. A
few months of living in Kaeleer weren't enough to over-
come survival tactics that had been learned from the time
she had gotten out of the cradle.

"When a warrior sees something strange, he—or she—
should report to—her—superiors," Hallevar said in a firm
but gentle voice. "That's one of the ways a young warrior
gains experience."

"Yes, sir," Jillian whispered.

"That was a fine first report, Jillian," Lucivar said. "Now
go back to your chores."

Jillian's shoulders went back. Her eyes shown with pleasure. "Yes, sir."

None of them spoke until the girl had gone back inside.

"Sounds like a compulsion spell," Falonar said quietly.

"Yes," Lucivar replied grimly, "it does. Falonar, keep an
eye on things here."

"You're going to Luthvian's?" Hallevar asked quickly as
Lucivar stepped away from them. "Then I'm going with you."

"No, you're not," Falonar said. "Kohlvar, you bring everyone up close to the eyries. Hallevar, you have the most
influence with the youngsters. Keep a tight leash on them."

"And where will you be?" Lucivar asked too softly.

Falonar squared off to face him. "*I'm* going with you."

*   *   *

They found Palanar on the ground outside the kitchen door.

"I'll look after him," Falonar said. "You go on."

Calling in his Eyrien war blade, Lucivar kicked open the kitchen door and lunged into the room. The stink inside gagged him, reminded him too strongly of carrion.

That thought catapulted him through the other downstairs rooms. Finding them empty, he surged up the stairs. He kicked the bedroom door open—and saw Luthvian. He probed the room swiftly to make sure no one was waiting for the moment when he dropped his guard, then he knelt beside the body.

At first he thought she was still alive. The wounds he could see were bad, but there would have been more blood if she had bled out. When he brushed her hair away from her neck, he saw why there wasn't a lot of blood.

He rested a hand on her head. All right. The body was dead, but she was strong enough to make the transition to demon-dead. If there was any sign that she was still there, fresh blood would strengthen her.

He probed cautiously so that he wouldn't punch through her inner barriers and inadvertently finish the kill.

Just outside her inner barriers was an odd little bubble of power. He paused, considered. The bubble had a feeling of emotional warmth that made him suspect. It wasn't the sort of feelings he associated with Luthvian. But there was nothing he could detect that made him believe he would be in danger, so he brushed a psychic tendril against it, lightly.

Lucivar . . . I was wrong about Marian. You chose well. I wish you both happy.

Tears stung his eyes. He brushed against the inner barriers. They opened with no resistance. He searched for her, searched for the least little flicker of her spirit. Nothing.

Luthvian had returned to the Darkness.

One tear spilled over. "Hell's fire, Luthvian," he said in a broken voice. "Why did you have to wait until you were dead to tell me that? Why—"

"Lucivar!"

He shot to his feet, responding to the grief and anger in Falonar's voice. He paused at the door, looked back. "May the Darkness embrace you, Mother."

Falonar was waiting for him in the kitchen.

"Palanar?" Lucivar asked.

Falonar shook his head. He didn't need to ask about Luthvian. "I saw that." He pointed to a folded sheet of paper on the table.

Lucivar stared at the paper that had his name on it. He didn't recognize the handwriting and felt an instinctive revulsion against touching it. Using Craft, he unfolded the paper, read it, and stormed out the door.

"Lucivar!" Falonar shouted, running after him. "Where are you going?"

"Get back to the eyries," Lucivar said as he strapped the fighting gauntlets over his forearms. "You're in charge now, Prince Falonar."

"Where are you going?"

Lucivar rose to the killing edge, felt the sweet, cold rage wash through him. "I'm going to get my wife and son away from those bitches."

12 / Kaeleer

The attack started the moment Falonar returned to the eyries. His Sapphire shield snapped up around him a second before an arrow would have gone through his back. He called in his longbow, nocked an arrow, added a bit of Sapphire power to the head, and let it fly.

He took a moment to probe the area and assess the enemy. Then he swore viciously. There was a full company of Eyrien warriors out there. None of them wore a Jewel darker than the Green, so his Sapphire Jewels would balance the odds a little, but his own warriors were far outnumbered. Every man would go down fighting, but that wasn't going to save the women and children.

"The communal eyrie!" Hallevar shouted as he herded women and children in that direction. "Move! Move!"

Smart move, Falonar thought approvingly as he let another arrow fly. It was big enough to hold all of them and give his warriors one concentrated battleground instead of scattered ones.

His shield deflected a dozen more arrows. Having risen to the killing edge, he embraced the cold rage and fought with a mind cleansed of emotions. *His* arrows found their targets.

Someone screamed. Looking to his left, he saw Nurian struggling with an Eyrien Warlord. He started to turn, but before he could draw his bow, another warrior rushed at him with a bladed stick. Vanishing the bow and arrow, he called in his own bladed stick and met the attack. As he danced back and looked for an opening, Nurian screamed again.

Screw honor. This was war. When his adversary came at him again, he met the blow with a dirty, nasty maneuver he'd recently learned from Lucivar that dispatched the enemy with a vengeance.

Even as he turned, expecting to be too late to save the Healer, he heard Jillian shout, "Down, Nurian!"

Hearing Jillian changed Nurian from helpless woman to apprentice warrior. She kicked viciously at the Warlord's groin at the same time she threw herself backward. The kick didn't land solidly, but it was enough to startle the man into letting go of her, and the unexpected move threw him off-balance. As he tried to right himself, an arrow whizzed through the air and buried itself in his chest.

Jillian was already nocking another arrow and taking aim while Nurian scrambled to her feet and ran, hunched over to stay out of the line of fire.

He threw a Sapphire shield in front of Jillian just in time to stop the arrows that would have gone right through her. "Retreat!" he shouted, ready to foam at the mouth when Jillian calmly sent another arrow flying. "Damn you, warrior, *retreat*!"

That startled her, but it was Nurian's shout that made her run.

Ready to cover their retreat, Falonar glanced back—and swore every vicious curse he knew. Nurian was now standing braced to fight with nothing but an Eyrien stick. Not even a *bladed* stick. What in the name of Hell did the woman think she could do with that? Did she think a warrior was going to come at her barehanded? Fool. *Idiot.*

He backed toward her, always watching for the next attack. "Retreat," he snarled at her—and then noticed that Jillian, instead of running all the way to the communal eyrie, had stopped halfway there to take up a rearguard position. "Disobey me again and I'll personally whip the skin off your backs. *Both of you.* Now *retreat*!"

They responded the same way any Eyrien warrior would

have—they ignored the threat and held their positions. So *he* retreated, forcing them back with him. *That* they were willing to do. Lucivar must have been out of his mind to think a *woman* would obey a sensible order. Which made Falonar extremely grateful that Surreal wasn't there. The Darkness only knew how he could have held *her* back in this fight.

When they got close enough to the communal eyrie, Hallevar grabbed Jillian and Kohlvar practically threw Nurian threw the doorway. Falonar was the last one in. As soon as he crossed the threshold, he filled the doorway with a Sapphire shield so that they would be protected but still have a good view. Some of the men had taken up positions at the shielded downstairs' windows. Others had gone to the upper rooms. The women and children were all huddled in the main community room.

Hallevar joined him at the door. "You think they're regrouping?"

"I don't know."

Behind them, he heard Tamnar say a bit resentfully, "Well, *little warrior*, looks like you made your first kill."

He and Hallevar both turned and blasted the same message at Tamnar. *SHUT UP!*

The boy flinched, looked shocked at the harsh reprimand, then slunk over to the window Kohlvar guarded.

Jillian stared at them, her normally brown skin an unhealthy gray. "I killed him?"

Before Falonar could phrase a cautious reply, Hallevar snorted. "You just scratched him enough to let Nurian get away."

Some of the tension drained out of the girl. "Oh. That's . . . Oh."

"You take a backup position over there," Hallevar said, pointing to a far corner of the room.

"Okay," Jillian said, sounding a little dazed.

Falonar turned back to look out the doorway. "She put that arrow right through the bastard's heart," he said, keeping his voice quiet.

"No reason for her to know that right now," Hallevar replied just as quietly. "Let her believe she just nicked him. We can't afford to have her freeze up if it comes down to that."

"If it comes down to that," Falonar said softly as he settled in to wait.

13 / Kaeleer

Saetan prowled the corridors of the Keep, too restless to stay in one place, too edgy to tolerate being around anyone.

Lucivar should have been back *hours* ago. He knew Lucivar had slipped out of the Keep late that morning to find out what was delaying Marian's and Daemonar's arrival, but the afternoon was waning, and there was no sign of any of them.

He doubted anyone else had noticed. The coven and the boyos were gathered in one of the large sitting rooms, just as they had gathered every day since Jaenelle had ordered them to remain at the Keep. So they wouldn't realize Lucivar was gone. And Jaenelle and Daemon . . . Well, they weren't likely to have noticed either.

Surreal had noticed Lucivar's absence, but she'd shrugged it off, saying he was probably with Prothvar and Mephis. Which made him realize that he hadn't seen either of *them* lately.

Somehow he had to find a way to make Jaenelle listen to him, had to find out why she was keeping such a stranglehold on all of them. Whether they acknowledged it or not, they were at war. The Queens and males in the First Circle weren't going to tolerate staying there indefinitely while their people were fighting. *Something* had to change. *Someone* had to act.

14 / Kaeleer

Falonar accepted the mug of ale Kohlvar handed to him.

"Makes no sense," Kohlvar said, shaking his head. "No direct attacks anymore, no efforts at a siege, just a few arrows now and then to make sure we know they're still out there."

"They've got us pinned down," Falonar replied. "We're outnumbered, and they know it."

"But what's the sense of pinning us down?"

We can't go anywhere, Falonar thought. *We can't report anything.*

"What's the sense?" Kohlvar repeated.

"I don't know. But I expect we'll find out sooner or later."

*   *   *

The answer came at twilight. One Warlord openly approached the communal eyrie, his hands held away from his sides, away from his weapons.

"I have a message," he shouted, holding up a white envelope.

"Put it on the ground," Falonar shouted back.

The Warlord shrugged, set the envelope on the ground, then placed a small rock over it to keep it from blowing away. He walked back the way he had come.

A few minutes later, Falonar watched the Eyrien company take flight.

He waited another hour before he used Craft to bring the envelope to the doorway. Still standing on the other side of the Sapphire shield, he created a ball of witchlight to illuminate the writing, the name of the recipient.

Dread shivered through him. It was the same handwriting as the note that had been left for Lucivar. But this one was addressed to the High Lord.

He called Kohlvar, Rothvar, Zaranar, and Hallevar over. "I'm going to take that to the Keep and give my report."

"Could be a trap," Hallevar said. "They could be waiting for you to make a move."

Yes, he was sure it *was* a trap—but not for him.

"I don't think they're going to bother us anymore, but maintain a watch. Stay sharp. Don't let *anyone* in, no matter who they are. I'll stay at the Keep until morning. If I come back before that . . . do your best to kill me."

They understood him. If he came back before that, they should assume he was being controlled and respond accordingly.

"May the Darkness protect you," Hallevar said.

Falonar passed through the Sapphire shield. Taking the envelope, he launched himself skyward and headed for the Keep.

15 / Kaeleer

Saetan stared at the sheet of paper. Too many feelings crowded him, so he pushed them all aside.

I have your son.
Hekatah

Which also meant she had Marian and Daemonar, since that was the only bait she could have used to provoke Lucivar into going to Hayll.

Now Lucivar was being used as the bait for *him.*

He understood the game. Hekatah and Dorothea would be willing to trade: him for Lucivar, Marian, and Daemonar.

Of course, they wouldn't let Lucivar go, *couldn't* let him go. As soon as he got Marian and Daemonar safely out of reach, he'd turn on Hekatah and Dorothea with all the destructive power that was in him.

So this was a false bargain right from the beginning.

He could go to Hayll and destroy Dorothea and Hekatah. Two Red-Jeweled Priestesses were no match for a Black-Jeweled Warlord Prince. He could go there, throw a Black shield around Lucivar, Marian, and Daemonar to keep them safe, then unleash his strength—and kill every living thing for miles around him.

But it wouldn't stop the war. Not now. Maybe it never would have. And it was the war that had to be stopped, not just the two witches who had started it.

So he would play their game . . . because it would finally give him the weapon he needed.

Everything has a price.

He removed the Black-Jeweled pendant and set it on the desk. He removed the Steward's ring from his left hand— the ring that contained the same Ebony shield Jaenelle had put into the Rings of Honor.

Even if Daemon was influencing Jaenelle, even if he *was* the reason she was resisting a formal declaration of war, even *he* couldn't stop her reacting. Not to this.

Don't think. Be an instrument.

By walking into the trap Dorothea and Hekatah had set for him, he was going to unleash the one thing he *knew* would bring out the explosive, savage side of Jaenelle—his own pain.

Of course, he would never be the same after those two bitches were done with him. He would never . . .

He opened the desk drawer, caressed the lavender-scented envelope. "Sometimes duty walks a road where the heart can't follow. I'm sorry, Sylvia. It would have been an honor to be your husband. I'm sorry."

He closed the drawer, picked up his cape, and quietly left the Keep.

16 / Kaeleer

Daemon glided through the Keep's corridors. He'd spent the past several hours making three months' worth of tonics for Karla, according to the instructions Jaenelle had given him. When he'd questioned her, reminding her that healing tonics that had blood in them would lose their potency over that amount of time, she had told him she had calculated that so the potency would taper off the way it needed to. And when he'd ask why . . .

Well, it was to be expected that she would be drained by unleashing the amount of power needed to stop Dorothea and Hekatah *completely*. The fact that it would take her three months to recover worried him. And now that she was so close to finishing . . . whatever it was . . . he was also worried that the boyos might finally slip the leash and throw themselves into battle.

They were feeling too hostile toward him just then to listen to anything he might say, but he hoped Saetan would still be reasonable. He was fairly sure he could say enough for the High Lord to understand that Jaenelle's evasion had a purpose, that all they needed was a few more days. A few more days and the threat to Kaeleer would end, the threat Dorothea and Hekatah had always been to the Blood would end.

He knocked on Saetan's door, then went in cautiously when it was Surreal who said, "Come in."

She was standing behind the small desk. Falonar stood beside her, looking tired and angry. Surreal didn't look tired, and she was a long way past angry. "Look at this," she said.

Even from where he stood, he could see the pendant and the Steward's ring. Slipping his hands into his trouser pockets, he walked around the desk, silently acknowledging the emotional cut when she deliberately moved away from him. He read the message and felt a claw-sharp chill rip down his back.

"*Now* are you finally going to do something?" Surreal

asked, slamming her hands on the desk. "They're not killing strangers anymore. You can't keep your distance anymore. *Those bitches have your father and brother.*"

It cost him dearly, but he managed to get that bored tone in his voice. "Lucivar and Saetan chose to take the risk when they disobeyed orders. It doesn't change anything." *Couldn't* change anything. Not if Jaenelle was going to save Kaeleer.

"They've also got Marian and Daemonar."

Of course they did. He felt concerned about Marian, but not really worried. If Marian were raped or harmed in any way, not even a Ring of Obedience would stop Lucivar from starting a full-scale slaughter. So he wasn't really worried about Marian, but just the thought of Daemonar in those bitches' hands for even an hour . . . "There's bound to be some kind of ransom demand," he said dismissively. "We'll see what we can accommodate."

"Accommodate?" Surreal said. "*Accommodate?* Don't you know what Dorothea and Hekatah will do to them?"

Of course he knew, far better than she did.

Surreal's voice filled with venom. "Are you at least going to tell Jaenelle?"

"Yes, I suppose the Lady will have to be told about this inconvenience." He walked out of the room while Surreal was still sputtering curses.

He wished she had cried. He wished she had shouted, screamed, raged, swore, wept bitterly. He didn't know what to do with this still woman he had cradled on his lap for the past hour.

He had told her as gently as he could. She had said nothing. Just put her head on his shoulder and turned inward, going down so deep into the abyss he couldn't even feel her.

So he held her. Sometimes his hands stroked, caressed— not to arouse her but to relax her. He *could* have drawn her back with sex, but it would have violated the trust she had in him, and *that* he wouldn't do. When his hand had rested on her chest, it was to reassure himself that her heart was still beating. Each warm breath against his throat was an unspoken promise that she would return to him.

Finally, after almost two hours had passed, she stirred. "What do you think will happen now?" she asked as if there had been no time at all between the question and his news.

"Even riding the Black Winds, it would have taken Saetan a couple of hours or more to get to Hayll. We don't know when he left—"

"But he would have gotten there by now."

"Yes." He paused, thought it through again. "Lucivar and Saetan aren't the prize. They're the bait. And bait becomes less valuable if it's damaged. So I think they're safe enough for the moment."

"Dorothea and Hekatah expect me to surrender Kaeleer in order to get Lucivar and Papa back, don't they?" When he didn't answer, Jaenelle raised her head and studied him. "No. That would never do, would it? In order to hold on to Kaeleer, they have to be able to control me, use my strength to rule."

"Yes. Lucivar and Saetan are the bait. You're the prize." Daemon brushed her hair away from her face. "How close are you to finishing your . . . spell?" He knew it was far more than that, but it was as good a word as any.

"A few more hours." She stirred a little more. "I should get back to it."

His hold on her tightened. "Not yet. Sit with me a little while longer. Please."

She relaxed against him. "We'll get them back, Daemon."

Father. Brother. He closed his eyes and pressed his cheek against her head, needing the warmth and contact. "Yes," he murmured, "we'll get them back."

17 / Kaeleer

Ladvarian studied the chamber that would be Witch's home for a while. An old carpet that he had brought from the Hall covered the stone floor. He had also taken a couple of lamps that used candle-lights and lots of scented candles. The narrow bed Tersa had given him was in the center of the chamber. The trunk was beside it and held a few changes of clothes, a couple of the books Jaenelle liked to read when she needed to snuggle up and rest for a day, her favorite music crystals, and some grooming things.

He had brought no pictures because three walls and the ceiling of the chamber were covered with layers of healing webs. The back of the chamber was filled with the tangled web of dreams and visions that had shaped the living myth, dreams made flesh, Witch.

Is it ready? he respectfully asked the large golden spider who was the Weaver of Dreams.

Web is ready, the Arachnian Queen replied, delicately brushing a leg against one of the drops of blood sealed in shielded water bubbles. *I add memories now. But . . . Need human memories.*

Ladvarian bristled. *She was *our* dream more than theirs.*

*But theirs, too. Need kindred *and* human memories for this Witch.*

Ladvarian's heart sank. It had been easy with the kindred. He had told them what was required and that it was for the Lady. That's all the kindred had needed to know. But humans would want to know why, why, why. They would take time to persuade—and time was something he didn't have.

The Strange One will help you, the spider said.

*But the Lady knows packs of humans, whole *herds* of humans. How—*

The First Circle have strong memories. They will be enough. Ask the Gray Black Widow. For a human, she is a good weaver.

She meant Karla. Yes. If he could persuade Karla . . .

Wait for the right time to ask. After Witch has gone to her own web. The humans will listen better then.

I'll go to the Keep now and wait. Ladvarian looked around one more time. There was nothing left to do. The chamber was ready. The tangled web was ready. The kindred who belonged to the Lady's court were gathered on the Arachnians' island to give their strength to the Weaver's web when the time came.

One more thing, the spider said. *Gray dog. You know this dog?*

An image appeared in Ladvarian's mind. *That's Graysfang. He's a wolf.*

Send him to me. There is something he must learn.

18 / Terreille

It was a war camp, not the sort of place he would have looked for Hekatah or Dorothea. Around the wide perimeter, metal stakes had been driven into the ground every few yards. Embedded in the stakes were two crystals, one on each side, spelled so that anything going between them would break their contact with the crystal in the next stake and would alert the guards. The camp itself had clusters of tents for the guards, a few small wooden cabins built close together near the camp's center, and two wooden huts that had heavily barred windows and layers of guard spells around them. In front of the cabins were six thick wooden stakes that had heavy chains attached to them. For prisoners. For bait.

As soon as he walked past the perimeter stakes, they knew he was coming. On the journey there, he had thought again about what he was going to do. He could kill Hekatah and Dorothea. He could unleash the strength of his Black Jewels, destroy everyone in the camp, and take Lucivar, Marian, and Daemonar home. But it wouldn't stop the war. Terreille needed to be confronted with a power that would terrify the people sufficiently that they wouldn't *dare* fight against it. So it always came back to provoking Jaenelle enough for her to unleash her Ebony power and give the Terreilleans a reason to stay in their own Realm.

As he walked toward the center of the camp, guards followed him. No one approached him or tried to touch him.

Round candle-lights set on top of tall metal poles lit the bloodstained bare ground at the exact center of the camp. Lucivar was chained to the last stake. The lash wounds on his chest and thighs had scabbed over and didn't appear to be deep enough to cause him serious harm. There were bruises on his face, but those, too, would cause no permanent damage.

Saetan stopped at the edge of the light. He hadn't seen Hekatah in ten years—hardly more than a breath of time for someone who had lived as long as he had. And he had known her for most of those years. Even so, despite Dorothea standing beside her, she had withered so much, *decayed* so much, he wasn't really sure it was her until she spoke.

"Saetan."

"Hekatah." He walked to the center of the bare ground.

"You've come to bargain?" Hekatah asked politely.

He nodded. "A life for a life."

She smiled. "For *lives*. We'll throw the bitch and the babe into the bargain. We don't really have any use for them."

Did she think he didn't know they would never give up Daemonar? They had been striving for centuries to get a child out of Lucivar or Daemon that they could control and breed in order to bring back a darker bloodline.

"My life for theirs," he said. *Everything has a price.*

"NO!" Lucivar shouted, struggling against the spelled chains. *"Kill them!"*

Ignoring Lucivar, he focused on Hekatah. "Do we have a bargain?"

"For a chance to see the High Lord humbled?" Hekatah said sweetly. "Oh, yes, we have a bargain. As soon as you're restrained, I'll set the others free. I swear it on my word of honor."

They ordered him to strip—and he did.

Removing his Black-Jeweled ring, he tossed it on the ground. He had put a tight shield around it so that no one could actually touch it. If he needed to call it back to him, he didn't want their foulness absorbed by the gold.

As two guards chained him to the center post, Hekatah slipped a Ring of Obedience over his organ.

"You look well for someone your age," she said, stepping back to give his naked body a thorough inspection.

He smiled gently. "Unfortunately, darling, I can't say the same about you."

Viciousness twisted Hekatah's face. "It's time you learned a lesson, *High Lord*." She raised her hand at the same time Dorothea, with a look of perverted glee, raised hers.

Lucivar had once tried to explain to the boyos why a Ring of Obedience could force a powerful male to submit, so Saetan thought he was ready for it.

Nothing could have prepared him for the pain that filled his cock and balls before it spread through his body. His nerves were on fire, while agony settled between his legs. He couldn't fight it, could barely think.

His sons had endured this, had *fought* against Dorothea's control knowing that *this* was waiting after every act of defiance. For centuries, they had endured this. How could a man not become twisted by this? How . . .

He screamed—and kept on screaming until his body just shut down.

19 / Kaeleer

Surreal paced back and forth in Karla's sitting room, growing angrier by the minute. She wasn't sure why she'd chosen to vent her frustrations to Karla. Maybe it was because Karla had seemed so damned indifferent to everything that had been happening.

All right, that wasn't fair. The woman was grieving for her cousin, Morton, not to mention that she was slowly recovering from a vicious poisoning. Even so . . .

"The bastard sounded like it was an inconvenience that would interfere with his manicure," Surreal raged at Karla. " 'We'll see what we can accommodate.' Hell's fire, it's his father and brother!"

"You don't know what he intends to do," Karla said blandly.

The blandness pushed Surreal's temper up another notch. "He doesn't plan to do anything!"

"How do you know?" `

Surreal sputtered, swore, paced. "It's as if he and Jaenelle *want* us to lose this war."

For the first time, temper heated Karla's voice. "Don't be an ass."

"Now, look, sugar—"

"No, *you* look," Karla snapped. "It's about time all of you looked and thought and remembered a few things. The boyos' instincts are pushing them toward battle. They can't change that any more than they can change being male. And the coven is made up of Queens whose instincts are urging them to protect their people."

"Which is exactly what they should be doing!" Surreal shouted. "And you don't seem to have that problem," she added nastily. Then she glanced at Karla's covered legs and regretted the words.

"When Jaenelle was fifteen," Karla said, "the Dark Council tried to say that Uncle Saetan was unfit to be her legal guardian. They decided to appoint someone else. And she said they could 'when the sun next rises.' Do you know what happened?"

Finally standing still, Surreal shook her head.

"The sun didn't rise for three days," Karla said mildly. "It didn't rise until the Council rescinded their decision."

Surreal sank to the floor. "Mother Night," she whispered.

"Jaenelle didn't want a court, didn't want to rule. The only reason she became the Queen of Ebon Askavi was to stop the Terreilleans who were coming into the kindred Territories and slaughtering the kindred. Do you really think a woman who would do those things has spent the past three weeks wringing her hands and hoping this will all go away? I don't. She needs us here for a reason—and she'll tell us when it's time to tell us." Karla paused. "And I'll tell you one other thing, just between us: sometimes a friend must become an enemy in order to remain a friend."

Karla was talking about Daemon. Surreal thought for a moment, then shook her head. "The way he's been acting—"

"Daemon Sadi is totally committed to Witch. Whatever he does, he does for her."

"You don't know that."

"Don't I?" Karla said too softly.

Black Widow. The words bloomed in Surreal's mind until there wasn't room for anything else. Black Widow. Maybe Karla *wasn't* indifferent to what was happening. Maybe she had *seen* something in a tangled web. "Are you sure about Sadi?"

"No," Karla replied. "But I'm willing to consider the possibility that what he says in public may be very different from what he does in private."

Surreal raked her fingers through her hair. "Well, Hell's fire, if Daemon and Jaenelle *were* planning something, they could at least tell the court."

"I was poisoned by a member of my court," Karla said quietly. "And let's not forget Jaenelle's grandmother, because I'm sure Jaenelle hasn't. So tell me, Surreal, if you were trying to find a way to totally destroy those two bitches, who would *you* trust?"

"She could have trusted the High Lord."

"And where is he right now?" Karla asked.

Surreal didn't say anything, since they both knew the answer.

20 / Terreille

"I think it's time to let Jaenelle know you're here," Hekatah said, circling behind Saetan. "I think we should send a little gift."

He felt her grab the little finger of his left hand. He felt the knife cut through skin and bone. And he felt rage when she dropped to her knees and clamped her mouth over the wound to drink his blood. A Guardian's blood.

Gathering his strength, he sent a blast of heat down his arm, psychic fire that cauterized the wound.

Hekatah jerked away from him, screaming.

While he had the chance, he used a little healing Craft to cleanse the wound and seal up the flesh enough to keep infection at bay.

Hekatah kept screaming. Dorothea rushed out of her cabin. Guards came running from every direction.

Finally the screaming stopped. He heard Hekatah scrabble for something on the ground, then slowly get to her feet. As she circled around him, he saw what the blast of power had done. Since her mouth had been clamped on the wound, the psychic fire had kept going after it cauterized the blood vessels. It had melted part of her jaw, grotesquely reshaping her face.

In one hand, she held his little finger. In the other, she held the knife. "You're going to pay for that," she said in a slurred voice.

"No," Dorothea said, stepping forward. "You said yourself that we have to keep the damage to a minimum until Jaenelle is contained."

Hekatah turned toward Dorothea. Saetan felt sure the sick revulsion on Dorothea's face would drive Hekatah past any ability to think rationally.

"Until Jaenelle is contained," Hekatah said with effort. "But . . . that doesn't mean . . . he can't pay." Turning toward him, she raised her hand.

For the second time, the agony from the Ring of Obedience ripped through him. That was devastating enough. Hearing Lucivar's pain-filled, but still enraged, war cry as Hekatah also punished the son for the deeds of the father produced an agony in him that cut far deeper.

21 / Kaeleer

Daemon wished Surreal hadn't been around when Geoffrey brought the small, ornately carved box that had been delivered to the Keep in Terreille. He *had* suggested that, since the verbal message had said it was a "gift" for Jaenelle, Surreal's presence wasn't required. She had countered by saying she was family and had just as much right to know what was going on as he or Jaenelle did. Which, unfortunately, was true.

"Do you want me to open it?" he asked Jaenelle when she had just stood there staring at the box for several minutes.

"No," she said too calmly. Using Craft, she flipped the lid off the box.

The three of them stared at the little finger nestled in a bed of silk—a little finger with a long, black-tinted nail.

"Well, sugar, I'd say that message is to the point," Surreal said as she stared at Jaenelle. "How many more pieces do you need to get back *before you do something*? We're running out of time!"

"Yes," Jaenelle said. "It's time."

She's in shock, Daemon thought. Then he looked at her eyes—and couldn't suppress the shudder. They were sapphire ice. But behind the ice was a Queen who had been pushed far beyond even the cold rage males were capable of unleashing. Because he was looking for it, because he could descend far enough into the abyss to feel it, he sensed that Hekatah's little gift had fully awakened the feral side, the *deadly* side of Witch. She was no longer a young woman who had received her father's finger as a demand for her surrender; she was a predator studying the bait laid out by an enemy.

Dorothea and Hekatah had seen the young woman. They had no idea who they were *really* dealing with.

"Come with me," Jaenelle said, lightly touching his arm before she walked out of the room.

Even through his shirt and jacket, her hand felt so cold it burned.

Careful to keep his eyes and expression bland, he looked at Surreal—and felt a little dismayed by the fury that looked back at him. That was when he realized that, despite being chilled to the bone, the room was still warm.

Jaenelle had given no outward warning of the rage just underneath the surface, no indication of power being gathered for a strike. Nothing.

He glanced at the finger again, felt his stomach clench. Then he walked out of the room.

Damn them both, Surreal thought as she stared at the finger in the box. Oh, there had been a little flicker of dismay in Sadi's face when he first saw it, but that had disappeared quickly enough. And from Jaenelle? Nothing. Hell's fire! She had shown more temper and concern when Aaron had been cornered by Vania! At least then there had been that freezing, terrifying rage. But the woman gets *a piece of her father* sent to her and . . . nothing. Not a damn thing. No reaction at all.

Well, fine. If that's the way those two wanted to play the game, that was just fine. *She* wore a Gray Jewel and *she* was a skilled assassin. There was no reason she couldn't slip into Terreille and get Lucivar and the High Lord—and Marian and Daemonar—away from those two bitches.

Surreal bit her lower lip. Well, getting *all* of them out in one piece *might* be a problem.

All right, so she'd think about it a little, work up some kind of plan. At least *she* was going to do something!

And maybe, while she was thinking, she would mention this little incident to Karla to see if the Black Widow still thought there was more going on than *nothing*.

By the time Daemon reached her workroom, the ice in Jaenelle's eyes had shattered into razor-edged shards, and he saw something in them that terrified him: cold, undiluted hatred.

"What do you expect will happen now?" Jaenelle asked too calmly.

Daemon slipped his hands into his trouser pockets to hide the trembling. He quietly cleared his throat. "I doubt anything more will happen until the messenger returns to Hayll and reports the delivery of the box. It's almost midmorning now. They aren't going to expect you to be capable of making any decisions immediately. So we've got a few hours. Maybe a little more than that."

Jaenelle paced slowly. She seemed to be arguing with

herself. Finally she sighed—as if she'd lost the argument—and looked at him. "The Weaver of Dreams sent me a message. She said the triangle must remain together in order to survive, that the other two sides weren't strong enough without the strength of the mirror—and the mirror would keep them *all* safe."

"The mirror?" Daemon asked cautiously.

"You are your father's mirror, Daemon. You're one side of the triangle."

The memory flashed in his mind of Tersa, years ago, tracing a triangle in the palm of his hand, over and over, while she had explained the mystery of the Blood's four-sided triangle.

"Father, brother, lover," he murmured. Three sides. And the fourth side was the triangle's center, the one who ruled all three.

"Exactly," Jaenelle replied.

"You want me to go to Hayll."

"Yes."

He nodded slowly, suddenly feeling like he was on a very thin, shaky footbridge, and one false step would send him plummeting into a chasm he would never escape. "If I walked in to try another exchange of prisoners, that would buy a few more hours."

"I never said anything about you handing yourself over to them," Jaenelle snapped. Her face had been pale since she'd seen Saetan's finger. Now it got paler. "Daemon, I need seventy-two hours."

"Sev—But everything is ready. All you would need to do is gather your strength and unleash it."

"I need seventy-two hours."

He stared at her, slowly coming to terms with what she was telling him. In a controlled dive into the abyss, he could descend to the level of his Black Jewels in a few minutes and gather his full strength. It was going to take her *seventy-two hours* to do the same thing.

Hell's fire, Mother Night, and may the Darkness be merciful.

But there was no way for him to . . .

He saw the knowledge in her eyes—and fought against the shame it produced in him. He should have known he couldn't hide the Sadist from Witch. And he finally understood what she was asking of him.

Unable to meet her eyes anymore, he turned away and began his own slow prowl around the room.

It was just a game. A dirty, vicious game—the kind the Sadist had always played so well. As he gave that part of himself free rein, the plan took shape as easily as breathing.

But . . . Everything has a price. If he was going to lose the companionship of almost everyone he had ever cared about, the reward would have to justify the cost.

"I can do this," he crooned, slowly circling around her. "I can keep Dorothea and Hekatah off-balance enough to keep the others safe and also prevent those *Ladies* from giving the orders to send the Terreillean armies into Kaeleer. I can buy you seventy-two hours, Jaenelle. But it's going to cost me because I'm going to do things I may never be forgiven for, so I want something in return."

He could taste her slight bafflement before she said, "All right."

"I don't want to wear the Consort's ring anymore."

A slash of pain, quickly stifled. "All right."

"I want a wedding ring in its place."

A flash of joy, immediately followed by sorrow. She smiled at him at the same time her eyes filled with tears. "It would be wonderful."

She meant that. So why the sorrow, why the anguish? He would have to deal with that when he got back.

His temper was already getting edgy, dangerous. "I'll take that as a 'yes.' There are things I'll need that I can't create well enough for this game."

"Just tell me what you need, Daemon."

He didn't want to do this. Didn't want to go back to that kind of life, not even for seventy-two hours. He was going to mutilate the life he'd begun to build here, and the coven, the boyos, they would never—

"Do you trust me?" he snapped.

"Yes."

No hesitation, no doubts.

He finally stopped moving and faced her. "Do you know how desperately I love you?"

Her voice shook when she answered, "As much as I love you?"

He held her, held on to her as his lifeline, his anchor. It would be all right. As long as he had *her*, it would be all right.

Finally, reluctantly, he eased back. "Come on, we've got a lot of work to do."

"That's the last of it," Jaenelle said several hours later. She carefully packed the box that held all the spelled items she had created for him. "Almost the last of it."

Daemon sipped the coffee he had brewed strong enough to bite. Physically, he was tired. Mentally, he was reeling. As Jaenelle created each of the spells he had asked for, he'd had to learn how to use them—which meant she'd explained the process to him as she created one, then had him practice with it while she created the ones he would take with him. She'd reviewed his efforts, given more instructions on how to hone the effect—and never once asked him what he intended to do, for which he was grateful. Of course, he didn't know exactly what *she* was going to do either. There were some things one Black Widow did not ask another.

Jaenelle held up a vial about the size of her index finger that was filled with dark powder. "This is a stimulant. A strong one. One dose will keep you on your feet for about six hours. You can mix it with any kind of liquid—" She eyed the coffee. "—but if you mix it with something brewed like *that* it's going to have more kick."

"That's one dose?" Daemon asked. Then he bit his tongue to keep from laughing and wished he could have a picture of the look on her face.

"There are enough doses in here for the next three days and then some," she said dryly.

"Well, I'd better find out what it does." Daemon held out the mug of coffee.

She opened the vial, tapped it lightly over the mug. The sprinkle of powder dissolved instantly.

He took a sip. A little nutty, just a little sharp. Actually quite—

He wheezed. His body suddenly had a kind of battlefield alertness, a fierce need to *move*. His mind was no longer hazed by mental fatigue. After the first few explosive seconds, he felt himself settle down, but there remained that bright reservoir of energy.

He drained the mug, waited a few seconds. No physical

changes, just the feeling that the reservoir got delightfully bigger.

Jaenelle carefully packed the vial into the box. "Everything has a price, Daemon," she said firmly.

That sobered him. "It's addictive?"

The look she gave him could have cut a man in half. "No, it is not. *I* use this sometimes—which you will *not* mention to any of the family. They'd throw three kinds of fits if they knew. This will keep you going, even if you don't get any food or sleep, but if you don't renew the dose every six hours, your feet are going to go out from under you and you'd better be prepared to sleep for a day."

"In other words, if I miss a dose, I'm not going to be able to flog myself awake again no matter what's going on around me."

She nodded.

"All right, I'll remember."

She held up another vial, this one full of a dark liquid. "This is a tonic for Saetan. I figured he's going to be weakened physically, so I made it strong. It's going to have a kick like a team of draft horses. Add it to an equal amount of liquid—wine or fresh blood."

"If I use the stimulant, can I use my blood for that tonic?"

"Yes," Jaenelle said, almost managing to keep her lips from twitching. "But if you *do* use your blood, make sure you pour it down his throat before you tell him what it is because it'll kick like *two* teams of draft horses—and he will not be happy with you for the first couple of minutes."

"Fair enough." He just hoped Saetan would be in good enough condition that he could howl about being dosed.

Jaenelle took a deep breath, let it out slowly. "That's it then."

Daemon set the mug down on the worktable. "I want to supervise making up the food pack. It won't take long. Will you wait for me?"

Her smile didn't reach her haunted sapphire eyes. "I'll wait."

"Prince Ssadi."

Daemon hesitated, turned toward the voice. "Draca."

She held out one hand, closed in a loose fist. Obediently, he put his hand under hers. When she opened her hand, colored bangles poured into his—the kind of bangles women sewed on dresses to catch the light.

Baffled, he looked at the bangles, then at her.

"When the time iss right, give thesse to Ssactan. He will undersstand."

She knows, Daemon thought. *She knows, but . . .* No, Draca wouldn't say anything to the coven or the boyos. The Seneschal of Ebon Askavi would keep her own council for her own reasons.

As she walked away, he slipped the bangles into his jacket pocket.

Surreal jumped when the door to her room flew open.

"What in the name of Hell do you think you're doing?" Daemon demanded, slamming the door.

"What does it look like I'm doing?" Surreal snapped. Silently, she swore. A few more minutes and she would have been able to slip away undetected.

"It *looks* like you're about to ruin several hours of careful planning," Daemon snapped back.

That stopped her. "What planning?" she asked suspiciously.

He swore with a creative vileness that surprised her. "What do you think I've been doing since we got that *gift* this morning? And what did you think *you'd* be able to do, going in alone?"

"I've been an assassin for a lot of years, Sadi. I could have—"

"One-on-one kills," he snarled. "That's not going to get you very far in an armed camp. And if you unleash the Gray to get rid of the guards, you can be sure the four people you're going in for will be dead by the time you reach them."

"You don't know—"

"I do know," Daemon shouted. "I grew up under that bitch's control. I *do* know."

Her anger couldn't match his, especially when he'd been able to put his finger on every doubt she had about succeeding. "You have a better idea?"

"Yes, Surreal, I have a better idea," Daemon replied coldly.

Surreal licked her lips, took a careful breath. "I could

help, create a diversion or something. Hell's fire, Daemon, those people are my family, too, the first family I've ever had. They mean something to me. Let me help."

Something queer filled his eyes as he stared at her. "Yes," he said in a silky croon, "I think you could be very helpful." His voice shifted, became irritated and efficient as he looked over the supplies piled on her bed. "At least you had the good sense to realize you would need to bring your own food and water since you won't be able to trust consuming anything that might be there." He headed for the door. "I'll need a couple more hours. Then we'll go."

"But—" The look he gave her had her backing down. "A couple of hours," she agreed.

It wasn't until he was gone that she began to wonder just what it was she had agreed to do.

Little fool, Daemon thought as he stormed back to Jaenelle's workroom. *Idiot.* If the kitchen staff hadn't mentioned that Surreal had requested a similar food pack, he wouldn't have known she was planning to go to Hayll, wouldn't have been prepared to deal with her presence. Oh, he could use her help in this game. It hadn't taken him more than a minute to recognize how many ways she could help. But, damn it, if she'd gone in and gotten everyone riled before he arrived . . . He had to buy Jaenelle seventy-two hours. A straight, clean fight would have gotten the others out, but it wouldn't have done *that.*

So he would play out his game—and Surreal would have a chance to dance with the Sadist.

He walked into the workroom and snarled at Jaenelle, "I'll need a couple more items."

Her eyes widened when he told her what he wanted, but she didn't say anything except, "I think I'd better give you a Ring that has a shield *no one* can get through."

Since he figured both Lucivar and Surreal would want to tear his heart out in a few hours' time, he thought that was an excellent idea.

The three of them stood outside the room that held the Dark Altar at the Keep.

Jaenelle hugged Surreal. "May the Darkness embrace you, Sister."

"We'll get them back," Surreal said, returning the hug. "Count on it." Glancing at Daemon, she went into the Altar's room and quietly closed the door.

Daemon just looked at Jaenelle, his heart too full to say anything. Besides, words seemed so inadequate at the moment. He brushed a thumb across her cheek, kissed her gently. Then he took a deep breath. "The game begins at midnight."

"And at midnight, seventy-two hours later, you're going to be riding the Winds back to the Keep in Terreille. No stops, no delays." She paused, waited for him to nod agreement, then added, "Don't ride any Wind darker than the Red. The others will be unstable."

It took effort to keep his jaw from dropping. A strong witch storm could create a disturbance on *part* of the psychic roadways through the Darkness, could even throw someone off the Web to be lost in the Darkness, but "unstable" sounded much, much worse.

"All right," he finally said. "We'll stay on the Red."

"Daemon," Jaenelle said softly, "I want you to promise me something."

"Anything."

Her eyes filled with tears. It took her a moment to regain control. "Thirteen years ago, you gave everything you had in order to help me."

"And I'll give you everything again," he replied just as softly.

She shook her head fiercely. "No. No more sacrifices, Daemon. Not from you. That's what I want you to promise me." She swallowed hard. "The Keep is going to be the only safe place. I want your promise that, at the appointed hour, you'll be on your way there. No matter who you have to walk away from, no matter who you have to leave behind, *you must get to the Keep before dawn.* Promise me, Daemon." She gripped his arm hard enough to hurt. "I have to know you'll be safe. Promise me."

Gently, he removed her hand, then raised it to place a kiss in her palm—and smiled. "I'm not going to do anything that will make me late for my own wedding."

Pain flashed in her eyes, making him wonder if she really *wanted* to marry him. No. He wouldn't begin to doubt, couldn't *afford* to doubt. "I'll come back to you," he said. "I swear it."

She gave him a brief, fierce kiss. "See that you do."

She looked pale and exhausted. There were dark smudges under her eyes. She had never looked more beautiful to him.

"I'll see you in a few days."

"Good-bye, Daemon. I love you."

As he approached the Dark Altar that was a Gate between the Realms, he didn't find Jaenelle's last words reassuring.

22 / Kaeleer

Karla eased herself into a chair in Jaenelle's sitting room. She could use Craft to float herself from place to place, and could even stand on her own now for a little while with the help of two canes. But channeling power through her body left her quickly exhausted, and standing made her legs ache. Still, the daily cup of Jaenelle's tonic *was* working. But she had an uneasy feeling she would need her strength for something else very soon.

It was the first time since Jaenelle had refused to allow Kaeleer to go to war that Karla had seen her. But even now, when *Jaenelle* had summoned her and Gabrielle, the Queen of Ebon Askavi was keeping her back to them, just staring out the window.

"I need the two of you to keep the boyos leashed for another few days," Jaenelle said quietly. "It won't be easy, but it's necessary."

"Why?" Gabrielle demanded. "Hell's fire, Jaenelle, we need to gather into armies and *fight*. Scattered the way we are now, we're barely holding our own and we aren't even fighting the armies that are bound to come in from Terreille, just the Terreilleans who were already in Kaeleer. The *bastards*. It's time to go to war. We *have* to go to war. It's not just the people who are dying. The *land* is being destroyed, too."

"The Queens can heal the land," Jaenelle replied, still not looking at them. "That is the Queens' special gift. And not as many of our people have died as you seem to think."

"No," Gabrielle said bitterly, "they're just dying of shame because they've been ordered to abandon their land."

"They can survive a little shame."

Karla laid a hand on Gabrielle's arm. Trying to keep her voice reasonable, she said, "I don't think there's any choice now, Jaenelle. If we don't stop retreating and start attacking, we aren't going to have a place to take a stand when the Terreillean armies *do* get here."

"They won't receive orders to enter Kaeleer for a few more days. By then, it won't make any difference."

"Because we'll be forced to surrender," Gabrielle snapped.

Karla's hand tightened on Gabrielle's arm. She didn't have much strength, but the gesture was enough to leash the other Queen's temper—at least for the moment.

"Is Kaeleer finally going to war with Terreille?" she asked.

"No," Jaenelle said. "Kaeleer will not go to war with Terreille."

It was the slight inflection that made ice run through Karla's body. The way Gabrielle's arm tensed under her hand, she knew the other woman had heard it, too.

"Then who *is* going to war with Terreille?"

Jaenelle turned around.

Gabrielle sucked in her breath.

For the first time, they were seeing the dream beneath the flesh.

Karla stared at the pointed ears that had come from the Dea al Mon, the hands with sheathed claws that had come from the Tigre, the hooves peeking out from beneath the black gown that could have come from the centaurs or the horses or the unicorns. Most of all, she stared at the tiny spiral horn.

The living myth. Dreams made flesh. But, oh, had any of them really thought about who the dreamers had been?

No wonder the kindred love her. No wonder we've all loved her.

Karla quietly cleared her throat to ask the question she suddenly hoped wouldn't be answered. "Who *is* going to war with Terreille?"

"I am," Witch said.

CHAPTER FIFTEEN

1 / Terreille

Half-blinded by the pain inflicted on him during the past two days, Saetan watched Hekatah approach and give him a long, slow study. Whenever the whim had struck either of them, she and Dorothea had used the Ring of Obedience on him, but more carefully now, stopping just before the moment when he would have fainted from the pain. Worse, for him, they had left him chained to the post through the daylight hours. Already weakened by pain, the afternoon sun had drained his psychic strength and stabbed at his eyes, producing a headache so violent even the pain from the Ring couldn't engulf it.

Bit by bit, pain had chewed away all the revitalizing effects Jaenelle's tonics had produced in him, changing his body back to where it had been when he'd first met her—closer to the demon-dead than to the living.

If he could have made a fast transition from Guardian to demon-dead, he might have considered it—the kind of transition Andulvar and Prothvar had made on the battlefield all those long centuries ago. They had both been so deep in battle fury, they hadn't even realized they had received deathblows. If he could have done it that way, he might have. It would be easy enough to slit a vein and bleed himself out, and there would be less pain. But he would be more vulnerable, and without a supply of fresh blood, the sunlight would weaken him to the point that, when Jaenelle finally came, he would be a liability to her instead of finding some way to fight with her.

When Jaenelle finally came. *If* Jaenelle ever came. She should have reacted by now, should have been there by now—if she was coming at all.

"I think it's time to send Jaenelle another little gift," Hekatah said, her girlish voice now slurred by the misshapen jaw. "Another finger?" She used the same tone another woman might use when trying to decide the merits of serving one dish over another at dinner. "Perhaps a toe this time. No, too insignificant. An eye? Too disfiguring. We don't want her to start thinking you've become too repulsive to rescue." Her eyes focused on his balls—and she smiled. "It's dead meat now, but it will still be useful for *this* anyway."

He didn't react. Wouldn't allow himself to react. It *was* dead meat now—the last part revitalized, the first part to die. He wouldn't react. And he wouldn't think of Sylvia. Not now. Not ever again.

With their eyes locked on each other, Hekatah stepped closer, closer. One of her hands stroked him, caressed him, closed around him to hold him for the knife.

An enraged shriek tore through the normal nighttime sounds.

Hekatah jumped back and whirled toward the sound.

Surreal came flying into the camp as if she'd been tossed by a huge hand. Her feet hit the ground first, but she couldn't stop the forward momentum. She tucked and rolled, coming up on her knees facing the darkness beyond the area illuminated by candle-lights.

"YOU COLD-BLOODED, HEARTLESS BASTARD!" Surreal screamed. "YOU GUTLESS SON OF A WHORING BITCH!"

Dorothea burst out of her cabin, shouting, "Guards! *Guards!*"

The guards rushed in from three sides of the camp. No one came out of the darkness facing them.

"GUARDS!" Dorothea shouted again.

From out of that darkness, a deep, amused voice said, "They aren't going to answer you, darling. They've been permanently detained."

Daemon Sadi stepped out of the darkness, stopping at the edge of the light. His black hair was a little windmussed. His hands were casually tucked in his trouser pockets. His black jacket was open, revealing the white silk shirt that was unbuttoned to the waist. The Black Jewel around his neck glittered with power. His golden eyes glittered, too.

Seeing that queer glitter in Daemon's eyes, Saetan shivered. Something was wrong here. *Very* wrong.

Hekatah turned halfway, resting the knife against Saetan's belly. "Take one more step and I'll gut him—and kill the Eyrien, too."

"Go ahead," Daemon said pleasantly as he walked into the camp. "It'll save me the trouble of arranging a couple of careful accidents, which I would have had to have done soon anyway since the Steward and the First Escort were becoming . . . troublesome. So, you kill them, I destroy you—and then I return to Kaeleer to console the grieving Queen. Yes, that will work out quite nicely. You'll be blamed for their deaths, and Jaenelle will never look at me and wonder why I'm the only male left whom she can depend on."

"You're forgetting about the Master of the Guard," Hekatah said.

Daemon smiled a gentle, brutal smile. "No, I haven't. I didn't forget about Prothvar or Mephis either. They're no longer a concern."

For a moment, Saetan thought Hekatah *had* gutted him. But while the wound wasn't physical, the pain *was*. "No," he said. "No. You couldn't have."

Daemon laughed. "Couldn't I? Then where are they, old man?"

Because he had wondered the same thing, Saetan couldn't answer that. But he still found himself denying it. "You couldn't have. *They're your family.*"

"My family," Daemon said thoughtfully. "How convenient that they decided to become 'family' after I became the Consort to the strongest Queen in the history of the Blood."

"That's not true," Saetan said, straining forward despite the knife Hekatah still held against his belly. It was mad to be arguing about this, but all his instincts shouted at him that it had to be *now*, that there might not be another chance to alter that look in Daemon's eyes.

"Isn't it?" Daemon said bitterly. "Then where were they 1,700 years ago when I was a child? Where were *you*? Where were *any* of you during all the years between then and now? Don't talk to me about *family*, High Lord."

Saetan sagged against the post. Mother Night, every worry he'd had about Daemon's loyalty was coming true.

"How very touching," Hekatah sneered. "Do you expect us to believe that? You're your father's son."

Daemon's gold eyes fastened on Hekatah. "I think it's more accurate to say I'm the man my father *might* have been if he'd had the balls for it."

"Don't listen to him," Dorothea said suddenly. "It's a trick, a trap. He's *lying.*"

"It seems to be his day for it," Surreal muttered bitterly.

Giving Surreal a brief, dismissive glance, Daemon shifted his attention to Dorothea. "Hello, darling. You look like a hag. It suits you."

Dorothea hissed.

"I brought you a present," Daemon said, glancing at Surreal again.

Dorothea looked at Surreal's pointed ears and sneered. "I've heard of her. She's nothing but a whore."

"Yes," Daemon agreed mildly, "she's a first-class slut who will spread her legs for anything that will pay her. She's also your granddaughter. Kartane's child. The only one he'll ever sire. The only continuation of *your* bloodline."

"No slut is *my* granddaughter," Dorothea snarled.

Daemon raised one eyebrow. "Really, darling, I thought that would be the convincing argument. The only difference between you is she's under a male most of the time while you're on top of him. But your legs are spread just as wide." He paused. "Well, there is *one* other difference. Since she was getting paid for it, *she* had to acquire some skill in bed."

Dorothea shook with rage. "Guards! Seize him!"

Twenty men surged forward, then dropped in their tracks.

Daemon just smiled. "Perhaps I should kill the rest of them now to eliminate further annoyances."

Hekatah carefully lowered the knife. "Why are you here, Sadi?"

"Your little schemes are interfering with my plans, and that annoys me."

"Terreille is going to war with Kaeleer. That's hardly a 'little scheme.' "

"Well, that all depends on whether you have the power to win, doesn't it?" Daemon crooned. "However, I'm not interested in ruling a Realm that's been devastated by a war, so I decided it was time we had a little talk."

Dorothea jumped forward. "Don't listen to him!"

"How can *you* rule a Realm?" Hekatah asked, ignoring Dorothea.

Daemon's smile became colder, crueler. "I control the witch who has the strength to kill every living thing in the Realm of Terreille."

"NO!" Saetan shouted. "You *do not* control the Queen."

When Daemon's eyes fixed on him, he started to shiver again.

"Don't I?" Daemon purred. "Haven't you wondered why she didn't respond to the 'gift,' High Lord? Oh, she was greatly distressed. Hasn't done anything but weep since your finger arrived. But she isn't here—and she isn't going to be because she values having my cock inside her more than she values you. Any of you." For the first time, Daemon glanced at Lucivar.

Saetan shook his head. "No. You can't do this, Daemon."

"Don't tell me what I can do. You had your chance, old man, and you didn't have the balls to take it. Now it's *my* turn, and I intend to rule."

"That's just another lie," Dorothea snapped. "You've never been interested in ruling."

Daemon turned searing, cold anger on her. "What would *you* know about what I wanted, bitch? You never offered me a chance to rule *anything*. You just wanted to use my strength without ever offering anything in return."

"I did offer you something!"

"What? *You?* You had your use of me, Dorothea. How could you imagine enduring more of that would be any kind of reward?"

"You *bastard*! You—" She took a step toward him, her hand raised like a claw.

A blow from a phantom hand knocked her off her feet. She fell on top of Surreal, who swore viciously and pushed her off.

Tearing his eyes away from Daemon, Saetan looked at Hekatah—and realized she was shaking, but it wasn't from anger.

"What is it you want, Sadi?" Hekatah said, unable to keep her voice steady.

A long, chilling moment passed before Daemon turned his attention back to her. "I came to negotiate on my Queen's behalf."

"I told you," Dorothea muttered—but she didn't try to get up.

"And what will you tell your Queen?" Hekatah asked

"That I arrived too late to save any of them. I'm sure I can prod her into a suitably violent reaction."

"She'll destroy more than us if she unleashes that kind of power."

Daemon's smile was a satisfied one. "Exactly. She'll destroy everything. And once all of you are gone . . . Well, there *will* have to be a few more battles in Kaeleer to eliminate the more troublesome males in the court. But after that, I think things will settle down quite nicely." He turned and started to walk away.

He'll never get her to destroy everyone in Terreille, Saetan thought, closing his eyes against the sick feelings churning in his stomach. *He'll never twist her* that *much. Not Jaenelle.*

"Wait," Hekatah said.

Saetan opened his eyes.

Daemon was almost at the edge of the light. Turning, he raised one eyebrow in inquiry.

"Was that the only reason you came here?" Hekatah asked.

Daemon glanced at Lucivar again and smiled. "No. I thought I would settle a few debts while I was here."

Hekatah returned the smile. "Then, perhaps, Prince, we do have something to talk about. But not right now. Why don't you indulge yourself while I—while Dorothea and I think about how we might settle this amicably between us."

"I'm sure I can find something amusing to do to pass the time," Daemon said. He walked out of the light, disappeared into the darkness.

Hekatah looked at Saetan. It wasn't possible for him to keep his feelings hidden right now, to keep his face blank.

Dorothea got to her feet and pointed at Surreal. "Secure that bitch," she snapped at a couple of guards. Then she turned to Hekatah. "You can't really believe Sadi."

"The High Lord does," Hekatah said quietly. "And *that's* very interesting." She hissed when Dorothea started to protest. "We'll discuss this in private."

She walked to her cabin with Dorothea reluctantly following.

After chaining Surreal to the post on Saetan's left, the guards gathered up the dead men, and, with uneasy glances at the surrounding darkness, finally returned to their duties.

"Your son's a cold-blooded bastard," Surreal said quietly.

Saetan thought about the look in Daemon's eyes. He thought about the man he should have known well—and didn't know at all. Closing his eyes, he rested his head against the post, and said, "I only have one son now—and he's Eyrien."

"Hello, Prick."

Lucivar turned his head, watched Daemon glide out of the darkness and circle around to stand directly in front of him.

He had watched that initial game closely, waiting for some sign from Daemon that it was time to attack. The spelled chains couldn't have held him by themselves, and, unlike Saetan, the pain from the Ring of Obedience didn't debilitate him for long—at least, it didn't drain him the way it seemed to drain the High Lord. No, what had made him hold back and wait was the threat to Marian and Daemonar. There was always a guard inside the far hut that was being used as one of the prisons, and that guard had orders to kill his wife and son if he broke free. So he had waited, especially after Saetan had surrendered to those two bitches, because he had realized that Saetan had known there wouldn't be an exchange, had walked in expecting to become a prisoner, and had had a reason for doing it.

So when he saw Daemon, he figured the game was about to begin. But now, seeing that bored, sleepy, *terrifying* look . . . He'd danced with the Sadist enough times in the past to know that look meant they were all in serious trouble.

"Hello, Bastard," he said carefully.

Daemon stepped closer. His fingertips drifted up Lucivar's arm, over the shoulder, traced the collarbone.

"What's the game?" Lucivar asked quietly. Then he shivered as Daemon's fingers drifted up his neck, along his jaw.

"It's simple enough," Daemon crooned, brushing a finger over Lucivar's lower lip. "You're going to die, and I'm going to rule." He met Lucivar's eyes and smiled. "Do you know what it's like in the Twisted Kingdom, Prick? Do you have any idea? I spent eight years in that torment because of you."

"You forgave the debt," Lucivar snarled softly. "I gave you the chance to settle it, and you chose to forgive it."

Daemon's hand gently settled on Lucivar's neck. He leaned forward until his lips almost brushed Lucivar's. "Did you really think I would forgive you?"

From the far hut, they both heard a child's outraged howl.

Daemon stepped back. Smiled. Slipped his hands into his trouser pockets. "You're going to pay for those years, Prick," Daemon said softly. "You're going to pay dearly."

Lucivar's heart pounded in his throat as Daemon glided toward the hut that held Marian and Daemonar. "Bastard? Bastard, wait. *I'm* the one who owes the debt. You can't . . . Daemon? *Daemon!*"

Daemon walked into the hut. A moment later, the guard hurried out.

"DAEMON!"

A few minutes after that, Lucivar heard his son scream.

Dorothea's hands closed into fists. "I'm telling you, it's a trick of some kind. I *know* Sadi."

"Do you?" Hekatah snapped.

I think it's more accurate to say I'm the man my father might have been if he'd had the balls for it.

Yes, she had been able to sense the ruthlessness, the ambition, the cruel sexuality in Daemon Sadi. It frightened her a little. It excited her even more.

"He's never been interested in using his strength to acquire power. He fought against every attempt I made to bring him around."

"That's because you handled him wrong," Hekatah snarled. "If you had doted on Sadi the way you had doted on that excuse for a son—"

"You used to think it was amusing that I was playing bedroom games with the High Lord's boy. You said it would make a man out of him."

And it had. It had honed Sadi's cruelty, his taste for perverse pleasure. She had sensed that, too. Just as she had sensed that it wouldn't be easy to get around his deep hatred for Dorothea. Well, she wouldn't let that interfere with

her *own* ambitions. Besides, Dorothea was becoming difficult, unreliable. She would have had to eliminate the bitch
after the war was won anyway.

"I tell you, he's up to something," Dorothea insisted.
"And you're just letting him wander around the camp to
do who knows what."

"What am I supposed to do?" Hekatah snapped. "Without any leverage, we can't go up against the Black and
expect to win."

"We've *got* leverage," Dorothea said through clenched
teeth.

Hekatah let out a nasty laugh. "What leverage? If he
really *has* destroyed Andulvar, Prothvar, and Mephis, he's
not going to squirm because Saetan's guts are spilling out
on the ground."

"You picked the wrong man, the wrong threat," Dorothea said irritably, waving a hand. "He may not give a
damn about Saetan, but he's always buckled when Lucivar
was threatened. Lucivar's been the one chain we could
count on to hold Sadi. If you threatened—" She paused,
sniffed, looked toward the door, and said uneasily, "What's
that smell?"

"What's that smell?" Surreal muttered. It was well past
midnight. Were the guards roasting some meat for tomorrow's meals? Possibly, but she couldn't imagine anyone
wanting to eat anything that smelled that vile. "Do you
smell it?" She turned her head to look at Saetan—and
didn't like what she saw. Not one little bit. Since Daemon
walked out of the camp the first time, the High Lord had
just been staring straight ahead. Just staring. "Uncle
Saetan?"

He turned his head, slowly. His eyes focused on her—
too slowly.

Checking to make sure there weren't any guards around
at the moment, she leaned toward him as much as she
could. "Uncle Saetan, this isn't exactly the time to start
taking mental side trips. We've got to think of a way to get
out of here."

"I'm sorry you're here, Surreal," he said in a worn-out
voice. "Truly, I am sorry."

Me, too. "Lucivar's got the physical strength, and I can

handle myself in a fight, but you've got the experience to come up with a plan that can use that strength to our best advantage."

He just looked at her. The smile that finally curved his lips was gently bitter. "Sweetheart . . . I've gotten very old in the past two days."

She could see that, and it scared her. Without him, she wasn't sure they *could* get out of there.

Hearing a door open, she immediately straightened up and looked away from him.

"Hell's fire," Dorothea said irritably, "what's that smell?" She stepped between the posts that held Saetan and Surreal.

Surreal clenched her teeth. She wore a Gray Jewel; Dorothea wore a Red. It would be easy enough to slip under Dorothea's inner barriers and weave a death spell—something nasty so that, when it triggered, the screams and confusion might give them a chance to get away.

She began a careful descent so that no one would notice it, but before she reached the depth of her Gray Jewel, another door opened.

The vile smell intensified, making her gag.

Daemon Sadi strolled out of the prison hut, his hands in his trouser pockets. He kept moving until he reached the center of the lighted area. He didn't look at them. His glittering eyes were focused intently on Lucivar, who stared back at him.

No one dared move.

Finally, Daemon looked toward the prison hut and said pleasantly, "Marian, darling, come out and show your foolish husband the price for my years in the Twisted Kingdom."

Two naked . . . *things* . . . floated out of the hut into the light. An hour ago, they had been a woman and a small boy. Now . . .

Surreal began panting in an effort to keep her stomach down. Mother Night, Mother Night, Mother Night.

Marian's fingers and feet were gone. So was the long, lovely hair. Daemonar's eyes were gone, as well as his hands and feet. Their wings were so crisped, the slight movement of floating made pieces break off. And their skin . . .

Smiling that cold, cruel smile, the Sadist released his hold on Marian and Daemonar. The little boy hit the ground with a *thump* and began screaming. Marian landed on the stumps of her feet and fell. When she landed, her skin split, and . . .

Not blood, Surreal realized as she stared with numb, sick fascination. Cooking juices oozed out from those splits in the skin.

The Sadist hadn't just burned them, he had *cooked* them—and they were still alive. Not even demon-dead, *alive*.

"Lucivar," Marian whispered hoarsely as she tried to crawl toward her husband. "Lucivar."

Lucivar screamed, but the scream of pain changed to an Eyrien war cry. Chains snapped as he exploded away from the post, charging right at Daemon. When he had covered half the distance, a hard psychic blow knocked him off his feet, sent him rolling back toward the post. He surged to his feet, rushed at Daemon again—and was struck down again. And again. And again.

When he couldn't get to his feet, he crawled toward Daemon, his teeth bared, his eyes filled with hate.

Sadi reached down, grabbed Daemonar's arm, and twisted it off the way another man would twist off a drumstick.

That got Lucivar to his feet. When he charged this time, he slammed into a Black shield and went to his knees.

Daemon just watched him and smiled.

He tried to break through the shield, tried to smash his way through it, claw his way through it, battered himself against it—and finally just braced himself against it, crying.

"Daemon," he pleaded. "Daemon . . . show a little mercy."

"You want mercy?" Daemon replied gently. With predatory speed, he stepped on Daemonar's head.

The skull smashed like an eggshell.

Daemon walked over to Marian, who was still whispering, still trying to crawl. Even over Lucivar's anguished howls, the rest of them could hear the bones snap when Daemon stepped on her neck.

Using Daemonar's arm as a pointer, Sadi gestured elegantly at the two bodies, all the while watching Lucivar and smiling. "They're both still strong enough to make the transition to demon-dead," he said pleasantly. "It's doubtful the brat is going to remember much of anything, but your wife's last thoughts of you . . . How kindly will she remember you, Prick, knowing you were the cause of this?"

"Finish it," Lucivar begged. "Let them go."

"Everything has a price, Prick. Pay the price, and I'll let them go."

"What do you want from me," Lucivar said in a broken voice. "Just tell me what you want from me."

Daemon's smile turned colder, meaner. "Prove you can be a good boy. Crawl back to the post."

Lucivar crawled.

Two of the guards who had been standing beyond the lighted area, watching, approached Lucivar and helped him to his feet while two others replaced the broken chains.

They were very gentle with him when they secured him to the post.

Lucivar looked at Daemon with grief-dulled eyes. "Satisfied?"

"Yes," Daemon said too softly. "I'm satisfied."

Surreal felt a flick of dark power, then another. She reached out to Marian, almost terrified that her psychic touch would get an answer. But there was nothing, *no one*, left.

That was when she finally realized she was crying, *had* been crying.

Dropping Daemonar's arm, Sadi used a handkerchief to meticulously wipe the grease from his hand. Then, walking over to Surreal, he used the same handkerchief to wipe the tears from her face.

She almost puked on him.

"Don't waste your tears on *them*, little witch," Daemon said quietly. "*You're* next."

She watched him walk away, disappear once more into the darkness. *I may be next, you cold-hearted bastard, but I won't go down without a fight. I can't win against you, but I swear by all that I am that I won't go down without a fight.*

Saetan closed his eyes, unable to bear the sight of the still figures lying a few feet away from him.

*I knew he was dangerous, but I didn't know he had this
in him. I helped him, encouraged him. Oh, witch-child, what
kind of monster did I allow into your bed, into your heart?*

As soon as they returned to Hekatah's cabin, Dorothea
fell into the nearest chair. She had done some cruel, vicious
things in her life, but this . . .

She shuddered.

Hekatah braced her hands on the table. "Do you still
think he'll buckle if we threaten Lucivar?" she asked in a
shaky voice.

"No," Dorothea replied in a voice just as shaky. "I don't
know what he'll do anymore." For centuries, the Blood in
Terreille had called him the Sadist. Now she finally understood why.

2 / Kaeleer

Karla watched Tersa build strange creations with brown
wooden building blocks. She was grateful for the older
woman's presence, and knew Gabrielle felt the same way.

Jaenelle had disappeared shortly after she had talked to
them. They, in turn, had talked to the rest of the coven,
only telling them that the boyos needed to be held back
for a few more days. They hadn't told the others about
Witch's intention of going to war with Terreille—alone.
They had understood the unspoken command when Jaenelle had finally shown them the dream that lived beneath
the human skin.

So the coven, unhappy but united, had rounded up the
boyos before any of them could slip the leash. It hadn't
been easy, and the males' hostility toward what they considered a betrayal had been vicious enough to make Karla
wonder if any of the marriages in the First Circle would
survive. Some of those marriages *might* have been destroyed right there and then if Tersa hadn't come along
and scolded the boyos for their lack of courtesy. Since the
males weren't willing to attack *her,* they had given in.

Almost twenty-four hours of enforced togetherness
hadn't made things any easier, but it was the only way to
ensure the males' continued presence. Even by the Keep's

standards, the sitting room the coven had chosen as a place of confinement was a large room with several clusters of furniture and lots of pacing room—and it wasn't big enough. The coven mostly kept to the chairs and couches to avoid being snarled at by a pacing male. And when the boyos weren't pacing, they were huddled together, muttering.

"How many days are we going to have to do this?" Karla muttered to herself.

"As many as it takes," Tersa replied quietly. She studied her newest creation for a minute, then knocked it down.

The wooden blocks clattered on the long table in front of the couch, but no one jumped this time, having gotten used to the noise. No one even paid much attention to Tersa's odd creations. The boyos, in an attempt to prove they *could* be courteous, had admired and inquired about the first few . . . structures . . . but when Tersa's replies became more and more confusing, they finally backed off and left her alone.

In fact, Karla would have bet they weren't paying attention to much of anything going on in the room—until Ladvarian came in and trotted over to her.

The Sceltie looked unbearably weary, and there was a deep sadness in his brown eyes—and just a bit of an accusation.

Karla? Ladvarian said.

"Little Brother," Karla replied.

Two bowls appeared on the small table next to Karla's chair. One was filled with . . .

Karla carefully picked one up, studied it.

. . . bubbles of water that had protective shields around them to form a kind of skin. The other bowl had one red bubble.

I need a drop of blood from each of you, Ladvarian said.

"Why?" Karla asked as she studied the bubble. It was a brilliant little piece of Craft.

For Jaenelle.

Hearing that, Chaosti jumped in. "If Jaenelle wants something from us right now, she can ask us herself."

"*Chaosti,*" Gabrielle hissed.

Chaosti snarled at her.

Ladvarian cringed at the anger in the room, but his eyes never left Karla.

"Why?" Karla asked.

"Why why why," Tersa said irritably as she knocked over the building blocks. "Humans can't even give a little gift without asking why why why. It is for your Queen. What more do you need to know?" Then, as if the outburst had never happened, she began arranging blocks again.

Karla shivered as she stared at Ladvarian. There were two ways to interpret "for Jaenelle." Either the dog was just the courier and was bringing these drops of blood to Jaenelle because *she* needed them for something . . . or Ladvarian wanted them *for Jaenelle*. But how to ask the right questions and get something more than an evasive answer. Because she was certain Ladvarian would become evasive if she pushed too hard.

"I'm not sure I can give you a drop of blood, little Brother," Karla said carefully. "My blood is still a bit tainted from the poison."

"That will have no effect on this," Tersa said absently as she used Craft to hold blocks in the air. "But what is in your *heart* . . . Yes, that *will* affect a great deal."

"Why?" Karla asked—and then winced when Tersa just looked at her. She turned her attention back to Ladvarian. "So, that's all we have to do? Just put a drop of blood into each bubble?"

*When you give the blood, you must think about Jaenelle. *Good* thoughts,* he added in a growl as he glanced at the other males.

Karla shook her head. "I don't understand. Why—"

"Because the Blood will sing to the Blood," Tersa answered quietly. "Because blood is the memory's river."

Exasperated, Karla looked at Tersa, but it was the structure that caught her eye first.

A spiral. A glistening black spiral.

Then the brown wooden blocks crashed down on the table.

Karla, Gabrielle said softly.

I saw it. She looked at Tersa, who looked back at her with frighteningly clear-sighted eyes. *She knows. Mother Night, whatever is going to happen . . . Tersa knows. And so does Ladvarian.*

And knowing that much, there was no longer any need to ask "why."

Glancing at Ladvarian for permission, Karla sent out the most delicate psychic tendril she could create and lightly touched the red bubble.

Ladvarian, as a puppy, being taught by Jaenelle to air walk. Being brushed and petted. Being taught . . .

She backed away. Those memories were private, the best he had to give.

She swallowed hard—and tasted tears. "What Jaenelle is trying to do . . . Is it dangerous?"

Yes, Ladvarian answered.

"Have other kindred given this gift?"

All the kindred who know her.

And I'll bet none of them asked why why why. Karla looked at the rest of the First Circle. No trace of anger. Not anymore. They would think about Jaenelle's actions over the past few weeks and reach the right conclusion.

"All right, little Brother," Karla said. Before she could use her thumbnail to prick a finger, Gabrielle touched her shoulder.

"I think . . ." Gabrielle hesitated, took a deep breath. "I think this should be done as ritual."

So that it would be as powerful as they could make it. "Yes, you're right." Karla set the clear bubble back into the bowl.

"I'll get what we need," Gabrielle said.

"I'll go with you," Morghann said.

As Gabrielle and Morghann walked past the males, Chaosti and Khary reached out, each one giving his wife a gentle touch of apology before stepping aside.

With a weary sigh, Ladvarian moved out of the way and lay down.

Tersa stood up.

"Tersa?" Karla said. "Aren't you going to give the gift?"

Those clear-sighted eyes looked into her. Then Tersa smiled, said, "I already have," and left the room.

That was enough to tell Karla who had shown the kindred how to create those brilliant little pieces of Craft.

Watching the males shift places and take up their usual protective stance, Karla's eyes filled with tears, and she wished, futilely, that Morton could have been standing among them.

We'll be all right, she thought when she saw Aaron wrap his arms around Kalush. *The harsh words will be forgiven, and we'll be all right.*

But would Jaenelle?

3 / Terreille

"It's your turn, little bitch," Daemon said as he unfastened the chains from the post.

Surreal stared at him. It was after midnight—was, in fact, almost twenty-four hours since he had killed Marian and Daemonar. The day had been quiet enough. Sadi had prowled around the camp, making everyone nervous, and Dorothea and Hekatah had played least-in-sight.

"What are you going to do with the bitch?" Dorothea said, approaching the posts.

Until now.

Daemon looked at Dorothea and smiled. "Well, darling, I'm going to use her to give you what you've always wanted."

"Meaning what?" Dorothea asked uneasily.

"Meaning," Daemon purred, "that I'm going to break your slut of a granddaughter. And then I'm going to mount her until she's seeded with my child. She's ripe for it. It'll catch. And I'll make sure she has all the incentive she needs not to try to abort it. Your bloodline and me, Dorothea. Exactly what you've wanted from me. And all you'll have to overlook is the fact that the result might have pointed ears."

Laughing, he dragged Surreal into the same hut that had held Marian and Daemonar.

She waited until he had turned to close the door before she called in her stiletto and launched herself at him. He spun around, raised an arm to block the knife. She twisted, bringing the knife in under his arm, intending to drive it between his ribs up to the hilt. Instead, the knife hit a shield, slid right past him, and went into the door.

Before she could yank the knife out of the wood, Daemon grabbed her, shoved her back to the center of the small room. Screaming, she launched herself at him again. He caught her hands and roughly pushed her back until her knees hit the edge of the narrow bed. She went down with him on top of her.

He rolled off immediately, sprang to his feet. "That's enough."

She leaped off the bed and hurled every curse she knew at the top of her lungs before she lunged at him again.

He pushed her away and swore viciously. "Damn it, Surreal, *that's enough.*"

"If you think I'm going to spread my legs for you, you'd better think again, *Sadist.*"

"Shut up, Surreal," Daemon said quietly but intensely.

She felt the shields go up around the hut. Not just a Black protective shield but a Black aural shield as well. Which meant no one could hear what was happening inside.

He took a deep breath, raked his fingers through his hair. "Well," he said dryly, "that little performance ought to convince the bitches that something is happening in here."

She had been gathering herself to spring at him again, intending to go for his balls this time. But that tone and those words sounded so . . . *Daemon* . . . that she paused. And remembered Karla's warning about a friend who becomes an enemy in order to remain a friend.

He eyed her, then approached warily. "Let's see your wrists."

She held out her hands, watching him—and saw the fury in his eyes when he snapped off the manacles and looked at the raw skin underneath.

Surreal huffed. "Damn it, Sadi, what kind of game are you playing?"

"A vicious one," he replied, calling in a leather box. He looked through it, pulled out a jar, and handed it to her. "Put that on your wrists."

She opened the jar, sniffed. A Healer's ointment. While she applied it to her wrists, he called in another box. There were several balls of clay sitting in nests of paper. Two of the nests were empty.

"Do you still have the food pack you brought?"

"Yes. I haven't had a chance to eat any of it," she added tartly.

"Then eat something now," he said, still looking through

the box. "I'd give you some from mine, but I gave most of
it to Marian."

A chill went down Surreal's spine. There was a funny
buzzing in her head. "To Marian?"

"Do you remember the shack we stopped at when we
got to Hayll?"

"Yes." Of course she remembered it. It was a couple of
miles away from the camp. That was where Daemon had
changed into the Sadist. One minute he had been carefully
explaining about the sentries and the perimeter stakes that
would alert the guards, and the next thing she knew, she
was tied up and he was purring threats about how she
should have stayed under Falonar and stayed out of his
way. He had scared her, badly. And the fact that he had
made her furious now. "You could have told me, you son
of a bitch."

He looked up. "Would you have been as convincing?"

She bristled, insulted. "You're damn right I would have
been."

"Well, we're going to have a chance to find out. You
said you wanted to help, Surreal. That you were willing to
be a diversion."

She *had* said that, but she'd thought she would have
known *when* she was being a diversion. "So?"

"So now you will be." He approached her, held up a
small gold hoop. "Listen carefully. This will produce the
illusion that you're broken." He slipped the hoop through
one of the links of the necklace that held her Gray Jewel.
"No one will be able to detect that you're still wearing the
Gray unless you use it. If you *do* need to use it, then don't
hesitate. I'll figure out some way to deal with things here."

"The High Lord will know I'm not broken."

Daemon shook his head as he turned back to search for
something else in the box. "You'd have to wear Jewels
darker than the Black to be able to detect that spell."

Darker than the *Black*? Sadi couldn't make a spell like
that. Which meant . . .

Mother Night.

"This"—Daemon held up a tiny crystal vial before at-
taching it to the necklace—"will convince anyone who
thinks to check that you're not only fertile but you're now

pregnant. A Healer would be able to tell within twenty-four hours," he added, answering her unspoken question.

Lifting the necklace, Surreal studied the vial. "You asked Jaenelle to create an illusion that I was pregnant with your child?"

She saw his face tighten.

Yes, he had asked Jaenelle. And it had hurt him to ask.

Looking to change the subject, she pointed to the balls of clay. "What are those?"

"The raw spells to create shadows."

Shadows. Illusions that could be made to fool someone into believing the person in front of them was real.

"Marian and Daemonar," she said weakly, staring at the two empty nests of paper.

"Yes," he replied sharply.

She hissed at him. "You didn't trust me, a *whore,* to put on a good show, but you figured *Lucivar* would be convin—" Her voice trailed away. "He doesn't know, does he?"

"No," Daemon said quietly, "he doesn't know."

Her legs weakened so abruptly, she sat on the floor. "Hell's fire, Mother Night, and may the Darkness be merciful."

"I know." Daemon hesitated. "I'm buying time, Surreal. I have got to buy enough time and still get everyone out of here. In order to make Dorothea and Hekatah believe Marian and Daemonar were dead, Lucivar had to believe it."

"Mother Night." Surreal rested her forehead on her knees. "What's worth paying a price like this?"

"My Queen needs the time in order to save Kaeleer."

"Oh, shit, Sadi." She looked up at him. "Tell me something. Even though you knew it was an illusion, how did you keep your stomach down afterward?"

He swallowed hard. "I didn't."

"You're mad," she muttered as she climbed to her feet.

"I serve," he said sharply.

Sometimes, for a male, it amounted to the same thing.

"All right," she said as she hooked her hair behind her pointed ears. "What do you need me to do?"

He hesitated, then started to hedge. "It's dangerous."

"Daemon," she said patiently, "what do you need?" When he still didn't answer, she took a guess. "You want me to wander around the camp whimpering and looking like a woman who's been raped out of her mind and is now terrified of what will happen to her if she miscarries the child that was produced from that rape. Right?"

"Yes," he said faintly.

"And then what?"

"Marian and Daemonar are at that shack. Slip out of camp tomorrow night, pick them up, and then go to the Keep. Don't stop, don't go anywhere else. Get to the Keep. You'll have to ride the Red Wind. The darker ones are unstable."

"Un—Never mind, I don't want to know about that." She thought everything through carefully. Yes, she could play this out. A woman that broken would spend a lot of time hiding, so letting people get glimpses of her throughout the day would be enough—and would hide the fact that she had disappeared.

Daemon reached for one of the balls of clay.

"What's that for?" Surreal asked.

"You would have fought for as long as you could," Daemon said, not looking at her. "You would look like you'd fought. After I create the illusion, you can carry this and—"

"No." Surreal shrugged out of her jacket and started unbuttoning her shirt. "You can't play all of this out with illusions. Not if you want to convince Dorothea and Hekatah long enough to buy the time Jaenelle needs."

His eyes turned hard yellow. "I'll give up a great deal for this, Surreal, but I'm *not* going to break my vow of fidelity."

"I know," she replied quietly. "That's not what I meant."

"Then what *did* you mean?" Daemon snapped.

She took a deep breath to steady herself. "You have to make the bruises real."

4 / Kaeleer

Calling in the bowl, Ladvarian placed it carefully on the chamber floor and watched the Arachnian Queen delicately touch the little bubbles now filled with blood and memories.

Is good, the spider said with approval. *Good memories. Strong memories. As strong as kindred.*

Ladvarian looked at the bowl that sat in front of the huge tangled web. There were still a lot of the kindred's gifts left in the bowl. It wasn't a fast thing the Weaver was doing.

You must rest, the spider said as she selected a bubble from the humans' offerings and floated up to a thread in the web. *All kindred must rest. Must be strong when the time comes to anchor the dream to flesh.*

Will you have enough time to add all the memories? Ladvarian asked respectfully.

The Weaver of Dreams didn't reply for a long time. Then, *Enough. Just enough.*

5 / Terreille

The whimpering wasn't all feigned.

But, Hell's fire, Surreal thought as she wandered aimlessly around the camp, she hadn't expected to have to goad Daemon quite *that* much before he finally got down to business. And she'd understood that the anger behind his teeth and hands was because he'd had to touch a woman besides Jaenelle in a few intimate places. But, shit, he didn't have to bite her breast quite *that* hard.

On the other hand, he had chosen his marks very carefully. Judging by the look in people's eyes when they saw her, the bruises were impressive, but none of them impeded movement or would freeze a muscle if she had to fight.

The hardest part had been seeing the hatred in Saetan's eyes. She'd wanted to tell him. Oh, how she'd wanted to say something, anything, to get that look out of his eyes. And she might have if Daemon hadn't chosen that moment to glide by and make a devastatingly cutting remark. After that, throughout the rest of the morning, she had avoided the High Lord—and she hadn't dared get anywhere near Lucivar.

But she had made sure that Dorothea had seen her. She'd felt the bitch trying to probe her to find out if she was really broken and really pregnant. Apparently the illusion spells had held up because Dorothea gently suggested that she lie down for a while and rest. The bitch was almost drooling over the idea of being able to get her hands on *any* child sired by Sadi.

She'd go back and hide for a little while, wait until sunset, then put in an appearance so that Hekatah could sniff around her. Then all she had to do was slip past the sentries and the perimeter markers, pick up Marian and Daemonar, and get them home. That was all she . . . *Shit.*

She hadn't been paying attention to exactly where she was going—and now found herself staring right into Lucivar's eyes.

He had spent the morning watching her whenever she appeared. It was a good act, but it was just a little off. Not that anyone else would have noticed. Oh, he was sure Dorothea and Hekatah and plenty of the guards had seen broken witches, but he doubted any of them had ever paid any attention to those women after the breaking. He, on the other hand, had taken care of a few of them in a number of courts. He hadn't been able to stop the breaking, but he'd taken care of them afterward. And they all had one thing in common: the first day or two after they were broken, they were cold. They huddled up in shawls and blankets, stayed close to any source of heat that was available to them.

But there was Surreal, wandering through the camp, wearing nothing over a shirt that seemed torn in all the right places to display some impressive bruises. And that made him think about a lot of things.

"You should put on a jacket, sweetheart," he said gently.

"Jacket?" Surreal said feebly while her hands tried to cover some of the rips in the shirt.

"A jacket. You're cold."

"Oh. No I'm—"

"Cold."

She shivered then, but it wasn't from cold, it was from nerves.

"You don't have to carry that bastard's child," Lucivar said quietly. "You can abort it. A broken witch still has that much power. And once you're barren, there's no reason for anyone to look in your direction."

"I can't," Surreal said fearfully. "I can't. He would be

so mad at me and . . . " She looked at the spot where Marian and Daemonar had died.

He wondered if he was wrong, if her mind really *was* so torn apart she didn't quite feel the cold yet. If *that* was true, then he understood the fear in her voice now. She was afraid the Sadist would do the same thing to her that he had done to Marian and Daemonar.

But what he saw in her eyes when she looked at him again wasn't fear, it was hot frustration.

The blood in his veins, which had felt so sluggish since he had crawled back to the post two nights ago, raged through him once again.

"Surreal . . ." He saw Daemon appear on the other side of the circle of bare ground a moment before she did.

With an almost-convincing cry, Surreal ran off.

Lucivar stared at Daemon. From across the distance, Daemon returned the stare.

"You bastard," Lucivar whispered. Daemon wouldn't have heard the words, but it didn't matter. Sadi would know what had been said.

Daemon walked away.

Lucivar leaned his head back against the post and closed his eyes.

If Surreal wasn't broken, if this was all a game, then Marian and Daemonar . . .

He should have remembered that about the Sadist. He, better than anyone else there, knew how vicious Daemon could be, but the Sadist had *never* harmed an innocent, had never hurt a child.

He had been waiting for the signal, but the game had begun before Daemon had walked into the camp. Still, he had played his part well—and would continue to do so.

Because understanding and forgiving were two very different things.

6 / Terreille

Drifting in a pain-hazed doze, Saetan felt the cup against his lips. The first swallow he took out of reflex, the second out of greed. As the taste of fresh blood filled his mouth, the Black power in it flowed through him, offering strength.

Hold on, a deep voice whispered in his mind. *You have to hold on. Please.*

He heard the weariness in that voice. He heard a son's plea to a father, and he responded. Being the man he was, he couldn't do otherwise. So he pushed his way through the haze of pain.

When he opened his eyes, all he saw was waning daylight, and he wondered if he'd just dreamed the plea he'd heard in Daemon's voice.

But he could still taste the dark, rich, fresh blood.

Closing his eyes again, he let his mind drift.

He was standing in an enormous cavern somewhere in the heart of Ebon Askavi. Etched in the floor was a huge web lined with silver. In the center where all the tether lines met was an iridescent Jewel the size of his hand, a Jewel that blended the colors of all the other Jewels. At the end of each tether line was an iridescent Jewel chip the size of his thumbnail.

He had been in this place once before, on the night when he had linked with Daemon in order to draw Jaenelle back to her body.

But there was something else in the cavern now.

Stretching across that silver web on the floor were three massive, connected tangled webs that rose from about a foot from the floor to almost twice his height. In the center of each web was an Ebony Jewel.

Witch stood in front of those webs, wearing that black spidersilk gown, holding the scepter that held two Ebony Jewels and the spiral horn Kaetien had gifted her with when he'd been killed five years ago.

Behind the webs were dozens of demon-dead. One of them approached the webs, smiled, then faded. At the moment the person faded, a little star the same color as the person's Jewel bloomed on the middle web.

Puzzled, he moved to get a better look at the tangled webs.

The first one repulsed him. The threads looked swollen, moldy, tainted. At the end of every single tether line of that web was an Ebony Jewel chip.

The middle one was beautiful, filled with thousands of those little colored stars and a sprinkling of Black and Ebony Jewel chips.

The last one was a simple web, perfect in its symmetry, made of gray, ebon-gray, and black threads. It, too, had Black and Ebony Jewel chips that had been carefully placed on the threads to form a spiral.

He glanced at Witch, but she was focused on the task, so he shifted again to watch.

He saw Char, the leader of the cildru dyathe, approach the webs. The boy grinned at him, waved a jaunty good-bye, and faded to become another bright star.

Titian approached him, kissed his cheek. "I'm proud to have known you, High Lord." She walked over to the webs and faded.

As he watched her, something nagged at him. Something about the structure of those webs. But before he could figure it out, Dujae, the artist who had given the coven drawing lessons, approached him.

"Thank you, High Lord," the huge man said. "Thank you for allowing me to know the Ladies. All the portraits I have done of them are at the Hall in Kaeleer now. My gift to you."

"Thank you, Dujae," he replied, puzzled.

As Dujae walked away, Prothvar stepped up. "It's a different kind of battlefield, but it's a good way to fight. Take care of the waif, Uncle Saetan." Prothvar hugged him.

Cassandra came next. Cassandra, whom he hadn't seen since the first party when they had all met the coven and the boyos.

She smiled at him, a sad smile, then pressed her hand against his cheek. "I wish I had been a better friend. May the Darkness embrace you, Saetan." She kissed him. When she faded, a glorious Black star began to shine in the middle web.

"Mephis," he said when his eldest son approached. "Mephis, what—"

Mephis smiled and hugged him. "I was proud to have you for a father, and honored to know you as a man. I'm not sure I ever told you that. I wanted you to know. Good-bye, Father. I love you."

"And I love you, Mephis," he said, holding on hard as he felt grief swell inside him.

When Mephis faded into the web, the only one left of the demon-dead was Andulvar.

"Andulvar, what's going on?"

"And the Blood will sing to the Blood," Andulvar replied. "Like to like." He looked at the webs. "She found a way to identify those who have been tainted from those who still honor the ways of the Blood. But she needed help to keep those who followed the old ways from being swept away with the rest when she unleashes. That's what the demon-dead will do—our strength will anchor the living. We'll burn out in the doing, but as Prothvar said, it's a good way to fight."

Andulvar smiled at him. "Take care of yourself, SaDiablo. And take care of those pups of yours. Both of them. Just remember that your mirror truly is your mirror. You only have to look to see the truth." Andulvar hugged him. "No man could have asked for a better friend or a better Brother. Hold on. Fight. You have the hardest burden, but your sons will help you."

Andulvar walked to the webs. He spread his dark wings, raised his arms . . . and faded.

As he blinked back tears, Jaenelle walked over to him. He wrapped his arms around her. "Witch-child . . ."

She shook her head, kissed him, and smiled. But her eyes were filled with tears.

"Thank you for being my father. It was glorious, Saetan." Then she leaned close and whispered in his ear, "Take care of Daemon. Please. He'll need you."

She didn't fade into the web, she just disappeared.

Wiping the tears with the back of his hand, he approached the webs and studied them carefully.

The first web, the moldy web, were the Blood tainted by Dorothea and Hekatah. The second web, with all its Jewel stars, were the Blood who still honored the old ways. The third web, with its spiral, was Witch.

As he continued to study the webs, he began to shake his head, slowly at first, then faster and faster. "No, no, no, witch-child," he muttered. "You can't connect them like this. If you unleash your full strength . . ."

It would blast through the large Ebony Jewel in the center of the first web, travel through all the strands, sweep up all the minds that resonated with those strands, then hit all the Ebony chips, meeting a smaller portion of itself in a devastating collision of power that would destroy anyone caught in *it. Then it would continue on to the next web, barely diminished.*

The middle web, with all those thousands of beads of power, would provide tremendous resistance as·her strength swept through it. The demon-dead, providing a shield and anchor for the living, would absorb some of her power as it flooded over them, but not all of those thousands of beads of power would be enough. That unleashed strength would continue on to the third web and . . .

The power would flow through that perfect symmetry, burn out the web, and shatter every Jewel chip as it came blasting back through the spiral. And once the last Jewel chip shattered, the only thing left to reabsorb the rest of the power would be . . .

"NO, witch-child," he shouted, turning round and round, searching for her. "No! A backlash like that will rip you apart! Jaenelle!"

He turned back to the webs. Maybe, if he could link himself to Witch's web somehow, draw every drop of reserve power out of his Birthright Red Jewels and his Black . . . Maybe he could shield her enough to keep her safe when the rest of that explosion of power came screaming back at her.

He took a step forward . . .

. . . and everything faded.

Saetan opened his eyes. Deep twilight. Almost night.

A dream? Just a dream? No. He had been a Black Widow too long not to know the difference between a dream and a vision. But it was fading. He couldn't *quite* remember, and there was something about that vision that was desperately important for him to remember.

That was when he noticed Daemon standing a few feet in front of him, watching him with frightening intensity.

Just remember that your mirror truly is your mirror. You only have to look to see the truth.

Andulvar's words. Andulvar's warning.

So, with eyes blinded by tears, he looked at his mirror, his namesake, his true heir. And saw.

Still watching him, Daemon reached into his jacket pocket. His hand came out as a loose fist. He opened his fingers, tipped his hand.

Little colored bangles, the kind women sewed on dresses to catch the light, spilled to the ground.

Saetan stared at them. They chilled him, but he couldn't say why.

And when he looked up again at Daemon . . . He could almost hear the unspoken plea to think, to know, to remember. But his mind was still too full of the other vision that had turned elusive.

Daemon walked away.

Saetan closed his eyes. Bangles and webs. If he could find the connection, he would also find the answers.

7 / Terreille

Surreal swore silently as she stared at the perimeter stakes. There had to be a trick to getting past them. Hell's fire, Daemon had gotten them into the camp without anyone realizing it, but she'd still been too stunned by his shift into the Sadist to pay much attention. And he'd gotten Marian and Daemonar *out* without anyone realizing it.

Could it be as simple as jumping over them so the contact between the crystals wasn't broken? No, she would have remembered *that*.

"What are you doing out here?" a voice demanded.

Shit.

She turned to face the sentry who was moving toward her. She was too far away from the camp for anyone to believe she was just a broken witch wandering around. But she had to try to convince this bastard. Or kill him quietly. If she ended up in a fight and used her Gray Jewels, Daemon would know she'd run into trouble and alter the rest of his plans. And *that* would allow those bitches to realize they'd been tricked and *really* start the war.

"The hut's lost," she said, waving her hand in a vague gesture.

He came closer, his eyes full of suspicion and doubt. "Answer me, bitch. Why are you out here?"

"The *hut's* lost," she repeated, doing her best to imitate the way Tersa's mind tended to meander. She pointed. "It should be near that fuzzy post, but it wandered off."

The sentry looked in that direction. "That's a *tree,* you

stupid bitch. Now—" He stopped, raked her body with his eyes, then smiled. Looking around to make sure no one else was nearby, he reached for her.

She took a step back, placed a protective hand over her abdomen, and shook her head. "Can't touch another male. He'll get mad at me if I touch another male."

The sentry gave her an evil grin. "Well, he's not going to know, is he?"

Surreal hesitated. That would certainly get her close enough to ram a knife between his ribs, but it would also take time she didn't have. The Gray Jewels then, and a fast kill—and may the Darkness help Sadi with whatever was going to happen in the camp afterward.

Down, Surreal!

She felt hind legs brush against her back as she dove.

A moment later, the sentry lay dead, his throat torn out.

A sight shield faded, revealing the blood-splashed wolf.

"Graysfang?" Surreal whispered. She touched the Jewel beneath her shirt. Gray's fang. The High Lord had been right.

Skirting the dead sentry, she reached for the wolf.

Wait, Graysfang said.

That's when she saw the small golden bump between his ears. The bump lifted, floated to the nearest perimeter stake, and uncurled its legs.

Surreal stared at the small gold spider as it busily spun a simple tangled web between two of the stakes. When it was done, it picked its way to the center of the web.

The sentry vanished. There was no trace of blood on the ground.

They will not find him now, Graysfang said. *They can only see what the web lets them see.* He gently closed his teeth around Surreal's arm and started tugging her.

"What about the spider?"

She will stay to guard the web. Hurry, Surreal.

She shook her arm free of his teeth. It would be easier to keep up with him if she wasn't hunched over. Switching to a communication thread, she asked, *What are you doing here? How did you get through the perimeter stakes?*

Humans are foolish. The meat trail is unguarded. Too many legs moving on the trail. The humans got tired of baring their fangs when it was only meat.

Meat trail? Oh, *game* trail. *How did you know about the trail? How did you find me?*

The Weaver of Dreams told me to learn the two-legged cat's scent and follow his tracks. He is a good hunter, Graysfang added with approval. *There is much feline in him. Kaelas says so.*

Sadi, with the predatory grace even the kindred recognized. Graysfang had followed Sadi. *Who's this Weaver?* She got a quick image of a large golden spider—and stumbled.

Damn fool of an idiot wolf. It was bad enough that he had gone to Arachna and brought a *small* spider back with him. But to deal with the *Queen* . . .

She asked me, Surreal, Graysfang said meekly when she snarled at him. *It's a bad thing to refuse the Weaver.*

Surreal gritted her teeth and picked up the pace. *We'll talk about it later.*

As soon as she saw the game trail, she recognized the place. This was where Daemon had brought them through the camp's perimeter. *I couldn't have found this place again by myself.*

You have a small snout, the wolf said kindly. *You cannot smell tracks.*

Surreal looked at Graysfang—at Gray's fang—and smiled.

"Let's go," she whispered. "Do you know the way to the shack?"

I know.

An hour later, she, Marian, Daemonar, and Graysfang were riding the Red Wind to the Keep.

8 / Terreille

"I think it's time we had a little talk," Hekatah said, trying to smile coyly at Daemon.

"Really?"

Oh, the arrogance, the surliness, the *meanness* in that voice. If his father had been even half the man the son was . . .

"It takes so long for a Realm to recover from a war, it would be foolish to go through with it if it can be avoided," she said, reaching up to caress his face as she wove a seduction spell around him.

He stepped back. "Don't ever touch me without my permission," he snarled softly. "Not even Jaenelle is allowed to touch me without my permission."

"And she submits?"

He smiled that cold, brutal smile. "She submits to a great many things—and begs for more."

Hekatah looked into his glazed eyes and shivered with excitement. The air was filled with the earthy tang of sex. She had him. He just didn't know it yet. "A partnership would serve us both well."

"But you already have a partner, Hekatah—one I will not deal with in any way."

She waved a hand dismissively. "She can be taken care of easily enough." She paused. "Darling Dorothea hasn't been sleeping well. I think I'll give her a little cup of something that will help."

He stared at her with those glazed eyes, a man aroused to the point of being frightening—and terribly exciting.

"In that case . . ." Daemon's hands cupped her face. His lips brushed against hers.

She was disappointed by the gentleness—until he *really* kissed her. Mean, dominating, unforgiving, demanding, painfully exciting.

But she was demon-dead. Her body *couldn't* respond that way, couldn't . . .

She drowned in that kiss, staggered by sensations her body hadn't felt in centuries.

He finally raised his head.

She stared at him. "How . . . It isn't possible."

"I think we've just proved that's a lie," Daemon crooned. "I punish women who lie to me."

"Do you?" Hekatah whispered, swaying. She couldn't look away from the cruel pleasure in his eyes. "I'll take care of Dorothea."

He kissed her again. This time she felt the mockery in the gentleness. There was nothing gentle about him. Nothing.

"I'll take care of Dorothea," she said again. "And then we'll be partners."

"And I promise you, darling," Daemon purred, "you're going to get everything you deserve."

9 / Terreille

Dorothea woke up late in the morning and groaned at the pain in her belly. It felt like a year's worth of moontime cramps had settled in her gut. She couldn't get sick now. *Couldn't.* Maybe a cup of herbal tea or some broth. Hell's fire, she was cold. Why was she so damn cold?

Shivering, she dragged herself out of bed—and fell.

After the shock came fear as she remembered the brew Hekatah had made for her last night. To help her sleep. What had she been thinking of not to test something that came from Hekatah's hand?

She hadn't been thinking. Hadn't . . .

That bitch. That walking piece of carrion must have used a compulsion spell on her to get her to drink it—and then to forget that she'd been *ordered* to drink it.

Her muscles constricted, twisted.

Not sick. Poisoned.

She needed help. She needed . . .

Her cabin door opened and closed.

Gasping from the effort, she rolled onto her side and stared at Daemon Sadi.

"Daemon," she whimpered, trying to hold out a hand toward him. "Daemon . . . help . . ."

He just stood there, studying her. Then he smiled. "Looks like witchblood was part of last night's little brew," he said pleasantly.

She couldn't draw a full breath. "You did this. *You* did this."

"You were becoming a problem, darling. It's nothing personal."

She felt the pain of the insult even through the physical pain. "Hekatah . . ."

"Yes," Daemon purred, "Hekatah. Now, don't worry, darling. I've put an aural and a protective shield around your cabin, so you'll be quite undisturbed for the rest of the day."

He walked out of the cabin.

She tried to crawl to the door, tried to scream for help. Couldn't do either.

It didn't take long for her world to become nothing but pain.

* * *

Daemon closed the door of the prison hut he'd been using whenever he needed to stay somewhere for a little while. Reaching into his jacket pocket, he withdrew the Jewels he'd gone to Dorothea's cabin to retrieve—Saetan's Black ring; Lucivar's pendant, ring, and Ring of Honor. He knew her well, knew exactly where to probe for a hiding place. It hadn't taken him more than a minute to slip around her guard spells and lift the Jewels while he stood there and talked to her.

He studied the Jewels and sighed with relief. Both men had put strong shields around the jewelry before handing them over to those bitches, so there was no way the pieces could have been tampered with or tainted. Still . . .

Setting the Jewels into the washbasin, he poured water over them, added some astringent herbs for cleansing, then let them soak.

This would be the last day, the last night. He could endure it that much longer. *Had* to endure it.

He closed his eyes. *Soon, sweetheart. A few more hours and I'll be on my way home, on my way back to you. And then we'll be married.*

Picturing Jaenelle slipping the plain gold wedding ring onto his finger, he smiled.

And then he remembered the seduction spell Hekatah had woven around him. Oh, he'd been aware of it, could have easily broken it—but he had let his body respond to it while he touched Hekatah. Kissed Hekatah. Hated Hekatah.

Just a game. A nasty, vicious game.

He barely made it to the chamber pot before he was quietly, but thoroughly, sick.

10 / Terreille

"It's your turn, Prick."

Because he was looking for it, because he knew *what* to look for, Lucivar saw the sick desperation in Daemon's eyes.

So he remained passive while Daemon unchained him and led him into the other prison hut, the one closest to them. And he stayed impassive while Daemon feverishly rumpled the small bed.

Then he let out an anguished Eyrien war cry that startled Daemon badly enough to fall onto the bed.

"Hell's fire, Prick," Daemon muttered as he stood up.

"Convincing enough?" Lucivar asked mildly.

Daemon froze.

All the masks dropped away. Lucivar saw a man physically and emotionally exhausted, a man barely able to stay on his feet.

"Why?" he asked quietly.

"I had to buy Jaenelle some time. I needed your hate to do it."

That simple. That painful. Daemon would regret it, deeply regret it, but he wouldn't hesitate to rip out his brother's heart if that's what Jaenelle needed from him. Which was exactly what he had done.

"You're here with Jaenelle's consent," Lucivar said, wanting the confirmation.

"I'm here at her command."

"To play out this game."

"To play out this game," Daemon agreed quietly.

Lucivar nodded, let out a bitter laugh. "Well, Bastard, you've played a good game." He paused, then said coldly, "Where are Marian and Daemonar?"

Daemon's hand shook a little as he raked his fingers through his hair. "Since Surreal didn't have to blast anyone with the Gray to get away from here, I have to assume she safely reached the hiding place where I had left them. They're all at the Keep by now."

Lucivar let that sink in, allowed himself a moment's relief and joy. "So now what happens?"

"Now I create a shadow of you, and you head for the Keep. Stay on the Red Wind. The darker ones are unstable."

Shadows. Daemon never could have created shadows that convincing. Not by himself. And Jaenelle . . . Jaenelle, having grown up around Andulvar and Prothvar, would have expected an Eyrien warrior to be able to accept the pain of the battlefield, no matter what that battlefield looked like.

"What do you need?" Lucivar asked.

Daemon hesitated. "Some hair, skin, and blood."

"Then let's play the game through."

They worked together in silence. The only sound Lucivar made during that time was a sigh of relief when Daemon slipped the Ring of Honor over his cock and used it to remove the Ring of Obedience in a way that wouldn't be detected.

Putting on the Ebon-gray Jewels Daemon had returned to him, he watched the final steps to the spell that would create a shadow of himself. And shuddered when he saw the tormented, anguished creature whose lips were pulled back in a rictus grin.

"Hell's fire, Bastard," Lucivar said, feeling queasy. "What was it you did to me that I would have ended up looking like *that*?"

"I don't know," Daemon replied wearily. "But I'm sure Hekatah can imagine something." He hesitated, swallowed hard. "Look, Prick, for once in your life, just do as you're told. Get to the Keep. Everyone who matters the most to you is waiting for you there."

"Not everyone," Lucivar said softly.

"I'll get the High Lord out." Dacmon waited.

Lucivar knew what Daemon was waiting for, what he hoped for. He wanted to be told that Saetan wasn't the only one left who mattered.

Lucivar said nothing.

Daemon looked away, and said wearily, "Let's go. There's one more game to play."

11 / Terreille

Saetan stared at the bangles lying on the ground. Why had Daemon made such a point of them? And why did they chill him so much?

He hissed in frustration, then jolted at the sibilant sound.

"You wish to undersstand thiss?" Draca had asked.

Bangles floating in a tank of water. Draca holding an egg-shaped stone attached to a thin silk cord. "A sspiral."

The stone moving in a circular motion, spiraling, spiraling, until all the water was in motion, all the bangles caught.

"A whirlpool," Geoffrey had said.

"No," Draca had replied. *"A maelsstrom. . . . Sshe will almosst alwayss sspiral. . . . You cannot alter her nature. . . . But the maelsstrom. . . . Sshield her, Ssaetan. Sshield her with your sstrength and your love and perhapss it will never happen."*

"And if it does?" he had asked.

"It will be the end of the Blood."

End of the Blood.

End of . . .

Those bangles weren't a message from Daemon, they were a warning from *Draca.* Jaenelle was spiraling down to her full strength to unleash the maelstrom. The end of the Blood. Was that why she had insisted that the First Circle remain at the Keep? Because it would be the only place that could withstand that devastating power? No. Jaenelle didn't like to kill. She wouldn't destroy all the Blood if she could . . .

Damn it. *Damn it,* he needed to draw that vision back. Needed to see those webs again in order to remember that one important thing that was eluding him. Deliberately eluding him. A veil had been drawn across that vision to keep him from remembering that one thing until it was too late.

But if she *was* going to unleash the maelstrom, what in the name of Hell was Daemon doing *here?*

Stalling. Buying time. Keeping Dorothea and Hekatah distracted. Playing games to . . . Marian and Daemonar. Then Surreal. He'd heard Lucivar cry out a couple of hours ago, but there had been no sign of him since then. Which only left . . .

A shadow fell across the bangles.

He looked up into Daemon's glazed eyes.

"It's time to dance," Daemon crooned.

·He might have said something, but he could smell Hekatah nearby. So he let Daemon lead him into the prison hut, said nothing while he was tied to the bed.

When Daemon stretched out beside him, he whispered, "When does the game end?"

Daemon tensed, swallowed hard. "In a couple more hours," he said, keeping his voice low. "At midnight." He laid a hand gently on Saetan's chest. "Nothing's going to happen. Just—"

They both heard someone brush against the door, both knew who was listening.

Saetan shook his head. Everything has a price. "Make it convincing, Daemon," he whispered.

He saw the sick resignation and the apology in Daemon's eyes before his son kissed him.

And he learned why the Blood called Daemon the Sadist.

Saetan lay on his side, staring at the wall.

Daemon had actually done very little. *Very* little. But he'd managed to convince that bitch who had hovered outside the door that a son was raping his own father without actually doing anything that would prevent either of them from being able to look the other in the eye. A rather impressive display of skill.

And very brief. He'd been concerned about that, but when Daemon walked out of the hut, he'd heard a murmured comment and Hekatah's delighted, abrasive laugh.

So, while Daemon continued to prowl and keep the camp on edge, he'd had time to rest, to gather his strength, to think.

The game ended at midnight. What was the significance of midnight? Well, it was called the witching hour, that moment suspended between one day and the next. And it would be seventy-two hours from the time Daemon appeared in the camp.

Saetan jerked upright. Seventy-two hours.

Confined to a sitting room in the Keep, he had paced. "From sunset to sunrise. That's how long an Offering takes. For the White, for the Black, that's how long it takes."

"For the Prince of the Darkness," Tersa had said as she pushed around the pieces of a puzzle. "But for the Queen?"

When Jaenelle had made the Offering to the Darkness, it had taken her three days. *Seventy-two hours.*

"Mother Night," he whispered, shifting into a sitting position.

The door opened. Daemon rushed in and dropped a bundle of clothing on the bed.

Before Saetan could say anything, one of Daemon's hands was clamped behind his head and the other was holding a cup to his lips, pouring warm liquid down his throat. He had no choice but to swallow or choke. He swallowed. A moment later, he wished he had choked.

"Hell's fire, what did you just give me?" he gasped as he bent over and pressed his forehead to his knees.

"A tonic," Daemon said, vigorously rubbing Saetan's back.

"Stop that," Saetan snapped. He turned his head just enough to glare at Daemon. "*Whose* tonic?"

"Jaenelle's—with my blood added."

Saetan swore softly, viciously, with great sincerity.

Daemon winced and muttered, "She said it would kick like two teams of draft horses."

"Only someone who's never had to drink one of these little tonics would describe it that mildly."

Daemon went down on his knees in front of Saetan and busily undid the chains. "I couldn't search for your clothes, so I brought you these. They should fit well enough."

Saetan gritted his teeth as Daemon massaged his legs and feet. "Where did you get them?"

"Off a guard. He won't be needing them."

"Damn things probably have lice."

"Deal with it," Daemon growled. Taking a ball of clay out of his jacket pocket, he rolled it into a stubby cylinder, then carefully forced the Ring of Obedience to open enough to slide off Saetan's organ. It clamped down on the clay with the same viciousness it had clamped down on flesh.

Setting the cylinder on the bed, Daemon glanced at Saetan's organ and sucked in a breath.

"It doesn't matter," Saetan said quietly. "I'm a Guardian. I'm past that part of my life."

"But—" Daemon pressed his lips together. "Get these on." After helping Saetan into the trousers, he knelt again to deal with the socks and boots. "It's almost midnight. We'll be cutting it close since we've got to cover a bit of ground in order to reach the nearest strand of the Winds. But in a few more hours, we'll be at the Keep. We'll be home."

The desperate eagerness in Daemon's eyes tore the veil off the vision.

Two webs. One moldy, tainted. The other beautiful, full of shining beads of power.

She had found a way to separate those who lived by the ways of the Blood from those who had been perverted by Hekatah and Dorothea.

But the third web . . .

She was a Queen, and a Queen wouldn't ask for what she herself wouldn't give. And perhaps it was also the only selfish thing she'd ever done. By sacrificing herself, she wouldn't have to carry the burden of all the lives she was about to destroy. But . . .

He doesn't know. You didn't tell him. He came here expecting you to be waiting for him when he got back. Oh, witch-child.

Which is why she had asked him to take care of Daemon, why she had known he would need to.

Maybe it wasn't too late. Maybe there was still a way to stop it, to stop her.

"Let's go," he said abruptly.

Daemon put a sight shield over both of them, and they slipped away from the camp.

By the time they reached the place where they could catch the Winds, a cold, sharp wind had begun to blow.

Saetan stopped, drew a breath through his mouth, tasted the air.

"It's just the wind," Daemon said.

"No," Saetan replied grimly, "it's not. Let's go."

12 / Terreille

Two hours later, Hekatah burst into Dorothea's cabin, waving a stubby clay cylinder. "We've been tricked. They're all gone. That thing in the prison hut isn't Lucivar, it's some kind of illusion. And Saetan . . ." She hurled the cylinder across the room. "That bastard Sadi *lied* to us."

Lying on the floor where she'd been all day, Dorothea stared at Hekatah. As her bowels released more bloody flux, she started to laugh.

13 / Kaeleer

A storm had been gathering all night—thunder, lightning, wind. Now, as dawn approached, the wind had turned fierce, sounding almost as if it had a voice.

"Come," Tersa said, helping Karla over to a couch. "You

must lie down now. Morghann, come over here and lie on the floor."

"What's going on?" Khardeen asked as Morghann obediently lay down on the floor near the couch. He retrieved a pillow and slipped it under his wife's head.

"It would be better for all of you to sit on the floor. Even the Keep will feel this storm."

The First Circle glanced at each other uneasily and obeyed.

"What is it?" Karla asked when Tersa placed an arm protectively over her and rested the other hand on Morghann's shoulder.

"The day has come for the debts to be called in and for the Blood to answer for what they've become."

"I don't understand," Karla said. "What does the storm mean?"

Lightning flashed. The wind howled.

Tersa closed her eyes—and smiled. "She is coming."

14 / Terreille

He'd cut it too close. He hadn't expected the ride on the Winds to be that rough or that Saetan's physical endurance would give out so fast—or his own. They'd had to drop from the Red Wind to the Sapphire and finally, on the last part of the journey, down to the Green.

They couldn't land at the Keep itself. Some kind of shields had come down all around the place. So he'd homed in on Lucivar's Ebon-gray Jewel—and the one small place in the shields that Lucivar was using his Jewels to keep open—and dropped them from the Winds as close as he could. It hadn't been close enough, not for two exhausted men trying to scramble up a steep mountain path.

Now, with the gate in sight and Lucivar's mental urging to hurry, Daemon half carried Saetan up the slope, fighting a fierce, howling wind for every step.

Almost there. Almost. Almost.

The sky was getting lighter. The sun would lift above the horizon at any moment.

Hurry. Hurry.

"Saetan! SAE-TANNNN!"

Daemon looked behind them. Hekatah was scrambling up the slope. The bitch must have ridden the Red Wind all the way in order to get there right behind them.

Not wasting his breath to swear, he picked up the pace as best as could, dragging Saetan with him.

"Sadi!" Hekatah screamed. "You lying bastard!"

"MOVE!" Lucivar shouted. He was using Craft to hold the gate open, straining physically and mentally to keep it from closing and locking them out.

Closer. Almost there. Almost.

Daemon grabbed the bars of the gate, used the strength in his Black Jewel to hold it open. "Get him inside," he said, shoving Saetan at Lucivar. Then he turned and waited.

Hekatah came up the slope, stopped a few feet away. "You lying bastard."

Daemon smiled. "I didn't lie, darling. I told you you were going to get everything you deserved." He let go of the gate. It slammed shut, and the last shield came down over it.

As he turned and ran across the open courtyard, he heard Hekatah screaming. And he heard a wild howling, a sound full of joy and pain, rage and celebration.

He crossed the threshold into the safety of the Keep a moment before Jaenelle unleashed the maelstrom.

You musst wake, said a deep, sibilant voice. *You musst wake.*

Daemon opened his eyes. It took him a moment to understand why everything looked a little . . . *strange* . . . and readjust. It took him another moment to confirm that he was still distantly linked to his body—and that his body was lying on the cold stone floor of the Keep where he and Lucivar and Saetan had fallen when Jaenelle unleashed her full strength.

You are the triangle who helped sshape the web of dreamss. Now you musst hold the dream. There iss not much time.

Groaning, he sat up and looked around. And was instantly wide-awake.

Mother Night, where are we?

He reached over Saetan's prone body and shook Lucivar.

Hell's fire, Bastard, Lucivar said. He raised his head. *Shit.*

Both of them reached for Saetan, shook him awake.

Father, wake up. We're in trouble. Daemon said.

Now what? Saetan growled. He raised himself up on his elbows. His eyes widened. *Mother Night.*

And may the Darkness be merciful, Lucivar added. *Where are we?*

Somewhere in the abyss. I think.

Climbing carefully to their feet, they looked around.

They were standing on the edge of a deep, wide chasm. Stretching across the chasm was an Opal web. Below them were webs the colors of the darker Jewels. Above them were webs the colors of the lighter Jewels.

What are we doing here? Lucivar asked.

We're the triangle who helped shape the dream, Daemon said. *We're supposed to hold the dream.*

Don't go cryptic on me, Bastard, Lucivar growled.

Daemon snarled at him.

Saetan raised his hand. They both fell silent.

Who told you that? Saetan asked.

A sibilant voice. Daemon paused. *It sounded like Draca, but it was male.*

Saetan nodded. *Lorn.* He looked around again.

Far, far, far above them, lightning flashed.

Why did Jaenelle ask you to come to Hayll, Daemon? Saetan asked.

She said that the triangle had to remain together in order to survive. That the mirror had the strength to keep the other two safe.

She saw that in a tangled web?

No. The Weaver of Dreams told her.

Lucivar began to swear.

Saetan's look was sharp, penetrating, thoughtful.

The lightning flashed a little closer.

Father, brother, lover, Saetan said softly.

Daemon nodded, remembering the triangle Tersa had traced on his palm. *The father came first. The brother stands between.* When they both looked at him, he shifted uneasily. *Something Tersa said once.*

Warnings from Tersa, the Arachnian Queen, and Draca, Saetan said. *A man might ignore one at his own peril, but all three?* He shook his head slowly. *I think not.*

The lightning flashed a little closer.

That's all well and good, Lucivar growled, *but I would prefer a straightforward order.*

*Thesse webss are the besst magic I can give you,"' Lorn said irritably. *Usse them to hold the dream. If sshe breakss through all of them, sshe will return to the Darknesss. You will losse her.*

Lucivar puffed out a breath. *That's clear enough. So where—* He looked up as the lightning flashed again. *What's that?*

They all looked up, waited for the next flash—and saw the small dark speck plummeting toward the webs.

Jaenelle, Daemon whispered.

She'll rip right through them, Saetan said. *We'll have to use our own strength to try to slow her speed.*

All right, Lucivar said. *How do we go?*

Saetan looked at Daemon, then at Lucivar. *Father, brother, lover.* He didn't wait for an answer. He exploded upward, racing to intercept Witch before she hit the White web.

Lucivar watched for a moment, then turned to the webs, his eyes narrowed. *If she hits them in the center, she'll break through them. So we'll roll her.* He clamped a hand on Daemon's shoulder, pointed with the other hand. *Not so close to the edge that you'll risk hitting the chasm walls, but away from the center. Then twist and roll while you're using your own strength as a brake.*

Daemon looked at the webs. *What will that do?*

For one thing, the countermovement should slow the speed. And if she gets wrapped in the webs—

We'll form a cocoon of power.

Lucivar nodded. *I'll go up to the Rose. I don't know how much strength Saetan has left. If he's still able to hold her, I can add my strength to his. If not . . . *

Where should I be? Daemon asked, willing to defer to Lucivar's ability and fighting experience.

The Green. I should be able to hold her that far. Lucivar hesitated. *Good luck, Bastard.*

And you, Prick.

Lucivar soared upward.

A moment later, Daemon heard Saetan's roar of defiance as the White web shattered. In the flash, he could see two small figures falling, falling.

He floated down to the Green web.

The Yellow web shattered. Then the Tiger Eye.

He heard Lucivar's war cry.

As the Rose web shattered, he saw a twirl of color as Lucivar rolled, fighting against the speed of the fall.

They hit the Summer-sky. Holding on to Witch's legs, Lucivar rolled the other way, catching most of the web before they crashed through.

The Purple Dusk. The Opal.

Daemon met him halfway between the Opal and the Green.

Let go, Prick, before you shatter the Ebon-gray.

With a cry that was part defiant, part pain, and part fear, Lucivar let go.

Rage filled Daemon. Love drove him. He and Witch hit the Green web. He rolled, but he didn't have Lucivar's skill. They broke through close to the middle of the web. He kept rolling so that when they hit the Sapphire, they were close to the edge. He rolled the other way, wrapping her in the web's power.

They broke through the Sapphire, but they weren't falling as fast now. He had a little more time to brace, to plan, to pour the strength of his Black Jewels into fighting the fall.

They hit the Red, rolled, clung for a second before falling to the Gray. Only half the Gray strands broke immediately. He strained back as hard as he could. When the other half broke, he rolled them *upward* while the web swung them down toward the Ebon-gray. He pulled against the swing, slowing it, slowing it.

When the other side of the Gray broke, they sailed down to the Ebon-gray. The web sagged when they landed, then stretched, then stretched a little more before the strands began to break.

His Black Jewels were almost drained, but he held on, held on, held on as they floated onto the Black web.

And nothing happened.

Shaking, shivering, Daemon stared at the Black web, not quite daring to believe.

It took him a minute to get his hands to unlock from their grip. When he was finally able to let go, he floated cautiously above the web. Near her shoulder, he noticed two small broken strands. Very carefully, he smoothed the Black strands over the other colors that cocooned her.

He could barely see her, only just enough to make out the tiny spiral horn. But that was enough.

We did it, he whispered as his eyes filled. *We did it.*

Yess, Lorn said very quietly. *You have done well.*

Daemon looked up, looked around. When he looked back at Witch, she faded.

Everything faded.

15 / Terreille

Saetan opened his eyes, tried to move, and found himself trapped by two warm bodies curled up around him. His sons.

Oh, witch-child. I hope it was worth the price.

He tried to move again, growled when he couldn't, and finally jabbed Lucivar with an elbow.

Lucivar just growled back and cuddled closer.

He shoved at Lucivar again because he couldn't, even in this small way, push Daemon aside. Not now.

Lucivar's growl turned into a snarl, but he finally stirred. And that woke Daemon.

"I'm delighted you find me such a comfortable pillow," Saetan said dryly, "but a man my age prefers not to sleep on a cold stone floor."

"Neither does a man *my* age," Lucivar grumbled, getting to his feet. He rolled his shoulders, stretched his back.

Daemon sat up with a groan.

Watching him, Saetan saw the light fill Daemon's eyes, the joy, the eagerness. It broke his heart.

He accepted Daemon's help in getting to his feet—and noted Lucivar's coolness toward his brother. That would change. Would *have* to change. But Lucivar wouldn't be approachable until he'd seen Marian and Daemonar, so there was no point in sparking that Eyrien temper. Besides, he was too damn tired to take on Lucivar right now.

As he walked to the doors, they fell into step on either side of him.

Twilight. The whole day had passed.

They walked across the open courtyard. Lucivar opened the gate.

A gust of wind made something flutter, catching Saetan's attention. A scrap of cloth from a woman's gown. Hekatah's gown.

He didn't mention it.

"I don't have the strength right now," he said quietly. "Would you two . . ."

Lucivar looked toward the south, Daemon toward the north. After a minute, their faces had the same grim, deliberately calm expression.

"There are a few Blood," Daemon said slowly. "Not many."

"The same," Lucivar said.

A few. Only a few. Sweet Darkness, let them get a different answer in Kaeleer. "Let's go home."

He felt the difference as soon as they walked through the Gate between the Realms. When they walked out of the Altar Room, Daemon and Lucivar both looked in the direction that would lead them to the First Circle—and the others.

He turned in the opposite direction, not quite ready to deal with what was going to come. "Come with me." Reluctantly, they obeyed.

He led them to a low-walled terrace that overlooked Riada, the closest Blood village.

Daemon looked down at the village. Lucivar looked in the direction of the Eyrien community.

Daemon sighed with relief. "I don't know how many people had lived there yesterday, but there are still a lot of Blood there."

"Falonar!" Lucivar cried. He looked at them and grinned. "The whole community. They're all right. Badly shaken up, but all right."

"Thank the Darkness," Saetan whispered. The tears came, as much from pride as grief. Prothvar had said it was a different kind of battlefield but a good one to fight on. He'd been right. It *was* a worthy battlefield. Instead of seeing more friends join the demon-dead. they had gone knowing those friends would live. Char, Dujae, Morton, Titian, Cassandra, Prothvar, Mephis, Andulvar. He would miss them. Mother Night. how he would miss them. "And the Blood shall sing to the Blood. You sang the song well, my friends. You sang it well."

He would have to tell Lucivar and Daemon—and Surreal—about this, too. But not yet. Not now.

He dreaded it, but he knew he couldn't hold either of them back much longer. "Come on, puppies. I'm sure the coven's going to have a few things to say about this."

It was worse than he'd expected.

The coven and the boyos fell all over Lucivar, who had his arms wrapped around Marian and Daemonar. Daemon they greeted with cool reserve. Except Karla, who had said, "Kiss kiss," and then *had* kissed him. And Surreal, who had given Daemon a cool stare, and said, "You look like shit, Sadi." He would have lashed out at her for that if Daemon hadn't commented dryly that her compliments were as effusive as ever—and if she hadn't grinned at the remark.

And Tersa, who had held her son's face between her hands and looked into his eyes. "It will be all right, Daemon," she had said gently. "Trust one who sees. It *will* be all right."

Saetan wasn't sure Daemon noticed the coolness, wasn't sure he even noticed who had greeted him and who hadn't. His eyes kept scanning the room for someone who wasn't there—someone who wasn't going to be there.

He was trying to think of a reasonable excuse to get Daemon away from the others when Geoffrey appeared at the door. "Your presence is requested at the Dark Throne. Draca would like to see you."

As they filed out of the room, Saetan stepped in beside Lucivar. "Stay close to your brother," he said quietly.

"I think it would be better—"

"Don't think, Prince, just follow orders."

Lucivar gave him a measuring look, then moved ahead to catch up with Daemon.

Surreal tucked her arm through his. "Lucivar's pissed?"

"That's one way of putting it," Saetan replied dryly.

"If you think it will help, I could give him a good kick in the balls. Although I have a feeling that when Marian realizes what he's pissed about, she'll do a better job than either of us can."

Saetan let out a groaning chuckle. "Now *that* will be interesting." Then he sobered. "Daemon played the same game with you."

"Yes, he did. But sometimes the best way to fool an enemy is to convince a friend."

"Your mother said almost the same thing to me once—after she punched me."

"Really?" Surreal smiled. "It must run in the family."

He decided it was better not to ask her to clarify that.

Baffled, Daemon waited for whatever announcement Draca was going to make. Not that it mattered. He would have to slip away to Amdarh in the next few days, talk to that jeweler, Banard, about designing a wedding ring for Jaenelle. He'd gotten her some earrings there for Winsol and had liked what he'd seen of the man's work.

Her birthday would be coming up soon. Would she mind having a wedding on her birthday? Well, maybe *he* would. He didn't really want to share the celebration of their wedding day with anything else. But they could have it soon after that. She would still be tired, still be recovering from this spell, but they could find a quiet place for the honeymoon. It didn't matter where.

Where was she? Maybe she was already in her room, recovering. Maybe that's what Draca was going to tell them—that Jaenelle had prevented the war, that Kaeleer was safe. As soon as this announcement was over, he'd slip up to her room and snuggle in next to her. Well, he'd take a bath first. He wasn't exactly smelling his best at the moment.

Where *was* she?

Then he looked at Lorn and felt a flicker of uneasiness.

No. They had saved her. The triangle *had* saved her. She'd expended so much of herself, had risen so far out of herself she'd been plummeting back down, but they had stopped the fall. They *had* stopped the fall.

Lucivar came up beside him, close enough to brush

shoulders with him. Saetan stepped up on his other side with Surreal close by.

Draca picked something up from the Throne's seat, hesitated, then turned to face them.

Daemon froze.

She was holding Jaenelle's scepter. But the metal was all twisted, and the two Ebony Jewels were shattered. Not just drained. *Shattered.* So was the spiral horn.

"The Queen of Ebon Asskavi iss gone," Draca said quietly. "The Dark Court no longer existss."

Someone began screaming. A scream full of panic, rage, denial, pain.

It wasn't until Lucivar and Saetan grabbed him and held him back that he realized the person who was screaming was himself.

16 / Kaeleer

"What was the point of it?" Gabrielle demanded angrily while the tears fell unheeded. "What was the point of offering the memories if they weren't going to do any good?"

Surreal raked her fingers through her hair and decided smacking someone probably wasn't going to help much. Well, it would make *her* feel better. Thank the Darkness she and Uncle Saetan had been able to heavily sedate Daemon. He couldn't have tolerated any of this right now.

She would have liked to have found out more about this memory thing, but she was more intrigued by the fact that Tersa seemed too calm and undisturbed—and also a little angry. It would take someone mucking up something very important to make Tersa angry.

"Yes, Tersa," Karla said testily, "what *was* the point?"

"Blood is the memory's river. And the Blood shall sing to the Blood," Tersa replied.

Gabrielle said something succinct and obscene.

"Shut up, Gabrielle," Surreal snapped.

Tersa was sitting on the long table in front of the couch, next to a pile of wooden building blocks. Surreal crouched down beside her. "What were the memories for?" she asked quietly.

Tersa brushed her tangled hair away from her face. "To

feed the web of dreams. It was no longer complete. It had lived, it had grown."

"But she's gone!" Morghann wailed.

"The Queen is gone," Tersa said with some heat. "Is that all she was to you?"

"No," Karla said. "She was Jaenelle. That was enough."

"Exactly," Tersa said. "It is still enough."

Surreal jolted, hardly daring to hope. She touched Tersa's hand, waited until she was sure she had the woman's attention. "The Queen is gone, but Jaenelle isn't?"

Tersa hesitated. "It's too soon to know. But the triangle kept the dream from returning to the Darkness, and now the kindred are fighting to hold the dream to the flesh."

That brought protests from Gabrielle and Karla.

"Wait a minute," Gabrielle said, glancing at Karla, who nodded. "If Jaenelle is hurt and needs a Healer, she should have *us*."

"No," Tersa said, her anger breaking free. "She should *not* have you. *You* could not look at what was done to that flesh and believe it could still live. But the kindred do not doubt. *The kindred will not believe anything else.* That is why, if it can be done, they are the ones who can do it." She jumped up and ran out of the room.

Surreal waited a moment, then followed. She didn't find Tersa, but she found Graysfang hovering nearby, whining anxiously.

She studied the wolf. Kindred do not doubt. They would sink in and fight for that dream with fangs and claws and never give it up. Well, she would never have a snout that could smell tracks, but she could damn well learn how to be as stubborn as a wolf. She would sink her teeth into the belief that Jaenelle was simply recovering somewhere private after performing an extremely difficult spell. She would sink in and hold on to that.

For Jaenelle's sake.

For Daemon's sake.

And for her own sake, because she wanted her friend to come back.

CHAPTER
SIXTEEN

1 / Kaeleer

Daemon walked down the steps that led to the garden in the Hall, the garden that had two statues.

When he woke up from the sedative Surreal and Saetan had given him, he had asked to leave the Keep. They had gone with him. So had Tersa.

Lucivar hadn't.

That had been a week ago.

He wasn't sure what he'd done during the days since. They had simply passed. And at night . . .

At night, he crept from his own bed into Jaenelle's because it was the only place he could sleep. Her scent was there, and in the dark, he could almost believe that she was simply away for a little while, that he would wake one morning and find her cuddled up next to him.

He stared at the statue of the male, with its paw/hand curved protectively above the sleeping woman. Part human, part beast. Savagery protecting beauty. But now he saw something else in its eyes: the anguish, the price that sometimes had to be paid.

He turned away from it, walked over to the other statue, stared at the woman's face—that familiar, beloved face—for a long, long time.

The tears came—again. The pain was always there.

"Tersa keeps telling me that it will be all right, to trust one who sees," he told the statue. "Surreal keeps telling me not to give up, that the kindred will be able to bring you back. And I want to believe that. I *need* to believe that. But when I ask Tersa about you directly, she hesitates, says it's too soon to know, says the kindred are fighting to hold the dream to the flesh. *Fighting* to hold the dream to the flesh." He laughed bitterly. "They're not fighting to hold the dream to flesh, Jaenelle. They're fighting to put enough of you together again for there to be something *for the dream to come back to.* And you knew what would happen, didn't you? When you decided to do this, *you knew.*"

He paced, circled, came back to the statue.

"I did it for you," he said quietly. "I bought the time, I played the game. For you." His breathing hitched, came out in a sob. "I knew I would have to do some things that wouldn't be forgiven. I *knew* it when you asked me to go to Hayll, but I did it anyway. F-for you. Because I was going to come back to you, and the rest of it wouldn't matter. B-because I was coming back to *you.* But you sent me there knowing you wouldn't be here when I got back, knowing . . ." He sank to his knees. "You said no sacrifices. You made me promise I wouldn't make any sacrifices. But what do you call this, Jaenelle? *What do you call this?* When I got back, we were going to get *m-married.* . . . And you left me. Damn you, Jaenelle, I did this for you, *and you left me.* You left me."

He collapsed on the grass near the statue, sobbing.

Lucivar rested a fist against the stone wall and bowed his head.

Mother Night. Daemon had gone into that game expecting to come back for his own wedding. *Mother Night.*

He was here because Marian had ripped into him that morning, giving him the full thrust of the temper that lived beneath her quiet nature. She'd told him that, yes, he'd been hurt, but he'd been hurt *to save them.* She'd asked him if he would have preferred losing a wife or son in truth in order for his feelings to be spared. And she'd told him that the man she had married would have the courage to forgive.

That had brought him here.

But now . . .

When they'd both been slaves in Terreille, he and Daemon had played games before, had used each other, had hurt each other. Sometimes they'd done it to relieve their own pain, sometimes it had been for a better reason. But they'd always been able to look past those games and forgive the hurt *because there had been no one else.* They'd fought with each other, but they'd also fought *for* each other.

He had other people now, a wider circle to love. A wife, a son. Maybe that had made the difference. He didn't *need* Daemon. But, Hell's fire, Daemon needed *him* right now.

But it was more than that. Thirteen years ago, he had wrongfully accused Daemon of killing Jaenelle. That had been the first hard shove that had ended with Daemon spending eight years in the Twisted Kingdom, lost in madness. And Daemon had forgiven him because, he'd said, he'd already grieved for a brother once and didn't want to do it again.

Daemon had believed a painful lie for thirteen years. *He'd* believed one for a couple of days. Marian had been right to rip into him.

So he would do what he could to mend things, for his own sake as well as for Daemon's. Because, during those long centuries of slavery when they'd had no one but each other, their anger had sometimes flared to moments of hate, but underneath there had always been love.

Pushing away from the wall, Lucivar walked down the steps, knelt in the grass beside Daemon. He touched his brother's shoulder.

Daemon looked at him out of a face devastated by grief before lunging into the open arms.

"I want her back," Daemon cried. "Oh, Lucivar, *I want her back.*"

Lucivar held on tight as his own tears fell. "I know, old son. I know."

2 / Kaeleer

"You're *leaving*?" Lucivar leaped to his feet and stared at Saetan. "What do you mean, 'leaving'? To go where?" Pacing behind the two chairs in front of the blackwood desk, he pointed an accusing finger at his father. "You are *not* going to the Dark Realm. *There's no one left there.* And you are *not* going to be alone."

"Lucivar," Saetan said quietly. "Lucivar, please listen."

"When the sun shines in Hell."

Prick, Daemon said on an Ebon-gray spear thread.

And why in the name of Hell are you just sitting there? Lucivar demanded. *He's your father, too.*

Daemon bit back exasperation. *Let him talk, Prick. If we don't like what we hear, then we'll do something about it.* "You're leaving because of Sylvia?" he asked Saetan.

Lucivar froze, swore softly, then settled back into the chair.

"That's part of it," Saetan said. "A Guardian isn't meant to be among the living. Not that way." He hesitated, then added, "If I stay . . . I can't stay and be a friend and encourage her to . . . She deserves to be with someone who can give her more than I can now."

"You could come to Ebon Rih and live with us," Lucivar said.

"Thank you, Lucivar, but no. I've . . ." Saetan took a deep breath. "I've been offered a position at the Keep as assistant historian/librarian. Geoffrey says he's starting to feel his years, and it's my fault that he's had more work now than he's ever had because I'm the one who introduced the coven to the Keep's library, and it's time I started making myself useful."

"The Keep is only a mountain away from our eyrie," Lucivar said.

"You will not bring Daemonar to the library."

Lucivar gave Saetan a sharp smile. "Did you bring me there when I was his age?"

"Once," Saetan said dryly. "And Geoffrey still reminds me of that little adventure on occasion." He glanced at Daemon. "I'll come and visit both of you, just to find out how much trouble you're causing."

Daemon felt a tension ease. He wanted to see his father, but not at Ebon Askavi. He would never again set foot in the Keep.

"The family owns three counties in Dhemlan," Saetan said. "I've divided them between you. Daemon, I'm giving you the Hall and all the land and tithes that go with it. Lucivar, you'll have the land that's near the Askavi border. The other property you'll own together."

"I don't need land," Lucivar protested.

"You're still the Warlord Prince of Ebon Rih because the people *want* you to be the Warlord Prince of Ebon Rih. But Daemonar may not want to rule—or you may have other sons or daughters who want a different kind of life. You'll be the caretaker of that land because the SaDiablo family *has been* the caretaker of that land for thousands of years. Is that understood?"

"Yes, sir," Lucivar said quietly.

"And you?" Saetan said, pointedly looking at Daemon.

"Yes, sir," he replied just as quietly. Well, that explained why Saetan had insisted on spending the past two months teaching him the family business. He'd thought it was just a way to keep him occupied and too busy to think too much.

He'd welcomed the work, especially when he realized that Saetan had shouldered the burden of helping Geoffrey with a far more difficult task. He and Lucivar had been told the results, but he knew he couldn't have tolerated accumulating the information.

Over forty percent of the Blood in Terreille were gone. Completely gone. Another thirty percent had been broken back to basic Craft. The Blood who were left in Terreille were reeling from the devastation—and the sudden freedom.

He hadn't asked what had happened to Alexandra, Leland, and Philip—and Saetan hadn't offered the information. Or if he had, it had only been to Wilhelmina.

The numbers were about the same in Little Terreille as they were for the Realm of Terreille. But the rest of Kaeleer was mostly untouched—except for Glacia. Karla was struggling to reunite her people and re-form her court. The taint Dorothea and Hekatah had spread in the Blood might have been destroyed, but the scars remained.

Everything has a price.

"What about Jaenelle's house in Maghre?" Lucivar asked.

Daemon shook his head. "Let Wilhelmina have it. She's decided to settle in Scelt, and—"

"The house was leased for Jaenelle," Saetan said firmly. "It remains for Jaenelle. If you have no objections to Wilhelmina living there until she finds a place of her own, so be it."

Daemon backed down. He loved that house, too, but he

wasn't sure he could ever live there again. And he wasn't really sure if Saetan truly believed Jaenelle *was* coming back or if his father just wasn't willing to do anything that would acknowledge that she *wasn't.* After all, it had been two months now with no news of any kind, just Tersa's continued—and useless—assurance that it would be all right. "Is that it?"

He read the message in Saetan's eyes. "I'll be with you in a minute," he said to Lucivar when his brother rose and looked at him.

When they were alone, Saetan said carefully, "I know how you feel about Ebon Askavi now."

Daemon rushed in. "I truly hope you will come to visit, Father, because I'll never set foot in the Keep again."

Saetan said gently, "You have to go one more time. Draca wants to see you."

3 / Kaeleer

"There iss ssomething I want to sshow you." Draca unlocked a door and stepped aside.

Daemon walked into a huge room that was a portrait gallery. Dozens upon dozens of paintings hung on the walls.

At first, he saw only one. The last one.

Unable to look at it, he turned his back to it and began to study the rest of them in order. Some were very, very old, but all of them had been exquisitely done. As he slowly walked around the room, he realized the portraits spanned the species who made up the Blood—and they were all female.

When he reached the last one, he studied Jaenelle's portrait for a long time, then looked at the signature. Dujae. Of course.

He turned and looked at Draca.

"They were all dreamss made flessh, Prince," Draca said gently. "Some only had one kind of dreamer, otherss were a bridge. Thesse were Witch."

"But—" Daemon looked at the portraits again. "I don't see Cassandra's portrait here."

"Sshe wass a Black-Jeweled witch, the Queen of Ebon

Asskavi. But sshe wass not Witch. Sshe wass not dreamss made flessh."

He shook his head. "Witch wears the Black. She's always a Black-Jeweled Queen."

"No. That iss not alwayss the dream, Daemon. There have been quiet dreamss and sstrong dreamss. There have been Queenss and ssongmakerss." She paused, waited. "Your dream wass to be Conssort to the Queen of Ebon Asskavi. Iss that not true?"

Daemon's heart began to pound. "I thought they were the same. I thought Witch and the Queen of Ebon Askavi were the same."

"And if they are not?"

Tears stung his eyes. "If they hadn't been the same, if I'd had to choose between the Queen and Jaenelle . . . I never would have set foot in this place. Excuse me, Draca. I—"

He started to rush past her, but he saw her hand move as if to hold him back. He could have avoided her easily, but, being who she was, he couldn't be that disrespectful.

Her ancient hand moved slowly, came to rest on his arm.

"The Queen of Ebon Asskavi iss gone," she said very quietly. "But sshe who iss Kaeleer'ss Heart, sshe who iss Witch, sstill livess."

4 / Kaeleer

"You'll take the income I've provided for you," Saetan snarled as he and Surreal walked through one of the Hall's gardens. He'd thought this would be a simple task, something to occupy a bit of time while he waited for Daemon to return from the Keep.

Surreal snarled back. "I don't need a damn income from you."

He stopped and turned on her. "Are you or are you not family?"

She stepped up to him until they were toe to toe. "Yes, I'm family, but—"

"Then take the damn income!" he shouted.

"Why?" she shouted back.

"Because I love you!" he roared. "And I want to give you that much."

She swore at him.

Hell's fire, why were his children all so *stubborn*?

He leashed his temper. "It's a gift, Surreal. Please take it."

She hooked her hair behind her ears. "If you're going to put it *that* way . . ."

A wolf raised its voice in an odd series of yips and howls.

"That's not Graysfang," Surreal said.

Saetan tensed. "No. It's one of the pack from the north woods."

Worry filled her eyes. "One of them has come back? Why does it sound like that?"

"The Tigre use drums to signal messages—just for fun things, a dance, an impromptu gathering," Saetan replied absently. "The wolves became intrigued by it and developed a few particular howls of their own."

The same series of yips and howls came again.

"Graysfang could have mentioned that," Surreal grumbled. "What's that one mean?"

"It means there's a message that should be heeded."

The wolf raised its voice again in a different song. Then another wolf joined in. And another. And another.

Listening, he started to cry—and laugh. There was only one reason the wolves raised their voices in quite that way.

Surreal gripped his arm. "Uncle Saetan, what is it?"

"It's a song of celebration. Jaenelle has come back."

5 / Kaeleer

It was early autumn, almost a year since he'd first come to Kaeleer.

Daemon carefully landed the small Coach in the meadow and stepped out. At the edge of the meadow, Ladvarian waited for him.

For weeks, he had raged and pleaded, begged and sworn. It hadn't done any good. Draca had insisted that she didn't know exactly where the kindred had hidden Jaenelle. She had also insisted that the healing was still very delicate and a strong presence—and difficult emotions—could easily interfere. Finally, exasperated, she had suggested that he make himself useful.

So he'd thrown himself into work. And every evening he had written a letter to Jaenelle, telling her about his day, pouring out his love. Two or three times a week, he went to the Keep and annoyed Draca.

Now, finally, the message had come. The kindred had done all they could. The healing wasn't complete, but the rest would take time, and she should be in a warm human den now.

So he'd been told where to bring the Coach that would take Jaenelle back to the Hall.

He crossed the meadow, stopped a few feet in front of Ladvarian. The Sceltie looked too thin, but there was joy—and wariness—in the brown eyes.

"Ladvarian," Daemon said quietly, respectfully.

Daemon. Ladvarian shifted uneasily. *Human males . . . Some human males pay too much attention to the outside.*

He understood the warning, heard the fear. And now he understood why they hadn't let him come sooner—they'd been afraid he wouldn't be able to stand what he saw. They were still afraid.

"It doesn't matter, Ladvarian," he said gently. "It doesn't matter."

The Sceltie studied him. *She is very fragile.*

"I know." Draca had drummed that into him before she'd let him come.

She sleeps a lot.

He smiled dryly. "I've hardly slept at all."

Satisfied, Ladvarian turned. *This way. Be careful. There are many guard webs.*

Looking around, he saw the tangled webs that could ensnare a person's mind and draw him into peculiar dreams—or hideous nightmares.

He walked carefully.

They walked for several minutes before they came to a path that led to a sheltered cove. A large tent was set up well back from the waterline. The colored fabric would keep out most of the sun but seemed loosely woven enough to let in air.

Closer to the water were several poorly made sand castles. Watching Kaelas trying to pack sand with one of those huge paws made him smile.

The front flaps of the tent were pulled back, revealing the woman sleeping inside. She wore a long skirt of swirling colors. The amethyst-colored shirt was unbuttoned and had slid to her sides, displaying her from the waist up.

Daemon took one look at her and bolted away from the tent.

He stopped a few yards away and just tried to draw a normal breath while his stomach twisted wildly.

The kindred had done their very best. They had given months of focused, single-minded devotion to produce this much healing. He never *ever* wanted to know what she had looked like when they had brought her here.

He felt Ladvarian come up behind him. Since the Sceltie *had* seen what she had looked like, the dog probably couldn't understand his reaction. "Ladvarian . . ."

She rose from the healing webs too soon, Ladvarian said in a voice that was bitter and accusing. *Because of you.*

Daemon turned slowly, his heart bleeding from the verbal wound.

*We *tried* to tell her you weren't hurt. We *tried* to tell her that she had to stay down in the healing webs longer. We *tried* to tell her that the Stra—that Tersa would tell you that she was coming back, that the High Lord would take care of his pup. But she kept saying that you were hurting and that she had promised. She stayed in the webs long enough for her insides to heal and then she rose. But when she saw . . .*

Daemon closed his eyes. No. Sweet Darkness, *no*. She would have been in pain, would have suffered. And she wouldn't have if she'd stayed down in the healing webs.

"Tersa did tell me," he said in a broken voice. "Over and over again. But . . . all I knew for certain was that Jaenelle had promised to marry me and then had left me, and . . ." He couldn't go on.

Maybe we could have told you, Ladvarian said reluctantly after a long silence. *We didn't think humans would believe that she could heal—at least, wouldn't believe enough. But, maybe, if we had told you about all the webs, you *could* have believed.*

Not likely. No matter how much he would have *wanted* to believe, the doubts would have crept in—and might have destroyed everything he wanted to save. "Tersa told me it would be all right. I didn't listen."

More silence. Then, *It is hard to listen when your paw is caught in a trap.*

That understanding, that much forgiveness, hurt. He looked at the Sceltie, needing to see the truth. "Ladvarian . . . did I cripple her?"

No, Ladvarian said gently. *She *will* heal, Prince. She is healing more and more every day. It will just take longer.*

Daemon walked back to the tent, stepped inside.

This time, he only saw Jaenelle.

She's all there, Ladvarian said anxiously.

Nodding, Daemon slipped off his shoes and jacket, then carefully stretched out beside her, propped on one elbow so that he could look at her. He reached out, tentatively brushed his fingers over her short golden hair, almost afraid to touch even that much. She was so fragile. So terribly, terribly fragile. But alive.

We had to crop her fur.

Considering the condition she must have been in, it was a practical solution to grooming problems the kindred must have faced.

His fingers brushed over her cheek. Her face, although horribly thin, was the same.

Then he noticed the Jewel resting on her chest. At first, he thought it was a Purple Dusk. Then, in its depths, he saw glints of Rose, Summer-sky, and Opal. Green, Sapphire, and Red. Gray and Ebon-gray. And just a hint of Black.

It's called Twilight's Dawn, Ladvarian said. *There's no other Jewel like it.* Then the Sceltie retreated, leaving him alone with her.

He watched her while she slept. Just watched her. After a while, he found the courage to let his fingers explore a little.

Ladvarian was right. She was all there, but she was barely more than a thin sheath of skin over organs and bones.

As one finger delicately traced her nipple, he stopped, thought about the open shirt, then looked at the beach where Ladvarian stood near Kaelas, watching him. *She didn't know I was coming, did she?*

No, Ladvarian replied.

He didn't have to ask why. If he hadn't been able to accept what he saw, the kindred would never have told her he had come—and Ladvarian would have taken her somewhere else, to *someone* else to heal over the winter months.

He knew *his* answer to that. He loved her, and all he wanted was to be with her. But, despite what Ladvarian had said . . . *because* of what Ladvarian had said . . . he was no longer sure she would want *him*.

Then she stirred a little, and he knew he wasn't going anywhere unless she sent him away.

Carefully bracing himself so that he wouldn't hurt her, he leaned over and brushed his lips against hers.

He raised his head. Her haunted sapphire eyes stared at him.

"Daemon?" There was so much uncertainty in her voice.

"Hello, sweetheart," he said, his voice husky with the effort not to cry. "I've missed you."

Her hand moved slowly, with effort, until it rested against his face. Her lips curved into a smile. "Daemon."

This time, when she said his name, it sounded like a promise, like a lovely caress.

Fantasy from
ANNE BISHOP

Return to the world of The Black Jewels

THE INVISIBLE RING
Anne Bishop

In this darkly mesmerizing tale from the world of
The Black Jewels, a young Warlord is auctioned off as a
pleasure slave to a notorious queen. He fears he will share
the fate of her other slaves, but the Gray Lady may not be
what she seems.

DREAMS MADE FLESH
Anne Bishop

Set in the realm of The Black Jewels trilogy, this
collection features four brand-new revelatory stories of
Jaenelle and her kindred.

THE TIR ALAINN TRILOGY

by
Anne Bishop

The Pillars of the World
"Bishop only adds luster to her reputation for
fine fantasy." —*Booklist*

Shadows and Light
"Plenty of thrills, faerie magic, human nastiness,
and romance." —*Locus*

The House of Gaian
"A vivid fantasy world....Beautiful." —*BookBrowser*

Available wherever books are sold or at
penguin.com

BELLADONNA

Anne Bishop

The thrilling follow-up to *Sebastian*

The Eater of the World continues to spread its dark influence across the realm of Ephemera, corrupting people's souls with doubts and fears. Only Glorianna Belladonna possesses the ability to thwart the Eater's plans. But she has been branded a rogue, and stands alone against the encroaching enity.

Penguin Group (USA) Online

What will you be reading tomorrow?

Tom Clancy, Patricia Cornwell, W.E.B. Griffin,
Nora Roberts, William Gibson, Robin Cook,
Brian Jacques, Catherine Coulter, Stephen King,
Dean Koontz, Ken Follett, Clive Cussler,
Eric Jerome Dickey, John Sandford,
Terry McMillan, Sue Monk Kidd, Amy Tan,
J. R. Ward, Laurell K. Hamilton,
Charlaine Harris, Christine Feehan...

You'll find them all at
penguin.com

*Read excerpts and newsletters,
find tour schedules and reading group guides,
and enter contests.*

Subscribe to Penguin Group (USA) newsletters
and get an exclusive inside look
at exciting new titles and the authors you love
long before everyone else does.

PENGUIN GROUP (USA)
us.penguingroup.com